"Get up!" murmured Sikes, trembling with rage, and drawing the pistol from his pocket. "Or I'll strew your brains upon the grass."

"For God's sake let me go!" cried Oliver, "let me run away and die in the fields. I will never come near London; never, never! Oh! Pray have mercy on me, and do not make me steal. For the love of all the bright angels that rest in Heaven, have mercy upon me!"

A Background Note about *Oliver Twist*

Oliver Twist is set in the early 1800s, in London and nearby towns. During this time, known as the Victorian Era, relief for the poor was administered by officials for the parish, which was similar to a county. Poor people either lived in the workhouse, in terrible conditions meant to deter them from staying, or they lived on their own and sometimes received "outdoor relief," which the upper classes disapproved of.

Labor laws did not prohibit children from working, and so they were often exploited by employers and their families. The society highly valued work, especially the middle classes, who had risen to a better standard of living because of the Industrial Revolution. They considered work of any sort better than charitable assistance.

Oliver Twist

Charles Dickens

Edited, and with an Afterword,
by Mary Ann Fugate

 THE TOWNSEND LIBRARY

OLIVER TWIST

TP THE TOWNSEND LIBRARY

For more titles in the Townsend Library,
visit our website: **www.townsendpress.com**

All new material in this edition is
copyright © 2007 by Townsend Press.
Printed in the United States of America

0 9 8 7 6 5 4 3 2 1

ISBN 13: 978-1-59194-083-8
ISBN 10: 1-59194-083-4

Library of Congress Control Number:
2006935806

CONTENTS

Among other public buildings in a certain town, there was one common to most towns, great or small: a workhouse. And in this workhouse was born the item of mortality known as Oliver Twist.

Although being born in a workhouse is not the most fortunate circumstance that can possibly befall a human being, in this particular instance, it was the best thing for Oliver Twist that could have occurred. There was considerable difficulty getting Oliver to take on the job of respiration. For some time he lay gasping on a little wool mattress, poised between this world and the next, the balance in favor of the latter.

There being nobody nearby but an old pauper woman, who was rather misty with beer, and a parish surgeon, Oliver and Nature fought out the point between them. The result was that, after a few struggles, Oliver breathed, sneezed, and proceeded to alert the workhouse of its new burden, by setting up a loud cry.

As Oliver gave this first proof of the free and proper action of his lungs, the patchwork coverlet that was carelessly flung over the iron bedstead rustled. The pale face of a young woman raised feebly from the pillow, and a faint voice said, "Let me see the child, and then die."

As the young woman spoke, the surgeon rose, and advancing to the bed, said, with more kindness than might have been expected of him, "Oh, you must not talk about dying yet."

"Lor bless her dear heart, no!" interjected the nurse. "When she has lived as long as I have, sir, and had thirteen children of her own, and all of 'em dead except two, and them in the wurkus with me, she'll know better than to talk on in that way! Think what it is to be a mother, there's a dear young lamb."

The patient shook her head, and stretched out her hand towards the child. The surgeon deposited it in her arms. She pressed her cold white lips passionately on its forehead, gazed wildly round, shuddered, fell back—and died. They rubbed her chest, hands, and temples, but the blood had stopped forever.

"It's all over, Mrs. Thingummy!" said the surgeon at last.

"Ah, poor dear, so it is!" said the nurse, as she stooped to take up the child.

"You needn't mind sending up to me, if the child cries, nurse," said the surgeon. "It's likely it will be troublesome. Give it a little gruel if it is." He put on his hat, and added, "she was a good-looking girl, too. Where did she come from?"

"She was brought here last night," replied the old woman. "She was found lying in the street. She had walked some distance, for her shoes were worn to pieces. But where she came from, or where she was going, nobody knows."

The surgeon leaned over the body, and raised the left hand. "The old story," he said, shaking his head. "No wedding ring, I see. Ah! Good night!"

The medical gentleman walked away to dinner, and the nurse sat down on a low chair before the fire, and proceeded to dress the infant.

What an excellent example of the power of dress, young Oliver Twist was! Wrapped in the blanket, he might have been the child of a nobleman or a beggar. But now that he was enveloped in the old calico robes that had grown yellow from use, he fell into his place at once—the orphan of a workhouse—the humble, half-starved drudge—to be cuffed and buffeted through the world—despised by all, and pitied by none.

Oliver cried lustily. If he could have known that he was an orphan, left to the tender mercies of church wardens and overseers, perhaps he would have cried the louder.

CHAPTER 2

Oliver was sent off to a branch workhouse, where twenty or thirty other juvenile offenders against the poor laws rolled about the floor all day, without the inconvenience of too much food or too much clothing, under the guidance of an elderly woman.

She received the culprits for the sum of seven-pence-halfpenny per small head per week, a good round diet for a child. But the elderly woman knew what was good for children, and she had an accurate perception of what was good for herself. So, she used the greater part of the weekly stipend for her own needs, and raised the children on a smaller allowance than was originally provided for them.

A rather unfortunate result usually accompanied the system of the woman caring for Oliver Twist. At the moment when a child had learned to exist upon the smallest possible portion of the weakest possible food, it did happen in eight and a half cases out of ten, either that it sickened from want and cold, or fell into the fire from neglect, or got half-smothered by accident. In any of these cases, the miserable little being was usually summoned into another world.

Occasionally, after a parish child had been inadvertently scalded to death when there happened to be a washing—though the accident was scarce, a washing being rare in the farm—the jury would take it into their heads to ask troublesome questions. But this rudeness was overcome by the evidence of the surgeon, and the testimony of the beadle. The former always opened the body and found nothing inside (which was probable indeed), and the latter invariably promised whatever the parish wanted. Besides, the board made periodical visits to the farm, and always sent the beadle the day before, to say they were going. The children were neat and clean when they went, and what more would the people have!

Nevertheless, this system of farming did not produce an extraordinary crop. Oliver Twist's ninth birthday found him a pale thin child, somewhat small in stature and circumference. But nature had implanted a good sturdy spirit in Oliver, and it may have been responsible for his having any ninth birthday at all. He was spending it in the coal cellar with a select party of two other young gentleman, who, after receiving a sound thrashing, had been locked up for claiming to be hungry. Meanwhile, Mrs. Mann, the good lady of the house, was unexpectedly startled by the arrival of Mr. Bumble, the beadle, striving to undo the latch of the garden gate.

"Goodness gracious! Is that you, Mr. Bumble, sir?" said Mrs. Mann, thrusting her head out of the window in seeming ecstasies of joy. "(Susan, take Oliver and them two brats upstairs, and wash 'em directly.)—Mr. Bumble, how glad I am to see you!"

Now, Mr. Bumble was a fat, bad-tempered man. So, instead of responding to this open-hearted greeting, he gave the little gate a tremendous shake, and then a kick, which could have been delivered from no leg but a beadle's.

"Lor, only think!" said Mrs. Mann, running out—"That I should have forgotten that the gate was bolted on the inside, on account of them dear children! Walk in, sir, pray, Mr. Bumble, do, sir."

"Do you think this respectful or proper conduct, Mrs. Mann," inquired Mr. Bumble, grasping his cane, "to keep the parish officers waiting at your garden gate, when they come here upon porochial business with the porochial orphans? Are you aweer, Mrs. Mann, that you are, as I may say, a porochial delegate, and a stipendiary?"

"Mr. Bumble, I was only telling one or two of the dear children as is so fond of you, that it was you coming," replied Mrs. Mann with great humility.

"Well, Mrs. Mann," he replied in a calmer tone, "it may be as you say. Lead the way in, Mrs. Mann, for I come on business, and have something to say."

Mrs. Mann ushered the beadle into a small parlor, where she placed a seat for him and ceremoniously put his cocked hat and cane on the table before him. Mr. Bumble wiped his forehead, glanced complacently at the cocked hat, and smiled.

"Now don't you be offended at what I'm going to say," observed Mrs. Mann, with captivating sweetness. "You've had a long walk, or I wouldn't mention it. Now, will you take a little drop of somethink, Mr. Bumble?"

"Not a drop," said Mr. Bumble, waving his right hand in a dignified manner.

"I think you will," said Mrs. Mann, who had noticed the tone of the refusal, and the accompanying gesture. "Just a leetle drop."

"What is it?" inquired the beadle.

"Why, it's what I'm obliged to keep in the house, to put into the blessed infants' medicine, when they ain't well, Mr. Bumble," replied Mrs. Mann as she opened a corner cupboard, and took down a bottle and glass. "I'll not deceive you, Mr. B. It's gin."

"Do you give the children medicine, Mrs. Mann?" inquired Bumble, following with his eyes the interesting process of mixing.

"Ah, that I do, dear as it is," replied the nurse. "I couldn't see 'em suffer before my eyes, you know sir."

"No," said Mr. Bumble approvingly, "you could not. You are a humane woman, Mrs. Mann. I shall mention it to the board, Mrs. Mann. I drink your health with cheerfulness," and he swallowed half of his drink.

"And now about business," said the beadle. "The child that was half-baptized Oliver Twist is nine years old today."

"Bless him!" said Mrs. Mann, inflaming her left eye with the corner of her apron.

"And despite a reward of ten pound, which was afterwards increased to twenty pound, and the most supernat'ral exertions on the part of this parish," said Bumble, "we have never been able to discover who is his father, or his mother's origin, name, or condition."

Mrs. Mann asked, "How comes he to have any name at all, then?"

The beadle drew himself up with great pride, and said, "I inwented it."

"You, Mr. Bumble!"

"I, Mrs. Mann. We name our foundlings in alphabetical order. The last was a S—Swubble, I named him. This was a T—Twist, I named him. The next one will be Unwin, and the next Vilkins."

"Why, you're quite a literary character, sir!" said Mrs. Mann.

"Well," said the beadle, "perhaps I may be." He

finished the gin and water, and added, "Oliver being now too old to remain here, the board have determined to have him back into the house. So let me see him at once."

"I'll fetch him directly," said Mrs. Mann. Oliver, having had by this time as much dirt removed as could be scrubbed off in one washing, was led into the room.

"Make a bow to the gentleman, Oliver," said Mrs. Mann.

Oliver made a bow.

"Will you go along with me, Oliver?" said Mr. Bumble, in a majestic voice.

Oliver was about to say that he would go along with anybody with great readiness, when, glancing upwards, he caught sight of Mrs. Mann, who had got behind the beadle's chair, and was shaking her fist at him with a furious expression. He took the hint at once, for the fist had been too often impressed upon his body not to be deeply impressed upon his memory.

"Will she go with me?" inquired poor Oliver.

"No, she can't," replied Mr. Bumble. "But she'll come and see you sometimes."

This was no great consolation to the child. Young as he was, however, he had sense enough to make a show of great regret at going away. Mrs. Mann gave him a thousand embraces, and, what Oliver wanted a great deal more, a piece of bread and butter, lest he should seem too hungry when he got to the workhouse.

Oliver was then led away by Mr. Bumble from the wretched home where one kind word or look had never lit the gloom of his infant years. And yet he burst into an agony of childish grief, as the cottage gate closed after him. Wretched as were the little companions in misery he was leaving behind, they were the only friends he had ever known. A sense of his loneliness in the great wide world sank into the child's heart for the first time.

Mr. Bumble walked on with long strides. Little Oliver, firmly grasping his gold-laced cuff, trotted beside him.

Oliver had not been within the walls of the workhouse a quarter of an hour, and had scarcely consumed a second slice of bread, when Mr. Bumble, who had handed him over to the care of an old woman, returned. He informed Oliver that he was to appear before the board immediately.

Mr. Bumble gave him a tap on the head with his cane to wake him up, and another on the back to make him lively. He then conducted him into a large white-washed room, where eight or ten fat gentlemen were sitting round a table. At the top of the table, seated in an armchair rather higher than the rest, was a particularly fat gentleman with a round, red face.

"Bow to the board," said Bumble. Oliver brushed away two or three tears that were lingering in his eyes, and seeing no board but the table, fortunately bowed to that.

"What's your name, boy?" said the gentleman in the high chair.

Oliver was frightened at the sight of so many gentlemen, which made him tremble, and the beadle gave him another tap behind, which made him cry. These two causes made him answer in a low and hesitating voice, whereupon a gentleman in a white waistcoat said he was a fool.

"Boy," said the gentleman in the high chair, "listen to me. You know you've got no father or mother, and that you were brought up by the parish?"

"Yes, sir," replied Oliver, weeping bitterly.

"What are you crying for?" inquired the gentleman in the white waistcoat.

"I hope you say your prayers every night," said another gentleman in a gruff voice, "and pray for the people who feed you, and take care of you—like a Christian."

"Yes, sir," stammered the boy. The gentleman who spoke last was absolutely right. It would have been very like a Christian, and a marvelously good Christian too, if Oliver had prayed for the people who fed and took care of him. But he hadn't, because nobody had taught him.

"Well! You have come here to be educated, and taught a useful trade," said the red-faced gentleman in the high chair.

"So you'll begin to pick oakum tomorrow morning at six o'clock," added the surly one in the white waistcoat.

For the combination of both these blessings in the one simple process of picking oakum, Oliver bowed low, and was then hurried away to a large room, where, on a rough, hard bed, he sobbed himself to sleep.

Poor Oliver! He little thought, as he lay sleeping, that the board had arrived at a decision that would determine his fortune. But they had.

The members of this board were philosophical men, and when they turned their attention to the workhouse, they found out at once that the poor people liked it! It was a regular place of public entertainment for the poorer classes, a tavern where there was nothing to pay, where it was all play and no work.

So the board established the rule that all poor people should have the choice of being starved by a gradual process in the house, or by a quick one out of it. They contracted with the water works to lay on an unlimited supply of water, and with a corn factory to supply small quantities of oatmeal, and issued three meals of thin gruel a day, with an onion twice a week, and half a roll on Sundays. They made a great many other wise and humane regulations: kindly undertook to divorce poor married people; and, instead of compelling a man to support his family, took his family away from him, and made him a bachelor!

For the first six months after Oliver Twist arrived, the system was in full operation. It was rather expensive at first, because of the increase in the undertaker's bill, and the necessity of taking in the clothes of all the paupers, which fluttered loosely on their wasted bodies. But the population of the workhouse thinned as well as the paupers themselves, and the board were in ecstasies.

The boys were fed in a large stone hall, with a pot at one end, out of which the master, assisted by one or two women, ladled the gruel at mealtimes. Of this festive meal each boy had one bowl, and no more—except on occasions of great public rejoicing, when he had two ounces and a quarter of bread besides.

The bowls never wanted washing. The boys polished them with their spoons till they shone again. When they had performed this operation (which never took long, the spoons being nearly as large as the bowls), they would sit staring at the pot with eager eyes, meanwhile sucking their fingers most diligently, to catch any spare gruel.

Oliver Twist and his companions suffered the tortures of slow starvation for three months. At last they got so voracious and wild with hunger, that a council was held, and lots were cast on who should walk up to the master after supper that evening, and ask for more. It fell to Oliver Twist.

The evening arrived, and the boys took their places. The master, in his cook's uniform, stationed himself at the pot. His pauper assistants arranged themselves behind him. The gruel was served out, and a long grace was said. The gruel disappeared, and the boys whispered to each other, and winked at Oliver, while his neighbors nudged him. He was desperate with hunger, and reckless with misery. He rose from the table, and, advancing to the master, basin and spoon in hand, said, somewhat alarmed at his own audacity, "Please, sir, I want some more."

The master, a fat, healthy man, turned pale, gazing in stupefied astonishment on the small rebel for some seconds, and then clung for support to the pot. The assistants were paralyzed with wonder, the boys with fear.

"What!" said the master at length, in a faint voice.

"Please, sir," replied Oliver, "I want some more."

The master aimed a blow at Oliver's head with the ladle, grabbed his arms, and shrieked aloud for the beadle.

The board were sitting in solemn meeting when Mr. Bumble rushed into the room, and addressing the gentleman in the high chair, said, "Mr. Limbkins, I beg your pardon, sir! Oliver Twist has asked for more!"

There was a general start. Horror struck every face.

"For more!" said Mr. Limbkins. "Compose yourself, Bumble. Do I understand that he asked for more, after he had eaten the supper allotted to him?"

"He did, sir," replied Bumble.

"That boy will be hung," said the gentleman in the white waistcoat. "I know that boy will be hung."

Nobody contradicted the gentleman's opinion. Oliver was ordered into confinement, and a sign was next morning posted outside the gate, offering a reward of five pounds to anybody who would take Oliver Twist off the hands of the parish. In other words, five pounds and Oliver Twist were offered to any man or woman who wanted an apprentice to any trade, business, or calling.

CHAPTER 3

For a week, Oliver remained a prisoner in the dark room where he had been put by the wisdom of the board. He cried bitterly all day. When the dismal night came on, he spread his little hands before his eyes to shut out the darkness, and crouching in the corner, tried to sleep. Whenever he woke with a start, trembling, he would draw himself closer to the wall, as if its cold hard surface were a protection in the gloom and loneliness that surrounded him.

As for exercise, it was nice cold weather, and he was allowed to wash himself every morning under the pump in the yard, in the presence of Mr. Bumble, who prevented his catching cold by repeated applications of the cane. As for society, he was carried every other day into the hall where the boys dined, and there flogged as a public warning. And for religious consolation, he was kicked into the same room every evening at prayer time. There he was permitted to listen to the prayers of the boys, containing a special clause, inserted by the board, in which they asked to be made good, virtuous, and obedient, and to be guarded from the sins of Oliver Twist.

It happened one morning, while Oliver was enjoying these comforts, that Mr. Bumble encountered Mr. Sowerberry, the undertaker, at the gate.

Mr. Sowerberry was a tall gaunt, large-jointed man, dressed in a suit of threadbare black. His features were not naturally cheerful, but he appeared generally agreeable as he shook Mr. Bumble's hand.

"I have taken the measure of the two women that died last night, Mr. Bumble," said the undertaker.

"You'll make your fortune, Mr. Sowerberry," said the beadle, tapping the undertaker on the shoulder, in a friendly manner, with his cane.

"Think so?" said the undertaker. "The prices allowed by the board are small, Mr. Bumble."

"So are the coffins," replied the beadle, with as close to a laugh as a great official ought to indulge in.

Mr. Sowerberry was much tickled at this, and he laughed a long time without stopping. "Well, well, Mr. Bumble," he said at length, "there's no denying that since the new system of feeding has come in, the coffins are narrower and more shallow than they used to be. But we must have some profit, Mr. Bumble. Well-seasoned timber is an expensive article, sir, and all the iron handles come by canal from Birmingham."

"Well," said Mr. Bumble, "every trade has its drawbacks. A fair profit is, of course, allowable."

"Of course," replied the undertaker. "And I must say, that I have to contend against one great disadvantage, which is that all the stout people go off the quickest. The people who have been better off are the first to sink when they come into the workhouse. Let me tell you, Mr. Bumble, that three or four inches over one's calculation makes a great hole in one's profits, especially when one has a family to provide for, sir."

As Mr. Sowerberry said this, Mr. Bumble thought it advisable to change the subject. Oliver Twist being uppermost in his mind, he turned to him.

"By the way," said Mr. Bumble, "you don't know anybody who wants a boy, do you? A porochial 'prentis, who is at present a dead weight round the porochial throat? Liberal terms, Mr. Sowerberry?" As Mr. Bumble spoke, he raised his cane to the bill above him, and gave three distinct raps upon the words "five pounds."

"Gadso!" said the undertaker. "That's just the thing I wanted to speak to you about. I was thinking that if I pay so much towards 'em, I've a right to get as much out of 'em as I can, Mr. Bumble. And so— I think I'll take the boy myself."

It was arranged that Oliver should go to Mr. Sowerberry that evening "upon liking"—a phrase that means that if the master finds, after a short trial, that he can get enough work out of a boy without putting too much food into him, he shall have him for good, to do what he likes with.

When little Oliver was taken before "the gentle-men" that evening, and informed that he was to go as general house-lad to a coffin-maker's, and that if he complained of his situation, or ever came back to the parish again, he would be sent to sea, there to be drowned, or knocked on the head, as the case might be, he showed so little emotion, that they pro-nounced him a hardened young rascal, and ordered Mr. Bumble to remove him immediately.

The simple fact was that Oliver, instead of pos-sessing too little feeling, possessed rather too much. He was being reduced, for life, to a state of brutal stupidity and sullenness by the ill-treatment he had suffered. Having heard the news of his destination in perfect silence, he pulled his cap over his eyes, and once more attaching himself to Mr. Bumble's coat cuff, was led away to a new scene of suffering.

For some time, Mr. Bumble drew Oliver along

without notice or remark. As they drew near to their destination, however, Mr. Bumble thought it best to look down, and see that the boy was in good order for inspection by his new master.

"Oliver!" said Mr. Bumble.

"Yes, sir," replied Oliver, in a low, tremulous voice.

"Pull that cap off your eyes, and hold up your head, sir."

Although Oliver did so at once, and passed the back of his unoccupied hand briskly across his eyes, he left a tear in them when he looked up at his escort. As Mr. Bumble gazed sternly upon him, it rolled down his cheek. It was followed by another, and another. Withdrawing his other hand from Mr. Bumble's, he covered his face, and wept until the tears sprang out from between his chin and bony fingers.

"Well!" exclaimed Mr. Bumble, stopping short, and darting a horrible look at his little charge. "Of all the ungrateful, and worst-disposed boys as ever I see, Oliver, you are the—"

"No, no, sir," sobbed Oliver, clinging to the beadle's hand. "No, no, sir, I will be good. Indeed, I will, sir! I am a very little boy, sir, and it is so—so—"

"So what?" inquired Mr. Bumble in amazement.

"So lonely, sir!" cried the child. "Everybody hates me. Oh! Sir, don't pray be cross to me!" The child looked in his companion's face with tears of real agony.

Mr. Bumble regarded Oliver's helpless look with some astonishment, and cleared his throat a few times. After muttering something about "that troublesome cough," he bade Oliver dry his eyes and be a good boy. Then once more taking his hand, he walked on with him in silence.

The undertaker, who had just closed the shutters of his shop, was making some entries in his daybook by the light of an appropriately dismal candle, when Mr. Bumble entered.

"Aha!" said the undertaker, looking up from the book. "Is that you, Bumble?"

"No one else, Mr. Sowerberry," replied the beadle. "Here! I've brought the boy." Oliver made a bow.

"Oh!" said the undertaker, raising the candle above his head to get a better view of Oliver. "Mrs. Sowerberry, will you have the goodness to come here a moment, my dear?"

A short, squeezed-up woman, with a quarrelsome face emerged from a little room behind the shop.

"My dear," said Mr. Sowerberry, "this is the boy from the workhouse that I told you of." Oliver bowed again.

"Dear me!" said the undertaker's wife, "he's very small."

"Why, he is rather small," replied Mr. Bumble, looking at Oliver as if it were his fault that he was no bigger. "There's no denying it. But he'll grow, Mrs. Sowerberry."

"Ah! I dare say he will," replied the lady, "on our food and our drink. I see no saving in parish children, for they always cost more to keep than they're worth. However, men always think they know best. Get downstairs, little bag o' bones." The undertaker's wife opened a side door, and pushed Oliver down a steep flight of stairs into a stone cell, damp and dark. It was the ante room to the coal cellar and kitchen, wherein sat an untidy girl, in shoes down at heel, and worn blue wool stockings.

"Here, Charlotte," said Mr. Sowerberry, who had followed Oliver down, "give this boy some of the cold bits that were put by for Trip. He hasn't come home since the morning, so he may go without 'em. I dare say the boy isn't too dainty to eat 'em—are you, boy?"

Oliver, whose eyes had glistened at the mention of food, replied in the negative, and a plateful of scraps was set before him. He clutched at the food that the dog had neglected, and tore into the bits with all the ferocity of famine.

"Well," said the undertaker's wife when Oliver had finished his supper, which she had regarded with fearful thoughts of his future appetite, "are you done?"

There being nothing edible within his reach, Oliver replied in the affirmative.

"Then come with me," said Mrs. Sowerberry, taking up a dirty lamp, and leading the way upstairs. "Your bed's under the counter. You don't mind sleeping among the coffins, I suppose? But it doesn't much matter whether you do, for you can't sleep anywhere else."

Oliver lingered no longer, but meekly followed his new mistress.

CHAPTER 4

Oliver, left to himself in the undertaker's shop, gazed timidly about him with a feeling of dread, which many people a good deal older than he will understand. An unfinished coffin, which stood in the middle of the shop, looked so gloomy and death-like that a cold tremble came over him. He almost expected to see some frightful form slowly rear its head, to drive him mad with terror.

Against the wall leaned a long row of elm boards cut in the same shape, looking in the dim light like high-shouldered ghosts with their hands in their pants pockets. Coffin plates, elm chips, bright-headed nails, and shreds of black cloth lay scattered on the floor. The shop was hot, and the atmosphere seemed tainted with the smell of coffins. The recess beneath the counter, in which his mattress lay, looked like a grave.

Nor were these the only dismal feelings that depressed Oliver. He was alone in a strange place, and had no friends to care for, or to care for him. The absence of no loved and well-remembered face sank heavily into his heart.

He wished, as he crept into his narrow bed, that it were his coffin, and that he could be lain in a calm and lasting sleep in the churchyard ground, with the tall grass waving gently above his head, and the sound of the old deep bell to soothe him in his sleep.

He was awakened in the morning by a loud kicking at the outside of the shop door, which, before he could huddle on his clothes, was repeated, in an angry manner, about twenty-five times. When he began to undo the chain, the legs stopped, and a voice began.

"Open the door, will yer?" cried the voice.

"I will, directly, sir," replied Oliver, undoing the chain, and turning the key.

"I suppose yer the new boy, ain't yer?" said the voice through the keyhole.

"Yes, sir," replied Oliver.

"Then I'll whop yer when I get in," said the voice, "you just see if I don't, my work'us brat!" and having made this obliging promise, the voice began to whistle.

Oliver did not entertain the smallest doubt that the owner of the voice, whoever he might be, would redeem his pledge most honorably. He drew back the bolts with a trembling hand, and opened the door.

Nobody did he see but a big charity-boy, sitting on a post in front of the house, eating a slice of bread and butter.

"I beg your pardon, sir," said Oliver at length, seeing no other visitor. "Did you knock?"

"I kicked," replied the charity-boy.

"Did you want a coffin, sir?" inquired Oliver, innocently.

At this, the charity-boy looked monstrously fierce, and said that Oliver would want one before long, if he cut jokes with his superiors in that way.

"Yer don't know who I am, I suppose, Work'us?" said the charity-boy, descending from the top of the post.

"No, sir," rejoined Oliver.

"I'm Mister Noah Claypole," said the charity-boy, "and you're under me. Take down the shutters, yer idle young ruffian!" With this, Mr. Claypole administered a kick to Oliver, and entered the shop with a dignified air, which did him great credit. It is difficult for a large-headed, small-eyed youth, of lumbering build and heavy face, to look dignified under any circumstances.

Oliver, having taken down the shutters, and broken a pane of glass in his effort to stagger away beneath the weight of the first one, was graciously assisted by Noah, who consoled him with the assurance that "he'd catch it." Mr. Sowerberry and Mrs. Sowerberry came down soon after. Oliver, having "caught it," followed that young gentleman down the stairs to breakfast.

"Come near the fire, Noah," said Charlotte. "I saved a nice little bit of bacon for you from master's breakfast. Oliver, shut that door, and take them bits that I've put out on the cover of the bread pan. Take it away to that box, and drink it there, and make haste, for they'll want you to mind the shop. D'ye hear?"

"D'ye hear, Work'us?" said Noah Claypole.

"Noah!" said Charlotte, "what a rude creature you are! Why don't you let the boy alone?"

"Let him alone!" said Noah. "Why everybody lets him alone enough. Neither his father nor his mother will ever interfere with him. All his relations let him have his own way pretty well. Eh, Charlotte?"

"Oh, you queer soul!" said Charlotte, bursting into a hearty laugh, in which she was joined by Noah. Then they both looked scornfully at poor Oliver Twist, as he sat shivering on the box in the coldest corner of the room, and ate the stale pieces that had been specially reserved for him.

Mr. and Mrs. Sowerberry—the shop being shut up—were taking their supper in the little back parlor, when Mr. Sowerberry, after several dutiful glances at his wife, said, "My dear—" He was going to say more, but he stopped short.

"Well," said Mrs. Sowerberry, sharply.

"Nothing, my dear, nothing," said Mr. Sowerberry.

"Ugh, you brute!" said Mrs. Sowerberry.

"Not at all, my dear," said Mr. Sowerberry humbly. "I thought you didn't want to hear, my dear. I was only going to say—"

"Oh, don't tell me what you were going to say," interposed Mrs. Sowerberry. "I am nobody, so don't consult me, please. I don't want to intrude upon your secrets." As Mrs. Sowerberry said this, she gave a hysterical laugh, which threatened violent consequences.

"But, my dear," said Mr. Sowerberry, "I want to ask your advice."

"No, don't ask mine," replied Mrs. Sowerberry, in an affected manner. "Ask somebody else's." Here, there was another hysterical laugh, which frightened Mr. Sowerberry, and at once reduced him to begging, as a special favor, to be allowed to say what Mrs. Sowerberry was most curious to hear. After a short duration, the permission was most graciously granted.

"It's only about young Twist, my dear," said Mr. Sowerberry. "A good-looking boy, my dear."

"He need be, for he eats enough," observed the lady.

"There's an interesting expression of melancholy

in his face, my dear," resumed Mr. Sowerberry. "He would make a delightful mute."

Mrs. Sowerberry looked up with an expression of considerable wonderment. Mr. Sowerberry noticed it and proceeded.

"I don't mean a regular mute to attend grown-up people, my dear, but only for children's practice. It would be new to have a mute in proportion, my dear. It would have a superb effect."

Mrs. Sowerberry, who had a good deal of taste in the undertaking way, was much struck by the novelty of this idea. But, as it would have compromised her dignity to have said so, she merely inquired, why such an obvious suggestion had not presented itself to her husband's mind before? Mr. Sowerberry rightly perceived this as an agreement to his proposition. Therefore Oliver would be at once initiated into the mysteries of the trade, accompanying his master on the next occasion of his services.

The occasion was not long in coming. Half an hour after breakfast the next morning, Mr. Bumble entered the shop and drew forth his large leather pocketbook, from which he selected a small scrap of paper, which he handed over to Sowerberry.

"Aha!" said the undertaker, glancing over it with a lively expression, "an order for a coffin, eh?"

"For a coffin first, and a porochial funeral afterwards," replied Mr. Bumble, fastening the strap of the pocketbook.

"Bayton," said the undertaker. "I never heard the name before."

Bumble shook his head, as he replied, "Obstinate people, Mr. Sowerberry. Proud, too, I'm afraid, sir."

"Proud, eh?" exclaimed Mr. Sowerberry with a sneer. "Come, that's too much."

"Oh, it's sickening," replied the beadle.

"So it is," agreed the undertaker.

"We only heard of the family the night before last," said the beadle. "A woman who lodges in the same house asked the porochial committee to send the porochial surgeon to see a woman who was very sick. He had gone out to dinner, but his 'prentice, who is a clever lad, sent 'em some medicine."

"Ah, there's promptness," said the undertaker.

"Promptness, indeed!" replied the beadle. "But what's the ungrateful behavior of these rebels, sir? Why, the husband sends back word that the medicine won't suit his wife's complaint, and so she shan't take it! Good, strong, wholesome medicine, that was given with great success to two Irish laborers and a coal heaver, only a week before—and he sends back word that she shan't take it, sir!"

Mr. Bumble struck the counter sharply with his cane, and became flushed with indignation.

"Well," said the undertaker, "I ne—ver—did—"

"No, nor nobody never did! But now she's dead, we've got to bury her, and the sooner it's done, the better."

Thus saying, Mr. Bumble put on his cocked hat wrong side first, in a fever of excitement, and flounced out of the shop.

"Why, he was so angry, Oliver, that he forgot even to ask after you!" said Mr. Sowerberry.

"Yes, sir," replied Oliver, who had carefully kept himself out of sight during the interview, and was shaking from head to foot at the sound of Mr. Bumble's voice.

"Well," said Mr. Sowerberry, taking up his hat, "the sooner this job is done, the better. Noah, look after the shop. Oliver, put on your cap, and come with me."

They walked for some time through the most crowded part of the town. Then, going down a narrow street more dirty and miserable than any they had yet passed through, paused to look for the right house. Many of the rough boards that made up doors and window shutters had been wrenched from their positions, to create an opening wide enough for the passage of a human body. The gutter was stagnant and filthy, and the very rats, which here and there lay putrefying in its rottenness, were starved by famine.

There was neither knocker nor bell handle at the open door where Oliver and his master stopped. So, groping his way cautiously through the dark passage, and bidding Oliver keep close to him and not be afraid, the undertaker climbed to the top of the first flight of stairs. Stumbling against a door on the landing, he rapped at it with his knuckles.

It was opened by a young girl of thirteen or fourteen. The undertaker at once saw enough of what the room contained to know this was the right place. He stepped in, and Oliver followed him.

There was no fire in the room, but a man and an old woman were crouching over the empty stove. There were some ragged children in another corner, and in a small recess, opposite the door, there lay upon the ground something covered with an old blanket. Oliver shuddered as he cast his eyes towards the place, and crept involuntarily closer to his master. Though it was covered up, the boy knew that it was a corpse.

The man's face was thin and pale, his hair and beard grizzly, his eyes bloodshot. The old woman's face was wrinkled. Her two remaining teeth protruded over her underlip, and her eyes were bright and piercing. Oliver was afraid to look at either her or the man. They seemed so like the rats he had seen outside.

"Nobody shall go near her," said the man, starting fiercely up. "Keep back! Damn you, keep back, if you've a life to lose!"

"Nonsense, my good man," said the undertaker, who was used to misery in all its shapes.

"I tell you," said the man, clenching his hands, and stamping furiously on the floor, "I won't have her put into the ground. She couldn't rest there. The worms would worry her, she is so worn away."

The undertaker offered no reply to this raving, but producing a tape from his pocket, knelt down for a moment by the side of the body.

"Ah!" said the man, bursting into tears, and sinking on his knees at the feet of the dead woman, "kneel round her, every one of you, and mark my words! I say she was starved to death. I never knew how bad she was, till the fever came upon her, and then her bones were starting through the skin. There was neither fire nor candle—she died in the dark! She couldn't even see her children's faces, though we heard her gasping out their names. I begged for her in the streets, and they sent me to prison. When I came back, she was dying. I swear it before the God that saw it! They starved her!" He twined his hands in his hair, and, with a loud scream, rolled upon the floor, the foam covering his lips.

The terrified children cried bitterly, but the old woman, who had hitherto remained as quiet as if she had been deaf to all that passed, menaced them into silence. Then she tottered towards the undertaker.

"She was my daughter," said the old woman, nodding her head in the direction of the corpse and speaking with an idiotic leer. "Lord! Well, it is strange that I who gave birth to her, and was a woman then, should be alive and merry now, and she lying there so cold and stiff! It's as good as a play—as good as a play!"

As the wretched creature mumbled and chuckled in her hideous merriment, the undertaker turned to go away.

"Stop, stop!" said the old woman in a loud whisper. "Will she be buried tomorrow, or next day, or tonight? I laid her out, and I must walk, you know. Send me a good warm cloak, for it is bitter cold. We should have cake and wine, too, before we go! Never mind—send some bread—only a loaf of bread and a cup of water. Shall we have some bread, dear?" she said eagerly, catching at the undertaker's coat.

"Yes, yes," said the undertaker, "Anything you like!" He disengaged himself from the old woman's grasp, and, drawing Oliver after him, hurried away.

The next day, the family having been meanwhile relieved with a half loaf and a piece of cheese, Oliver and his master returned to the miserable abode. Mr. Bumble had already arrived, accompanied by four men from the workhouse, who were to act as bearers. An old black cloak had been thrown over the rags of the old woman and the man, and the bare coffin was hoisted on the shoulders of the bearers, and carried into the street.

"Now, you must put your best foot foremost, old lady!" whispered Sowerberry in the old woman's ear. "We are rather late, and it won't do to keep the clergyman waiting. Move on, my men!"

The bearers trotted on under their light burden, and the two mourners kept as near them as they could. Mr. Bumble and Sowerberry walked at a smart pace in front, and Oliver ran by the side.

However, when they reached the obscure corner of the churchyard where the parish graves were made, the clergyman had not arrived. The clerk, who was sitting by the vestry-room fire, seemed to think it might be an hour or so before he came. So, they put the bier on the brink of the grave, and the two mourners waited patiently with a cold rain drizzling down, while the ragged boys whom the spectacle had attracted into the churchyard jumped backward and forward over the coffin. Mr. Sowerberry and Bumble, being personal friends of the clerk, sat by the fire with him, and read the paper.

At length, after more than an hour, Mr. Bumble, Sowerberry, and the clerk were seen running towards the grave. Immediately afterwards, the clergyman appeared. Mr. Bumble then thrashed a boy or two, to keep up appearances. The reverend gentleman, having read as much of the burial service as could be compressed into four minutes, walked away again.

"Now, Bill!" said Sowerberry to the grave digger. "Fill up!"

It was no difficult task, for the grave was so full that the uppermost coffin was within a few feet of the surface. The grave digger shoveled in the earth, stamped it loosely down with his feet, shouldered his spade, and then walked off, followed by the boys, who murmured loud complaints at the fun being over so soon.

"Come, my good fellow!" said Bumble, tapping the man on the back. "They want to shut up the yard."

The man, who had never once moved since he had taken his station by the grave side, started, raised his head, and stared at the person who had addressed him. He walked forward for a few paces and fell down in a swoon. The crazy old woman was too much occupied in bewailing the loss of her cloak, which the undertaker had taken off, to pay him any attention. So they threw a can of cold water over him, and when he came to, they saw him safely out of the churchyard, locked the gate, and departed on their different ways.

"Well, Oliver," said Sowerberry, as they walked home, "how do you like it?"

"Not much, sir," replied Oliver, with considerable hesitation.

"Ah, you'll get used to it in time, Oliver," said Sowerberry.

Oliver wondered, in his own mind, whether it had taken a long time for Mr. Sowerberry to get used to it. But he thought it better not to ask the question. He walked back to the shop, thinking over all he had seen and heard.

CHAPTER 5

The month's trial over, Oliver was formally apprenticed. It was a nice sickly season just at this time, and coffins were doing well. The oldest inhabitants could not remember when measles had been so prevalent, or so fatal to infants. In the course of a few weeks, Oliver acquired a great deal of experience. The success of Mr. Sowerberry's idea exceeded even his highest hopes. Oliver headed many mournful processions, in a hatband reaching down to his knees, to the indescribable admiration and emotion of all the mothers in the town.

He continued meekly to submit to the ill-treatment of Noah Claypole, who used him far worse than before, now that his envy was roused by seeing the new boy promoted, while he, the old one, remained where he was. Charlotte treated Oliver ill, because Noah did, and Mrs. Sowerberry was his decided enemy, because Mr. Sowerberry was disposed to be his friend. So, between these three on one side, and a glut of funerals on the other, Oliver was not altogether comfortable.

One day, Oliver and Noah had gone to the kitchen to dine upon a small joint of mutton. Charlotte was quickly called away, and Noah Claypole, being hungry and vicious, decided to devote the time to aggravating young Oliver Twist.

Noah put his feet on the tablecloth, pulled Oliver's hair, twitched his ears, and called him a "sneak." Furthermore, he announced his intention of

coming to see him hanged, whenever that desirable
event should take place. And in order to make Oliver
cry, he did what many sometimes do to this day, when
they want to be funny. He got rather personal.

"Work'us," said Noah, "how's your mother?"

"She's dead," replied Oliver. "Don't you say
anything about her to me!"

Oliver's color rose as he said this. He breathed
quickly, and there was a curious working of the
mouth and nostrils, which Noah thought must fore-
shadow a violent fit of crying.

"What did she die of, Work'us?" said Noah.

"Of a broken heart, some of our old nurses told
me," replied Oliver, more as if he were talking to
himself, than answering Noah. "I think I know what
it must be to die of that!"

"Work'us," said Noah, as a tear rolled down
Oliver's cheek. "What's set you a snivelling now?"

"Not you," replied Oliver, sharply. "Don't say
anything more to me about her. You'd better not!"

"Better not!" exclaimed Noah. "Work'us, don't
be impudent. Your mother was a nice 'un she was."
And here, Noah nodded his head expressively, curled
up as much of his small red nose as possible.

"Yer know, Work'us," continued Noah, speaking in a jeering tone of affected pity. "It can't be
helped now, and I am sorry for it. I'm sure we all are,
and pity yer very much. But yer must know, Work'us,
yer mother was a regular right-down bad 'un."

"What did you say?" inquired Oliver, looking up
quickly.

"A regular right-down bad 'un, Work'us,"
replied Noah, coolly. "And it's a great deal better
that she died when she did, or else she'd have been
hard laboring in Bridewell, or transported, or hung,

which is more likely than either, isn't it?"

Crimson with fury, Oliver started up, overthrew the chair and table, seized Noah by the throat and shook him till his teeth chattered in his head. Then, collecting his whole force into one heavy blow, he felled him to the ground.

A minute ago, the boy had looked the mild, dejected creature that harsh treatment had made him. But his spirit was roused at last, and the cruel insult to his dead mother had set his blood on fire. His whole person changed, as he stood glaring over the cowardly tormentor who now lay crouching at his feet, and he felt an energy he had never known before.

"He'll murder me!" blubbered Noah. "Charlotte! Missis! Here's the new boy a murdering me! Help! Oliver's gone mad! Char—lotte!"

Noah's shouts were responded to by a loud scream from Charlotte, and a louder one from Mrs. Sowerberry. The first woman rushed into the kitchen by a side door, while the latter paused on the staircase till she was quite certain that it was necessary for the preservation of human life to come further down.

"Oh, you little wretch!" screamed Charlotte, seizing Oliver with her utmost force, which was about equal to that of a moderately strong man in particularly good training. "Oh, you little un-grate-ful, mur-de-rous, hor-rid villain!" And between every syllable, Charlotte gave Oliver a blow with all her might, accompanying it with a scream, for the benefit of society.

Lest Charlotte's fist should not calm Oliver's wrath, Mrs. Sowerberry plunged into the kitchen, and held him with one hand, while she scratched his face with the other. Noah rose from the ground, and pommelled him behind.

When they were all wearied out, and could tear and beat no longer, they dragged Oliver, struggling and shouting, into the dust cellar, and there locked him up. This being done, Mrs. Sowerberry sank into a chair, and burst into tears.

"Bless her, she's going off!" said Charlotte. "A glass of water, Noah, dear."

"Oh! Charlotte," said Mrs. Sowerberry, speaking as well as she could as Noah poured the cold water over her head and shoulders. "Oh! Charlotte, what a mercy we have not all been murdered in our beds!"

"Mercy indeed, ma'am," was the reply. "I only hope this'll teach master not to have any more of these dreadful creatures that are born to be murderers and robbers from their cradle. Poor Noah! He was all but killed, ma'am, when I come in."

"Poor fellow!" said Mrs. Sowerberry, looking piteously on the charity-boy.

Noah, whose top waistcoat button might have been somewhere on a level with the crown of Oliver's head, performed some affecting tears and sniffs.

"What's to be done!" exclaimed Mrs. Sowerberry. "Your master's not at home, and he'll kick that door down in ten minutes." Oliver's vigorous plunges against the bit of timber in question made this event highly probable.

"I don't know, ma'am," said Charlotte, "unless we send for the police officers."

"No, no," said Mrs. Sowerberry. "Run to Mr. Bumble, Noah, and tell him to come here directly, and not to lose a minute. Never mind your cap! Make haste!"

Noah stopped to make no reply, but started off at his fullest speed.

CHAPTER 6

Noah Claypole ran along the streets and paused not once for breath, until he reached the workhouse gate. Having rested here, for a minute or so, to collect a good burst of sobs and an imposing show of tears and terror, he knocked loudly at the gate. He presented such a rueful face to the aged pauper who opened it that he started back in astonishment.

"Why, what's the matter with the boy?" said the old pauper.

"Mr. Bumble!" cried Noah, with dismay, and in tones so loud and agitated that Mr. Bumble himself, who happened to be nearby, rushed into the yard without his cocked hat.

"Oh, Mr. Bumble, sir!" said Noah: "Oliver, sir—Oliver has—"

"What? What?" interrupted Mr. Bumble, with a gleam of pleasure in his metallic eyes. "Not run away, has he, Noah?"

"No, sir, but he's turned wicious," replied Noah. "He tried to murder me, sir, and then he tried to murder Charlotte and missis. Oh! What dreadful pain it is!" And here, Noah twisted his body into a variety of eel-like positions, giving the impression that he had sustained severe internal injury and damage.

When Noah saw that the information paralyzed Mr. Bumble, he bewailed his dreadful wounds ten times louder than before. And, when he observed a gentleman in a white waistcoat crossing the yard, he was more tragic in his lamentations than ever.

The gentleman turned angrily round, and inquired what that young cur was howling for.

"It's a poor boy from the free-school, sir," replied Mr. Bumble, "who has been nearly murdered by young Twist."

"I knew it!" exclaimed the gentleman, stopping short. "I felt a strange premonition from the first that the young savage would come to be hung!"

"He has likewise attempted, sir, to murder the female servant," said Mr. Bumble, with a face of ashy paleness.

"And his missis," interposed Mr. Claypole.

"And his master, too, I think you said, Noah?" added Mr. Bumble.

"No! He's out, or he would have murdered him," replied Noah. "He said he wanted to."

"Ah! Said he wanted to, did he, my boy?" inquired the gentleman in the white waistcoat.

"Yes, sir," replied Noah. "And please, sir, missis wants to know whether Mr. Bumble can step up there, directly, and flog him—'cause master's out."

"Certainly, my boy," said the gentleman in the white waistcoat, smiling and patting Noah's head, which was about three inches higher than his own. "You're a good boy. Here's a penny for you. Bumble, just step up to Sowerberry's with your cane, and see what's best to be done. Don't spare him, Bumble."

"No, I will not, sir," replied the beadle. And the cocked hat and cane having been, by this time, adjusted to their owner's satisfaction, Mr. Bumble and Noah Claypole ran with all speed to the undertaker's shop.

Here the position of affairs had not at all

improved. Sowerberry had not yet returned, and Oliver continued to kick, with undiminished vigor, at the cellar door. The accounts of his ferocity were so startling that Mr. Bumble judged it prudent to talk before opening the door. He gave a kick at the outside, and, then, applying his mouth to the key-hole, said, in a deep and impressive tone, "Oliver!"

"You let me out!" replied Oliver, from the inside.

"Do you know this voice, Oliver?" said Mr. Bumble.

"Yes," replied Oliver.

"Ain't you afraid of it, sir?" said Mr. Bumble.

"No!" replied Oliver, boldly.

An answer so different from the one he had expected staggered Mr. Bumble. He stepped back from the keyhole and looked from one to another of the three bystanders, in mute astonishment.

"Oh, Mr. Bumble, he must be mad," said Mrs. Sowerberry. "No boy in half his senses could venture to speak so to you."

"It's not madness, ma'am," replied Mr. Bumble, after a few moments of deep meditation. "It's meat."

"What?" exclaimed Mrs. Sowerberry.

"Meat, ma'am, meat," replied Bumble, with stern emphasis. "You've overfed him, ma'am. You've raised an artificial soul and spirit in him, ma'am, unbecoming a person of his condition. What have paupers to do with soul or spirit? It's quite enough that we let 'em have live bodies. If you had kept the boy on gruel, ma'am, this would never have happened."

"Dear, dear!" ejaculated Mrs. Sowerberry, piously raising her eyes to the kitchen ceiling. "This comes of being liberal!"

"Ah!" said Mr. Bumble, "the only thing that can be done now is to leave him in the cellar for a day or so, till he's a little starved down. Then take him out, and keep him on gruel all through the apprenticeship. He comes of a bad family. Excitable natures, Mrs. Sowerberry! The doctor said that mother of his made her way here against difficulties and pain that would have killed any well-disposed woman weeks before."

At this point, Oliver, just hearing enough to know that some allusion was being made to his mother, recommenced kicking, with a violence that rendered every other sound inaudible. Sowerberry returned at this juncture. Oliver's offense having been explained to him, with such exaggerations as the ladies thought best calculated to rouse his ire, he unlocked the cellar door in a twinkling, and dragged his rebellious apprentice out by the collar.

Oliver's clothes had been torn in the beating he had received. His face was bruised and scratched, and his hair scattered over his forehead. The angry flush had not disappeared, however, when he was pulled out of his prison. He scowled boldly at Noah and looked quite undismayed.

"You are a nice young fellow, ain't you?" said Sowerberry, giving Oliver a box on the ear.

"He called my mother names," replied Oliver.

"And what if he did, you ungrateful wretch?" said Mrs. Sowerberry. "She deserved what he said, and worse."

"She didn't," said Oliver.

"She did," said Mrs. Sowerberry.

"It's a lie!" said Oliver.

Mrs. Sowerberry burst into a flood of tears, which left Mr. Sowerberry no alternative. If he had hesitated for one instant to punish Oliver most severely, he would have been an unnatural husband and a base imitation of a man. He was kindly disposed towards the boy. The flood of tears, however, left him no choice, so he at once gave him a drubbing, which satisfied even Mrs. Sowerberry.

For the rest of the day, Oliver was shut up in the back kitchen with water and a slice of bread. At night, Mrs. Sowerberry, after making various remarks about his mother outside the door, ordered him upstairs to his dismal bed.

It was not until he was left alone in the silence of the gloomy workshop that Oliver gave way to his feelings. He had listened to their taunts with a look of contempt. He had borne the lash without a cry, for he felt that pride swelling in his heart that would have kept down a shriek to the last, though they had roasted him alive. But now, when there were none to see or hear him, he fell upon his knees on the floor. Hiding his face in his hands, he wept such tears as few so young ever have cause to pour out!

For a long time, Oliver remained motionless in this attitude. The candle was burning low when he rose to his feet. Having gazed cautiously round him and listened intently, he gently undid the fastenings of the door, and looked out.

It was a cold, dark night. The stars seemed, to the boy's eyes, farther from the earth than he had ever seen them before. There was no wind, and the somber shadows thrown by the trees upon the ground looked death-like. He softly reclosed the door and tied up in a handkerchief the few articles of clothing he had. Then he sat himself down upon a bench to wait for morning.

With the first ray of light that struggled through the crevices in the shutters, Oliver arose and again unbarred the door. After one timid look around, he closed it behind him and was in the open street.

He looked to the right and to the left, uncertain whither to fly.

He remembered seeing the wagons as they went out, toiling up the hill. He took the same route, and arriving at a footpath across the fields, he struck into it, and walked quickly on. Along this same footpath, Oliver had trotted beside Mr. Bumble, when he first brought him to the workhouse from the farm. His heart beat quickly when he thought of this, and he half resolved to turn back. He had come a long way, though, and should lose a great deal of time by doing so. Besides, it was so early that there was little fear of his being seen, so he walked on.

When he reached the house, he stopped, and peeped into the garden. One of his former companions was weeding one of the little beds. Oliver felt glad to see him. They had been beaten, and starved and shut up together, many a time.

"Hush, Dick!" said Oliver, as the boy ran to the gate, and thrust his thin arm between the rails to greet him. "Is any one up?"

"Nobody but me," replied the child.

"You musn't say you saw me, Dick," said Oliver. "I am running away. They beat and ill-used me, Dick, and I am going to seek my fortune. How pale you are!"

"I heard the doctor tell them I was dying," replied the child with a faint smile. "I am very glad to see you, but don't stop!"

"Yes, I will, to say good b'ye to you," replied Oliver. "I shall see you again, Dick. I know I shall! You will be well and happy!"

"I hope so," replied the child. "After I am dead, but not before. I know the doctor must be right, Oliver, because I dream so much of Heaven, and Angels, and kind faces that I never see when I am awake. Kiss me," said the child, climbing up the low gate, and flinging his little arms round Oliver's neck. "Good b'ye! God bless you!"

The blessing was the first that Oliver had ever heard invoked upon his head. Through the struggles and sufferings, and troubles and changes of his life, he never once forgot it.

CHAPTER 7

Oliver reached the end of the bypath and once more gained the highroad. It was eight o'clock now. Though he was nearly five miles away from the town, he ran, and hid behind the hedges by turns till noon, fearing that he might be pursued and overtaken. Then he sat down to rest by the side of a milestone, and began to think, for the first time, where he had better go and try to live.

The stone by which he was seated advertised that it was just seventy miles from that spot to London.

London!—nobody—not even Mr. Bumble— could ever find him there! He had often heard the old men in the workhouse, too, say that no lad of spirit need want in London. It was the very place for a homeless boy. He jumped upon his feet, and again walked forward.

Oliver walked twenty miles that day, and all that time tasted nothing but the crust of dry bread, and a few drinks of water, which he begged at the cottage doors by the roadside. When the night came, he went into a meadow and decided to lie there till morning. He felt frightened at first, for the wind moaned dismally over the empty fields. He was cold and hungry, and more alone than he had ever felt before. Being tired with his walk, however, he soon fell asleep and forgot his troubles.

He felt cold and stiff when he got up next morning, and so hungry that he was obliged to exchange his only penny for a small loaf in the first village through which he passed. He had walked no more than twelve miles when night closed in again. His feet were sore, and his legs so weak that they trembled beneath him. Another night spent sleeping in the bleak damp air made him worse. When he set forward on his journey next morning, he could hardly crawl along.

He waited at the bottom of a steep hill till a stagecoach came up, and then begged from the outside passengers, but there were few who took any notice of him. Even those told him to wait till they got to the top of the hill, and then let them see how far he could run for a halfpenny. Poor Oliver tried to keep up with the coach a little way, but was unable to do it, because of his fatigue and sore feet. When the passengers saw this, they put their halfpence back into their pockets again, declaring that he was an idle young dog, and didn't deserve anything. The coach rattled away and left only a cloud of dust behind.

In some villages, large painted boards were fixed up, warning all persons who begged within the district that they would be sent to jail. This frightened Oliver, and made him glad to move on. In others, he would stand about the inn-yards, and look mournfully at every one who passed, until the landlady ordered one of the post-boys to drive that strange boy out of the place, for she was sure he had come to steal something. If he begged at a farmer's house, they threatened to set the dog on him. When he showed his nose in a shop, they talked about the beadle—which brought Oliver's heart into his mouth—often the only thing he had there, for many hours.

In fact, if it had not been for a good-hearted

turnpike man, and a benevolent old lady, Oliver would most assuredly have fallen dead upon the King's highway. The turnpike man gave him a meal of bread and cheese, and the old lady, who had a shipwrecked grandson wandering barefoot in some distant part of the earth, took pity upon the poor orphan, and gave him what little she could afford—and more—with such kind and gentle words, and such tears of sympathy and compassion, that they sank deeper into Oliver's soul than all the sufferings he had ever undergone.

Early on the seventh morning after he had left his native place, Oliver limped slowly into the little town of Barnet. Not a soul had awakened to the business of the day. The sun was rising in all its splendid beauty, but the light only served to show the boy his own lonesomeness and desolation, as he sat, with bleeding feet and covered with dust, upon a doorstep.

By degrees, the shutters were opened, and people began passing to and fro. Some few stopped to gaze at Oliver for a moment or two, or turned round to stare at him as they hurried by. But none troubled themselves to inquire how he came there.

He had been crouching on the step for some time, wondering at the great number of taverns, gazing listlessly at the coaches as they passed through, and thinking how strange it seemed that they could do with ease, in a few hours, what it had taken him a whole week of courage and determination beyond his years to accomplish. Then he observed that a boy, who had passed him carelessly some minutes before, had returned, and was now surveying him most earnestly from the opposite side of the way. Oliver raised his head, and returned his steady look. Upon this, the boy crossed over, and walking close up to Oliver, said, "Hullo, my covey! What's the row?"

The boy was about his own age, but one of the queerest looking boys that Oliver had even seen. He was a snub-nosed, flat-browed, common-faced boy enough, and as dirty a juvenile as one would wish to see. But he had about him all the airs and manners of a man. He was short for his age, with rather bow legs, and little, sharp, ugly eyes. His hat was stuck on the top of his head so lightly that it threatened to fall off every moment—and would have done so, if he had not every now and then given his head a sudden twitch, which brought it back to its old place again. He wore a man's coat, which reached nearly to his heels. He had turned the cuffs back, halfway up his arm, to get his hands out of the sleeves. He was as swaggering a young gentleman as ever stood four feet six.

"Hullo, my covey! What's the row?" said this strange young gentleman to Oliver.

"I am very hungry and tired," replied Oliver, the tears standing in his eyes as he spoke. "I have been walking these seven days."

"Walking for sivin days!" said the young gentleman. "Beak's order, eh? But," he added, noticing Oliver's look of surprise, "I suppose you don't know what a beak is, my flash com-pan-i-on."

Oliver mildly replied that he had always heard a bird's mouth described by the term in question.

"My eyes, how green!" exclaimed the young gentleman. "Why, a beak's a madgst'rate, and when you walk by a beak's order, it's not straight forerd, but always agoing up, and niver a coming down agin.

Was you never on the mill?"

"What mill?" inquired Oliver.

"What mill! Why, the mill—the mill as takes up so little room that it'll work inside a stone jug, and always goes better when the wind's low with people, than when it's high, acos then they can't get work-men. But come," said the young gentleman, "you want grub, and you shall have it. I'm at low-water-mark myself—only one bob and a magpie. But, as far as it goes, I'll fork out and stump. Up with you on your pins. There! Now then!"

The young gentleman took Oliver to an adjacent shop, where he purchased a ready-dressed ham and a half-quarter loaf, the ham being kept clean and pre-served from dust by pulling out a portion of the bread, and stuffing it therein. Taking the bread under his arm, the young gentleman turned into a small public house, and led the way to a tap room in the rear of the premises. Here, a pot of beer was brought in, by direction of the mysterious youth, and Oliver made a long and hearty meal, during which the strange boy eyed him with great attention.

"Going to London?" said the strange boy, when Oliver had finished.

"Yes."

"Got any lodgings?"

"No."

"Money?"

"No."

The strange boy whistled and put his arms into his pockets, as far as the big coat sleeves would let them go.

"Do you live in London?" inquired Oliver.

"I do, when I'm at home," replied the boy. "I

suppose you want some place to sleep in tonight, don't you?"

"I do, indeed," answered Oliver. "I have not slept under a roof since I left the country."

"Don't fret your eyelids on that score," said the young gentleman. "I've got to be in London tonight, and I know a 'spectable old gentleman who lives there, wot'll give you lodgings for nothink, and never ask for the change—that is, if any genelman he knows interduces you."

This unexpected offer of shelter was too tempting to be resisted, especially as it was immediately followed up by the assurance that the old gentleman would doubtless provide Oliver with comfortable work. This led to a more friendly and confidential dialogue, from which Oliver discovered that his friend's name was Jack Dawkins, and that he was a protege of the elderly gentleman.

Mr. Dawkins's appearance did not say a great deal in favor of the comforts that his patron provided. But, as he had a rather flighty way of talking, and furthermore said that he was known by the nickname "The Artful Dodger," Oliver concluded that, being of a careless turn, the moral teachings of his benefactor had been thrown away upon him. He secretly resolved to cultivate the good opinion of the old gentleman as quickly as possible, and, if he found the Dodger incorrigible, as he more than half suspected he should, to decline the honor of his further acquaintance.

As Jack Dawkins objected to their entering London before nightfall, it was nearly eleven o'clock when they reached the turnpike at Islington. They crossed from the Angel into St. John's Road; struck down the small street which terminates at Sadler's Wells Theatre; through Exmouth Street and Coppice Row; across the ground that once bore the name of Hockley-in-the-Hole; thence into Little Saffron Hill; and so into Saffron Hill the Great, along which the Dodger walked at a rapid pace.

Oliver could not help glancing on either side of the way as he passed along. A dirtier or more wretched place he had never seen. The street was narrow and muddy, and the air was filled with filthy odors.

There were a good many small shops, but the only stock in trade appeared to be heaps of children, who, even at that time of night, were crawling in and out at the doors, or screaming from the inside. The sole places that seemed to prosper amid the general blight of the place were the taverns. Covered ways and yards disclosed little knots of houses, where drunken men and women positively wallowed in filth. From several of the doorways, ill-looking fellows were cautiously emerging.

Oliver was just considering whether he hadn't better run away, when they reached the bottom of the hill. His conductor, catching him by the arm, pushed open the door of a house near Field Lane, and, drawing him into the passage, closed it behind them.

"Now, then!" cried a voice from below, in reply to a whistle from the Dodger.

"Plummy and slam!" was the reply.

This seemed to be some watchword that all was right, for the light of a feeble candle gleamed on the wall at the remote end of the passage. A man's face peeped out, from where a balustrade of the old kitchen staircase had broken away.

"There's two of you," said the man, thrusting the candle farther out, and shielding his eyes with his hand. "Who's the t'other one?"

"A new pal," replied Jack Dawkins, pulling Oliver forward.

"Where did he come from?"

"Greenland. Is Fagin upstairs?"

"Yes, he's a sortin' the wipes. Up with you!" The candle was drawn back, and the face disappeared.

Oliver, groping his way with one hand, and having the other firmly grasped by his companion, ascended with much difficulty the dark and broken stairs.

Dawkins threw open the door of a backroom, and drew Oliver in after him.

The walls and ceiling of the room were perfectly black with age and dirt. There was a table before the fire, upon which were a candle, stuck in a ginger-beer bottle, two or three pewter pots, a loaf and butter, and a plate. In a frying pan, which was on the fire, some sausages were cooking. Standing over them, with a toasting fork in his hand, was an old shriveled Jew, whose repulsive face was obscured by a quantity of matted red hair. He was dressed in a greasy flannel gown and seemed to be dividing his attention between the frying pan and the clothes-horse, over which a great number of silk handkerchiefs were hanging. Several rough beds made of old sacks were huddled side by side on the floor.

Seated round the table were four boys, none older than the Dodger, smoking long clay pipes, and drinking spirits with the air of middle-aged men. These all crowded about their associate as he whispered a few words to the Jew, and then turned round and grinned at Oliver. So did the Jew himself, toasting fork in hand.

"This is him, Fagin," said Jack Dawkins, "my friend Oliver Twist."

The Jew grinned, and, making a low bow to Oliver, took him by the hand, and hoped he should have the honor of his intimate acquaintance. Upon this, the young gentleman with the pipes came round him, and shook both his hands hard—especially the one in which he held his little bundle. One young gentleman was anxious to hang up his cap for him; and another was so obliging as to put his hands in his pockets.

"We are glad to see you, Oliver," said the Jew. "Dodger, take off the sausages, and draw a tub near the fire for Oliver. Ah, you're staring at the pocket handkerchiefs! There are a good many of 'em, ain't there? We've just looked 'em out, ready for the wash. Ha! ha! ha!"

The latter part of this speech was hailed by a boisterous shout from all the hopeful pupils of the merry old gentleman, and then they sat down to supper.

Oliver ate his share, and the Jew then mixed him a glass of hot gin and water, telling him he must drink it off directly, because another gentleman wanted the tumbler. Oliver did as he was told. Immediately afterwards he felt himself gently lifted onto one of the sacks, and then he sank into a deep sleep.

CHAPTER 8

It was late next morning when Oliver awoke from a long sleep. There was no one in the room but the old Jew, who was boiling some coffee in a saucepan for breakfast, and whistling softly to himself as he stirred it with an iron spoon.

Oliver was not thoroughly awake, however. So, when the Jew turned round and looked at him, and called him by his name, he did not answer. He was to all appearances asleep.

After satisfying himself on this point, the Jew stepped gently to the door, which he fastened. He then drew forth, from some trap in the floor, a small box. His eyes glistened as he raised the lid and looked in. He took from it a magnificent gold watch, sparkling with jewels.

"Aha!" said the Jew, shrugging up his shoulders, and distorting every feature with a hideous grin. "Clever dogs! Staunch to the last! Never told the old parson where they were. Never poached upon old Fagin! And why should they? It wouldn't have loosened the knot, or kept the drop up a minute longer. No! Fine fellows!"

With these muttered reflections, the Jew once more deposited the watch in its place of safety. At least half a dozen more items were drawn forth from the same box, and surveyed with equal pleasure—rings, brooches, bracelets, and other articles of jewelery, of magnificent materials, and costly workmanship.

Having replaced these trinkets, the Jew took out

another one, so small that it lay in the palm of his hand. There seemed to be some small inscription on it, for the Jew laid it flat upon the table, and shading it with his hand, pored over it, long and earnestly. At length he put it down, as if despairing of success. Leaning back in his chair, he muttered, "What a fine thing capital punishment is! Dead men never repent or bring awkward stories to light. Ah, it's a fine thing for the trade! Five of 'em strung up in a row, and none left to talk!"

As the Jew uttered these words, his bright dark eyes fell on Oliver's face. The boy's eyes were fixed on his in mute curiosity, enough to show the old man that he had been observed.

He closed the lid of the box with a loud crash, and, laying his hand on a bread knife, started furiously up. Even in his terror, though, Oliver could see that the knife quivered in the air.

"What's that?" said the Jew. "What do you watch me for? Why are you awake? What have you seen? Speak out, boy! Quick—for your life."

"I wasn't able to sleep any longer, sir," replied Oliver, meekly. "I am sorry if I have disturbed you, sir."

"You were not awake an hour ago?" said the Jew, scowling fiercely on the boy.

"No, indeed!" replied Oliver.

"Are you sure?" cried the Jew, with a threatening attitude.

"Upon my word I was not, sir," replied Oliver, earnestly.

"Of course I know that, my dear!" said the Jew, abruptly resuming his old manner. "I only tried to frighten you. You're a brave boy. Ha!" The Jew rubbed his hands with a chuckle, but glanced uneasily at the box.

"Did you see any of these pretty things, my dear?" said the Jew, laying his hand upon it.

"Yes, sir," replied Oliver.

"Ah!" said the Jew, turning rather pale. "They—they're mine, Oliver, my little property. All I have to live upon, in my old age. The folks call me a miser, my dear."

Oliver thought the old gentleman must be a decided miser to live in such a dirty place, with so many watches. But, thinking that perhaps his fondness for the Dodger and the other boys cost him a good deal of money, he only cast a respectful look at the Jew, and asked if he might get up.

"Certainly, my dear," replied the old gentleman. "There's a pitcher of water in the corner by the door. Bring it here, and I'll give you a basin to wash in, my dear."

Oliver got up, walked across the room and stooped to raise the pitcher. When he turned his head, the box was gone.

He had scarcely washed himself and made everything tidy when the Dodger returned, accompanied by a sprightly young friend, whom Oliver had seen smoking on the previous night, and who was now formally introduced to him as Charley Bates. The four sat down to breakfast, with coffee and some hot rolls and ham that the Dodger had brought home in the crown of his hat.

"Well," said the Jew, glancing slyly at Oliver, and addressing himself to the Dodger, "I hope you've been at work this morning, my dears?"

"Hard," replied the Dodger.

"As nails," added Charley Bates.

"Good boys!" said the Jew. "What have you got?"

"A couple of pocketbooks," replied the Dodger.

"Lined?" inquired the Jew, with eagerness.

"Pretty well," replied the Dodger, producing two pocketbooks, one green, and the other red.

"Not so heavy as they might be," said the Jew, after looking at the insides carefully, "but neat and nicely made. Ingenious workman, ain't he, Oliver?"

"Indeed, sir," said Oliver. Mr. Charles Bates laughed uproariously, much to the amazement of Oliver, who saw nothing to laugh at.

"And what have you got, my dear?" said Fagin to Charley Bates.

"Wipes," replied Master Bates, producing four pocket handkerchiefs.

"Well," said the Jew, inspecting them closely. "They're good ones. The marks shall be picked out with a needle, and we'll teach Oliver how to do it. Shall us, Oliver?"

"If you please, sir," said Oliver.

"You'd like to be able to make pocket handkerchiefs as easy as Charley Bates, wouldn't you, my dear?" said the Jew.

"Very much, indeed, if you'll teach me, sir," replied Oliver.

Master Bates burst into another laugh, which, meeting the coffee he was drinking, and carrying it down some wrong channel, nearly ended in his premature suffocation.

"He is so jolly green!" said Charley when he recovered.

The Dodger said nothing, but he smoothed

Oliver's hair over his eyes, and said he'd know better, by and by. The old gentleman, observing Oliver's color mounting, changed the subject by asking whether there had been much of a crowd at the execution that morning. This made Oliver wonder more and more, for it was plain from the replies of the two boys that they had both been there. Oliver naturally wondered how they could possibly have found time to be so industrious.

When the breakfast was cleared away, the merry old gentleman and the two boys played at a curious game. The merry old gentleman, placing a snuffbox in one pocket of his trousers, a note case in the other, and a watch in his waistcoat pocket, with a guard chain round his neck, and sticking a mock diamond pin in his shirt, buttoned his coat tight round him, and putting his spectacle case and handkerchief in his pockets, trotted up and down the room with a stick, imitating an old gentleman walking about the streets. Sometimes he stopped at the fireplace, and sometimes at the door, pretending that he was staring with all his might into shop windows. At such times, he would look constantly round him, for fear of thieves, and would keep slapping all his pockets in turn, to see that he hadn't lost anything, in such a funny and natural manner that Oliver laughed till the tears ran down his face.

All this time, the two boys followed him closely about, getting out of his sight so nimbly, every time he turned round, that it was impossible to follow their motions. At last, the Dodger trod upon his toes, or ran upon his boot accidentally, while Charley Bates stumbled up against him, and in that one moment they took from him, with the most extraordinary rapidity, snuffbox, note case, watch-guard, chain, shirt pin, pocket handkerchief, even the spectacle case. If the old gentleman felt a hand in any one of his pockets, he cried out where it was. Then the game began all over again.

When this game had been played a great many times, a couple of young ladies named Bet and Nancy called to see the young gentlemen. They wore a good deal of hair, not very neatly fixed, and were rather untidy about the shoes and stockings. They were not exactly pretty, but they had a great deal of color in their faces, and looked quite stout and hearty. Being remarkably free and agreeable in their manners, Oliver thought them nice girls indeed.

The visitors stayed a long time. Spirits were produced, and the conversation took a convivial turn. At length, Charley Bates said it was time to pad the hoof. This, it occurred to Oliver, must be French for going out, for directly afterwards, the Dodger, Charley, and the two young ladies went away together, the amiable old Jew having given them money to spend.

"That's a pleasant life, isn't it?" said Fagin. "They have gone out for the day."

"Have they finished work, sir?" inquired Oliver.

"Yes," said the Jew, "that is, unless they should unexpectedly come across any, when they are out. They won't neglect it, if they do, my dear, depend upon it. Make 'em your models, my dear. Do everything they bid you, and take their advice in all matters—especially the Dodger's, my dear. He'll be a great man himself, and will make you one too, if you take after him. Is my handkerchief hanging out of my pocket, my dear?" said the Jew, stopping short.

"Yes, sir," said Oliver.

"See if you can take it out, without my feeling it, as you saw them do, when we were at play this morning."

Oliver held up the bottom of the pocket with one hand, as he had seen the Dodger hold it, and drew the handkerchief lightly out of it with the other.

"Is it gone?" cried the Jew.

"Here it is, sir," said Oliver, showing it in his hand.

"You're a clever boy, my dear," said the playful old gentleman, patting Oliver on the head approvingly. "I never saw a sharper lad. Here's a shilling for you. If you go on in this way, you'll be the greatest man of the time. And now come here, and I'll show you how to take the marks out of the handkerchiefs."

Oliver wondered what picking the old gentleman's pocket had to do with his chances of being a great man. But, thinking that the Jew, being so much his senior, must know best, he followed him quietly to the table, and was soon deeply involved in his new study.

CHAPTER 9

For many days, Oliver remained in the Jew's room, picking the marks out of the pocket handkerchiefs, and sometimes taking part in the game, which the two boys and the Jew played every morning. At length, he began to languish for fresh air, and begged the old gentleman to allow him to go out to work with his two companions.

Oliver had become anxious to be actively employed because of the old gentleman's stern morality. Whenever the Dodger or Charley Bates came home at night empty-handed, he would talk with great vehemence of the misery of lazy habits, and would send them supperless to bed. On one occasion, he even went so far as to knock them both down a flight of stairs.

One morning, Oliver obtained the permission he had so eagerly sought. There had been no handkerchiefs to work upon for two or three days, and the dinners had been rather meager. The old gentleman told Oliver he might go, and placed him under the joint guardianship of Charley Bates and the Dodger.

The three boys sallied out; the Dodger with his coat sleeves tucked up, and his hat cocked, as usual; Master Bates sauntering along with his hands in his pockets; and Oliver between them, wondering where they were going, and what branch of manufacture he would be instructed in first.

The pace at which they went was such a lazy saunter that Oliver soon began to think his

companions were going to deceive the old gentleman, by not going to work at all. The Dodger had a
vicious propensity, too, of pulling the caps from the
heads of small boys and tossing them down, while
Charley Bates pilfered apples and onions from the
stalls. These things looked so bad that Oliver was on
the point of going back home, when he saw a mysterious change of behavior on the part of the
Dodger.

They were just emerging from a narrow court
not far from the open square in Clerkenwell, when
the Dodger made a sudden stop, and, laying his finger on his lip, drew his companions back again, with
the greatest caution.

"What's the matter?" demanded Oliver.

"Hush!" replied the Dodger. "Do you see that
old man at the bookstall?"

"The old gentleman over the way?" said Oliver.
"Yes, I see him."

"He'll do," said the Doger.

"A prime plant," observed Master Charley
Bates.

The two boys walked stealthily across the road,
and slunk close behind the old gentleman. Oliver
walked a few paces after them, and stood looking on
in silent amazement.

The old gentleman was respectable-looking,
with a powdered head and gold spectacles. He was
dressed in a bottle-green coat with a black velvet collar, wore white trousers, and carried a smart bamboo
cane under his arm. He had taken up a book from
the stall, and there he stood, reading away, as hard as
if he were in his elbow chair, in his own study. It was
plain that he saw not the bookstall, nor the street,

nor the boys, nor, in short, anything but the book itself, which he was reading straight through, with the greatest eagerness.

To Oliver's horror and alarm, he saw the Dodger plunge his hand into the old gentleman's pocket, and draw from it a handkerchief! He handed it to Charley Bates, and both ran away round the corner at full speed!

In an instant the whole mystery of the handkerchiefs, and the watches, and the jewels, and the Jew, rushed upon the boy's mind.

He stood with the blood so tingling through all his veins from terror, that he felt as if he were in a burning fire. Then, confused and frightened, he took to his heels and made off as fast as he could lay his feet to the ground.

In the instant when Oliver began to run, the old gentleman, putting his hand to his pocket, and missing his handkerchief, turned sharp round. Seeing the boy scudding away at such a rapid pace, he naturally concluded him to be the culprit, and shouting "stop thief!" with all his might, made off after him, book in hand.

But the old gentleman was not the only person who raised the alarm. The Dodger and Master Bates, unwilling to attract public attention by running down the open street, had merely retired into the first doorway round the corner. They no sooner heard the cry, and saw Oliver running, than, guessing exactly how the matter stood, they leaped out, calling "stop thief!" too, and joined in the pursuit like good citizens.

Oliver was not acquainted with the beautiful axiom that self-preservation is the first law of nature.

If he had been, perhaps he would have been prepared for this. Not being prepared, however, it alarmed him the more. So away he went like the wind, with the old gentleman and the two boys roaring and shouting behind him.

"Stop thief!" There is a magic in the sound. The tradesman leaves his counter; the butcher throws down his tray; the baker his basket; the milkman his pail; the errand boy his parcels; the school boy his marbles. Away they run, yelling, knocking down the passengers as they turn the corners, rousing up the dogs, and astonishing the fowls.

"Stop thief!" The cry is taken up by a hundred voices, and the crowd grows at every turning. Away they fly, splashing through the mud, and rattling along the pavements. Up go the windows, out run the people, and, joining the rushing throng, swell the shout, and lend fresh vigor to the cry, "stop thief!"

One wretched breathless child, panting with exhaustion, terror in his looks, agony in his eyes, large drops of perspiration streaming down his face, strains every nerve to evade his pursuers, and as they follow on his track, and gain upon him every instant, they hail his decreasing strength with joy. "Stop thief!"

Stopped at last! A clever blow. He is down upon the pavement, and the crowd eagerly gather round him. "Stand aside!" "Give him a little air!" "Nonsense! He don't deserve it." "Where's the gentleman?" "Here he is, coming down the street." "Make room there for the gentleman!" "Is this the boy, sir!"

Oliver lay, covered with mud and dust, and bleeding from the mouth, looking wildly round upon the heap of faces that surrounded him. The old gentleman was pushed into the circle by the foremost of the pursuers.

"Yes," said the gentleman, "I am afraid it is the boy."

"Afraid!" murmured the crowd. "That's a good 'un!"

"Poor fellow!" said the gentleman, "he has hurt himself."

"*I* did that, sir," said a great lubberly fellow, stepping forward, "and I cut my knuckle agin' his mouth. I stopped him, sir."

The fellow touched his hat with a grin, expecting something for his pains. But the old gentleman, eyeing him with an expression of dislike, look anxiously round, as if he contemplated running away himself. A police officer (who is generally the last person to arrive in such cases) at that moment made his way through the crowd, and seized Oliver by the collar.

"Get up," said the man, roughly.

"It wasn't me, sir. Indeed, it was two other boys," said Oliver, clasping his hands passionately, and looking round. "They are here somewhere."

"Oh no, they ain't," said the officer. He meant this to be ironical, but it was true, for the Dodger and Charley Bates had gone down the first convenient street they came to.

"Come, get up!"

"Don't hurt him," said the old gentleman, compassionately.

"Oh no, I won't hurt him," replied the officer, tearing his jacket half off his back. "Will you stand upon your legs, you young devil?"

Oliver, who could hardly stand, made a shift to

raise himself on his feet, and was at once lugged along the streets by the jacket collar. The gentleman walked on with them, and as many of the crowd as could achieve the feat, got a little ahead, and stared back at Oliver from time to time. The boys shouted in triumph, and on they went.

CHAPTER 10

The crowd accompanied Oliver through two or three streets, and down a place called Mutton Hill. Then he was led beneath a low archway, and up a dirty court, into the police office by the back way. It was a small paved yard into which they turned, and here they encountered a stout man with a bunch of whiskers on his face, and a bunch of keys in his hand.

"What's the matter now?" said the man carelessly.

"A young pickpocket," replied the man who had Oliver.

"Are you the party that's been robbed, sir?" inquired the man with the keys.

"Yes, I am," replied the old gentleman, "but I am not sure that this boy actually took the handkerchief. I—I would rather not press the case."

"Must go before the magistrate now, sir," replied the man. "His worship will be disengaged in half a minute. Now, young gallows!"

This was an invitation for Oliver to enter a stone cell. Here he was searched, and nothing being found upon him, locked up.

The old gentleman looked almost as rueful as Oliver when the key grated in the lock. He turned with a sigh to the book, which had been the innocent cause of all this disturbance.

"There is something in that boy's face," said the old gentleman to himself as he walked slowly away, tapping his chin with the cover of the book in a thoughtful manner. "Can he be innocent? He looked like—by the bye," exclaimed the old gentleman, halting abruptly, and staring up into the sky, "Bless my soul!—where have I seen something like that look before?"

After musing for some minutes, the old gentleman walked, with the same meditative face, into a backroom opening from the yard. There, retiring into a corner, he called up before his mind's eye a vast array of faces over which a dusky curtain had hung for many years. "No," said the old gentleman, shaking his head, "it must be imagination."

He wandered over them again. There were the faces of friends, and foes, and of many almost strangers. There were the faces of young and blooming girls that were now old women; there were faces that the grave had changed and closed upon, but which the mind still dressed in their old freshness and beauty.

But the old gentleman could recall no one face of which Oliver's features bore a trace. So, he heaved a sigh over the recollections he awakened, and buried himself in the pages of the musty book.

He was roused by a touch on the shoulder, and a request from the man with the keys to follow him into the office. He was at once ushered into the imposing presence of the renowned Mr. Fang.

The office was a front parlor, with a paneled wall. Mr. Fang sat behind a bar opposite a sort of wooden pen, in which poor little trembling Oliver was already deposited. Mr. Fang was a lean, long-backed, stiff-necked, middle-sized man, with no great quantity of hair. His face was stern, and much flushed.

The old gentleman bowed respectfully, and advancing to the magistrate's desk with a card, said,

"That is my name and address, sir." He then withdrew a pace or two, and, with another polite and gentlemanly inclination of the head, waited to be questioned.

Mr. Fang looked up with an angry scowl. "Who are you?"

The old gentleman pointed, with some surprise, to his card.

"Officer!" said Mr. Fang, tossing the card contemptuously away. "Who is this fellow?"

"My name, sir," said the old gentleman, "is Brownlow. Permit me to inquire the name of the magistrate who offers an unprovoked insult to a respectable person, under the protection of the bench." Saying this, Mr. Brownlow looked around the office as if in search of some person who would afford him the required information.

"Officer!" said Mr. Fang, "what's this fellow charged with?"

"He's not charged at all, Your Worship," replied the officer. "He appears against this boy, Your Worship."

His worship knew this perfectly well, but it was a good annoyance, and a safe one.

"Appears against the boy, does he?" said Mr. Fang, surveying Mr. Brownlow contemptuously from head to foot. "Swear him!"

"Before I am sworn, I must beg to say one word," said Mr. Brownlow, "and that is, that I really never, without actual experience, could have believed—"

"Hold your tongue, sir!" said Mr. Fang, peremptorily.

"I will not, sir!" replied the old gentleman.

"Hold your tongue this instant, or I'll have you turned out of the office!" said Mr. Fang. "You're an insolent fellow. How dare you bully a magistrate!"

"What!" exclaimed the old gentleman, reddening.

"Swear this person!" said Fang to the clerk. "I'll not hear another word."

Mr. Brownlow's indignation was greatly roused. But reflecting that he might only injure the boy by giving vent to it, he suppressed his feelings and submitted to be sworn at once.

"Now," said Fang, "what's the charge against this boy? What have you got to say, sir?"

"I was standing at a bookstall—" Mr. Brownlow began.

"Hold your tongue, sir," said Mr. Fang. "Where's the policeman? Here, swear this policeman. Now, policeman, what is this?"

The policeman, with becoming humility, related how he had searched Oliver, and found nothing on his person, and how that was all he knew about it.

"Are there any witnesses?" inquired Mr. Fang.

"None, Your Worship," replied the policeman.

Mr. Fang sat silent for some minutes, and then, turning round to the prosecutor, said in a towering passion.

"Do you mean to state what your complaint against this boy is, man, or do you not? Now, if you stand there, refusing to give evidence, I'll punish you for disrespect to the bench. I will, by—"

By what, or by whom, nobody knows, for the clerk and jailer coughed loud, just at the right moment. And the former dropped a heavy book upon the floor, thus preventing the word from being heard—accidentally, of course.

With many interruptions and repeated insults, Mr. Brownlow contrived to state his case. He observed that, in the surprise of the moment, he had run after the boy because he saw him running away. And he expressed his hope that, if the magistrate should find him, although not actually the thief, to be connected with the thieves, he would deal as leniently with him as justice would allow.

"He has been hurt already," said the old gentleman in conclusion. "And I fear," he added, "I really fear that he is ill."

"Yes, I dare say!" said Mr. Fang, with a sneer. "Come, none of your tricks here, you young vagabond. What's your name?"

Oliver tried to reply but his tongue failed him. He was deadly pale, and the whole place seemed turning round and round.

"What's your name, you hardened scoundrel?" demanded Mr. Fang. "Officer, what's his name?"

This was addressed to a bluff old fellow, in a striped waistcoat, who was standing by the bar. He bent over Oliver, and repeated the inquiry. But finding him really incapable of understanding the question, and knowing that his not replying would only infuriate the magistrate the more, and add to the severity of his sentence, he hazarded a guess.

"He says his name's Tom White, Your Worship," said the kindhearted thief-taker.

"Oh, he won't speak out, won't he?" said Fang. "Very well. Where does he live?"

"Where he can, Your Worship," replied the officer, again pretending to receive Oliver's answer.

"Has he any parents?" inquired Mr. Fang.

"He says they died in his infancy, Your Worship,"

replied the officer, hazarding the usual reply.

At this point of the inquiry, Oliver raised his head, and, looking round with imploring eyes, murmured a feeble prayer for a drink of water.

"Stuff and nonsense!" said Mr. Fang. "Don't try to make a fool of me."

"I think he really is ill, Your Worship," said the officer.

"I know better," said Mr. Fang.

"Take care of him, Officer," said the old gentleman, raising his hands instinctively. "He'll fall down."

"Stand away, Officer," cried Fang. "Let him, if he likes."

Oliver availed himself of the kind permission, and fell to the floor in a fainting fit. The men in the office looked at each other, but no one dared to stir.

"I knew he was shamming," said Fang, as if this were incontestable proof of the fact. "Let him lie there. He'll soon be tired of that."

"How do you propose to deal with the case, sir?" inquired the clerk in a low voice.

"Summarily," replied Mr. Fang. "He stands committed for three months—hard labor of course. Clear the office."

A couple of men were preparing to carry the insensible boy to his cell, when an elderly man of decent but poor appearance, clad in an old suit of black, rushed hastily into the office, and advanced towards the bench.

"Stop! Don't take him away!" cried the newcomer, breathless with haste.

Mr. Fang was not a little indignant to see an unbidden guest enter in such irreverent disorder.

"Who is this? Turn this man out. Clear the

office!" cried Mr. Fang.

"I *will* speak," cried the man. "I will not be turned out. I saw it all. I keep the bookstall. I demand to be sworn. I will not be put down. Mr. Fang, you must hear me. You must not refuse, sir."

His manner was determined, and the matter was growing rather too serious to be hushed up.

"Swear the man," growled Mr. Fang with an ill grace. "Now, man, what have you got to say?"

"This," said the man. "I saw three boys: two others and the prisoner here, loitering on the opposite side of the way, when this gentleman was reading. The robbery was committed by another boy. I saw it done, and I saw that this boy was perfectly amazed and stupefied by it." Having by this time recovered a little breath, the worthy bookstall keeper proceeded to relate the exact circumstances of the robbery.

"Why didn't you come here before?" said Fang, after a pause.

"I hadn't a soul to mind the shop," replied the man. "Everybody who could have helped me had joined in the pursuit. I could get nobody till five minutes ago, and I've run here all the way."

"The prosecutor was reading, was he?" inquired Fang, after another pause.

"Yes," replied the man. "The book he has in his hand."

"Oh, that book, eh?" said Fang. "Is it paid for?"

"No, it is not," replied the man, with a smile.

"Dear me, I forgot all about it!" exclaimed the absent old gentleman, innocently.

"A nice person to bring a charge against a poor boy!" said Fang, with a comical effort to look

humane. "I consider, sir, that you have obtained possession of that book under suspicious and disrep-
utable circumstances. You may think yourself fortunate that the owner of the property declines to prosecute. Let this be a lesson to you, my man, or the law
will overtake you yet. The boy is discharged. Clear
the office!"

"D—n me!" cried the old gentleman, bursting
out with the rage he had kept down so long, "d—n
me! I'll—"

"Clear the office!" said the magistrate.
"Officers, do you hear? Clear the office!"

The indignant Mr. Brownlow was conveyed out,
with the book in one hand, and the bamboo cane in
the other, in a perfect frenzy of rage and defiance.
He reached the yard, and his passion vanished in a
moment. Little Oliver Twist lay on his back on the
pavement, with his shirt unbuttoned, and his temples bathed with water. His face was a deadly white,
and a cold tremble convulsed his whole frame.

"Poor boy!" said Mr. Brownlow, bending over
him. "Call a coach, somebody. Directly!"

A coach was obtained, and Oliver having been
carefully laid on the seat, the old gentleman got in
and sat himself on the other.

"May I accompany you?" said the bookstall
keeper, looking in.

"Bless me, yes, my dear sir," said Mr. Brownlow
quickly. "I forgot you. Dear, dear! I have this unhappy book still! Jump in. Poor fellow! There's no time
to lose."

The bookstall keeper got into the coach, and
away they drove.

CHAPTER 11

The coach rattled away, over nearly the same ground as that which Oliver had traversed when he first entered London in company with the Dodger. Turning a different way when it reached Islington, it stopped at length before a neat house, in a quiet shady street near Pentonville. Here, a bed was prepared, in which Mr. Brownlow saw his young charge carefully and comfortably deposited, and here, he was tended with a kindness that knew no bounds.

But, for many days, Oliver remained insensible to all the goodness of his new friends. The sun rose and sank, and rose and sank again, and many times after that. Still the boy lay stretched on his uneasy bed, dwindling away beneath the wasting heat of fever.

Weak, thin, and pallid, he awoke at last from what seemed to have been a long and troubled dream. Feebly raising himself in the bed, with his head resting on his trembling arm, he looked anxiously around.

"Where have I been brought to?" said Oliver. "This is not the place I went to sleep in."

He uttered these words in a feeble voice, being faint and weak, but they were overheard at once. The curtain at the bed's head was hastily drawn back, and a motherly old lady, neatly and precisely dressed, rose as she undrew it, from an armchair close by, in which she had been sitting at needlework.

"Hush, my dear," said the old lady softly. "You must be quiet, or you will be ill again. Lie down again." With those words, the old lady gently placed Oliver's head upon the pillow, and, smoothing back his hair from his forehead, looked so kindly in his face, that he could not help placing his little hand in hers, and drawing it round his neck.

"Save us!" said the old lady, with tears in her eyes. "What a grateful little dear it is. What would his mother feel if she could see him now!"

"Perhaps she does see me," whispered Oliver. "Perhaps she has sat by me. I almost feel as if she had."

"That was the fever, my dear," said the old lady mildly. She brought some cool stuff for Oliver to drink. Then, patting him on the cheek, told him he must lie very quiet, or he would be ill again.

So, Oliver kept still, partly because he was anxious to obey the kind old lady in all things, and partly because he was completely exhausted with what he had already said. He soon fell into a gentle doze, from which he was awakened by the light of a candle. A gentleman with a large and loud-ticking gold watch in his hand, who felt his pulse, said he was a great deal better.

"You *are* a great deal better, are you not, my dear?" said the gentleman.

"Yes, thank you, sir," replied Oliver.

"Yes, I know you are," said the gentleman: "You're hungry too, an't you?"

"No, sir," answered Oliver.

"Hem!" said the gentleman. "No, I know you're not. He is not hungry, Mrs. Bedwin," said the gentleman, looking wise.

The old lady made a respectful inclination of the head, which seemed to say that she thought the doctor was a clever man. The doctor appeared much of the same opinion himself.

"You feel sleepy, don't you, my dear?" said the doctor.

"No, sir," replied Oliver.

"No," said the doctor, with a shrewd and satisfied look. "You're not sleepy. Nor thirsty. Are you?"

"Yes, sir, rather thirsty," answered Oliver.

"Just as I expected, Mrs. Bedwin," said the doctor. "You may give him a little tea, ma'am, and some dry toast without any butter. Don't keep him too warm, ma'am; but be careful that you don't let him be too cold."

The old lady dropped a curtsy. The doctor, after tasting the cool stuff, and expressing a qualified approval of it, hurried away.

Oliver dozed off again, soon after this. When he awoke, it was nearly twelve o'clock. The old lady tenderly bade him good night shortly afterwards, and left him in charge of a fat old woman who had just come. After telling Oliver that she had come to sit up with him, she drew her chair close to the fire and went off into a series of short naps, checkered at frequent intervals with tumblings forward, and moans and chokings. These, however, had no worse effect than causing her to rub her nose hard, and then fall asleep again.

Oliver lay awake for some time, tracing with his languid eyes the intricate pattern of the paper on the wall. The darkness and the deep stillness of the room were solemn, and they brought into the boy's mind the thought that death had been hovering there, for many days and nights, and might yet fill it with the gloom and dread of his awful presence. So Oliver turned his face upon the pillow, and fervently prayed to Heaven. Gradually, he fell into a deep tranquil sleep.

It had been bright day, for hours, when Oliver opened his eyes; he felt cheerful and happy. The crisis of the disease was safely past. He belonged to the world again.

In three days' time he was able to sit in an easy chair, well propped up with pillows. As he was still too weak to walk, Mrs. Bedwin had him carried downstairs into the little housekeeper's room, which belonged to her. Having him set by the fireside, the good old lady sat herself down too.

"You're very kind to me, ma'am," said Oliver.

"Well, never you mind that, my dear," said the old lady. "That's got nothing to do with your broth, and it's full time you had it, for Mr. Brownlow may come in to see you this morning. We must get up our best looks, because the better we look, the more he'll be pleased." And with this, the old lady applied herself to warming up, in a little saucepan, a basin full of broth.

"Are you fond of pictures, dear?" inquired the old lady, seeing that Oliver had fixed his eyes most intently on a portrait that hung against the wall just opposite his chair.

"I don't quite know, ma'am," said Oliver, without taking his eyes from the canvas. "I have seen so few that I hardly know. What a beautiful, mild face that lady's is! Who is she?"

"Why, really, my dear, I don't know," answered the old lady in a good-humored manner. "It's not a likeness of anybody that you or I know, I expect. It seems to strike your fancy, dear."

"It is so pretty," replied Oliver.

"Why, sure you're not afraid of it?" said the old lady, observing the look of awe with which the child regarded the painting.

"Oh no, no," returned Oliver quickly, "but the eyes look so sorrowful, and where I sit, they seem fixed upon me. It makes my heart beat," added Oliver in a low voice, "as if it was alive, and wanted to speak to me, but couldn't."

"Lord save us!" exclaimed the old lady, starting, "don't talk in that way, child. You're weak and nervous after your illness. Let me wheel your chair round to the other side, and then you won't see it. There!" said the old lady.

Oliver *did* see it in his mind's eye as distinctly as if he had not altered his position, but he thought it better not to worry the kind old lady. So he smiled gently when she looked at him, and Mrs. Bedwin, satisfied that he felt more comfortable, salted and broke bits of toasted bread into the broth. Oliver got through it with extraordinary speed. He had scarcely swallowed the last spoonful, when there came a soft rap at the door. "Come in," said the old lady, and in walked Mr. Brownlow.

Now, the old gentleman came in as brisk as need be, but, he had no sooner raised his spectacles on his forehead to take a good long look at Oliver, than his face underwent a variety of odd contortions. Oliver looked worn and shadowy from sickness, and made an ineffectual attempt to stand up, out of respect to his benefactor, which terminated in his sinking back into the chair again. The fact is that Mr. Brownlow's heart, being large enough for any six ordinary gentlemen of humane disposition, forced a supply of tears into his eyes.

"Poor boy, poor boy!" said Mr. Brownlow, clearing his throat. "I'm rather hoarse this morning,

Mrs. Bedwin. I'm afraid I have caught cold."

"I hope not, sir," said Mrs. Bedwin.

But never mind that. How do you feel, my dear?" said Mr. Brownlow.

"Very happy, sir," replied Oliver. "And very grateful indeed, sir, for your goodness to me."

"Good boy," said Mr. Brownlow, stoutly. "Have you given him any nourishment, Bedwin?"

"He has just had a basin of strong broth, sir," replied Mrs. Bedwin.

"Ugh!" said Mr. Brownlow, with a slight shudder, "a couple of glasses of port wine would have done him a great deal more good. Wouldn't they, Tom White, eh?"

"My name is Oliver, sir," replied the little invalid, with a look of great astonishment.

"Oliver," said Mr. Brownlow. "Oliver what? Oliver White, eh?"

"No, sir, Twist, Oliver Twist."

"Queer name!" said the old gentleman. "What made you tell the magistrate your name was White?"

"I never told him so, sir," returned Oliver in amazement.

This sounded so like a falsehood, that the old gentleman looked somewhat sternly in Oliver's face, but there was truth in every one of its thin and sharpened lineaments.

"Some mistake," said Mr. Brownlow. But, although his motive for looking steadily at Oliver no longer existed, the old idea of the resemblance between his features and some familiar face came upon him so strongly, that he could not withdraw his gaze.

"I hope you are not angry with me, sir?" said Oliver, raising his eyes beseechingly.

"No," replied the old gentleman. "What's this? Bedwin, look there!"

As he spoke, he pointed hastily to the picture over Oliver's head, and then to the boy's face. There was its living copy. The eyes, the head, the mouth—every feature was the same. The expression was, for the instant, so precisely alike, that the minutest line seemed copied with startling accuracy!

Oliver knew not the cause of this sudden exclamation, for it startled him so much, he fainted away. This weakness on his part affords the narrative an opportunity of relieving the reader from suspense, on behalf of the two young pupils of the Merry Old Gentleman; and of recording—

When the general attention was fixed upon Oliver, the Dodger and Master Bates made immediately for their home by the shortest possible cut.

It was not until the two boys had run through a most intricate maze of narrow streets and courts, that they ventured to halt beneath a low and dark archway. Having remained silent here, just long enough to recover breath to speak, Master Bates burst into an uncontrollable fit of laughter, flung himself upon a doorstep, and rolled with glee.

"What's the matter?" inquired the Dodger.

"Ha! ha! ha!" roared Charley Bates.

"Hold your noise," remonstrated the Dodger, looking cautiously round. "Do you want to be grabbed, stupid?"

"I can't help it," said Charley, "To see him splitting away at that pace, and cutting round the corners, and knocking up again' the posts, and starting on again as if he was made of iron as well as them, and me with the wipe in my pocket, oh, my eye!" He again rolled upon the doorstep, and laughed louder than before.

"What'll Fagin say?" inquired the Dodger.

"Why, what should he say?" inquired Charley, stopping rather suddenly in his merriment.

Mr. Dawkins whistled for a couple of minutes, then, taking off his hat, scratched his head, and nodded thrice.

"What do you mean?" said Charley.

"Toor rul lol loo, gammon and spinnage, the frog he wouldn't, and high cockolorum," said the Dodger.

This was explanatory, but not satisfactory. Master Bates again said, "What do you mean?"

The Dodger made no reply, but thrust his tongue into his cheek, slapped the bridge of his nose some half-dozen times in a familiar but expressive manner, and turning on his heel, slunk down the court. Master Bates followed, with a thoughtful countenance.

The noise of footsteps on the creaking stairs roused the merry old gentleman as he sat over the fire. There was a rascally smile on his white face as he turned round, and looking sharply out from under his thick red eyebrows, bent his ear towards the door, and listened.

"Why, how's this?" muttered the Jew, "only two of 'em? Where's the third? They can't have got into trouble."

The footsteps approached nearer and reached the landing. The door was slowly opened, and the Dodger and Charley Bates entered, closing it behind them.

CHAPTER 12

"Where's Oliver?" said the Jew, rising with a menacing look.

The young thieves looked uneasily at each other but made no reply.

"What's become of the boy?" said the Jew, seizing the Dodger tightly by the collar. "Speak out, or I'll throttle you!"

"The traps have got him," said the Dodger, sullenly. "Let go o' me, will you!" And, swinging himself, at one jerk, clean out of the big coat, which he left in the Jew's hands, the Dodger snatched up the toasting fork, and made a pass at the old gentleman's waistcoat.

The Jew stepped back, and, seizing up the pot, prepared to hurl it at his assailant's head. But he suddenly altered its destination, and flung it full at Charley Bates.

"Who pitched that 'ere at me?" growled a deep voice. "I might have know'd that nobody but an infernal, rich, plundering, thundering old Jew could afford to throw away any drink but water. Wot's it all about, Fagin? D—me, if my neck handkercher an't lined with beer! Come in, you sneaking warmint— Wot are you stopping outside for, as if you was ashamed of your master! Come in!"

The man who growled out these words was a stout fellow of about five-and-thirty, in a black velveteen coat, soiled breeches, lace-up boots, and gray cotton stockings, which enclosed a bulky pair of legs.

He had a brown hat on his head, and a dirty hand-kerchief round his neck, which he used to smear the beer from his face as he spoke. His face was broad and heavy, with a beard of three days' growth, and two scowling eyes, one of which was discolored by a recent blow.

A white shaggy dog, with his face scratched and torn in twenty different places, skulked into the room.

"Why didn't you come in afore?" said the man. "You're getting too proud to own me afore company, are you? Lie down!"

This command was accompanied with a kick, which sent the animal to the other end of the room. He appeared well used to it, however, for he coiled himself up in a corner quietly, and, winking his ill-looking eyes twenty times in a minute, appeared to take a survey of the apartment.

"What are you up to? Ill-treating the boys, you covetous old fence?" said the man, seating himself deliberately. "I wonder they don't murder you! If I'd been your 'prentice, I'd have done it long ago, and—no, I couldn't have sold you afterwards, for you're fit for nothing but keeping as a curiosity of ugliness in a glass bottle, and I suppose they don't blow glass bottles large enough."

"Hush! Mr. Sikes," said the Jew, trembling, "don't speak so loud!"

"None of your mistering," replied the ruffian, "You know my name—out with it! I shan't disgrace it when the time comes."

"Well, then—Bill Sikes," said the Jew, with abject humility. "You seem out of humor."

"Perhaps I am," replied Sikes. "I should think

you was rather out of sorts too, unless you mean as little harm when you throw pewter pots about, as you do when you blab and—"

"Are you mad?" said the Jew, catching the man by the sleeve, and pointing towards the boys.

Mr. Sikes contented himself with tying an imaginary knot under his left ear, and jerking his head over on the right shoulder. He then demanded a glass of liquor.

"And mind you don't poison it," said Mr. Sikes, laying his hat upon the table.

After swallowing two glasses of spirits, Mr. Sikes took some notice of the young gentlemen, which led to a conversation about the cause and manner of Oliver's capture.

"I'm afraid," said the Jew, "that he may say something that will get us into trouble."

"That's very likely," returned Sikes with a malicious grin. "You're blowed upon, Fagin."

"And I'm afraid, you see," added the Jew, speaking as if he had not noticed the interruption—"if the game was up with us, it might be up with a good many more, and that it would come out rather worse for you than it would for me, my dear."

The man started, and turned round upon the Jew. But the old gentleman's shoulders were shrugged up to his ears, and his eyes were vacantly staring on the opposite wall.

There was a long pause. Every member of the respectable coterie appeared plunged in his own reflections.

"Somebody must find out wot's been done at the office," said Mr. Sikes in a much lower tone than he had taken since he came in.

The Jew nodded.

"If he hasn't peached, and is committed, there's no fear till he comes out again," said Mr. Sikes, "and then he must be taken care of. You must get hold of him somehow."

Again the Jew nodded.

The prudence of this line of action, indeed, was obvious. Unfortunately, there was one strong objection to its being adopted. This was that the Dodger, Charley Bates, Fagin, and Mr. William Sikes happened to entertain a violent antipathy to going near a police office for any reason whatsoever.

How long they might have sat and looked at each other, in a state of uncertainty, it is difficult to guess. But the sudden entrance of the two young ladies whom Oliver had seen on a former occasion caused the conversation to flow afresh.

"The very thing!" said the Jew. "Bet will go. Won't you, my dear?"

"Wheres?" inquired the young lady.

"Only just up to the office, my dear," said the Jew coaxingly.

The young lady did not positively affirm that she would not, but she merely expressed an emphatic and earnest desire to be "blessed" if she would.

The Jew's face fell. He turned from this young lady to the other female.

"Nancy, my dear," said the Jew in a soothing manner, "what do YOU say?"

"That it won't do. So it's no use a-trying it on, Fagin," replied Nancy.

"Why, you're just the person for it," reasoned Mr. Sikes, "nobody about here knows anything of you."

"And as I don't want 'em to, neither," replied

Nancy in the same composed manner, "it's rather more no than yes with me, Bill."

"She'll go, Fagin," said Sikes.

"No, she won't, Fagin," said Nancy.

"Yes, she will, Fagin," said Sikes.

And Mr. Sikes was right. By dint of alternate threats, promises, and bribes, the lady was ultimately prevailed upon to undertake the commission.

Accordingly, with a clean white apron tied over her gown, and her curl papers tucked up under a straw bonnet, both articles of dress being provided from the Jew's inexhaustible stock, Miss Nancy prepared to issue forth on her errand.

"Stop a minute, my dear," said the Jew, producing a little covered basket. "Carry that in one hand. It looks more respectable, my dear."

"Give her a door key to carry in her t'other one, Fagin," said Sikes, "it looks real and genuine like."

"So it does," said the Jew, hanging a large street-door key on the forefinger of the young lady's right hand.

"Oh, my brother! My poor, dear, sweet, innocent little brother!" exclaimed Nancy, bursting into tears, and wringing the little basket and the street-door key in an agony of distress. "Where have they taken him to! Oh, do have pity, and tell me what's been done with the dear boy, gentlemen!"

Having uttered those words in a most lamentable and heart-broken tone, to the delight of her hearers, Miss Nancy paused, winked to the company, nodded smilingly round, and disappeared.

"Ah, she's a clever girl," said the Jew, turning round to his young friends, and shaking his head gravely.

"She's a honor to her sex," said Mr. Sikes, filling his glass, and smiting the table with his enormous fist. "Here's to her health, and wishing they was all like her!"

While these remarks were being made about the accomplished Nancy, that young lady made her way to the police office. Entering by the back way, she went straight up to the bluff officer in the striped waistcoat, and with the most piteous wailings, demanded her own dear brother.

"I haven't got him, my dear," said the old man.

"Where is he?" screamed Nancy, in a distracted manner.

"Why, the gentleman's got him," replied the officer.

"What gentleman! Oh, gracious heavens!" exclaimed Nancy.

The old man informed the deeply affected sister that Oliver had been taken ill in the office, and discharged after a witness proved the robbery to have been committed by another boy, not in custody. The prosecutor had carried him away, in an insensible condition, to his own residence, somewhere in Pentonville.

In a dreadful state of doubt and uncertainty, the agonized young woman staggered to the gate, and then, exchanging her faltering walk for a swift run, returned by the most devious route she could think of to the domicile of the Jew.

Mr. Bill Sikes no sooner heard the account, than he hastily called up the white dog, and, putting on his hat, departed.

"We must know where he is, my dears. He must be found," said the Jew, greatly excited. "Charley, do nothing but skulk about, till you bring home some news of him! Nancy, my dear, I must have him found. I trust to you, my dear—to you and the Artful for everything!" added the Jew, unlocking a drawer with a shaking hand. "There's money, my dears. I shall shut up this shop tonight. You'll know where to find me! Don't stop here a minute. Not an instant, my dears!"

With these words, he pushed them from the room, and carefully double-locking and barring the door behind them, drew from its place of conceal-ment the box that he had unintentionally disclosed to Oliver. Then he hastily proceeded to hide the watches and jewelry beneath his clothing.

A rap at the door startled him in this occupation. "Who's there?" he cried in a shrill tone.

"Me!" replied the voice of the Dodger, through the keyhole.

"What now?" cried the Jew impatiently.

"Is he to be kidnapped to the other place, Nancy says?" inquired the Dodger.

"Yes," replied the Jew, "wherever she lays hands on him. Find him out, that's all. I shall know what to do next, never fear."

The boy murmured a reply, and hurried down-stairs after his companions.

"He has not peached so far," said the Jew. "If he means to blab us among his new friends, we may stop his mouth yet."

CHAPTER 13

After Oliver recovered from the faint into which Mr. Brownlow's abrupt exclamation had thrown him, the subject of the picture was carefully avoided. When he came down into the housekeeper's room next day, he cast an eager glance at the wall, in the hope of again looking on the face of the beautiful lady. But the picture had been removed.

"Ah!" said the housekeeper, watching the direction of Oliver's eyes. "It is gone, you see."

"I see it is ma'am," replied Oliver. "Why have they taken it away?"

"It has been taken down because Mr. Brownlow said, that as it seemed to worry you, perhaps it might prevent your getting well," rejoined the old lady.

"It didn't worry me, ma'am," said Oliver. "I liked to see it. I quite loved it."

"Well!" said the old lady, good-humoredly, "you get well as fast as ever you can, dear, and it shall be hung up again. I promise you that! Now, let us talk about something else."

This was all the information Oliver could obtain about the picture at that time. So he listened attentively to a great many stories she told him, about an amiable and handsome daughter of hers, who was married to an amiable and handsome man, and lived in the country; and about a son, who was clerk to a merchant in the West Indies; and who wrote such dutiful letters home four times a year, that it brought the tears into her eyes to talk about them. When the old lady had expounded a long time on the excellence of her children, and the merits of her kind good husband, who had been dead and gone just twenty-six years, it was time to have tea.

After tea she began to teach Oliver cribbage, which he learnt as quickly as she could teach. They played with great interest and gravity until it was time for the invalid to have some warm wine and water, with a slice of dry toast, and then to go cosily to bed.

They were happy days, those of Oliver's recovery. Everything was so quiet and orderly, and everybody so kind and gentle, that after the noise and turbulence in the midst of which he had always lived, it seemed like Heaven itself. He was no sooner strong enough to put his clothes on, than Mr. Brownlow provided a complete new suit, new cap, and new pair of shoes. As Oliver was told that he might do what he liked with the old clothes, he gave them to a servant who had been kind to him, and asked her to sell them and keep the money for herself. This she readily did, and, as Oliver looked out of the parlor window, and saw the peddler roll them up in his bag and walk away, he felt quite delighted to think that they were safely gone, and that there was now no possible danger of his ever being able to wear them again.

One evening, about a week after the affair of the picture, as he was sitting talking to Mrs. Bedwin, there came a message down from Mr. Brownlow, that if Oliver Twist felt pretty well, he should like to see him in his study.

"Bless us! Wash your hands, and let me part your hair nicely for you, child," said Mrs. Bedwin. "Dear heart alive! If we had known he would have asked for you, we would have put you a clean collar on, and made you as smart as sixpence!"

When ready, Oliver tapped at the study door. After Mr. Brownlow called to him to come in, he found himself in a little backroom, quite full of books, with a window looking into some pleasant gardens. There was a table drawn up before the window, at which Mr. Brownlow was seated reading. When he saw Oliver, he pushed the book away from him, and told him to come near the table, and sit down. Oliver complied, marveling where the people could be found to read such a great number of books as seemed to be written to make the world wiser.

"There are a good many books, are there not, my boy?" said Mr. Brownlow, observing the curiosity with which Oliver surveyed the shelves that reached from the floor to the ceiling.

"A great number, sir," replied Oliver. "I never saw so many."

"You shall read them, if you behave well," said the old gentleman kindly, "and you will like that, better than looking at the covers—that is, in some cases. How should you like to grow up a clever man, and write books, eh?"

"I think I would rather read them, sir," replied Oliver.

"Wouldn't you like to be a book writer?" said the old gentleman.

Oliver considered a little while, and at last said he should think it would be a much better thing to be a bookseller; upon which the old gentleman laughed heartily, and declared he had said a good thing. Oliver felt glad to have done so, though he by no means knew what it was.

"Well," said the old gentleman, composing his features. "Don't be afraid! We won't make an author of you, while there's an honest trade to be learnt, or brickmaking to turn to."

"Thank you, sir," said Oliver. At the earnest manner of his reply, the old gentleman laughed again.

"Now," said Mr. Brownlow, speaking in a much more serious manner than Oliver had ever known him assume yet, "I want you to pay great attention, my boy, to what I am going to say. I shall talk to you without any reserve, because I am sure you are well able to understand me, as many older persons would be."

"Oh, don't tell me you are going to send me away, sir, pray!" exclaimed Oliver, alarmed at the serious tone. "Don't turn me out of doors to wander in the streets again. Let me stay here, and be a servant. Don't send me back to the wretched place I came from. Have mercy upon a poor boy, sir!"

"My dear child," said the old gentleman, moved by the warmth of Oliver's sudden appeal, "you need not be afraid of my deserting you, unless you give me cause."

"I never, never will, sir," interposed Oliver.

"I hope not," rejoined the old gentleman. "I do not think you ever will. I have been deceived before, but I feel strongly disposed to trust you, nevertheless. I am more interested in your behalf than I can well account for, even to myself. The persons on whom I have bestowed my dearest love lie deep in their graves. But, although the happiness and delight of my life lie buried there too, I have not made a coffin of my heart, and sealed it up forever. Deep affliction has but strengthened my affections."

The old gentleman said this in a low voice, more

to himself than to his companion. As he remained silent for a short time afterwards, Oliver sat quite still.

"Well!" said the old gentleman at length, in a more cheerful tone, "I only say this, because you have a young heart, and knowing that I have suffered great pain and sorrow, you will be more careful, perhaps, not to wound me again. You say you are an orphan, without a friend in the world. All the inquiries I have been able to make confirm the statement. Let me hear your story—where you come from; who brought you up; and how you got into the company in which I found you. Speak the truth, and you shall not be friendless while I live."

Oliver's sobs prevented him from speaking for some minutes. When he was beginning to relate how he had been brought up at the farm, and carried to the workhouse by Mr. Bumble, a peculiarly impatient double-knock was heard at the street door, and the servant, running upstairs, announced Mr. Grimwig.

"Is he coming up?" inquired Mr. Brownlow.

"Yes, sir," replied the servant. "He asked if there were any muffins in the house, and, when I told him yes, he said he had come to tea."

Mr. Brownlow smiled, and, turning to Oliver, said that Mr. Grimwig was an old friend of his, and he must not mind his being a little rough in his manners. He was a worthy creature at heart.

"Shall I go downstairs, sir?" inquired Oliver.

"No," replied Mr. Brownlow, "I would rather you remained here."

At this moment, there walked into the room a stout old gentleman, rather lame in one leg, who was dressed in a blue coat, striped waistcoat, and a broad-brimmed white hat, with the sides turned up with green. The variety of shapes into which his face was twisted defy description. He had a manner of screwing his head on one side when he spoke, and of looking out of the corners of his eyes at the same time, which made him resemble a parrot. Holding out a small piece of orange peel at arm's length, he exclaimed, in a growling voice, "Do you see this! I can't call at a man's house but I find a piece of this poor surgeon's friend on the staircase. I've been lamed with orange peel once, and I know orange peel will be my death, or I'll be content to eat my own head, sir!"

This was the handsome offer with which Mr. Grimwig backed nearly every assertion he made. It was the more singular because Mr. Grimwig's head was such a particularly large one, that the hardiest man alive could hardly entertain a hope of being able to get through it at a sitting.

"I'll eat my head, sir," repeated Mr. Grimwig, striking his stick upon the ground. "Hallo! what's that!" looking at Oliver, and retreating a pace or two.

"This is young Oliver Twist, whom we were speaking about," said Mr. Brownlow.

Oliver bowed.

"You don't mean to say that's the boy who had the fever?" said Mr. Grimwig, recoiling a little more. "Wait a minute!" continued Mr. Grimwig, abruptly, "that's the boy who had the orange! If that's not the boy who had the orange, and threw this bit of peel upon the staircase, I'll eat my head, and his, too."

"No, he has not had one," said Mr. Brownlow,

laughing. "Come! Put down your hat, and speak to my young friend."

"I feel strongly on this subject, sir," said the irritable old gentleman, drawing off his gloves. "There's always orange peel on the pavement in our street. And I *know* it's put there by the surgeon's boy at the corner." Then, still keeping his stick in his hand, he sat down, and, opening a double eyeglass, took a view of Oliver, who colored, and bowed again.

"How are you, boy?" said Mr. Grimwig.

"A great deal better, thank you, sir," replied Oliver.

Mr. Brownlow, guessing that his singular friend was about to say something disagreeable, asked Oliver to step downstairs and tell Mrs. Bedwin they were ready for tea, which, since he did not half like the visitor's manner, he was happy to do.

"He is a nice-looking boy, is he not?" inquired Mr. Brownlow.

"I don't know," replied Mr. Grimwig, pettishly.

"Don't know?"

"No. I don't know. I never see any difference in boys. I only knew two sort of boys. Mealy boys and beef-faced boys."

"And which is Oliver?"

"Mealy. I know a friend who has a beef-faced boy. A fine boy, they call him, with a round head, and red cheeks, and glaring eyes. A horrid boy, with a body and limbs that appear to swell out of the seams of his blue clothes, with the appetite of a wolf. I know him! The wretch!"

"Come," said Mr. Brownlow, "these are not the characteristics of young Oliver Twist, so he needn't excite your wrath."

"They are not," replied Mr. Grimwig. "He may have worse. Where does he come from! Who is he? What is he? He has had a fever. What of that? Fevers are not peculiar to good people, are they? Bad people have fevers sometimes. I knew a man who was hung in Jamaica for murdering his master. He had had a fever six times. He wasn't recommended to mercy on that account."

Now, the fact was that, in the inmost recesses of his own heart, Mr. Grimwig felt that Oliver's appearance and manner were unusually compelling. But he had a strong appetite for contradiction, and, inwardly determining that no man should dictate to him whether a boy was well-looking, he had resolved, from the first, to oppose his friend.

When Mr. Brownlow admitted that he had postponed any investigation into Oliver's previous history until he thought the boy was strong enough to hear it, Mr. Grimwig chuckled maliciously. And he demanded whether the housekeeper was in the habit of counting the plates at night. Because if she didn't find a tablespoon or two missing some morning, why, he would be content to—and so forth.

All this, Mr. Brownlow bore with great good humor. After Oliver arrived with the tea, matters went on smoothly.

"And when are you going to hear a full, true, and particular account of the life and adventures of Oliver Twist?" asked Grimwig of Mr. Brownlow, at the conclusion of the meal, looking sideways at Oliver.

"Tomorrow morning," replied Mr. Brownlow. "I would rather he was alone with me at the time. Come up to me tomorrow morning at ten o'clock, my dear."

"Yes, sir," replied Oliver. He answered with some hesitation, because he was confused by Mr. Grimwig's looking so hard at him.

"I'll tell you what," whispered that gentleman to Mr. Brownlow, "he won't come up to you tomorrow morning. I saw him hesitate. He is deceiving you, my good friend."

"I'll swear he is not," replied Mr. Brownlow, warmly.

"If he is not," said Mr. Grimwig, "I'll—" and down went the stick.

"I'll answer for that boy's truth with my life!" said Mr. Brownlow, knocking the table.

"And I for his falsehood with my head!" rejoined Mr. Grimwig, knocking the table also.

"We shall see," said Mr. Brownlow, checking his rising anger.

"We will," replied Mr. Grimwig, with a provoking smile.

As fate would have it, Mrs. Bedwin chanced to bring in, at this moment, a small parcel of books, which Mr. Brownlow had that morning purchased of the bookstall keeper.

"Stop the boy, Mrs. Bedwin!" said Mr. Brownlow, "there is something to go back."

"He has gone, sir," replied Mrs. Bedwin.

"Call after him," said Mr. Brownlow. "He is a poor man, and they are not paid for. There are some books to be taken back, too."

The street door was opened. Oliver ran one way, and the girl ran another. Mrs. Bedwin stood on the step and screamed for the book-boy, but there was no boy in sight. Oliver and the girl returned, in a breathless state, to report that there were no tidings of him.

"Dear me, I am sorry for that," exclaimed Mr. Brownlow. "I particularly wished those books to be returned tonight."

"Send Oliver with them," said Mr. Grimwig, with an ironical smile. "He will be sure to deliver them safely, you know."

"Yes, do let me take them, if you please, sir," said Oliver. "I'll run all the way, sir."

The old gentleman was just going to say that Oliver should not go out on any account, when a most malicious cough from Mr. Grimwig determined him that he should. This would prove to him the injustice of his suspicions.

"You *shall* go, my dear," said the old gentleman. "The books are on a chair by my table. Fetch them down."

Oliver, delighted to be of use, brought down the books under his arm in a great bustle, and waited, cap in hand, to hear what message he was to take.

"You are to say," said Mr. Brownlow, glancing steadily at Grimwig. "You are to say that you have brought those books back, and that you have come to pay the four pound ten I owe him. This is a five-pound note, so you will have to bring me back ten shillings change."

"I won't be ten minutes, sir," said Oliver, eagerly. Having buttoned up the bank note in his jacket pocket, and placed the books carefully under his arm, he made a respectful bow, and left the room. Mrs. Bedwin followed him to the street door, giving him many directions about the nearest way, and the name of the bookseller, and the name of the street, all of which Oliver said he clearly understood.

"Bless his sweet face!" said the old lady, looking

after him. "I can't bear to let him go out of my sight."

"He'll be back in twenty minutes, at the longest," said Mr. Brownlow, pulling out his watch, and placing it on the table. "It will be dark by that time."

"Oh! You really expect him to come back, do you?" inquired Mr. Grimwig.

"Don't you?" asked Mr. Brownlow, smiling.

"No," he said, smiting the table with his fist, "I do not. The boy has a new suit of clothes on his back, a set of valuable books under his arm, and a five-pound note in his pocket. He'll join his old friends the thieves, and laugh at you. If ever that boy returns to this house, sir, I'll eat my head."

With these words he drew his chair closer to the table, and there the two friends sat, with the watch between them.

It grew so dark that the figures on the dial plate were scarcely discernible, but there the two old gentlemen continued to sit, in silence.

CHAPTER 14

In the gloomy parlor of a public house, in the filth-iest part of Little Saffron Hill, where no ray of sun ever shone, there sat, strongly impregnated with the smell of liquor, a man no experienced agent of the police would have hesitated to recognize as Mr. William Sikes. At his feet, sat a white-coated, red-eyed dog, who occupied himself, alternately, in wink-ing at his master with both eyes at the same time, and in licking a large, fresh cut on one side of his mouth, which appeared to be the result of some recent conflict.

"Keep quiet, you warmint!" said Mr. Sikes.

Mr. Sikes's dog, having faults of temper in com-mon with his owner, at once fixed his teeth in one of the half-boots. Having given it a hearty shake, he retired, growling, just escaping the pewter cup that Mr. Sikes leveled at his head.

"You would, would you?" said Sikes, seizing the poker in one hand, and deliberately opening with the other a large clasp knife, which he drew from his pocket. "Come here, you born devil! D'ye hear?"

The dog no doubt heard, because Mr. Sikes spoke in the harshest key of a harsh voice. But, appearing to object to having his throat cut, he remained where he was, and growled more fiercely than before, at the same time grasping the end of the poker between his teeth, and biting at it like a wild beast.

Dropping on his knees, Mr. Sikes began to assail the animal most furiously. The dog jumped from right to left, and from left to right, snapping, growling, and barking. The man thrust and swore, and struck and blasphemed. The struggle was reaching a most critical point for one or other, when, the door suddenly opening, the dog darted out.

"What the devil do you come between me and my dog for?" said Sikes, with a fierce gesture.

"I didn't know, my dear, I didn't know," replied Fagin, humbly.

"Didn't know, you white-livered thief!" growled Sikes. "Couldn't you hear the noise?"

"Not a sound of it, as I'm a living man, Bill," replied the Jew.

"Oh no! You hear nothing, you don't," retorted Sikes with a fierce sneer. "Sneaking in and out, so as nobody hears how you come or go! I wish you had been the dog, Fagin, half a minute ago."

"Why?" inquired the Jew with a forced smile.

"Cause the government that cares for the lives of such men as you, who haven't half the pluck of curs, lets a man kill a dog how he likes," replied Sikes, shutting up the knife. "That's why."

The Jew rubbed his hands, and, sitting down at the table, affected to laugh at the pleasantry of his friend. He was obviously ill at ease, however.

"Grin away," said Sikes, replacing the poker, and surveying him with savage contempt. "You'll never have the laugh at me, though. I've got the upper hand over you, Fagin, and, d—me, I'll keep it. If I go, you go. So take care of me."

"Well, my dear," said the Jew, "I know all that. We—we—have a mutual interest, Bill."

"Humph," said Sikes, as if he thought the interest lay rather more on the Jew's side than on his.

"Well, what have you got to say to me?"

"It's all passed safe through the melting pot," replied Fagin, "and this is your share. It's rather more than it ought to be, my dear. But I know you'll do me a good turn another time, and—"

"Stow that gammon," interposed the robber, impatiently. "Where is it? Hand over!"

"Yes, Bill, give me time," replied the Jew, soothingly. "Here it is! All safe!" As he spoke, he drew forth a small brown-paper packet. Sikes, snatching it from him, hastily opened it, and proceeded to count the sovereigns it contained.

"This is all, is it?" inquired Sikes.

"All," replied the Jew.

"You haven't opened the parcel and swallowed one or two, have you?" inquired Sikes, suspiciously. "Don't put on an injured look at the question. You've done it many a time. Ring the bell."

It was answered by another man, younger than Fagin, but nearly as vile and repulsive in appearance.

Bill Sikes merely pointed to the empty measure. The man, perfectly understanding the hint, retired to fill it, previously exchanging a remarkable look with Fagin, who raised his eyes for an instant, and shook his head in reply. It was lost upon Sikes, who was stooping at the moment to tie the bootlace that the dog had torn.

"Is anybody here, Barney?" inquired Fagin, speaking, now that Sikes was looking on, without raising his eyes from the ground.

"Dot a shoul," replied Barney, whose words made their way through the nose.

"Nobody?" inquired Fagin, in a tone of surprise, which perhaps might mean that Barney was at liberty to tell the truth.

"Dobody but Biss Dadsy," replied Barney.

"Nancy!" exclaimed Sikes. "Where? Strike me blind, if I don't honor that 'ere girl for her native talents."

"She's bid havid a plate of boiled beef id the bar," replied Barney.

"Send her here," said Sikes, pouring out a glass of liquor.

Barney presently returned, ushering in Nancy, who was decorated with the bonnet, apron, basket, and street-door key.

"You are on the scent, are you, Nancy?" inquired Sikes, proffering the glass.

"Yes, I am, Bill," replied the young lady, disposing of its contents, "and tired enough of it I am, too. The young brat's been ill and confined to the crib, and—"

"Ah, Nancy, dear!" said Fagin, looking up.

She suddenly checked herself, and with several gracious smiles upon Mr. Sikes, turned the conversation to other matters. In about ten minutes' time, Mr. Fagin was seized with a fit of coughing, upon which Nancy pulled her shawl over her shoulders, and declared it was time to go. Mr. Sikes, finding that he was walking a short part of her way himself, expressed his intention of accompanying her. They went away together, followed, at a little distance, by the dog.

The Jew thrust his head out of the room door when Sikes had left it; looked after him as he walked up the dark passage; shook his clenched fist; muttered a deep curse; and then, with a horrible grin, reseated himself at the table, where he was soon deeply absorbed in the interesting pages of the *Hue-and-Cry*.

Meanwhile, Oliver Twist, little dreaming that he was within so short a distance of the merry old gentleman, was on his way to the bookstall. When he got into Clerkenwell, he accidentally turned down a wrong street. But not discovering his mistake until he had got halfway down it, and knowing it must lead in the right direction, he did not think it worth while to turn back; and so marched on, as quickly as he could, with the books under his arm.

He was walking along, thinking how happy and contented he ought to feel, and how much he would give for only one look at poor little Dick, who, starved and beaten, might be weeping bitterly at that very moment, when he was startled by a young woman screaming. "Oh, my dear brother!" And he had hardly looked up, to see what the matter was, when he was stopped by having a pair of arms thrown tight round his neck.

"Don't," cried Oliver, struggling. "Let go of me. Who is it? What are you stopping me for?"

The only reply to this was a great number of loud lamentations from the young woman who had embraced him, and who had a little basket and a street-door key in her hand.

"Oh my gracious!" said the young woman, "I have found him! Oh! Oliver! Oh you naughty boy, to make me suffer such distress on your account! Come home, dear. Thank gracious goodness heavens, I've found him!" The young woman burst into a fit of crying, and got so dreadfully hysterical that a couple of women came up and asked if she needed a doctor.

"Oh, no, never mind," said the young woman, grasping Oliver's hand. "I'm better now. Come home directly, you cruel boy! Oh, ma'am," she said to one of the women, "he ran away, near a month ago, from his parents, who are hard-working and respectable people. He went and joined a set of thieves and bad characters, and almost broke his mother's heart."

"Young wretch!" said one woman.

"Go home, you little brute," said the other.

"I am not," replied Oliver, greatly alarmed. "I don't know her. I haven't any sister, or father and mother either. I'm an orphan. I live at Pentonville."

"Only hear him, how he braves it out!" cried the young woman.

"Why, it's Nancy!" exclaimed Oliver, and started back, in irrepressible astonishment.

"You see he knows me!" cried Nancy, appealing to the bystanders. "He can't help himself. Make him come home, or he'll kill his dear mother and father, and break my heart!"

"What the devil's this?" said a man, bursting out of a beer shop, with a white dog at his heels. "Young Oliver! Come home to your poor mother, you young dog!"

"I don't belong to them. I don't know them. Help! help!" cried Oliver, struggling in the man's powerful grasp.

"Help!" repeated the man. "Yes, I'll help you, you young rascal! What books are these? You've been a stealing 'em, have you? Give 'em here." With these words, the man tore the volumes from his grasp, and struck him on the head.

"That's right!" cried a looker-on. "That's the

only way of bringing him to his senses!"

"To be sure!" cried a sleepy-faced carpenter.

"It'll do him good!" said the two women.

"And he shall have it, too!" rejoined the man, administering another blow, and seizing Oliver by the collar. "Come on, you young villain!"

Weak with recent illness and stupefied by the blows and the suddenness of the attack, what could one poor child do! It was a low neighborhood and no help was near; resistance was useless. In another moment he was dragged into a labyrinth of dark narrow courts, and was forced along them at a rapid pace.

* * *

The gas lamps were lighted; Mrs. Bedwin was waiting anxiously at the open door; the servant had run up the street twenty times to see if there were any traces of Oliver; and still the two old gentlemen sat, perseveringly, in the dark parlor, with the watch between them.

CHAPTER 15

Sikes slackened his pace when they reached a large open cattle market, and he roughly commanded Oliver to take hold of Nancy's hand.

"Do you hear?" growled Sikes, as Oliver hesitated, and looked round.

They were in a dark corner, quite out of the way of passengers. Oliver saw that resistance would be of no avail. He held out his hand, which Nancy clasped tight in hers.

"Give me the other," said Sikes, seizing Oliver's unoccupied hand. "Here, Bull's-Eye!"

The dog looked up, and growled.

"See here, boy!" said Sikes, putting his other hand to Oliver's throat. "If he speaks ever so soft a word, hold him!"

The dog growled again, and licking his lips, eyed Oliver as if he were anxious to attach himself to his windpipe without delay.

Sikes regarded the animal with grim approval. "Now, you know what you've got to expect, boy, so call away. The dog will soon stop that game. Get on, young 'un!"

It was Smithfield that they were crossing, although it might have been Grosvenor Square, for all Oliver knew. The night was dark and foggy. The lights in the shops could scarcely struggle through the heavy mist, which thickened every moment and shrouded the streets and houses in gloom, rendering the strange place still stranger in Oliver's eyes.

They had hurried on a few paces, when a deep church-bell struck the hour.

"Eight o' clock, Bill," said Nancy, when the bell ceased.

"What's the good of telling me that. I can hear it, can't I!" replied Sikes.

"I wonder whether *they* can hear it," said Nancy.

"Of course they can," replied Sikes.

"Oh, Bill, such fine young chaps as them!"

"Yes, that's all you women think of," answered Sikes. "Fine young chaps! Well, they're as good as dead, so it don't much matter."

With this consolation, Mr. Sikes appeared to repress a rising tendency to jealousy, and, clasping Oliver's wrist more firmly, told him to step out again.

"Wait a minute!" said the girl. "I wouldn't hurry by, if it was you that was coming out to be hung, the next time eight o'clock struck, Bill. I'd walk round the place till I dropped, if the snow was on the ground, and I hadn't a shawl to cover me."

"And what good would that do?" inquired the unsentimental Mr. Sikes. "Unless you could pitch over a file and twenty yards of good stout rope, you might as well be walking fifty mile off, or not walking at all, for all the good it would do me. Come on, and don't stand preaching there."

The girl burst into a laugh, drew her shawl more closely round her, and they walked away. But Oliver felt her hand tremble, and, looking up in her face as they passed a gas lamp, saw that it had turned a deadly white.

At length they turned into a filthy narrow street, nearly full of old clothes shops. The dog stopped before the door of a shop that was closed and apparently untenable. The house was in a ruinous condition, and on the door was nailed a board, intimating that it was to let, which looked as if it had hung there for many years.

"All right," cried Sikes, glancing cautiously about.

Nancy stooped below the shutters, and Oliver heard the sound of a bell. They crossed to the opposite side of the street, and stood for a few moments under a lamp. A noise, as if a sash window were gently raised, was heard. Soon afterwards the door softly opened. Mr. Sikes then seized the terrified boy by the collar, and all three were quickly inside the house.

The passage was perfectly dark. They waited while the person who had let them in chained and barred the door.

"Let's have a glim," said Sikes.

"Stand still a moment, and I'll get you one," replied the voice. The receding footsteps of the speaker were heard, and, in another minute, the Artful Dodger appeared, holding a tallow candle.

The young gentleman did not stop to bestow any sign of recognition upon Oliver except a humorous grin. He beckoned the visitors to follow him down a flight of stairs. They crossed an empty kitchen, and, opening the door of a low earthy-smelling room, were received with a shout of laughter.

"Oh, my wig!" cried Master Charles Bates. "Here he is! Oh, Fagin, look at him! I can't bear it. Hold me, somebody, while I laugh it out."

With this irrepressible burst of mirth, Master Bates laid himself flat on the floor, and kicked convulsively for five minutes. Then jumping to his feet, and, advancing to Oliver, he viewed him round and round, while the Jew, taking off his nightcap, made a great number of low bows to the bewildered boy. The Artful, meantime, who seldom gave way to merriment when it interfered with business, rifled Oliver's pockets.

"Look at his togs, Fagin!" said Charley, putting the light so close to his new jacket as nearly to set him on fire. "Superfine cloth, and the heavy swell cut! And his books, too! Nothing but a gentleman, Fagin!"

"Delighted to see you looking so well, my dear," said the Jew, bowing with mock humility. "The Artful shall give you another suit, my dear, for fear you should spoil that Sunday one. Why didn't you write, my dear, and say you were coming? We'd have got something warm for supper."

At this, Master Bates roared again so loud, that Fagin himself relaxed, and even the Dodger smiled, and drew forth the five-pound note at that instant.

"Hallo, what's that?" inquired Sikes, stepping forward as the Jew seized the note. "That's mine, Fagin."

"No, my dear," said the Jew. "Mine, Bill. You shall have the books."

"If that ain't mine!" said Bill Sikes, putting on his hat with a determined air, "mine and Nancy's that is, I'll take the boy back again."

The Jew started. Oliver started too, hoping that the dispute might really end in his being taken back.

"Hand over, will you?" said Sikes.

"This is hardly fair, Bill. Hardly fair, is it, Nancy?" inquired the Jew.

"Fair, or not fair," retorted Sikes, "hand over, I

tell you! Do you think Nancy and me has got nothing else to do with our precious time but to spend it in scouting arter and kidnapping every young boy as gets grabbed through you? Give it here, you old skeleton, give it here!"

With this gentle remonstrance, Mr. Sikes plucked the note from between the Jew's finger and thumb, and, looking the old man coolly in the face, folded it up small, and tied it in his neckerchief.

"That's for our share of the trouble," said Sikes, "and not half enough, neither. You may keep the books, if you're fond of reading. If you ain't, sell 'em."

"They belong to the old gentleman," said Oliver, wringing his hands, "to the good, kind, old gentleman who took me into his house, and had me nursed, when I was near dying of the fever. Oh, pray send him back the books and money. Keep me here all my life long, but pray send them back. He'll think I stole them. All of them who were so kind to me will think I stole them. Oh, do have mercy upon me, and send them back!"

With these words, Oliver fell upon his knees at the Jew's feet and beat his hands together, in perfect desperation.

"The boy's right," remarked Fagin, looking round and knitting his shaggy eyebrows into a hard knot. "You're right, Oliver, they *will* think you have stolen 'em. Ha! ha!" chuckled the Jew, rubbing his hands, "it couldn't have happened better, if we had chosen our time!"

"Of course it couldn't," replied Sikes. "I know'd that, directly I see him coming through Clerkenwell, with the books under his arm. They're soft-hearted psalm singers, or they wouldn't have taken him in at all. They'll ask no questions after him, for fear they should be obliged to prosecute. He's safe enough."

Oliver had looked from one to the other, while these words were being spoken, as if he were bewildered, and could scarcely understand what passed. But when Bill Sikes concluded, he jumped suddenly to his feet, and tore wildly from the room, uttering shrieks for help, which made the bare old house echo to the roof.

"Keep back the dog, Bill!" cried Nancy, springing before the door, and closing it, as the Jew and his two pupils darted out in pursuit. "He'll tear the boy to pieces."

"Serve him right!" cried Sikes, struggling to disengage himself from the girl's grasp. "Stand off from me, or I'll split your head against the wall."

"I don't care about that, Bill," screamed the girl, struggling violently with the man, "the child shan't be torn down by the dog, unless you kill me first."

"Shan't he!" said Sikes, setting his teeth. "I'll soon do that, if you don't keep off."

He flung the girl from him to the further end of the room, just as the Jew and the two boys returned, dragging Oliver among them.

"What's the matter here!" said Fagin, looking round.

"The girl's gone mad, I think," replied Sikes, savagely.

"No, she hasn't," said Nancy, pale and breathless from the scuffle. "No, she hasn't, Fagin. Don't think it."

"Then keep quiet, will you?" said the Jew, with a threatening look.

"No, I won't do that, neither," replied Nancy,

speaking loudly. "Come! What do you think of that?"

Mr. Fagin felt tolerably certain that it would be rather unsafe to prolong any conversation with her. With the view of diverting the attention of the company, he turned to Oliver.

"So you wanted to get away, my dear, did you?" said the Jew, taking up a jagged and knotted club from a corner of the fireplace.

Oliver made no reply. But he watched the Jew's motions, and breathed quickly.

"Called for the police, did you?" sneered the Jew, catching the boy by the arm. "We'll cure you of that, my young master."

The Jew inflicted a smart blow on Oliver's shoulders with the club, and was raising it for a second, when the girl, rushing forward, wrested it from his hand. She flung it into the fire, with a force that brought some of the glowing coals whirling out into the room.

"I won't stand by and see it done, Fagin," cried the girl. "You've got the boy, and what more would you have?—Let him be—or I shall put that mark on some of you, that will bring me to the gallows before my time."

The girl stamped her foot violently on the floor as she vented this threat, her face quite colorless from the passion of rage into which she had gradually worked herself.

"Why, Nancy!" said the Jew, in a soothing tone. After a pause, during which he and Mr. Sikes had stared at one another in a disconcerted manner, "You—you're more clever than ever tonight. Ha! ha! My dear, you are acting beautifully."

"Am I!" said the girl. "Take care I don't overdo it. You will be the worse for it, Fagin, and so I tell you in good time to keep clear of me."

The Jew shrank involuntarily back a few paces and cast a glance, half-imploring and half-cowardly, at Sikes.

"What do you mean by this?" said Sikes to Nancy. "Burn my body! Do you know who you are, and what you are?"

"Oh, yes, I know all about it," replied the girl, laughing hysterically and shaking her head from side to side with indifference.

"Well, then, keep quiet," rejoined Sikes, with a growl like that he was accustomed to use when addressing his dog, "or I'll quiet you for a good long time to come."

The girl laughed again, and, darting a hasty look at Sikes, turned her face aside, and bit her lip till the blood came.

"You're a nice one," added Sikes, as he surveyed her with a contemptuous air, "to take up the humane and genteel side! A pretty subject for the child, as you call him, to make a friend of!"

"God Almighty help me, I am!" cried the girl passionately, "and I wish I had been struck dead in the street, before I had lent a hand in bringing him here. He's a thief, a liar, a devil, all that's bad, from this night forth. Isn't that enough for the old wretch, without blows?"

"Come, Sikes," said the Jew, motioning towards the boys, who were eagerly attentive to all that passed. "We must have civil words, Bill."

"Civil words!" cried the girl, whose passion was frightful to see. "You villain! Yes, you deserve 'em from me. I thieved for you when I was a child not half as old as this!" pointing to Oliver. "I have been in the same trade for twelve years since. Don't you know it? Speak out!"

"Well," replied the Jew, with an attempt at pacification, "and, if you have, it's your living!"

"Aye, it is!" returned the girl, pouring out the words in one continuous and vehement scream. "It is my living, and the cold, wet, dirty streets are my home. You're the wretch that drove me to them long ago, and that'll keep me there, day and night, till I die!"

"I shall do you a mischief worse than that, if you say much more!" interrupted the Jew.

The girl said nothing more, but, tearing her hair and dress in a transport of passion, made such a rush at the Jew as would probably have left marks of her revenge upon him, had not her wrists been seized by Sikes at the right moment. She made a few ineffectual struggles, and fainted.

"She's all right now," said Sikes, laying her down in a corner. "She's uncommon strong in the arms, when she's in this way."

The Jew wiped his forehead, and smiled, as if it were a relief to have the disturbance over.

"It's the worst of having to do with women," he said, "but they're clever, and we can't get on, in our line, without 'em. Charley, show Oliver to bed."

"I suppose he'd better not wear his best clothes tomorrow, Fagin, had he?" inquired Charley.

"Certainly not," replied the Jew.

Master Bates led Oliver into an adjacent kitchen, where there were two or three of the beds on which he had slept before. Here, with many uncontrollable bursts of laughter, he produced the identical old suit of clothes that Oliver had so much congratulated himself upon leaving off at Mr. Brownlow's.

"Put off the smart ones," said Charley, "and I'll give 'em to Fagin to take care of. What fun it is!"

Poor Oliver unwillingly complied. Master Bates rolled up the new clothes under his arm and departed from the room, leaving Oliver in the dark, and locking the door behind him.

CHAPTER 16

M<small>r.</small> Bumble walked up the High Street early in the morning. The beadle always carried his head high, but this morning it was higher than usual.

Mr. Bumble did not converse with the small shopkeepers and others who spoke to him as he passed along. He merely waved his hand, and did not stop until he reached the farm where Mrs. Mann tended the infant paupers.

"Drat that beadle!" said Mrs. Mann. "If it isn't him at this time in the morning! Lauk, Mr. Bumble, only think of its being you! Well, dear me, it IS a pleasure, this is! Come into the parlor, sir, please."

The first sentence was addressed to Susan, and the exclamations of delight were uttered to Mr. Bumble. The good lady unlocked the garden gate, and showed him into the house.

"Mrs. Mann, I am going to London."

"Lauk, Mr. Bumble!" cried Mrs. Mann, starting back.

"To London, ma'am," resumed the beadle, "by coach. I and two paupers, Mrs. Mann! A legal action is a coming on about a settlement, and the board has appointed me to dispose of the matter before the quarter sessions at Clerkenwell.

"And I question," added Mr. Bumble, drawing himself up, "whether the Clerkenwell Sessions will not find themselves in the wrong box before they have done with me."

Mrs. Mann appeared quite awed by his determined speech. At length she said, "You're going by coach, sir? I thought it was always usual to send them paupers in carts."

"That's when they're ill, Mrs. Mann," said the beadle. "We put the sick paupers into open carts in the rainy weather, to prevent their taking cold."

"Oh!" said Mrs. Mann.

"The opposition coach contracts for these two, and takes them cheap," said Mr. Bumble. "They are both in a low state, and we find it would come two pound cheaper to move 'em than to bury 'em—that is, if we can throw 'em upon another parish, which I think we shall be able to do, if they don't die upon the road to spite us. Ha! ha! ha!"

When Mr. Bumble had laughed a little while, his eyes again encountered the cocked hat, and he became grave.

"We are forgetting business, ma'am," said the beadle. "Here is your porochial stipend for the month."

Mr. Bumble produced some silver money rolled up in paper, from his pocketbook.

"Thank you, Mr. Bumble, sir, I am very much obliged to you, I'm sure."

Mr. Bumble nodded, and inquired how the children were.

"Bless their dear little hearts!" said Mrs. Mann with emotion, "they're as well as can be, the dears! Of course, except the two that died last week. And little Dick."

"Isn't that boy no better?" inquired Mr. Bumble.

Mrs. Mann shook her head.

"He's a ill-conditioned, wicious, bad-disposed

porochial child that," said Mr. Bumble angrily. "Where is he?"

"I'll bring him to you in one minute, sir," replied Mrs. Mann. "Here, you Dick!"

After some calling, Dick was discovered. Having had his face put under the pump, and dried upon Mrs. Mann's gown, he was led into the awful presence of Mr. Bumble.

The child was pale and thin, his cheeks were sunken, and his eyes large and bright. The scanty parish dress hung loosely on his feeble body, and his young limbs had wasted away, like those of an old man. He did not dare to lift his eyes from the floor, and he dreaded even to hear the beadle's voice.

"Can't you look at the gentleman, you obstinate boy?" said Mrs. Mann.

The child meekly raised his eyes, and encountered those of Mr. Bumble.

"What's the matter with you, porochial Dick?" inquired Mr. Bumble, with well-timed jocularity.

"Nothing, sir," replied the child faintly.

"I should think not," said Mrs. Mann.

"You want for nothing, I'm sure."

"I should like—" faltered the child.

"Hey-day!" interposed Mrs. Mann, "I suppose you're going to say that you DO want for something, now? Why, you little wretch—"

"Stop, Mrs. Mann, stop!" said the beadle, raising his hand with a show of authority. "Like what, sir, eh?"

"I should like," faltered the child, "if somebody that can write, would put a few words down for me on a piece of paper, and fold it up and seal it, and keep it for me, after I am laid in the ground. I should like to leave my dear love to poor Oliver Twist, and to let him know how often I have sat by myself and cried to think of his wandering about in the dark nights with nobody to help him. And I should like to tell him," said the child pressing his small hands together, and speaking with great fervor, "that I was glad to die when I was young, for, perhaps, if I had lived to be a man, and had grown old, my little sister who is in Heaven, might forget me, or be unlike me. It would be so much happier if we were both children there together."

Mr. Bumble surveyed the little speaker from head to foot with astonishment, and, turning to his companion, said, "That out-dacious Oliver has corrupted them all!"

"I couldn't have believed it, sir," said Mrs. Mann, looking malignantly at Dick. "I never see such a hardened little wretch!"

"Take him away, ma'am!" said Mr. Bumble imperiously. "This must be stated to the board, Mrs. Mann. Take him away, I can't bear the sight of him."

Dick was immediately taken away, and locked up in the coal cellar. Mr. Bumble shortly afterwards left to prepare for his journey.

At six o'clock next morning, Mr. Bumble took his place on the outside of the coach, accompanied by the criminals whose settlement was disputed. The two paupers persisted in shivering, and complaining of the cold, in a manner which, Mr. Bumble declared, caused his teeth to chatter in his head, and made him feel quite uncomfortable, although he had a greatcoat on.

In due course of time, they arrived in London. Having disposed of these evil-minded persons for the night, Mr. Bumble sat himself down in the house at which the coach stopped, and took a temperate dinner of steaks, oyster sauce, and porter. Then he drew his chair to the fire and composed himself to read the paper.

The first paragraph upon which Mr. Bumble's eye rested was the following advertisement.

"FIVE GUINEAS REWARD"

"Whereas a young boy, named Oliver Twist, absconded, or was enticed, on Thursday evening last, from his home, at Pentonville, and has not since been heard of. The above reward will be paid to any person who will give such information as will lead to the discovery of Oliver Twist, or throw any light upon his previous history, in which the advertiser is warmly interested."

And then followed a full description of Oliver's dress, person, appearance, and disappearance, with the name and address of Mr. Brownlow.

Mr. Bumble opened his eyes, read the advertisement three more times, and in five minutes was on his way to Pentonville.

"Is Mr. Brownlow at home?" inquired Mr. Bumble of the girl who opened the door.

To this inquiry the girl returned the rather evasive reply of "I don't know; where do you come from?"

Mr. Bumble no sooner uttered Oliver's name, in explanation of his errand, than Mrs. Bedwin, who had been listening at the parlor door, hastened into the passage in a breathless state.

"Come in," said the old lady. "I knew we should hear of him. Poor dear! I knew we should! I was certain of it. Bless his heart! I said so all along."

The worthy old lady hurried back into the parlor

again, and seating herself on a sofa, burst into tears. The girl, who was not quite so susceptible, had run upstairs meanwhile, and now returned with a request that Mr. Bumble would follow her immediately.

He was shown into the little back study, where sat Mr. Brownlow and his friend Mr. Grimwig, with decanters and glasses before them.

"Take a seat, will you?" said Mr. Brownlow.

Mr. Bumble sat himself down, while Mr. Brownlow moved the lamp, so as to obtain an uninterrupted view of the beadle's face, and said, with a little impatience, "Now, sir, you come in consequence of having seen the advertisement?"

"Yes, sir," said Mr. Bumble.

"And you are a beadle, are you not?" inquired Mr. Grimwig.

"I am a porochial beadle, gentlemen," rejoined Mr. Bumble proudly.

"Of course," observed Mr. Grimwig aside to his friend, "I knew he was. A beadle all over!"

Mr. Brownlow gently shook his head to impose silence on his friend, and resumed. "Do you know where this poor boy is now?"

"No more than nobody," replied Mr. Bumble.

"Well, what DO you know of him?" inquired the old gentleman. "Speak out, my friend, if you have anything to say."

"You don't happen to know any good of him, do you?" said Mr. Grimwig.

Mr. Bumble shook his head solemnly.

"You see?" said Mr. Grimwig, looking triumphantly at Mr. Brownlow.

Mr. Brownlow looked apprehensively at Mr. Bumble's pursed-up countenance, and asked him to communicate what he knew regarding Oliver, in as few words as possible.

It would be tedious if given in the beadle's words, occupying some twenty minutes in the telling. But the sum and substance of it was that Oliver was a foundling, born of low and vicious parents. That he had, from his birth, displayed no better qualities than treachery, ingratitude, and malice. That he had terminated his brief career by making a cowardly attack on an unoffending lad, and running away in the nighttime from his master's house. Folding his arms again, he then awaited Mr. Brownlow's observations.

"I fear it is all too true," said the old gentleman sorrowfully. "I would gladly have given you triple the money, if it had been favorable to the boy."

It is probable that if Mr. Bumble had had this information at an earlier period of the interview, he might have imparted a very different coloring to his little history. It was too late to do it now, however. So he shook his head gravely, and, pocketing the five guineas, withdrew.

Mr. Brownlow paced the room to and fro for some minutes, evidently much disturbed by the beadle's tale. At length he stopped, and rang the bell violently.

"Mrs. Bedwin," said Mr. Brownlow, when the housekeeper appeared, "that boy, Oliver, is an impostor."

"It cannot be," said the old lady energetically.

"I tell you he is," retorted the old gentleman. "What do you mean by can't be? We have just heard a full account of him from his birth. He has been a thorough little villain, all his life."

"I never will believe it, sir," replied the old lady, firmly. "Never!"

"You old women never believe anything but quack doctors, and lying storybooks," growled Mr. Grimwig. "I knew it all along. Why didn't you take my advise in the beginning? Bah!" And Mr. Grimwig poked the fire with a flourish.

"He was a dear, grateful, gentle child, sir," retorted Mrs. Bedwin, indignantly. "I know what children are, sir. People who can't say the same, shouldn't say anything about them. That's my opinion!"

This was a hard hit at Mr. Grimwig, who was a bachelor. The old lady tossed her head, and made ready for another speech, when she was stopped by Mr. Brownlow.

"Silence!" said the old gentleman, feigning an anger he was far from feeling. "Never let me hear the boy's name again. I rang to tell you that. Never, on any pretense, mind! You may leave the room, Mrs. Bedwin. Remember! I am in earnest."

There were sad hearts at Mr. Brownlow's that night.

Oliver's heart sank within him, when he thought of his good friends. It was well for him that he could not know what they had heard, or it might have broken outright.

CHAPTER 17

About noon next day, Fagin gave Oliver a long lecture on the sin of ingratitude. He laid great stress on the fact of his having taken Oliver in, and cherished him, when, without his timely aid, he might have perished with hunger. Also, he related the dismal history of a young lad whom he had similarly taken in, but who, proving unworthy of his confidence and willing to communicate with the police, had unfortunately come to be hanged one morning. Mr. Fagin lamented the wrong-headed and treacherous behavior of the young person in question, and concluded by drawing a rather disagreeable picture of the discomforts of hanging. With great friendliness, he expressed his anxious hopes that he might never be obliged to submit Oliver Twist to that unpleasant operation.

Little Oliver's blood ran cold as he listened to the words. He glanced timidly up, and met the Jew's searching look.

Smiling hideously, Fagin patted Oliver on the head, and said that if he kept himself quiet, and applied himself to business, they would be good friends yet. Then he went out, and locked the door behind him.

And so Oliver remained for the greater part of many days, seeing nobody between early morning and midnight, left to commune with his own thoughts, which never failed to revert with sadness to his kind friends.

After the lapse of a week or so, the Jew left the room door unlocked, and he was at liberty to wander about the house.

It was a dirty place. The rooms upstairs had great high wooden chimneypieces and large doors, with paneled walls and cornices to the ceiling. From all of these tokens Oliver concluded that a long time ago, before the old Jew was born, it had belonged to better people, and had perhaps been quite handsome, dismal and dreary as it looked now.

One afternoon, the Dodger and Master Bates going out that evening, the first young gentleman had some anxiety regarding his appearance. He condescendingly commanded Oliver to assist him with his clothes, straightaway.

Oliver was but too glad to make himself useful and have some faces, however bad, to look upon. Kneeling on the floor, while the Dodger sat upon the table so that he could take his foot in his lap, Oliver began cleaning his boots.

The Dodger looked down on Oliver with a thoughtful expression, and then said, half in abstraction, and half to Master Bates, "What a pity he isn't a prig!"

"Ah!" said Master Charles Bates, "he don't know what's good for him."

"I suppose you don't even know what a prig is?" said the Dodger mournfully.

"I think I know," replied Oliver, looking up. "It's a the—; you're one, are you not?" inquired Oliver, checking himself.

"I am," replied the Dodger. "I'd scorn to be anything else. So's Charley. So's Fagin. So's Sikes. So's Nancy. So's Bet. So we all are, down to the dog.

And he's the downiest one of the lot!"

"And the least given to peaching," added Charley Bates.

"He wouldn't so much as bark in a witness box. No, not if you tied him up in one, and left him there without wittles for a fortnight," said the Dodger.

"Not a bit of it," observed Charley.

"But this hasn't got anything to do with young Green here," added the Dodger.

"No more it has," said Charley. "Why don't you put yourself under Fagin, Oliver?"

"And make your fortun' out of hand?" added the Dodger, with a grin.

"And so be able to retire on your property, as I mean to," said Charley Bates.

"I don't like it," rejoined Oliver, timidly. "I wish they would let me go. I—I—would rather go."

"And Fagin would *rather* not!" rejoined Charley.

Oliver, thinking it might be dangerous to express his feelings more openly, only sighed, and went on with his boot cleaning.

"Go!" exclaimed the Dodger. "Why, where's your spirit? Don't you take any pride in yourself? Would you go and be dependent on your friends?"

"Oh, blow that!" said Master Bates, drawing two or three silk handkerchiefs from his pocket, and tossing them into a cupboard, "that's too mean."

"*I* couldn't do it," said the Dodger, with an air of haughty disgust.

"You can leave your friends, though," said Oliver with a half smile, "and let them be punished for what you did."

"That," rejoined the Dodger, with a wave of his pipe, "That was all out of consideration for Fagin, 'cause the traps know that we work together, and he might have got into trouble if we hadn't made our lucky. That was the move, wasn't it, Charley?"

Master Bates nodded.

"Look here!" said the Dodger, drawing forth a handful of shillings and halfpence. "Here's a jolly life! Here, catch hold. There's plenty more where they were took from. You won't, won't you? Oh, you precious flat!"

"It's naughty, ain't it, Oliver?" inquired Charley Bates. "He'll come to be scragged, won't he?" As he said it, Master Bates caught up an end of his neckerchief, and, holding it erect in the air, dropped his head on his shoulder, and jerked a curious sound through his teeth.

"You've been brought up bad," said the Dodger, surveying his boots with much satisfaction when Oliver had polished them. "Fagin will make something of you, though, or you'll be the first he ever had that turned out unprofitable. You'd better begin at once, for you'll come to the trade long before you think of it. You're only losing time, Oliver."

"And always put this in your pipe, Nolly," added the Dodger, as the Jew was heard unlocking the door above, "if you don't take pocket handkechers and watches, some other cove will, so that the coves that lose 'em will be all the worse, and you'll be all the worse, too."

"To be sure!" said the Jew, who had entered unseen by Oliver. "It all lies in a nutshell my dear, take the Dodger's word for it. He understands the philosophy of his trade." The old man chuckled with delight at his pupil's proficiency.

The Jew had returned home accompanied by Miss Betsy, and a gentleman who was addressed by the Dodger as Tom Chitling.

Mr. Chitling was older in years than the Dodger, being perhaps eighteen. He had small twinkling eyes, and a pock-marked face; wore a dark corduroy jacket, greasy trousers, and an apron. His wardrobe was rather out of repair, but he excused himself by stating that his "time" was only out an hour before. Having worn the regimentals for six weeks past, he had not been able to bestow any attention on his private clothes. Mr. Chitling added that the new way of fumigating clothes up yonder was unconstitutional, for it burnt holes in them, and there was no remedy against the County. Mr. Chitling wound up his observations by stating that he had not touched a drop of anything for forty-two moral long hardworking days, and that he was "as dry as a lime-basket."

"Where do you think the gentleman has come from, Oliver?" inquired the Jew, with a grin, as the other boys put a bottle of spirits on the table.

"I—I—don't know, sir," replied Oliver.

"Who's that?" inquired Tom Chitling, casting a contemptuous look at Oliver.

"A young friend of mine, my dear," replied the Jew.

"He's in luck, then," said the young man. "Never mind where I came from, young 'un. You'll find your way there, soon enough, I'll bet a crown!"

At this, the boys laughed. After some more jokes on the same subject, they exchanged a few short whispers with Fagin, and withdrew.

After some words apart between Mr. Chitling

and Fagin, they drew their chairs towards the fire. The Jew, telling Oliver to come and sit by him, led the conversation to topics such as the great advantages of the trade, the proficiency of the Dodger, the amiability of Charley Bates, and the liberality of the Jew himself.

From this day, Oliver was seldom left alone, but was placed in almost constant communication with the two boys, who played the old game with the Jew every day. At other times the old man would tell them stories of robberies he had committed in his younger days, mixed up with so much that was funny and curious, that Oliver could not help laughing heartily, in spite of all his better feelings.

In short, the wily old man had the boy in his sights. Having prepared his mind, by solitude and gloom, to prefer any society to the companionship of his own sad thoughts in such a dreary place, he was now slowly instilling into his soul the poison that he hoped would blacken it, and change its nature forever.

CHAPTER 18

It was a chill, damp, windy night when Fagin, with his greatcoat tight round his shriveled body, and the collar up over his ears so as to hide the lower part of his face, emerged from his den. The mud lay thick upon the stones, the rain fell sluggishly down, and everything felt cold and clammy to the touch. As he glided stealthily along, the hideous old man seemed like some loathsome reptile.

He went through many winding and narrow ways. Then, turning suddenly off to the left, he went down an alley lighted only by a single lamp at the farther end. At the door of a house he knocked. After a few muttered words with the person who opened it, he walked upstairs.

A dog growled as he touched the handle of a room door, and a man's voice demanded who was there.

"Only me, Bill," said the Jew, looking in.

"Bring in your body then," said Sikes.

"Well, my dear," replied the Jew.—"Ah! Nancy."

Mr. Fagin and his young friend had not met since she had interfered in behalf of Oliver. All doubts upon the subject, if he had any, were speedily removed by the young lady's behavior. She took her feet off the fender of the fireplace, pushed back her chair, and bade Fagin draw up his.

"It is cold, Nancy dear," said the Jew, as he warmed his skinny hands over the fire. "It seems to go right through one," added the old man, touching his side.

"It must be a piercer, if it finds its way through your heart," said Mr. Sikes. "I'm ready for business, so say what you've got to say."

"About the crib at Chertsey, Bill?" said the Jew, drawing his chair forward, and speaking in a low voice.

"Yes, wot about it?" inquired Sikes.

"When is it to be done, Bill, eh? Such plate, my dear, such plate!" said the Jew, rubbing his hands in a rapture of anticipation.

"Not at all," replied Sikes coldly. "At least it can't be a put-up job, as we expected."

"Then it hasn't been properly gone about," said the Jew, turning pale with anger. "Don't tell me!"

"But I will tell you," retorted Sikes. "Toby Crackit has been hanging about the place for a fortnight, and he can't get one of the servants in line. The old lady has had 'em these twenty years. If you were to give 'em five hundred pound, they wouldn't be in it."

"But do you mean to say, my dear," remonstrated the Jew, "that the women can't be got over by flash Toby Crackit? Think what women are, Bill."

"No, not even by flash Toby Crackit," replied Sikes. "He says he's worn sham whiskers, and a canary waistcoat, the whole blessed time he's been loitering down there, and it's all of no use."

"He should have tried mustachios and a pair of military trousers, my dear," said the Jew.

"So he did," rejoined Sikes, "and they warn't of no more use than the other."

The Jew looked blank at this information. After

ruminating for some minutes with his chin sunk on his breast, he raised his head and said, with a deep sigh, that if flash Toby Crackit reported aright, he feared the game was up.

"And yet," said the old man, dropping his hands on his knees, "it's a sad thing, my dear, to lose so much when we had set our hearts upon it."

"So it is," said Mr. Sikes. "Worse luck!"

A long silence ensued, during which the Jew was plunged in deep thought, with his face wrinkled into an expression of villainy. Sikes eyed him furtively from time to time. Nancy sat with her eyes fixed upon the fire, as if she had been deaf to all that passed.

"Fagin," said Sikes, abruptly breaking the stillness that prevailed. "Is it worth fifty shiners extra, if it's safely done from the outside?"

"Yes," said the Jew, rousing himself.

"Is it a bargain?" inquired Sikes.

"Yes, my dear, yes," rejoined the Jew, every muscle in his face working with the excitement.

"Then," said Sikes, "let it come off as soon as you like. Toby and me were over the garden wall the night afore last, sounding the panels of the door and shutters. There's one part we can crack, safe and softly."

"Which is that, Bill?" asked the Jew eagerly.

"Why," whispered Sikes, "as you cross the lawn—"

"Yes?" said the Jew, bending his head forward, with his eyes almost starting out of it.

"Umph!" cried Sikes, stopping short. "Never mind which part it is. You can't do it without me, I know. But it's best to be on the safe side when one deals with you."

"As you like, my dear, as you like," replied the Jew. "Is there no help wanted, but yours and Toby's?"

"None," said Sikes. "Cept a centerbit and a boy. The first we've both got. The second you must find us."

"A boy!" exclaimed the Jew. "Then it's a panel, eh?"

"Never mind wot it is!" replied Sikes. "I want a boy, and he musn't be a big 'un."

The Jew nodded his head towards Nancy, who was still gazing at the fire, and signed that he would have her told to leave the room. Sikes complied by requesting Miss Nancy to fetch him a jug of beer.

"You don't want any beer," said Nancy, folding her arms, and retaining her seat.

"I tell you I do!" replied Sikes.

"Nonsense," rejoined the girl coolly, "Go on, Fagin. I know what he's going to say, Bill. He needn't mind me."

"Why, you don't mind the old girl, do you, Fagin?" he asked. "You've known her long enough to trust her, or the Devil's in it. She ain't one to blab. Are you Nancy?"

"*I* should think not!" replied the young lady, drawing her chair up to the table, and putting her elbows upon it.

"No, my dear, I know you're not," said the Jew, "but I didn't know whether you mightn't p'r'aps be out of sorts, as you was the other night," replied the Jew.

At this confession, Miss Nancy burst into a loud laugh, and, swallowing a glass of brandy, shook her

head with an air of defiance, and burst into exclama-
tions like "Keep the game a-going!" "Never say die!"
These seemed to reassure both gentlemen, for the
Jew nodded his head with a satisfied air, as did Mr.
Sikes.

"Now, Fagin," said Nancy with a laugh. "Tell
Bill at once about Oliver!"

"Ha! You're the sharpest girl I ever saw!" said
the Jew.

"What about him?" demanded Sikes.

"He's the boy for you, my dear," replied the Jew
in a hoarse whisper.

"Have him, Bill!" said Nancy. "I would, if I was
in your place. He's only to open a door for you.
Depend upon it, he's a safe one, Bill."

"I know he is," rejoined Fagin. "He's been in
good training these last few weeks, and it's time he
began to work for his bread. Besides, the others are
all too big."

"Well, he is just the size I want," said Mr. Sikes,
ruminating.

"And will do everything you want, Bill, my
dear," interposed the Jew. "He can't help himself.
That is, if you frighten him enough."

"Frighten him!" echoed Sikes. "It'll be no sham
frightening, mind you. If there's anything queer
about him when we once get into the work, you
won't see him alive again, Fagin. Think of that
before you send him. Mark my words!" said the robber, poising a crowbar, which he had drawn from
under the bedstead.

"I've had my eye upon him, my dears. Once let
him feel that he is one of us, with the idea that he has
been a thief, and he's ours! Ours for his life. Oho! It

couldn't have come out better!" The old man crossed his arms upon his breast and literally hugged himself for joy.

"Ours!" said Sikes. "Yours, you mean."

"Perhaps I do, my dear," said the Jew, with a shrill chuckle.

"And wot," said Sikes, scowling fiercely, "wot makes you take so much pains about one chalk-faced kid, when you know there are fifty boys snoozing about Common Garden every night, as you might pick and choose from?"

"Because they're of no use to me, my dear," replied the Jew. "Their looks convict 'em when they get into trouble, and I lose 'em all. With this boy, properly managed, my dears, I could do what I couldn't with twenty of them. Besides," said the Jew, "he must be in the same boat with us. Now, how much better this is, than being obliged to put the poor leetle boy out of the way—which would be dangerous, and we should lose by it besides."

"When is it to be done?" asked Nancy.

"Ah, to be sure," said the Jew. "When is it to be done, Bill?"

"I planned with Toby, the night arter tomorrow," rejoined Sikes in a surly voice, "if he heerd nothing from me to the contrary."

"Good," said the Jew, "there's no moon. It's all arranged about bringing off the swag, is it?"

Sikes nodded.

"And about—"

"Ah, it's all planned," rejoined Sikes, interrupting him. "Never mind particulars. You'd better bring the boy here tomorrow night. I shall get off the stone an hour arter daybreak. Then you hold your tongue, and keep the melting pot ready."

It was decided that Nancy should repair to the Jew's next evening and bring Oliver away with her. If Fagin detected any reluctance for the task, he would be willing to accompany her. It was also arranged that poor Oliver should be unreservedly consigned to the custody of Mr. William Sikes, who should deal with him as he thought fit. Sikes would not be held responsible by the Jew for any mischance or evil that might be necessary to visit on the boy. And any representations made by Mr. Sikes on his return should be required to be confirmed, in all important particulars, by the testimony of flash Toby Crackit.

These preliminaries adjusted, Mr. Sikes proceeded to drink brandy at a furious rate, and to brandish the crowbar in an alarming manner. At length, in a fit of professional enthusiasm, he insisted upon producing his box of housebreaking tools. He had no sooner stumbled in with the box, and opened it for the purpose of explaining the nature of the various implements it contained, than he fell over the box upon the floor, and went to sleep where he fell.

"Good night, Nancy," said the Jew, muffling himself up as before.

"Good night."

Their eyes met, and the Jew scrutinized her. There was no flinching about the girl. She was as true and earnest in the matter as Toby Crackit himself could be.

The Jew again bade her good night, and, bestowing a sly kick upon the prostrate form of Mr. Sikes while her back was turned, groped downstairs.

"Always the way!" muttered the Jew to himself as he turned homeward. "The worst of these women is that a very little thing serves to call up some long-forgotten feeling. The best of them is that it never lasts. Ha! ha!"

Mr. Fagin wended his way, through mud and mire, to his gloomy abode, where the Dodger was sitting up, impatiently awaiting his return.

"Is Oliver a-bed? I want to speak to him," was his first remark.

"Hours ago," replied the Dodger, throwing open a door. "Here he is!"

The boy was lying, fast asleep, on a rude bed upon the floor, so pale with anxiety, sadness, and the closeness of his prison, that he looked like death, when life has just departed.

"Not now," said the Jew, turning softly away. "Tomorrow. Tomorrow."

CHAPTER 19

When Oliver awoke in the morning, he was a good deal surprised to find that a new pair of shoes, with strong thick soles, had been placed at his bedside, and that his old shoes had been removed. At first, he hoped that it might be the forerunner of his release. But the Jew told him that he was to be taken to the residence of Bill Sikes that night.

"To—to stay there, sir?" asked Oliver, anxiously.

"No, my dear." replied the Jew. "We shouldn't like to lose you. Don't be afraid, Oliver, you shall come back to us again."

The old man, who was stooping over the fire toasting a piece of bread, looked round and chuckled as if to show that he knew he would still be glad to get away if he could.

"Why, do you think, are you going to Sikes?" inquired Fagin.

"Indeed I don't know, sir," replied Oliver.

"Bah!" said the Jew, turning away with a disappointed expression. "Wait till Bill tells you, then."

The Jew seemed much vexed by Oliver's not expressing any greater curiosity on the subject, and he remained surly and silent till night, when he prepared to go out.

"You may burn a candle," said the Jew, putting one upon the table. "And here's a book for you to read, till they come to fetch you. Good night!"

"Good night!" replied Oliver, softly.

The Jew walked to the door, looking over his

shoulder at the boy as he went. Suddenly stopping, he called him by his name.

Oliver looked up and saw that the Jew was gazing fixedly at him from the dark end of the room.

"Take heed, Oliver! Take heed!" said the old man, shaking his right hand before him in a warning manner. "He's a rough man, and thinks nothing of blood when his own is up. Whatever happens, say nothing, and do what he bids you. Mind!" Placing a strong emphasis on the last word, and nodding his head, he left the room.

Oliver pondered, with a trembling heart, on the words he had just heard. He concluded that he had been selected to perform some ordinary menial offices for the housebreaker, until another boy, better suited for his purpose, could be engaged. He was too well accustomed to suffering to bewail the prospect of change very severely. With a heavy sigh, he took up the book which the Jew had left with him, and began to read.

It was a history of the lives and trials of great criminals. He read of dreadful crimes that made the blood run cold; of secret murders that had been committed by the wayside; of bodies hidden in deep pits and wells. Here, too, he read of men who, lying in their beds at dead of night, had been tempted by their own bad thoughts to such dreadful bloodshed that it made the flesh creep. The terrible descriptions were so real and vivid, that the pages seemed to turn red with gore, and the words upon them whispered by the spirits of the dead.

In a paroxysm of fear, the boy fell upon his knees and prayed Heaven to spare him from such deeds. He asked that he should die at once rather than be reserved for crimes so fearful and appalling. By degrees, he grew more calm, and requested, in a low and broken voice, that he might be rescued from his present dangers.

Just then a rustling noise aroused him.

"Who's there?" he cried, catching sight of a figure standing by the door. Oliver raised the candle above his head, and looked towards the door. It was Nancy.

"Put down the light," said the girl, turning away her head. "It hurts my eyes."

Oliver saw that she was pale, and gently inquired if she were ill. The girl threw herself into a chair, with her back towards him, and wrung her hands, but made no reply.

"God forgive me!" she cried after a while, "I never thought of this."

"Has anything happened?" asked Oliver. "Can I help you? I will if I can."

She rocked herself to and fro, and gasped for breath.

"Nancy!" cried Oliver, "What is it?"

The girl beat her hands upon her knees, and her feet upon the ground. Suddenly stopping, she drew her shawl close round her, and shivered with cold. At length she raised her head, and looked round.

"I don't know what comes over me sometimes," said she, pretending to busy herself in arranging her dress. "It's this damp dirty room, I think. Now, Nolly, dear, you are to go with me."

"What for?" asked Oliver, recoiling.

"What for?" echoed the girl, raising her eyes, and averting them again, the moment they encountered the boy's face. "Oh! For no harm."

"I don't believe it," said Oliver, who had watched her closely.

"Have it your own way," rejoined the girl, affecting to laugh. "For no good, then."

Oliver could see that he had some power over the girl's better feelings, and he thought of appealing to her compassion. But, then, he realized that many people were still in the streets. Someone might be found to believe his tale. So he stepped forward, and said, somewhat hastily, that he was ready.

His timing was not lost on his companion. She eyed him narrowly, while he spoke.

"Hush!" said the girl, stooping over him. "You can't help yourself. I have tried hard for you, but all to no purpose. You are hedged round and round. If ever you are to get loose from here, this is not the time."

Oliver looked up in her face with great surprise. She seemed to speak the truth. Her face was white and agitated, and she trembled with earnestness.

"I have saved you from being ill-used once, and I will again, and I do now," continued the girl. "Those who would have fetched you, if I had not, would have been far more rough than me. I have promised for your being quiet and silent. If you are not, you will only do harm to yourself and me too, and perhaps be my death. See here! I have borne all this for you already."

She pointed, hastily, to some livid bruises on her neck and arms, and continued.

"Remember this! And don't let me suffer more for you, just now. If I could help you, I would, but I have not the power. They don't mean to harm you. Whatever they make you do, is no fault of yours.

Hush! Every word from you is a blow for me. Give me your hand. Make haste!"

She caught the hand that Oliver instinctively placed in hers, and, blowing out the light, drew him after her up the stairs. A carriage was waiting. The girl pulled him in with her, and drew the curtains close. The driver wanted no directions, but lashed his horse into full speed.

The girl still held Oliver fast by the hand, and continued to pour into his ear the warnings and assurances she had already imparted. All was so quick and hurried, that he had scarcely time to recollect where he was, or how he came there, when the carriage stopped at the house where Sikes lived.

Oliver cast a hurried glance along the empty street, and a cry for help hung upon his lips. But the girl's voice was in his ear, beseeching him in such tones of agony to remember her, that he had not the heart to utter it. While he hesitated, the opportunity was gone. He was already in the house, and the door was shut.

"This way," said the girl, releasing her hold for the first time. "Bill!"

"Hallo!" replied Sikes, appearing at the head of the stairs with a candle. "Oh! That's the time of day. Come on!"

This was an uncommonly hearty welcome from a person of Mr. Sikes's temperament. Nancy, appearing much pleased by it, saluted him politely.

"Did he come quiet?" inquired Sikes when they had all reached the room, closing the door as he spoke.

"Like a lamb," rejoined Nancy.

"I'm glad to hear it," said Sikes, looking grimly

at Oliver. "Come here, young 'un, and let me read you a lecture."

Taking him by the shoulder, Sikes sat himself down by the table, and stood the boy in front of him.

"Now, first: do you know wot this is?" inquired Sikes, taking up a pocket pistol that lay on the table.

Oliver replied in the affirmative.

"Well, then, look here," continued Sikes. "This is powder, that 'ere's a bullet, and this is a little bit of a old hat for waddin'." He proceeded to load the pistol, with great deliberation.

"Now it's loaded," said Mr. Sikes, when he had finished.

"Yes, I see it is, sir," replied Oliver.

"Well," said the robber, grasping Oliver's wrist, and putting the barrel so close to his temple that they touched, at which moment the boy could not repress a start, "if you speak a word when you're out o'doors with me, except when I speak to you, that loading will be in your head without notice. And as near as I know, there isn't anybody as would be asking partickler arter you, if you *was* disposed of. D'ye hear me?"

"The short and the long of what you mean," said Nancy, speaking emphatically, "is, that if you're crossed by him in this job you have on hand, you'll prevent his ever telling tales afterwards, by shooting him through the head, and will take your chance of swinging for it, as you do for a great many other things in the way of business, every month of your life."

"That's it!" observed Mr. Sikes, approvingly. "Let's have some supper, and get a snooze before starting."

Nancy disappeared for a few minutes and presently returned with a pot of porter and a dish of sheep's heads. After supper ended, Mr. Sikes disposed of a couple of glasses of spirits and water, and threw himself on the bed, ordering Nancy to call him at five precisely. Oliver stretched himself in his clothes on a mattress upon the floor, and the girl, mending the fire, sat before it, ready to rouse them at the appointed time.

When Oliver awoke, the table was covered with tea things and Nancy was busily engaged in preparing breakfast. A sharp rain was beating against the window panes, and the sky looked black and cloudy.

"Now, then!" growled Sikes, as Oliver started up, "half-past five! Look sharp, or you'll get no breakfast, for it's late as it is."

Oliver took some breakfast, and then replied to a surly inquiry from Sikes by saying that he was quite ready.

Nancy, scarcely looking at the boy, threw him a handkerchief to tie round his throat. Sikes gave him a large rough cape to button over his shoulders. Thus attired, he gave his hand to the robber, who, pausing to show him with a menacing gesture that he had that same pistol in a side pocket of his greatcoat, clasped it firmly in his, and led him away.

Oliver turned when they reached the door, in the hope of meeting a look from the girl. But she had resumed her old seat in front of the fire, and sat perfectly motionless before it.

CHAPTER 20

It was raining hard when they got into the street. The night had been wet and large pools of water had collected in the road. The windows of the houses were all shut, and the streets through which they passed were noiseless and empty. But as they approached the city, the noise and traffic gradually increased. When they threaded the streets between Shoreditch and Smithfield, it had swelled into a roar of sound and bustle. It was as light as it was likely to be, till night came on again, and the busy morning of half the London population had begun.

They struck, by way of Chiswell Street, into Barbican, thence into Long Lane, and so into Smithfield, where they passed the shouts and chaos of the open livestock market. Sikes, dragging Oliver after him, elbowed his way through the thickest of the crowd, and bestowed little attention on the numerous sights and sounds, which so astonished the boy. He nodded, twice or thrice, to a passing friend and pressed steadily onward, until they were clear of the turmoil, and had made their way through Hosier Lane into Holborn.

"Now, young 'un!" said Sikes, looking up at the clock of St. Andrew's Church, "hard upon seven! you must step out. Come, don't lag behind already, Lazy-legs!"

Oliver, quickening his pace into a kind of trot between a fast walk and a run, kept up with the rapid strides of the housebreaker as well as he could.

They held their course at this rate, until they had passed Hyde Park corner, and were on their way to Kensington. Sikes relaxed his pace until an empty cart came up. Seeing "Hounslow" written on it, he asked the driver with as much civility as he could assume, if he would give them a lift as far as Isleworth.

"Jump up," said the man. "Is that your boy?"

"Yes, he's my boy," replied Sikes, looking hard at Oliver, and putting his hand abstractedly into the pocket where the pistol was.

"Your father walks rather too quick for you, don't he, my man?" inquired the driver, seeing that Oliver was out of breath.

"Not a bit of it," replied Sikes, interposing. "He's used to it. Here, take hold of my hand, Ned. In with you!"

Thus addressing Oliver, he helped him into the cart. The driver, pointing to a heap of sacks, told him to lie down there, and rest himself.

As they passed the different milestones, Oliver wondered, more and more, where his companion meant to take him. Kensington, Hammersmith, Chiswick, Kew Bridge, Brentford were all passed, and yet they went on as steadily as if they had only just begun their journey. At length, they came to a public house called the Coach and Horses. A little way beyond it, another road appeared to run off. And here, the cart stopped.

Sikes dismounted, holding Oliver by the hand all the while. Lifting him down, he bestowed a furious look upon him, and rapped the side pocket with his fist, in a significant manner.

"Goodbye, boy," said the man.

"He's sulky," replied Sikes, giving him a shake. "A young dog! Don't mind him."

"Not I!" rejoined the other, getting into his cart. "It's a fine day, after all." And he drove away.

Sikes waited until he had gone, and then, telling Oliver he might look about him if he wanted, once again led him onward on his journey.

Taking a right-hand road, they walked on for a long time, passing many large gardens and gentlemen's houses on both sides of the way, and stopping for nothing but a little beer, until they reached a town. Here against the wall of a house, Oliver saw written up in pretty large letters, "Hampton." They lingered about, in the fields, for some hours. At length they came back into the town, and, turning into an old public house with a defaced sign board, ordered some dinner by the kitchen fire.

Several rough men sat drinking and smoking. They took no notice of Oliver, and little of Sikes. As Sikes took little notice of them, he and his young comrade sat in a corner by themselves, without being much troubled by their company.

They had some cold meat for dinner, and sat so long after it, while Mr. Sikes indulged himself with three or four pipes, that Oliver began to feel quite certain they were not going any farther. Being much tired with the walk and getting up so early, he fell asleep.

It was quite dark when he was awakened by a push from Sikes. Rousing himself sufficiently to sit up and look about him, he found Sikes talking with a laboring man, over a pint of ale.

"So, you're going on to Lower Halliford, are you?" inquired Sikes.

"Yes, I am," replied the man, who seemed a little the worse—or better, as the case might be—for drinking, "and not slow about it neither. My horse hasn't got a load behind him going back, as he had coming up in the mornin', and he won't be long a-doing of it."

"Could you give my boy and me a lift as far as there?" demanded Sikes, pushing the ale towards his new friend.

"If you're going directly, I can," replied the man. "Are you going to Halliford?"

"Going on to Shepperton," replied Sikes.

"I'm your man, as far as I go," replied the other. "Is all paid, Becky?"

"Yes, the other gentleman's paid," replied the girl.

"I say!" said the man, "that won't do, you know."

"Why not?" rejoined Sikes. "You're a-going to accommodate us, and wot's to prevent my standing treat for a pint or so, in return?"

The stranger reflected upon this argument, seized Sikes by the hand, and declared he was a real good fellow. After the exchange of a few more compliments, they bade the company good night, and went out.

The night was very dark. A damp mist rose from the river, and spread itself over the dreary fields. It was piercing cold, too. All was gloomy and black. Not a word was spoken, for the driver had grown sleepy, and Sikes was in no mood to lead him into conversation. Oliver sat huddled in a corner of the cart, bewildered with alarm.

Sunbury was passed through, and they came again into the lonely road. Two or three miles more, and the cart stopped. Sikes alighted, took Oliver by the hand, and they once again walked on.

They turned into no house at Shepperton, as the weary boy had expected, but still kept walking on, in mud and darkness, through gloomy lanes, until they came within sight of the lights of a town. Oliver saw that the water was just below them, and that they were coming to the foot of a bridge.

Sikes kept straight on, until they were close upon the bridge, then turned suddenly down a bank upon the left.

"The water!" thought Oliver, turning sick with fear. "He has brought me to this lonely place to murder me!"

He was about to throw himself on the ground, and make one struggle for his young life, when he saw that they stood before a solitary house, all ruinous and decayed. There was a window on each side of the entrance, and one story above, but no light was visible.

Sikes, with Oliver's hand still in his, softly approached the low porch, and raised the latch. The door yielded to the pressure, and they passed in together.

CHAPTER 21

"Hallo!" cried a loud, hoarse voice, as soon as they set foot in the passage.

"Don't make such a row," said Sikes, bolting the door.

"My pal!" cried the same voice. "A glim, Barney! Show the gentleman in, Barney. Wake up first, if convenient."

The speaker appeared to throw a bootjack, or some such article, at the person he addressed, to rouse him from his slumber. There was an indistinct muttering, as of a man between sleep and awake.

"Do you hear?" cried the same voice. "There's Bill Sikes in the passage with nobody to do the civil to him, and you sleeping there, as if you took laudanum with your meals. Are you any fresher now, or do you want the iron candlestick to wake you thoroughly?"

A pair of slipshod feet shuffled hastily across the bare floor of the room, and there issued from a door on the right a feeble candle and the same individual who officiated as waiter at the public house on Saffron Hill.

"Bister Sikes!" exclaimed Barney, with real or counterfeit joy, "'cub id, sir."

"You get on first," said Sikes, putting Oliver in front of him. "Quicker! or I shall tread upon your heels."

Sikes pushed Oliver before him, and they entered a low dark room with a smoky fire, two or three broken chairs, a table, and an old couch, on

149

which, with his legs much higher than his head, a man was reposing at full length, smoking a long clay pipe. He was dressed in a smartly-cut coat, with large brass buttons, an orange neckerchief, a patterned waistcoat, and drab breeches. Mr. Crackit had no great quantity of hair, either upon his head or face. But what he had was reddish, and tortured into long corkscrew curls, through which he occasionally thrust some dirty fingers, ornamented with large common rings.

"Bill, my boy!" said Toby, turning his head towards the door, "I'm glad to see you. I was almost afraid you'd given it up, in which case I should have made a personal wentur. Hallo!"

Uttering this exclamation in a tone of great surprise, as his eyes rested on Oliver, Mr. Toby Crackit brought himself into a sitting posture, and demanded who that was.

"Only the boy!" replied Sikes, drawing a chair towards the fire.

"Wud of Bister Fagid's lads," exclaimed Barney, with a grin.

"Fagin's, eh!" exclaimed Toby, looking at Oliver. "Wot an inwalable boy that'll make, for the old ladies' pockets in chapels! His mug is a fortin' to him."

"There's enough of that," interposed Sikes, impatiently, and stooping over his friend, he whispered a few words in his ear, at which Mr. Crackit laughed immensely, and honored Oliver with a long stare of astonishment.

"Now," said Sikes, as he resumed his seat, "if you'll give us something to eat and drink while we're waiting, you'll put some heart in us. Sit down by the fire, younker, and rest yourself. You'll have to go out with us again tonight, though not far off."

Oliver looked at Sikes in timid wonder, and drawing a stool to the fire, sat with his aching head upon his hands, scarcely knowing what was passing around him.

"Here," said Toby, as Barney placed some fragments of food, and a bottle upon the table, "success to the crack!" He advanced to the table, filled a glass with spirits, and drank off its contents. Mr. Sikes did the same.

"A drain for the boy," said Toby, half-filling a wineglass. "Down with it, innocence."

"Indeed, I-" said Oliver, looking piteously up into the man's face.

"Down with it!" echoed Toby. "Do you think I don't know what's good for you? Tell him to drink it, Bill."

"He had better!" said Sikes clapping his hand upon his pocket. "Burn my body, if he isn't more trouble than a whole family of Dodgers. Drink it, you perwerse imp!"

Frightened by the menacing gestures of the two men, Oliver hastily swallowed the contents of the glass, and immediately fell into a violent fit of coughing, which delighted Toby Crackit and Barney, and even drew a smile from the surly Mr. Sikes.

This done, and Sikes having satisfied his appetite (Oliver could eat nothing but a small crust of bread), the two men laid themselves down on chairs for a short nap. Oliver retained his stool by the fire, while Barney wrapped in a blanket, and stretched himself on the floor.

They slept for some time, nobody stirring but Barney, who rose once or twice to throw coals on the fire. Oliver fell into a heavy doze, but he was roused by Toby Crackit jumping up and declaring it was half-past one.

In an instant, the other two were on their feet, and all were actively engaged in busy preparation. Sikes and his companion put on large dark shawls, and drew on their greatcoats. Barney brought forth several articles, which he hastily crammed into the pockets.

"Barkers for me, Barney," said Toby Crackit.

"Here they are," replied Barney, producing a pair of pistols.

"All right!" replied Toby, stowing them away. "The persuaders?"

"I've got 'em," replied Sikes.

"Crape, keys, centerbits, darkies—nothing forgotten?" inquired Toby, fastening a small crowbar to a loop inside the skirt of his coat.

"All right," rejoined his companion. "Bring bits of timber, Barney. That's the time of day."

With these words, he took a thick stick from Barney's hands, who, having delivered another to Toby, busied himself in fastening on Oliver's cape.

"Now then!" said Sikes, holding out his hand.

Oliver, who was completely stupefied by the unwonted exercise, and the air, and the drink, put his hand mechanically into Sikes.

"Take his other hand, Toby," said Sikes. "Look out, Barney."

The man went to the door, and returned to announce that all was quiet. The two robbers issued forth with Oliver between them.

It was now intensely dark. The fog was much heavier than it had been in the early part of the night, and Oliver's hair and eyebrows, within a few minutes after leaving the house, had become stiff with the half-frozen moisture that was floating about. They crossed the bridge, and kept on towards the lights he had seen before. They soon arrived at Chertsey.

"Slap through the town," whispered Sikes. "There'll be nobody in the way to see us."

They hurried through the main street of the little town, which at that late hour was wholly deserted. They cleared the town as the church bell struck two.

Quickening their pace, they turned up a road on the left. After walking about a quarter of a mile, they stopped before a detached house surrounded by a wall, to the top of which Toby climbed in a twinkling.

"The boy next," said Toby. "Hoist him up."

Before Oliver had time to look round, Sikes caught him under the arms, and in three or four seconds he and Toby were lying on the grass on the other side. Sikes followed directly. And they stole cautiously towards the house.

Now, for the first time, Oliver, almost mad with grief and terror, saw that housebreaking and robbery, if not murder, were the objects of the expedition. He clasped his hands together, and involuntarily uttered a subdued exclamation of horror. His limbs failed him, and he sank upon his knees.

"Get up!" murmured Sikes, trembling with rage, and drawing the pistol from his pocket. "Or I'll strew your brains upon the grass."

"For God's sake let me go!" cried Oliver, "let me run away and die in the fields. I will never come near London; never, never! Oh! Pray have mercy on me, and do not make me steal. For the love of all the bright angels that rest in Heaven, have mercy upon me!"

The man to whom this appeal was made swore a dreadful oath, and had cocked the pistol, when Toby, striking it from his grasp, placed his hand upon the boy's mouth, and dragged him to the house.

"Hush!" cried the man. "Say another word, and I'll do the business myself with a crack on the head. That makes no noise, and is quite as certain, and more genteel. Here, Bill, wrench the shutter open. He's game enough now. I've seen older hands of his age took the same way, for a minute or two, on a cold night."

Sikes, invoking terrific curses upon Fagin's head for sending Oliver on such an errand, plied the crowbar vigorously, but with little noise. After some delay, and some assistance from Toby, the shutter swung open on its hinges.

It was a little lattice window, about five feet and a half above the ground, at the back of the house, which belonged to a scullery at the end of the passage. The opening was so small that the occupants had probably not thought it worthwhile to defend it more securely. But it was large enough to admit a boy of Oliver's size, nevertheless. Mr. Sikes undid the fastening of the lattice, and it soon stood wide open also.

"Now listen," whispered Sikes, drawing a dark lantern from his pocket, and throwing the glare full on Oliver's face, "I'm a going to put you through there. Take this light. Go softly up the steps straight afore you, and along the little hall, to the street door. Unfasten it, and let us in."

"There's a bolt at the top you won't be able to reach," interposed Toby. "Stand upon one of the hall chairs."

Sikes imperiously commanded Crackit to get to work. Toby complied, first producing his lantern, and placing it on the ground. Then he planted himself firmly with his head against the wall beneath the window, and his hands upon his knees, so as to make a step of his back.

Sikes stepped upon him, put Oliver gently through the window with his feet first and planted him safely on the floor inside.

"Take this lantern," said Sikes, looking into the room. "You see the stairs afore you?"

Oliver, more dead than alive, gasped out, "Yes." Sikes, pointing to the street door with the pistol barrel, briefly advised him to take notice that he was within shot all the way, and that if he faltered, he would fall dead that instant.

"It's done in a minute," said Sikes, in the same low whisper. "Directly I let go of you, do your work. Hark!"

"What's that?" whispered the other man.

They listened intently.

"Nothing," said Sikes, releasing his hold of Oliver. "Now!"

In the short time he had had to collect his senses, the boy had firmly resolved that, whether he died in the attempt or not, he would make one effort to dart upstairs from the hall, and alarm the family. Filled with this idea, he advanced at once, but stealthily.

"Come back!" suddenly cried Sikes aloud. "Back! back!"

Scared by the sudden breaking of the dead stillness of the place, and by a loud cry which followed it, Oliver let his lantern fall, and knew not whether to advance or fly.

The cry was repeated—a light appeared—a vision of two terrified half-dressed men at the top of the stairs swam before his eyes—a flash—a loud noise—a smoke—a crash somewhere—and he staggered back.

Sikes had disappeared for an instant; but he was up again, and had him by the collar before the smoke had cleared away. He fired his own pistol after the men, who were already retreating, and dragged the boy up.

"Clasp your arm tighter," said Sikes, as he drew him through the window. "Give me a shawl here. They've hit him. Quick! How the boy bleeds!"

Then came the loud ringing of a bell, mingled with the noise of firearms, and the shouts of men, and the sensation of being carried over uneven ground at a rapid pace. And then, a cold deadly feeling crept over the boy's heart, and he saw or heard no more.

CHAPTER 22

The night was bitter cold. The snow lay on the ground, frozen into a hard thick crust, and a sharp wind howled abroad. Bleak, dark, and piercing cold, it was a night for the well-housed and fed to draw round the bright fire and thank God they were at home; and for the homeless, starving wretch to lay him down and die.

Such was the weather when Mrs. Corney, the matron of the workhouse that was the birthplace of Oliver Twist, sat herself down before a cheerful fire in her own little room, to solace herself with some tea.

She had just tasted her first cup, when she was disturbed by a soft tap at the door.

"Oh, come in with you!" said Mrs. Corney, sharply. "Some of the old women dying, I suppose. They always die when I'm at meals. Don't stand there, letting the cold air in. What's amiss now, eh?"

"Nothing, ma'am," replied a man's voice.

"Dear me!" exclaimed the matron, in a much sweeter tone, "is that Mr. Bumble?"

"At your service, ma'am," said Mr. Bumble, who now made his appearance, bearing the cocked hat in one hand and a bundle in the other.

"Hard weather, Mr. Bumble," said the matron.

"Hard, indeed, ma'am," replied the beadle. "Anti-porochial weather this, ma'am. Mrs. Corney, we have given away a matter of twenty quartern loaves and a cheese and a half, this blessed afternoon, and yet them paupers are not contented."

"Of course not. When would they be, Mr. Bumble?" said the matron, sipping her tea.

"When, indeed, ma'am!" rejoined Mr. Bumble. "Why here's one man that, in consideration of his wife and large family, has a quartern loaf and a good pound of cheese, full weight. Is he grateful, ma'am? Not a copper farthing's worth of it! What does he do, ma'am, but ask for a few coals! What would he do with coals? Toast his cheese with 'em and then come back for more. That's the way with these people, ma'am. Give 'em a apron full of coals today, and they'll come back for another, the day after tomorrow, as brazen as alabaster."

"It beats anything I could have believed," observed the matron emphatically. "But don't you think out-of-door relief a bad thing, anyway, Mr. Bumble?"

"Mrs. Corney," said the beadle, smiling, "out-of-door relief, properly managed, is the porochial safeguard. The great principle of out-of-door relief is, to give the paupers exactly what they don't want; and then they get tired of coming."

"But," said the beadle, stopping to unpack his bundle, "these are official secrets, ma'am; not to be spoken of, except, as I may say, among the porochial officers, such as ourselves. This is the port wine, ma'am, that the board ordered for the infirmary; real, fresh, genuine port wine; only out of the cask this forenoon; clear as a bell, and no sediment!"

Having held the first bottle up to the light, and shaken it well to test its excellence, Mr. Bumble placed them both on top of a chest of drawers, and took up his hat, as if to go.

"You'll have a cold walk, Mr. Bumble," said the

matron.

"It blows, ma'am," replied Mr. Bumble, turning up his coat collar, "enough to cut one's ears off."

The matron looked, from the little kettle, to the beadle, who was moving towards the door, and bashfully inquired whether he wouldn't take a cup of tea?

Mr. Bumble instantaneously turned back his collar again, laid his hat and stick upon a chair, and drew another chair up to the table. As he slowly seated himself, he looked at the lady. She fixed her eyes upon the little teapot. Mr. Bumble coughed, and slightly smiled.

Mrs. Corney rose to get another cup and saucer from the closet. As she sat down, her eyes once again encountered those of the gallant beadle. She colored, and applied herself to the task of making his tea. Again Mr. Bumble coughed—louder this time.

"Sweet? Mr. Bumble?" inquired the matron, taking up the sugar basin.

"Very sweet, indeed, ma'am," replied Mr. Bumble. He fixed his eyes on Mrs. Corney as he said this, and if ever a beadle looked tender, Mr. Bumble was that beadle at that moment.

The tea was made, and handed in silence. Mr. Bumble began to eat and drink, occasionally giving a deep sigh.

"You have a cat, ma'am, I see," said Mr. Bumble, glancing at one who, in the center of her family, was basking before the fire, "and kittens too, I declare!"

"I am so fond of them, Mr. Bumble, you can't think," replied the matron. "They're *so* happy, *so* frolicsome, and *so* cheerful, that they are quite companions for me."

"Very nice animals, ma'am," replied Mr. Bumble, approvingly, "so domestic."

"Oh, yes!" rejoined the matron with enthusiasm, "so fond of their home too, that it's quite a pleasure, I'm sure."

"Mrs. Corney, ma'am," said Mr. Bumble, slowly, and marking the time with his teaspoon, "Any cat, or kitten, that could live with you, ma'am, and *not* be fond of its home, must be an ass, ma'am."

"Oh, Mr. Bumble!" remonstrated Mrs. Corney.

"It's of no use disguising facts, ma'am," said Mr. Bumble, slowly flourishing the teaspoon with a kind of amorous dignity that made him doubly impressive. "I would drown it myself, with pleasure."

"Then you're a cruel man," said the matron vivaciously, as she held out her hand for the beadle's cup, "and a very hardhearted man besides."

"Hardhearted, ma'am?" said Mr. Bumble. He resigned his cup without another word, squeezed Mrs. Corney's little finger as she took it, and hitched his chair a little morsel farther from the fire.

Consequently, Mr. Bumble, moving his chair by little and little farther from the fire, soon began to diminish the distance between himself and the matron. Eventually, the two chairs touched, and when they did so, Mr. Bumble stopped.

Now, if the matron had moved her chair to the right, she would have been scorched by the fire, and if to the left, she must have fallen into Mr. Bumble's arms. So she remained where she was, and handed Mr. Bumble another cup of tea.

"Hardhearted, Mrs. Corney?" said Mr. Bumble, stirring his tea, and looking up into the matron's face. "Are *you* hardhearted, Mrs. Corney?"

"Dear me!" exclaimed the matron, "what a curious question from a single man. What can you want to know for, Mr. Bumble?"

The beadle drank his tea to the last drop, finished a piece of toast, whisked the crumbs off his knees, wiped his lips, and deliberately kissed the matron.

"Mr. Bumble!" cried that discreet lady in a whisper, for the fright was so great, that she had quite lost her voice. "Mr. Bumble, I shall scream!" Mr. Bumble made no reply, but in a slow and dignified manner, put his arm round the matron's waist.

The lady would have screamed at this additional boldness, but that exertion was rendered unnecessary by a hasty knocking at the door. Mr. Bumble darted, with much agility, to the wine bottles, and began dusting them with great violence, while the matron sharply demanded who was there.

"If you please, mistress," said a withered old female pauper, hideously ugly, putting her head in at the door, "Old Sally is a-going fast."

"Well, what's that to me?" angrily demanded the matron. "I can't keep her alive, can I?"

"No, no, mistress," replied the old woman, "nobody can. She's far beyond the reach of help. But she's troubled in her mind, and she says she has got something to tell, which you must hear. She'll never die quiet till you come, mistress."

The worthy Mrs. Corney muttered a variety of invectives against old women who couldn't even die without purposely annoying their betters. Muffling herself in a thick shawl, she briefly requested Mr. Bumble to stay till she came back, lest anything particular should occur. Bidding the messenger to walk fast, and not be all night hobbling up the stairs, she followed her from the room.

Mr. Bumble's conduct on being left to himself was rather inexplicable. He opened the closet, counted the teaspoons, weighed the sugar tongs, closely inspected a silver milk pot to ascertain that it was of the genuine metal, and, having satisfied his curiosity on these points, put on his cocked hat cornerwise, and danced with much gravity four times round the table.

Having gone through this extraordinary performance, he took off the cocked hat again, and, spreading himself before the fire with his back towards it, seemed to be mentally engaged in taking an exact inventory of the furniture.

CHAPTER 23

I t was a bare garret room, with a dim light burning at the farther end. There was another old woman watching by the bed, and the parish apothecary's apprentice was standing by the fire, making a toothpick out of a quill.

"Cold night, Mrs. Corney," said this young gentleman, as the matron entered.

"Very cold, indeed, sir," replied the mistress, in her most civil tones, and dropping a curtsy as she spoke.

"You should get better coals out of your contractors," said the apothecary's deputy, breaking a lump on the top of the fire with the rusty poker. "These are not at all the sort of thing for a cold night."

"They're the board's choosing, sir," returned the matron.

The conversation was here interrupted by a moan from the sick woman.

"If she lasts a couple of hours, I shall be surprised," said the apothecary's apprentice, intent upon the toothpick's point. "It's a breakup of the system altogether. Is she dozing, old lady?"

The attendant stooped over the bed to ascertain, and nodded.

"Then perhaps she'll go off in that way, if you don't make a row," said the young man. "Put the light on the floor. She won't see it there."

The attendant did as she was told. The mistress, with an expression of impatience, wrapped herself in her shawl, and sat at the foot of the bed.

The apothecary's apprentice, having completed the manufacture of the toothpick, planted himself in front of the fire and made good use of it for ten minutes or so. Then he wished Mrs. Corney joy of her job, and took himself off on tiptoe.

When they had sat in silence for some time, the two old women rose from the bed. Crouching over the fire, they held out their withered hands to catch the heat and began to converse in a low voice.

While they were thus employed, the matron, who had been impatiently watching until the dying woman should awaken from her stupor, joined them by the fire, and sharply asked how long she was to wait?

"Not long, mistress," replied the second woman. "We have none of us long to wait for Death. Patience! He'll be here soon enough for us all."

"Hold your tongue, you doting idiot!" said the matron sternly. "Martha, tell me. Has she been in this way before?"

"Often," answered the first woman.

"But will never be again," added the second one. "That is, she'll never wake again but once—and mind, mistress, that won't be for long!"

"Long or short," said the matron, snappishly, "she won't find me here when she does wake. Take care, both of you, how you worry me again for nothing. It's no part of my duty to see all the old women in the house die, and I won't. Mind that, you impudent old harridans!"

She was bouncing away when a cry from the two women, who had turned towards the bed, caused her to look round. The patient had raised herself upright, and was stretching her arms towards them.

"Who's that?" she cried, in a hollow voice.

"Hush, hush!" said one of the women, stooping over her. "Lie down!"

"I'll never lie down again alive!" said the woman, struggling. "I *will* tell her! Come here! Nearer! Let me whisper in your ear."

She clutched the matron by the arm, and forcing her into a chair by the bedside, was about to speak, when looking round, she caught sight of the two old women bending forward eagerly to listen.

"Turn them away," said the woman, drowsily. "Make haste!"

The superior pushed them from the room, closed the door, and returned to the bedside.

"Now listen to me," said the dying woman. "In this very bed, I once nursed a pretty young creetur that was brought into the house with her feet cut and bruised with walking, and all soiled with dust and blood. She gave birth to a boy, and died. I robbed her, so I did! She wasn't cold—I tell you she wasn't cold, when I stole it!"

"Stole what, for God's sake?" cried the matron.

"*It!*" replied the woman. "The only thing she had. She wanted clothes to keep her warm, and food to eat. But she had kept it safe, and had it in her bosom. It was gold, I tell you! Rich gold, that might have saved her life!"

"Gold!" echoed the matron, bending eagerly over the woman as she fell back. "Go on, go on—yes—what of it? Who was the mother?"

"She charged me to keep it safe," replied the woman with a groan, "and trusted me as the only woman about her. I stole it in my heart when she first showed it to me hanging round her neck. The child's death, perhaps, is on me besides! They would have treated him better, if they had known it all!"

"Known what?" asked the other. "Speak!"

"The boy grew so like his mother," said the woman, rambling on, "that I could never forget it when I saw his face. Poor girl! She was so young, too! Such a gentle lamb! Wait, there's more to tell. I have not told you all, have I?"

"No, no," replied the matron, inclining her head to catch the words, as they came more faintly from the dying woman. "Be quick, or it may be too late!"

"The mother," said the woman, making a more violent effort than before, "when the pains of death first came upon her, whispered in my ear that if her baby was born alive, and thrived, the day might come when it would not feel so much disgraced to hear its poor young mother named. "And oh, kind Heaven!" she said, folding her thin hands together, "whether it be boy or girl, raise up some friends for it in this troubled world, and take pity upon a lonely desolate child, abandoned to its mercy!"

"The boy's name?" demanded the matron.

"They *called* him Oliver," replied the woman, feebly. "The gold I stole was—"

"Yes, yes—what?" cried the other.

The matron bent eagerly over the woman to hear her reply, but drew back, instinctively, as she once again rose, slowly and stiffly, into a sitting posture. Then, clutching the coverlet with both hands, the woman muttered some indistinct sounds in her throat, and fell lifeless on the bed.

* * *

"Stone dead!" said one of the old women, hurrying in as soon as the door was opened.

"And nothing to tell, after all," rejoined the

matron, walking carelessly away.

The two crones, too busily occupied in the preparations for their dreadful duties to make any reply, were left alone, hovering about the body.

CHAPTER 24

Whle these things were passing in the country workhouse, Mr. Fagin sat in the old den—the same from which Oliver had been removed by the girl— brooding over a dull, smoky fire. He held a pair of bellows upon his knee, and he had fallen into deep thought.

At a table behind him sat the Artful Dodger, Master Charles Bates, and Mr. Chitling, all intent upon a game of cards. The Dodger, as occasion served, bestowed a variety of earnest glances at Mr. Chitling's cards. It being a cold night, the Dodger wore his hat, as was often his custom indoors. He also held a clay pipe between his teeth, which he only removed to apply for refreshment to a quart pot upon the table, filled with gin and water.

Master Bates was also attentive to the play, but he more frequently applied himself to the gin and water, and moreover indulged in many jests and irrelevant remarks. The Artful more than once took occasion to reason gravely with his companion upon these improprieties. Master Bates received these criticisms extremely well, merely requesting his friend to be "blowed," or to insert his head in a sack.

Master Bates and Mr. Chitling invariably lost, but instead of angering Master Bates, the loss appeared to give him the highest amusement. He laughed most uproariously at the end of every deal, and protested that he had never seen such a jolly game in all his born days.

"That's two doubles and the rub," said Mr. Chitling, with a long face, as he drew half-a-crown from his waistcoat pocket. "I never see such a feller as you, Jack. You win everything. Even when we've good cards, Charley and I can't make nothing of 'em."

This delighted Charley Bates so much, that his consequent shout of laughter roused the Jew from his reverie, and induced him to inquire what was the matter.

"Matter, Fagin!" cried Charley. "I wish you had watched the play. Tommy Chitling hasn't won a point, and I went partners with him against the Artful."

"Ay, ay!" said the Jew, with a grin, which showed that he was at no loss to understand the reason. "Try 'em again, Tom."

"No more of it for me, thank 'ee, Fagin," replied Mr. Chitling. "I've had enough. That 'ere Dodger has such a run of luck that there's no standing again' him."

"Ha! ha! my dear," replied the Jew, "you must get up very early in the morning, to win against the Dodger."

"Morning!" said Charley Bates, "you must put your boots on overnight, and have a telescope at each eye, and a opera glass between your shoulders, if you want to come over him."

Mr. Dawkins received these handsome compliments with much philosophy, and he proceeded to amuse himself by sketching a ground plan of Newgate on the table with the piece of chalk, whistling, meantime, with peculiar shrillness.

"How precious dull you are, Tommy!" said the Dodger, stopping short when there had been a long silence, and addressing Mr. Chitling. "What do you think he's thinking of, Fagin?"

"How should I know, my dear?" replied the Jew, looking round as he plied the bellows. "About his losses, maybe, or the little retirement in the country that he's just left, eh? Ha! ha! Is that it, my dear?"

"Not a bit of it," replied the Dodger, as Mr. Chitling was about to reply. "What do *you* say, Charley?"

"I should say," replied Master Bates, with a grin, "that he was uncommon sweet upon Betsy. See how he's a-blushing! Oh, my eye! Tommy Chitling's in love! Oh, Fagin! What a spree!"

Thoroughly overpowered with the notion of Mr. Chitling being the victim of the tender passion, Master Bates threw himself back in his chair with such violence, that he lost his balance, and pitched over upon the floor, where he lay until his laugh was over.

"Never mind him, my dear," said the Jew, winking at Mr. Dawkins, and giving Master Bates a reproving tap with the nozzle of the bellows. "Betsy's a fine girl. Stick with her, Tom. Do as she bids you, and you will make your fortune."

"So I *do* do as she bids me," replied Mr. Chitling. "I shouldn't have been caught, if it hadn't been for her advice. But it turned out a good job for you, didn't it, Fagin! And what's six weeks of it? It must come, some time or another, and why not in the wintertime when you don't want to go out a-walking so much, eh, Fagin?"

"Ah, to be sure, my dear," replied the Jew.

"You wouldn't mind it again, Tom, would you," asked the Dodger, winking upon Charley and the Jew, "if it made Bet all right?"

"I mean to say that I shouldn't," replied Tom, angrily. "There, now. Ah! Who'll say as much as that, I should like to know. Eh, Fagin?"

"Nobody, my dear," replied the Jew. "Not a soul, Tom. I don't know one of 'em that would do it besides you."

"I might have got clear off, if I'd split upon her, mightn't I, Fagin?" angrily pursued the poor half-witted dupe. "A word from me would have done it, wouldn't it, Fagin?"

"To be sure it would, my dear," replied the Jew.

"But I didn't blab it, did I, Fagin?" demanded Tom, pouring question upon question.

"No, no, to be sure," replied the Jew. "You were too stouthearted for that. A deal too stout, my dear!"

"Perhaps I was," rejoined Tom, looking round. "And if I was, what's to laugh at in that, eh, Fagin?"

The Jew, perceiving that Mr. Chitling was considerably roused, hastened to assure him that nobody was laughing. But, unfortunately, Charley, in opening his mouth to reply that he was never more serious in his life, was unable to prevent the escape of such a violent roar, that the abused Mr. Chitling rushed across the room and aimed a blow at the offender. Charley ducked to avoid it, and chose his time so well that it struck the chest of the merry old gentleman, and caused him to stagger to the wall, where he stood panting for breath, while Mr. Chitling looked on in intense dismay.

"Hark!" cried the Dodger at this moment, "I heard the bell." Catching up the light, he crept softly upstairs.

The bell was rung again, with some impatience,

while the party were in darkness. After a short pause, the Dodger reappeared, and whispered Fagin mysteriously.

"Yes," said the Jew. "Bring him down. Hush! Quiet, Charley! Gently, Tom! Scarce, scarce!"

There was no sound of their whereabouts, when the Dodger descended the stairs, bearing the light in his hand, and followed by a man in a coarse smock-frock, who, after casting a hurried glance round the room, pulled off a large wrapper which had concealed the lower portion of his face, and disclosed the haggard and unshorn features of flash Toby Crackit.

"How are you, Faguey?" said Toby, nodding to the Jew. With these words he drew a chair to the fire, and placed his feet upon the hob.

"See there, Faguey," he said, pointing disconsolately to his top boots, "not a bubble of blacking, by Jove! But don't look at me in that way, man. All in good time. I can't talk about business till I've eat and drank!"

The Jew motioned to the Dodger to place the eatables upon the table, and, seated himself opposite the housebreaker to wait.

Toby was by no means in a hurry to open the conversation. He ate with the utmost outwards indifference, until he could eat no more. Then, ordering the Dodger out, he closed the door, mixed a glass of spirits and water, and composed himself for talking.

"First and foremost, Faguey," said Toby.

"Yes, yes!" interposed the Jew, drawing up his chair.

"First and foremost, Faguey," said the house-breaker, "how's Bill?"

"What!" screamed the Jew, starting from his seat.

"Why, you don't mean to say—" began Toby, turning pale.

"Mean!" cried the Jew, stamping furiously on the ground. "Where are they? Sikes and the boy! Where are they? Where have they been? Where are they hiding? Why have they not been here?"

"The crack failed," said Toby faintly.

"I know it," replied the Jew, tearing a newspaper from his pocket and pointing to it. "What more?"

"They fired and hit the boy. We cut over the fields at the back, with him between us—straight as the crow flies—through hedge and ditch. They gave chase. The whole country was awake, and the dogs upon us."

"The boy!"

"Bill had him on his back, and scudded like the wind. We stopped to take him between us. His head hung down, and he was cold. They were close upon our heels. Every man for himself! We parted company, and left the youngster lying in a ditch. Alive or dead, that's all I know about him."

The Jew uttered a loud yell, and twining his hands in his hair, rushed from the room, and from the house.

CHAPTER 25

Avoiding, as much as was possible, all the main streets, and skulking only through the byways and alleys, Fagin at length emerged on Snow Hill. Here he walked even faster than before, and then turned into a narrow and dismal alley, called Field Lane, leading to Saffron Hill. He was well known to the sallow denizens of the lane. Those who were on the lookout to buy or sell, nodded, familiarly, as he passed along.

He stopped to address a salesman of small stature, who was smoking a pipe at his warehouse door. Pointing in the direction of Saffron Hill, Fagin inquired whether any one was up yonder tonight.

"At the Cripples?" inquired the man.

The Jew nodded.

"Let me see," pursued the merchant, reflecting. "Yes, there's some half-dozen of 'em gone in, that I knows. I don't think your friend's there."

"Sikes is not, I suppose?" inquired the Jew, disappointed.

The little man shook his head, looking amazingly sly. "Have you got anything in my line tonight?"

"Nothing tonight," said the Jew, turning away.

The Three Cripples, or rather the Cripples, as the establishment was familiarly known to its patrons, was the public house in which Mr. Sikes and his dog have already figured. Merely making a sign to a man at the bar, Fagin walked straight upstairs, and opening the door of a room, and softly insinuating himself into the chamber, looked anxiously about, shading his eyes with his hand, as if in search of some particular person.

The room was illuminated by two gaslights, and curtains of faded red were drawn. The ceiling was blackened, to prevent its color from being injured by the flaring of the lamps, and the place was so full of dense tobacco smoke, that at first it was scarcely possible to discern anything more. By degrees, however, as some of it cleared away through the open door, there appeared a large crowd, male and female, gathered round a long table. At the upper end sat a chairman with a hammer of office in his hand, while a professional gentleman with a bluish nose, and his face tied up for the benefit of a toothache, presided at a jingling piano in a remote corner.

As Fagin stepped softly in, the professional gentleman, running over the keys by way of prelude, occasioned a general cry of order for a song. A young lady proceeded to entertain the company with a ballad in four verses, between each of which the accompanist played the melody all through, as loud as he could.

Fagin looked eagerly from face to face while these proceedings were in progress, but apparently without finding the one he sought. Succeeding, at length, in catching the eye of the chairman, he beckoned to him slightly, and left the room, as quietly as he had entered it.

"What can I do for you, Mr. Fagin?" inquired the chairman, as he followed him out to the landing. "Won't you join us? They'll be delighted, every one of 'em."

The Jew shook his head impatiently, and said in a whisper, "Is *he* here?"

"No," replied the man.

"And no news of Barney?" inquired Fagin.

"None," replied the landlord of the Cripples. "He won't stir till it's all safe. Depend on it, they're on the scent down there. If he moved, he'd blow upon the thing at once. He's all right enough, Barney is, else I should have heard of him."

"Will *he* be here tonight?" asked the Jew, laying the same emphasis on the pronoun as before.

"Monks, do you mean?" inquired the landlord, hesitating.

"Hush!" said the Jew. "Yes."

"Certain," replied the man, drawing a gold watch from his fob. "I expected him here before now. If you'll wait ten minutes, he'll be—"

"No, no," said the Jew, hastily. "Tell him I came here to see him, and that he must come to me tonight. No, say tomorrow. As he is not here, tomorrow will be time enough."

"Good!" said the man. "Nothing more?"

"Not a word now," said the Jew, descending the stairs. The landlord returned to his guests.

The Jew was no sooner alone, than his face resumed its former expression of anxiety. After a brief reflection, he called a hack-cabriolet, and bade the man drive towards Bethnal Green. He dismissed him within some quarter of a mile of Mr. Sikes's residence, and performed the short remainder of the distance on foot.

Fagin crept softly upstairs, and entered. Nancy was alone, lying with her head upon the table, and her hair straggling over it.

"She has been drinking," thought the Jew, coolly, "or perhaps she is only miserable."

The old man turned to close the door, and the

noise roused the girl. She eyed his crafty face narrow-ly, as she asked of Toby Crackit's story. When it was concluded, she sank into her former attitude, but spoke not a word. She pushed the candle impatient-ly away, and once or twice as she feverishly changed her position, but this was all.

During the silence, the Jew looked restlessly about the room, as if to assure himself that there were no appearances of Sikes having covertly returned. Apparently satisfied with his inspection, he said in his most conciliatory tone, "And where should you think Bill was now, my dear?"

The girl moaned out some half-intelligible reply, that she could not tell, and seemed, from the smoth-ered noise that escaped her, to be crying.

"And the boy, too," said the Jew, straining his eyes to catch a glimpse of her face. "Poor leetle child! Left in a ditch, Nance, only think!"

"The child," said the girl, suddenly looking up, "is better where he is, than among us. If no harm comes to Bill from it, I hope he lies dead in the ditch and that his young bones may rot there."

"What!" cried the Jew, in amazement.

"Ay, I do," returned the girl, meeting his gaze. "I shall be glad to have him away from my eyes, and to know that the worst is over. I can't bear to have him about me. The sight of him turns me against myself, and all of you."

"Pooh!" said the Jew, scornfully. "You're drunk."

"Am I?" cried the girl bitterly. "It's no fault of yours, if I am not! You'd never have me anything else, if you had your will, except now—the humor doesn't suit you, does it?"

"No!" rejoined the Jew, furiously. "It does not."

"Change it, then!" responded the girl, with a laugh.

"Change it!" exclaimed the Jew, exasperated beyond all bounds by his companion's unexpected obstinacy, "I *will* change it! Listen to me, who with six words, can strangle Sikes as surely as if I had his bull's throat between my fingers now. If he comes back, and leaves the boy behind him, murder him yourself if you would have him escape a hanging. And do it the moment he sets foot in this room, or mind me, it will be too late!"

"What is all this?" cried the girl involuntarily.

"What is it?" pursued Fagin, mad with rage. "When the boy's worth hundreds of pounds to me, am I to lose what chance threw me, through the whims of a drunken gang that I could whistle away the lives of! And me bound, too, to a born devil that only wants the will, and has the power to, to—"

Panting for breath, the old man stammered for a word, and in that instant checked the torrent of his wrath, and changed his whole demeanor. A moment before, his face grown livid with passion, but now, he shrunk into a chair, and trembled with the fear of having disclosed some hidden villainy. After a short silence, he ventured to look round at his companion. He appeared somewhat reassured, on seeing her in the same listless attitude from which he had first roused her.

"Nancy, dear!" croaked the Jew, in his usual voice. "Did you mind me, dear?"

"Don't worry me now, Fagin!" replied the girl, raising her head languidly. "If Bill has not done it this time, he will another. He has done many a good job for you, and will do many more when he can. When he can't he won't, so no more about that."

"Regarding this boy, my dear?" said the Jew, rubbing the palms of his hands nervously together.

"The boy must take his chance with the rest," interrupted Nancy, hastily. "And I say again, I hope he is dead, and out of harm's way, and out of yours—that is, if Bill comes to no harm. And if Toby got clear off, Bill's pretty sure to be safe, for Bill's worth two of Toby any time."

"And about what I was saying, my dear?" observed the Jew, keeping his glistening eye steadily upon her.

"Your must say it all over again, if it's anything you want me to do," rejoined Nancy. "And if it is, you had better wait till tomorrow."

Fagin put several other questions, all to determine whether the girl had heard his unguarded hints. But she answered them so readily, and was so utterly unmoved by his searching looks, that his original impression of her being more than a trifle in liquor was confirmed.

Having eased his mind by this discovery, and having ascertained that Sikes had not returned, Mr. Fagin again turned his face homeward, leaving his young friend asleep, with her head upon the table.

It was within an hour of midnight, and a sharp wind scoured the streets. Fagin had reached his own corner, and was already fumbling in his pocket for the door key, when a dark figure emerged from a deep shadow, and, crossing the road, glided up to him unperceived.

"Fagin!" whispered a voice close to his ear.

"Ah!" said the Jew, turning quickly round, "is that—"

"Yes!" interrupted the stranger. "I have been

lingering here these two hours. Where the devil have you been?"

"On your business, my dear," replied the Jew, glancing uneasily at his companion. "On your business all night."

"Oh, of course!" said the stranger, with a sneer. "What's come of it?"

The Jew was about to reply, when the stranger, interrupting him, motioned to the house, remarking, that he had better say what he had got to say, under cover.

Fagin unlocked the door, and requested him to close it softly, while he got a light.

"It's as dark as the grave," said the man, groping forward a few steps. "Make haste!"

Fagin stealthily descended the kitchen stairs. After a short absence, he returned with a lighted candle, and the news that Toby Crackit was asleep in the backroom below, and that the boys were in the front one. Beckoning the man to follow him, he led the way upstairs.

"We can say the few words we've got to say in here, my dear," said the Jew, throwing open a door on the first floor. "And as there are holes in the shutters, and we never show lights to our neighbors, we'll set the candle on the stairs. There!"

With those words, the Jew led the way into the apartment, which contained only a broken armchair, and an old couch or sofa without covering. Upon this piece of furniture, the stranger sat himself with the air of a weary man, and the Jew drew up the armchair opposite. The candle outside threw a feeble reflection on one wall.

They conversed for some time in whispers. A

listener might easily have perceived that Fagin appeared to be defending himself against some remarks of the stranger, and that the latter was in a state of considerable irritation. They might have been talking, thus, for a quarter of an hour, when Monks—by which name the Jew had designated the strange man several times—said, raising his voice a little, "I tell you again, it was badly planned. Why not have kept him here among the rest, and made a sneaking, snivelling pickpocket of him at once?"

"Only hear him!" exclaimed the Jew, shrugging his shoulders.

"Why, do you mean to say you couldn't have done it, if you had chosen?" demanded Monks, sternly. "Haven't you done it, with other boys, scores of times? If you had had patience for a twelvemonth, at most, couldn't you have got him convicted, and sent safely out of the kingdom, perhaps for life?"

"Whose turn would that have served, my dear?" inquired the Jew humbly.

"Mine," replied Monks.

"But not mine," said the Jew, submissively. "He might have become of use to me. When there are two parties to a bargain, it is only reasonable that the interests of both should be consulted."

"What then?" demanded Monks.

"I saw it was not easy to train him to the business," replied the Jew. "He was not like other boys in the same circumstances."

"Curse him, no!" muttered the man, "or he would have been a thief, long ago."

"I had no hold upon him to make him worse," pursued the Jew, anxiously watching the face of his companion. "I had nothing to frighten him with, which we always must have in the beginning, or we labor in vain. What could I do? Send him out with the Dodger and Charley? We had enough of that, at first, my dear. I trembled for us all."

"*That* was not my doing," observed Monks.

"No, my dear!" renewed the Jew. "And I don't quarrel with it now. Because, if it had never happened, you might never have clapped eyes on the boy to notice him, and so led to the discovery that it was he you were looking for. Well! I got him back for you by means of the girl, and then *she* begins to favor him."

"Throttle the girl!" said Monks, impatiently.

"Why, we can't afford to do that just now, my dear," replied the Jew, smiling. "Besides, that sort of thing is not in our way, or, one of these days, I might be glad to have it done. As soon as the boy begins to harden, she'll care no more for him than for a block of wood. You want him made a thief. If he is alive, I can make him one from this time, and, if—if—" said the Jew, drawing nearer to the other—"it's not likely, mind you—but if the worst comes to the worst, and he is dead—"

"It's no fault of mine if he is!" interposed the other man, with a look of terror, and clasping the Jew's arm with trembling hands. "Mind that. Fagin! I had no hand in it. Anything but his death, I told you from the first. I won't shed blood. It's always found out, and haunts a man besides. If they shot him dead, I was not the cause. Do you hear me? Fire this infernal den! What's that?"

"What!" cried the Jew, as he sprung to his feet. "Where?"

"Yonder!" replied the man, glaring at the opposite wall. "A shadow! I saw the shadow of a woman, in a cloak and bonnet, pass along the wainscot like a breath!"

They rushed tumultuously from the room. The candle showed them only the empty staircase, and their own white faces. A profound silence reigned throughout the house.

"It's your fancy," said the Jew, taking up the light and turning to his companion.

"I'll swear I saw it!" replied Monks, trembling. "It was bending forward when I saw it first, and when I spoke, it darted away."

The Jew glanced contemptuously at the pale face of his associate, and ascended the stairs. They looked into all the rooms, which were cold, bare, and empty. They descended into the passage, and thence into the cellars below. The green damp hung upon the low walls, and all was still as death.

"What do you think now?" said the Jew, when they had regained the passage. "Besides ourselves, there's not a creature in the house except Toby and the boys. They're safe enough. See here!"

The Jew drew forth two keys from his pocket, and explained that when he first went downstairs, he had locked them in, to prevent any intrusion on the conference.

Now, Mr. Monks gave vent to several grim laughs, and confessed the shadow could only have been his excited imagination. He declined to renew the conversation, however, suddenly remembering that it was past one o'clock. And so the amiable couple parted.

CHAPTER 26

Mr. Bumble had re-counted the teaspoons, re-weighed the sugar tongs, made a closer inspection of the milk pot, and ascertained the exact condition of the furniture; and had repeated each process full half a dozen times, before he began to think that it was time for Mrs. Corney to return. As there were no sounds of Mrs. Corney's approach, he decided to inspect the interior of Mrs. Corney's chest of drawers.

Being filled with various garments of good fashion and texture, carefully preserved between two layers of old newspapers, speckled with dried lavender, the three long drawers gave him exceeding satisfaction. Arriving at the right-hand corner drawer, and beholding therein a small padlocked box, which, being shaken, gave forth a pleasant sound, as of the chinking of coin, Mr. Bumble returned with a stately walk to the fireplace. He said, with a grave and determined air, "I'll do it!"

He followed up this declaration by taking a view of his legs in profile, with much seeming pleasure and interest. He was still placidly engaged in this activity, when Mrs. Corney, hurrying into the room, threw herself on a chair by the fireside, and covering her eyes with one hand, placed the other over her heart, and gasped for breath.

"Mrs. Corney," said Mr. Bumble, stooping over the matron, "Has anything happened, ma'am? Pray answer me."

"Oh, Mr. Bumble!" cried the lady, "I have been

so dreadfully put out!"

"Put out, ma'am!" exclaimed Mr. Bumble, "Who has dared to—? I know! This is them wicious paupers! Take something, ma'am," said Mr. Bumble soothingly. "A little of the wine?"

"Not for the world!" replied Mrs. Corney. "I couldn't—oh! The top shelf in the right-hand corner—oh!" The good lady pointed, distractedly, to the cupboard. Mr. Bumble rushed to the closet, and, snatching a pint green-glass bottle from the shelf, filled a tea cup with its contents, and held it to the lady's lips.

"I'm better now," said Mrs. Corney, falling back, after drinking half of it.

Mr. Bumble raised his eyes piously to the ceiling in thankfulness, and, bringing them down again to the brim of the cup, lifted it to his nose.

"Peppermint," exclaimed Mrs. Corney, in a faint voice, smiling gently on the beadle as she spoke. "Try it! There's a little something else in it."

Mr. Bumble tasted the medicine with a doubtful look, smacked his lips, took another taste, and put the cup down empty.

"It's very comforting," said Mrs. Corney.

"Very much so indeed, ma'am," said the beadle. As he spoke, he drew a chair beside the matron, and tenderly inquired what had happened to distress her.

"Nothing," replied Mrs. Corney. "I am a foolish, excitable, weak creetur."

Mr. Bumble drew his chair a little closer. "Are you a weak creetur, Mrs. Corney?"

"We are all weak creeturs," said Mrs. Corney, laying down a general principle.

"So we are," said the beadle.

Mr. Bumble removed his left arm from the back of Mrs. Corney's chair, where it had previously rested, to Mrs. Corney's apron string, round which it gradually became entwined.

"This is a comfortable room, ma'am," said Mr. Bumble looking round. "Another room, and this, ma'am, would be a complete thing."

"It would be too much for one," murmured the lady.

"But not for two, ma'am," rejoined Mr. Bumble. "Eh, Mrs. Corney?"

Mrs. Corney lowered her head, when the beadle said this. The beadle lowered his, to get a view of Mrs. Corney's face. Mrs. Corney, with great propriety, turned her head away.

"The board allows you coals, don't they, Mrs. Corney?" inquired the beadle, affectionately pressing her hand.

"And candles," replied Mrs. Corney, slightly returning the pressure.

"Coals, candles, and house rent free," said Mr. Bumble. "Oh, Mrs. Corney, what an Angel you are!"

The lady sank into Mr. Bumble's arms, and that gentleman imprinted a passionate kiss upon her chaste nose.

"Such porochial perfection!" exclaimed Mr. Bumble, rapturously. "You know that Mr. Slout is worse tonight, my fascinator?"

"Yes," replied Mrs. Corney, bashfully.

"He can't live a week, the doctor says," pursued Mr. Bumble. "He is the master of this establishment. His death will cause a wacancy, which must be filled up. Oh, Mrs. Corney, what a prospect this opens!

What a opportunity for a jining of hearts and house-keepings!"

Mrs. Corney sobbed.

"The little word?" said Mr. Bumble, bending over the bashful beauty. "The one little, little, little word, my blessed Corney?"

"Ye—ye—yes!" sighed out the matron.

"One more," pursued the beadle. "Compose your darling feelings for only one more. When is it to come off?"

Mrs. Corney threw her arms around Mr. Bumble's neck, and said it might be as soon as he pleased, and that he was "a irresistible duck."

Matters being satisfactorily arranged, the contract was solemnly ratified in another teacupful of the peppermint mixture. While it was being disposed of, Mrs. Corney acquainted Mr. Bumble with the old woman's decease.

"Good," he said, sipping his peppermint. "I'll call at Sowerberry's as I go home, and tell him to send tomorrow morning. Was it that as frightened you, love?"

"It wasn't anything particular, dear," said the lady evasively.

"It must have been something, love," urged Mr. Bumble. "Won't you tell your own B.?"

"Not now," rejoined the lady. "After we're married, dear."

"After we're married!" exclaimed Mr. Bumble. "It wasn't any impudence from any of them male paupers as—"

"No, love!" interposed the lady, hastily.

"If I thought it was," continued Mr. Bumble, "if I thought as any one of 'em had dared to lift his wulgar eyes to that lovely face—"

"They wouldn't have dared to do it, love," responded the lady.

"They had better not!" said Mr. Bumble, clenching his fist. "Let me see any man, porochial or extra-porochial, as would presume to do it. I can tell him that he wouldn't do it a second time!"

As Mr. Bumble accompanied the threat with many warlike gestures, she was much touched with this proof of his devotion, and protested, with great admiration, that he was indeed a dove.

The dove then exchanged a long and affectionate embrace with his future partner, and once again braved the cold wind of the night. Bright visions of his future promotion served to occupy his mind until he reached the shop of the undertaker.

Now, Mr. and Mrs. Sowerberry having gone out to tea and supper, and Noah Claypole not being disposed to exert himself more than is necessary, the shop was not closed, although it was past the usual hour of shutting up. Mr. Bumble tapped with his cane on the counter several times. Attracting no attention, and seeing a light shining through the glass window of the little parlor at the back of the shop, he peeped in to see what was going forward.

The cloth was laid for supper; the table was covered with bread and butter, plates and glasses; a porter pot and a wine bottle. At one end of the table, Mr. Noah Claypole lolled in an easy chair, with his legs thrown over one of the arms, a knife in one hand, and a mass of buttered bread in the other. Close beside him stood Charlotte, opening oysters from a barrel. A more than ordinary redness in the region of the young gentleman's nose denoted that he was intoxicated.

"Here's a delicious fat one, Noah, dear!" said Charlotte. "Try him, do."

"What a delicious thing is an oyster!" remarked Mr. Claypole, after he had swallowed it. "What a pity it is, a number of 'em should ever make you feel uncomfortable, isn't it, Charlotte?"

"It's quite a cruelty," said Charlotte. "Have another. Here's one with such a beautiful, delicate beard!"

"I can't manage any more," said Noah. "I'm sorry. Come here, Charlotte, and I'll kiss yer."

"What!" said Mr. Bumble, bursting into the room. "Say that again, sir."

Charlotte uttered a scream, and hid her face in her apron. Mr. Claypole gazed at the beadle in drunken terror.

"Say it again, you wile, owdacious fellow!" said Mr. Bumble. "How dare you mention such a thing, sir? And how dare you encourage him, you insolent minx? Kiss her!" exclaimed Mr. Bumble, in strong indignation. "Faugh!"

"I didn't mean to do it!" said Noah, blubbering. "She's always a-kissing me, whether I like it or not."

"Oh, Noah," cried Charlotte, reproachfully.

"Yer know yer are!" retorted Noah. "She's always a-doin' it, Mr. Bumble, sir."

"Silence!" cried Mr. Bumble, sternly. "Take yourself downstairs, ma'am. Noah, you shut up the shop. Don't say another word till your master comes home, and, when he does come home, tell him that Mr. Bumble said he was to send an old woman's shell after breakfast tomorrow morning. Do you hear sir? Kissing!" cried Mr. Bumble, holding up his hands.

"The sin and wickedness of the lower orders in this porochial district is frightful! This country's ruined, and the character of the peasantry gone forever!" With these words, the beadle strode, with a lofty and gloomy air, from the undertaker's premises.

CHAPTER 27

Sikes rested the body of the wounded boy across his bended knee, and turned his head, for an instant, to look back at his pursuers.

The loud shouting of men vibrated through the air, and the barking of the neighboring dogs, roused by the sound of the alarm bell, resounded in every direction.

"Stop, you white-livered hound!" cried the robber, shouting after Toby Crackit, who, making the best use of his long legs, was already ahead. "Stop!"

The repetition of the word brought Toby to a dead standstill.

"Bear a hand with the boy," cried Sikes, beckoning furiously to his confederate. "Come back!"

Toby made a show of returning, but came slowly along.

"Quicker!" cried Sikes, laying the boy in a dry ditch at his feet, and drawing a pistol from his pocket.

At this moment the noise grew louder. Sikes, again looking round, could discern that the men who had given chase were already climbing the gate of the field in which he stood, and that a couple of dogs were some paces in advance of them.

"It's all up, Bill!" cried Toby. "Drop the kid, and show 'em your heels." With this parting advice, Mr. Crackit turned tail, and darted off at full speed. Sikes clenched his teeth, took one look around, threw over the form of Oliver the cape in which he had been hurriedly muffled, and ran along the front of the hedge, as if to distract the attention of those behind, from the spot where the boy lay. Then, whirling his pistol high into the air, he cleared the hedge at a bound, and was gone.

"Ho, ho, there!" cried a tremulous voice in the rear. "Pincher! Neptune! Come here, come here!"

The dogs, who, in common with their masters, seemed to have no particular relish for the sport in which they were engaged, readily answered to the command. Three men, who had by this time advanced some distance into the field, stopped to take counsel together.

"My orders," said the fattest man of the party, "is that we 'mediately go home again."

"I am agreeable to anything which is agreeable to Mr. Giles," said a shorter man, who was by no means of a slim figure, and who was very pale in the face.

"I shouldn't wish to appear ill-mannered, gentlemen," said the third, who had called the dogs back, "Mr. Giles ought to know."

"Certainly," replied the shorter man, "and whatever Mr. Giles says, it isn't our place to contradict him. No, no, I know my sitiwation!" His teeth chattered in his head as he spoke.

"You are afraid, Brittles," said Mr. Giles.

"I an't," said Brittles.

"You are," said Giles.

"You're a falsehood, Mr. Giles," said Brittles.

"You're a lie, Brittles," said Mr. Giles.

The third man brought the dispute to a close, most philosophically.

"I'll tell you what it is, gentlemen," said he, "we're all afraid."

"Speak for yourself, sir," said Mr. Giles, who was the palest of the party.

"So I do," replied the man. "It's natural and proper to be afraid, under such circumstances. I am."

"So am I," said Brittles, "only there's no call to tell a man he is, so bounceably."

This dialogue was held between the two men who had surprised the burglars, and a traveling tinker who had been sleeping in an outhouse, and who had been roused, together with his two mongrel curs, to join in the pursuit. Mr. Giles acted in the double capacity of butler and steward to the old lady of the mansion. Brittles was a lad of all-work, who, having entered her service a mere child, was treated as a promising young boy still, though he was something past thirty.

The three men hurried back to a tree, behind which they had left their lantern, lest its light should inform the thieves in what direction to fire. Catching up the light, they made the best of their way home, at a good round trot.

The air grew colder, as day came slowly on, and the mist rolled along the ground like a dense cloud of smoke. Then the rain came down, thick and fast, and pattered noisily among the leafless bushes. Still, Oliver lay motionless and insensible on the spot where Sikes had left him.

At length, the boy awoke with a low cry of pain. His left arm, rudely bandaged in a shawl, hung heavy and useless at his side, and the bandage was saturated with blood. He was so weak, that he could scarcely raise himself into a sitting posture. When he had done so, he looked feebly round for help, and groaned with pain. Urged by a creeping sickness at his heart, which seemed to warn him that if he stayed there, he must surely die, Oliver got upon his feet, and tried to walk. His head was dizzy, and he staggered to and fro like a drunken man. But he kept up, nevertheless, and, with his head drooping languidly on his breast, went stumbling onward, he knew not whither.

He looked about, and saw that at no great distance there was a house, which perhaps he could reach. Pitying his condition, they might have compassion on him. If they did not, it would be better, he thought, to die near human beings, than in the lonely open fields. He summoned all his strength for one last trial.

As he drew nearer to this house, a feeling come over him that he had seen it before. He remembered nothing of its details, but the shape and aspect of the building seemed familiar to him.

That garden wall! On the grass inside, he had fallen on his knees last night, and prayed for the two men's mercy. It was the very house they had attempted to rob.

Oliver felt such fear come over him when he recognized the place, that, for the instant, he forgot the agony of his wound, and thought only of flight. Flight! He could scarcely stand, and if he were in full possession of his best powers, whither could he fly?

He pushed against the garden gate, which swung open on its hinges. He tottered across the lawn, climbed the steps, knocked faintly at the door, and, his whole strength failing him, sunk down against one of the pillars of the little portico.

It happened that about this time, Mr. Giles, Brittles, and the tinker were having tea and sundries in the kitchen while Mr. Giles gave an account of the robbery, to which his audience (but especially the cook and housemaid) listened with breathless interest.

"It was about half-past two," said Mr. Giles, "when I woke up, and, turning round in my bed, I fancied I heerd a noise. I says, at first, 'This is illusion' and was composing myself off to sleep, when I heerd the noise again, distinct."

"What sort of a noise?" asked the cook.

"A kind of a busting noise," replied Mr. Giles, looking round him. "I turned down the clothes, sat up in bed, and listened."

The cook and housemaid simultaneously said "Lor!" and drew their chairs closer together.

"I heerd it now, quite apparent," resumed Mr. Giles. "'somebody,' I says, 'is forcing a door, or window. What's to be done? I'll call up that poor lad, Brittles, and save him from being murdered in his bed, or his throat,' I says, 'may be cut from his right ear to his left, without his ever knowing it.'"

Here, all eyes were turned upon Brittles, who fixed his upon the speaker, and stared at him, with his mouth wide open, and his face expressive of the most unmitigated horror.

"I tossed off the clothes," said Giles, "got softly out of bed, drew on a pair of—"

"Ladies present, Mr. Giles," murmured the tinker.

"*Of shoes*, sir," said Giles, "seized the loaded pistol, and walked on tiptoes to his room. 'Brittles,' I says, when I had woke him, 'don't be frightened!'"

"So you did," observed Brittles, in a low voice.

Mr. Giles continued. "We took a dark lantern, and groped our way downstairs in the pitch dark, like so."

Mr. Giles had risen from his seat, and taken two steps with his eyes shut, when he started violently, in common with the rest of the company, and hurried back to his chair. The cook and housemaid screamed.

"It was a knock," said Mr. Giles, assuming perfect serenity. "Open the door, somebody."

Nobody moved.

"It seems a strange sort of a thing, a knock coming at such a time in the morning," said Mr. Giles, surveying the pale faces which surrounded him. "But the door must be opened. Do you hear, somebody?"

Mr. Giles, as he spoke, looked at Brittles. But that young man made no reply. Mr. Giles directed an appealing glance at the tinker, but he had suddenly fallen asleep. The women were out of the question.

"If Brittles would rather open the door in the presence of witnesses," said Mr. Giles, after a short silence, "I am ready to make one."

"So am I," said the tinker, waking up, as suddenly as he had fallen asleep.

Brittles agreed on these terms, and the party took their way upstairs, with the dogs in front. The two women, who were afraid to stay below, brought up the rear. By the advice of Mr. Giles, they all talked loud, to warn any evil-disposed person outside, that they were strong in numbers.

Mr. Giles gave the word of command to open the door. Brittles obeyed, and the group, peeping over each other's shoulders, beheld no more formidable object than poor little Oliver Twist, speechless and exhausted, who raised his heavy eyes, and mutely solicited their compassion.

"A boy!" exclaimed Mr. Giles, valiantly, pushing the tinker into the background. "What's the matter with the—eh?—Why—Brittles—look here—don't you know?"

Brittles no sooner saw Oliver, than he uttered a loud cry. Mr. Giles, seizing the boy by one leg and one arm (fortunately not the broken limb), lugged him straight into the hall, and deposited him on the floor.

"Here's one of the thieves, ma'am!" bawled Giles, calling up the staircase. "Wounded, miss! I shot him, miss, and Brittles held the light."

The two women servants ran upstairs to carry the news that Mr. Giles had captured a robber, and the tinker busied himself in endeavoring to restore Oliver, lest he should die before he could be hanged. In the midst of all this noise and commotion, there was heard a sweet female voice, which quelled it in an instant.

"Giles!" whispered the voice from the stair-head.

"I'm here, miss," replied Mr. Giles. "Don't be frightened, miss, I ain't much injured. He didn't make a very desperate resistance, miss! I was soon too many for him."

"Hush!" replied the young lady, "you frighten my aunt as much as the thieves did. Is the poor creature much hurt?"

"Wounded desperate, miss," replied Giles.

"He looks as if he was a-going, miss," bawled Brittles. "Wouldn't you like to come and look at him, miss, in case he should?"

"Hush, pray!" rejoined the lady. "Wait quietly only one instant, while I speak to aunt."

With a footstep as soft and gentle as the voice, the speaker tripped away. She soon returned, with the direction that the wounded person was to be carried, carefully, upstairs to Mr. Giles's room, and that

Brittles was to saddle the pony and go instantly to Chertsey for a constable and doctor.

"But won't you take one look at him, first, miss?" asked Mr. Giles, with as much pride as if Oliver were some rare bird that he had skillfully brought down. "Not one little peep, miss?"

"Not now, for the world," replied the young lady. "Poor fellow! Oh! Treat him kindly, Giles, for my sake!"

The old servant looked up at the speaker, as she turned away, with a glance as proud and admiring as if she had been his own child. Then, bending over Oliver, he helped to carry him upstairs, with the care and solicitude of a woman.

CHAPTER 28

In a handsome room of old-fashioned comfort, there sat two ladies at a well-spread breakfast table. Mr. Giles, dressed in a full suit of black, waited upon them. Of the two ladies, one was well advanced in years, but the high-backed chair in which she sat was not more upright than she. Dressed in a quaint mixture of bygone costume, with some slight concessions to the prevailing taste, she sat with her hands folded on the table before her. Her eyes (and age had dimmed but little of their brightness) were attentively upon her young companion.

The younger lady was in the lovely bloom and springtime of womanhood, not past seventeen. Cast as she was in so slight and exquisite a mold, so mild and gentle, so pure and beautiful, earth seemed not her element, nor its rough creatures her fit companions. The intelligence that shone in her deep blue eye, and was stamped upon her face, seemed scarcely of her age, or of the world.

"And Brittles has been gone upwards of an hour, has he?" asked the old lady, after a pause.

"An hour and twelve minutes, ma'am," replied Mr. Giles.

"He is always slow," remarked the old lady.

"Brittles always was a slow boy, ma'am," replied the attendant. And seeing that Brittles had been a slow boy for upwards of thirty years, there appeared no great probability of his ever being a fast one.

Just then a gig drove up to the garden gate, out

of which jumped a fat gentleman, who ran straight up to the door. Getting quickly into the house by some mysterious process, he burst into the room, and nearly overturned Mr. Giles and the breakfast table together.

"I never heard of such a thing!" exclaimed the fat gentleman. "My dear Mrs. Maylie—bless my soul—in the silence of the night, too—I *never* heard of such a thing!"

With these expressions of condolence, the fat gentleman shook hands with both ladies, and drawing up a chair, inquired how they found themselves.

"You ought to be positively dead with the fright," said the fat gentleman. "Why didn't you send? Dear, dear! So unexpected! In the silence of the night, too!"

The doctor seemed especially troubled by the fact of the robbery having been unexpected, and attempted in the nighttime; as if it were the established custom of gentlemen in the housebreaking way to transact business at noon, and to make an appointment, by post, a day or two previous.

"And you, Miss Rose," said the doctor, turning to the young lady, "I—"

"Oh!" said Rose, interrupting him, "but there is a poor creature upstairs, whom Aunt wishes you to see."

"Ah, to be sure," replied the doctor, "so there is. Show me the way. I'll look in again, as I come down, Mrs. Maylie. That's the little window that he got in at, eh? Well, I couldn't have believed it!"

Talking all the way, he followed Mr. Giles upstairs.

The doctor was absent much longer than either

he or the ladies had anticipated. A large flat box was fetched out of the gig, and the servants ran up and down stairs perpetually. At length he returned, and, looking mysterious, closed the door.

"This is an extraordinary thing, Mrs. Maylie," said the doctor, standing with his back to the door, as if to keep it shut.

"He is not in danger, I hope?" said the old lady.

"I don't think he is," replied the doctor. "Have you seen the thief?"

"No," rejoined the old lady.

"Nor heard anything about him?"

"No."

"I beg your pardon, ma'am," interposed Mr. Giles, "but I was going to tell you about him when Doctor Losberne came in."

The fact was, that Mr. Giles had not, at first, been able to bring his mind to the confession that he had only shot a boy. Such commendations had been bestowed upon his bravery, that he could not, for the life of him, help postponing the explanation for a few delicious minutes.

"Rose wished to see the man," said Mrs. Maylie, "but I wouldn't hear of it."

"Humph!" rejoined the doctor. "There is nothing alarming in his appearance. Have you any objection to see him in my presence?"

"If it be necessary," replied the old lady, "certainly not."

"Then I think it is necessary," said the doctor. "He is perfectly quiet and comfortable now. Miss Rose, will you permit me? Not the slightest fear, I pledge you my honor!"

CHAPTER 29

The doctor led the ladies, with much ceremony and stateliness, upstairs.

"Now," said the doctor, in a whisper, as he softly turned the handle of a bedroom door, "let us hear what you think of him. He has not been shaved recently, but he don't look at all ferocious. Let me first see that he is in visiting order."

Stepping before them, he looked into the room. Motioning them to advance, he closed the door when they had entered, and gently drew back the curtains of the bed. Upon it, instead of the ruffian they had expected to behold, there lay a mere child, worn with pain and exhaustion, and sunk into a deep sleep. His wounded arm, bound and splintered up, was crossed upon his breast, and his head reclined upon the other arm, which was half-hidden by his long hair, as it streamed over the pillow.

The younger lady seated herself in a chair by the bedside, and gathered Oliver's hair from his face. As she stooped over him, her tears fell upon his forehead. The boy stirred, and smiled in his sleep, as though these gestures of pity and compassion had awakened some pleasant dream of a love and affection he had never known.

"What can this mean?" exclaimed the elder lady. "This poor child can never have been the pupil of robbers!"

"Vice," said the surgeon, replacing the curtain, "takes up her abode in many temples."

"But at so early an age!" urged Rose.

"My dear young lady," rejoined the surgeon, mournfully shaking his head, "crime, like death, is not confined to the old and withered alone. The youngest and fairest are too often its chosen victims."

"But, can you really believe that this delicate boy has been the voluntary associate of the worst outcasts of society?" said Rose.

The surgeon shook his head to show that he feared it was possible. Observing that they might disturb the patient, he led the way into an adjoining room.

"But even if he has been wicked," pursued Rose, "think how young he is. He may never have known a mother's love, or the comfort of a home. Abuse, or the want of bread may have driven him to men who have forced him to crime. Dear aunt, for mercy's sake, think of this, before you let them drag this sick child to a prison. Oh! As you love me, and know that I have never felt the want of parents in your goodness and affection, but that I might have done so, and might have been equally helpless as this poor child, have pity upon him before it is too late!"

"My dear love," said the elder lady, as she folded the weeping girl to her bosom, "do you think I would harm a hair of his head?"

"Oh, no!" replied Rose, eagerly.

"No, surely," said the old lady, "my days are drawing to their close. May mercy be shown to me as I show it to others! What can I do to save him, sir?"

"I think if you give me a full and unlimited commission to bully Giles, and that boy, Brittles, I can manage it. Giles is a faithful fellow and an old servant, I know, but you can make it up to him in a thousand ways, and reward him for being such a good shot besides. You don't object to that?"

"Unless there is some other way of preserving the child," replied Mrs. Maylie.

"There is no other," said the doctor. "No other, take my word for it."

"Then my aunt invests you with full power," said Rose, smiling through her tears.

"The boy will wake in an hour or so, I dare say," said the doctor, "and I think we may converse with him without danger. If, from what he says, we judge that he is a real and thorough bad one, he shall be left to his fate, without any further interference on my part. Is is a bargain?"

"He cannot be hardened in vice," said Rose. "It is impossible."

"Good," retorted the doctor. "Then so much the more reason for agreeing to my proposition."

Hour after hour passed on, and still Oliver slumbered heavily. It was evening, indeed, before the kindhearted doctor told them that he was at length sufficiently restored to be spoken to.

The conference was a long one. Oliver told them all his simple history, and was often compelled to stop, by pain and want of strength. It was a solemn thing to hear, in the darkened room, the feeble voice of a sick child recounting the evils that hard men had brought upon him.

Oliver's pillow was smoothed by gentle hands that night, and loveliness and virtue watched him as he slept. He felt calm and happy, and could have died without a murmur.

The doctor, after wiping his eyes, went downstairs to open upon Mr. Giles. And finding nobody about the parlors, he decided to look into the kitchen.

There were assembled the women servants, Mr. Brittles, Mr. Giles, the tinker, and the constable. The adventures of the previous night were still under discussion.

"Sit still!" said the doctor, waving his hand.

"Thank you, sir," said Mr. Giles. "How is the patient tonight, sir?"

"So-so," returned the doctor. "I am afraid you have got yourself into a scrape there, Mr. Giles."

"I hope you don't mean to say, sir," said Mr. Giles, trembling, "that he's going to die. If I thought it, I should never be happy again. I wouldn't cut a boy off, not for all the plate in the county, sir."

"That's not the point," said the doctor, mysteriously. "Mr. Giles, are you a Protestant?"

"Yes, sir, I hope so," faltered Mr. Giles, who had turned pale.

"And what are *you*, boy?" said the doctor, turning sharply upon Brittles.

"Lord bless me, sir!" replied Brittles, starting violently. "I'm the same as Mr. Giles, sir."

"Then tell me this," said the doctor, "both of you! Are you going to take upon yourselves to swear, that that boy upstairs is the boy that was put through the little window last night? Out with it!"

The doctor made this demand in such a dreadful tone of anger, that Giles and Brittles stared at each other in a state of stupefaction.

"Pay attention to the reply, constable, will you?" said the doctor. "Something may come of this before long."

The constable looked as wise as he could.

"It's a simple question of identity, you will observe," said the doctor. "Here's the house broken into, and a couple of men catch one moment's glimpse of a boy, in the midst of gunpowder smoke, and in all the distraction of alarm and darkness. Here's a boy comes to that same house, next morning, and because he happens to have his arm tied up, these men lay violent hands upon him—by doing which, they place his life in great danger—and swear he is the thief. Now, the question is, whether these men are justified by the fact. If not, in what situation do they place themselves?"

The constable nodded profoundly.

"I ask you again," thundered the doctor, "are you, on your solemn oaths, able to identify that boy?"

Brittles looked doubtfully at Mr. Giles; Mr. Giles looked doubtfully at Brittles; the constable put his hand behind his ear, to catch the reply; the two women and the tinker leaned forward to listen; the doctor glanced keenly round; when a ring was heard at the gate, and at the same moment, the sound of wheels.

"It's the Bow Street officers!" cried Brittles, taking up a candle. "Me and Mr. Giles sent for 'em this morning."

"What?" cried the doctor.

"Yes," replied Brittles, "I sent a message up by the coachman, and I only wonder they weren't here before, sir."

"You did, did you? Then confound your slow coaches down here," said the doctor, walking away.

CHAPTER 30

"Who's that?" inquired Brittles, opening the door a little way.

"Open the door," replied a man outside. "It's the officers from Bow Street, as was sent to today."

Much comforted by this assurance, Brittles opened the door to its full width, and confronted a portly man in a greatcoat, who walked in, without saying anything more, and wiped his shoes on the mat, as coolly as if he lived there.

"Just send somebody out to relieve my mate, will you, young man?" said the officer. "Have you got a coach house here, that you could put the gig up in, for five or ten minutes?"

Brittles pointed out the building, and the portly man stepped back to the garden gate, and helped his companion to put up the gig. This done, they returned to the house, and, being shown into a parlor, took off their greatcoats and hats.

The man who had knocked at the door was a stout personage of middle height, aged about fifty, with shiny black hair, half-whiskers, a round face, and sharp eyes. The other was a red-headed, bony man, in top boots, with a turned-up sinister-looking nose.

"Tell your governor that Blathers and Duff is here, will you?" said the stouter man, laying a pair of handcuffs on the table. "Oh! Good evening, master. Can I have a word or two with you in private, if you please?"

This was addressed to Mr. Losberne, who now made his appearance. Motioning Brittles to retire, he brought in the two ladies, and shut the door.

"This is the lady of the house," said Mr. Losberne, motioning towards Mrs. Maylie.

Mr. Blathers made a bow. Then he put his hat on the floor, and taking a chair, motioned to Duff to do the same.

"Now, with regard to this here robbery, master," said Blathers. "What are the circumstances?"

Mr. Losberne, who appeared desirous of gaining time, recounted them at great length. Messrs. Blathers and Duff looked very knowing meanwhile, and occasionally exchanged a nod.

"I can't say, for certain, till I see the work, of course," said Blathers, "but my opinion at once is that this wasn't done by a countryman, eh, Duff?"

"Certainly not," replied Duff.

"Now, what is this, about this here boy that the servants are a-talking on?" said Blathers.

"Nothing at all," replied the doctor. "One of the frightened servants chose to take it into his head that he had something to do with this attempt to break into the house. But it's nonsense, sheer absurdity."

"Very easy disposed of, if it is," remarked Duff.

"What he says is quite correct," observed Blathers, nodding his head, and playing carelessly with the handcuffs, as if they were a pair of castanets. "Who is the boy? What account does he give of himself? Where did he come from? He didn't drop out of the clouds, did he, master?"

"Of course not," replied the doctor, with a nervous glance at the two ladies. "I know his whole history, but we can talk about that presently. You would like, first, to see the place where the thieves made their attempt, I suppose?"

"Certainly," rejoined Mr. Blathers. "We had better inspect the premises first, and examine the servants afterwards. That's the usual way of doing business."

Lights were then procured, and everyone went into the little room at the end of the passage and looked out at the window; and afterwards went round by way of the lawn, and looked in at the window; and after that, had a candle handed out to inspect the shutter with; and after that, a lantern to trace the footsteps with; and after that, a pitchfork to poke the bushes with.

This done, they came in again, and Mr. Giles and Brittles were put through a melodramatic representation of their share in the previous night's adventures, which they performed some six times over. Then Blathers and Duff cleared the room, and held a long council together.

Meanwhile, the doctor walked up and down the next room in an uneasy state, and Mrs. Maylie and Rose looked on with anxious faces.

"Upon my word," he said, making a halt, "I hardly know what to do."

"Surely," said Rose, "the poor child's story, faithfully repeated to these men, will be sufficient to exonerate him."

"I doubt it, my dear young lady," said the doctor, shaking his head. "I don't think it would exonerate him, either with them, or with legal functionaries of a higher grade. What is he, after all, they would say? A runaway. Judged by mere worldly considerations and probabilities, his story is a doubtful one."

"You believe it, surely?" interrupted Rose.

"I believe it, strange as it is," rejoined the doctor. "But I don't think it is exactly the tale for a practical police officer, nevertheless. Viewed with their eyes, there are many ugly points about it. He can only prove the parts that look ill, and none of those that look well. On his own showing, you see, he has been the companion of thieves for some time past; he has been carried to a police officer, on a charge of picking a gentleman's pocket; he has been taken away, forcibly, from that gentleman's house, to a place that he cannot describe or point out. He is brought down to Chertsey, by men who seem to have taken a violent fancy to him, and is put through a window to rob a house; and then, just at the very moment when he is going to alarm the inmates, and so do the very thing that would set him all to rights, there rushes into the way a blundering dog of a half-bred butler, and shoots him! As if on purpose to prevent his doing any good for himself! Don't you see all this?"

"I see it, of course," replied Rose, smiling at the doctor's impetuosity. "But still I do not see anything in it to incriminate the poor child."

"No," replied the doctor, "of course not! Bless the bright eyes of your sex! They never see, whether for good or bad, more than one side of any question."

Having given vent to this opinion, the doctor put his hands into his pockets, and walked up and down the room with even greater rapidity than before.

"The more I think of it," said the doctor, "the more I see that it will occasion endless trouble and difficulty if we put these men in possession of the boy's real story. I am certain it will not be believed, and even if they can do nothing to him in the end, still the dragging it forward, and giving publicity to all the doubts that will be cast upon it, must interfere, materially, with your benevolent plan of rescuing him from misery."

"Oh! What is to be done?" cried Rose. "Dear, dear! Why did they send for these people?"

"Why, indeed!" exclaimed Mrs. Maylie. "I would not have had them here, for the world."

"All I know is," said Mr. Losberne, at last, sitting down with a kind of desperate calmness, "that we must try and carry it off with a bold face. The object is a good one, and that must be our excuse. The boy has strong symptoms of fever upon him, and is in no condition to be talked to any more; that's one comfort. We must make the best of it; and if bad be the best, it is no fault of ours. Come in!"

"Well, master," said Blathers, entering the room followed by his colleague, and making the door fast, before he said any more. "This warn't a put-up thing."

"And what the devil's a put-up thing?" demanded the doctor, impatiently.

"We call it a put-up robbery, ladies," said Blathers, turning to them, "when the servants is in it."

"Nobody suspected them, in this case," said Mrs. Maylie.

"We find it was a town hand," said Blathers, continuing his report, "for the style of work is first-rate."

"Wery pretty indeed it is," remarked Duff, in an undertone.

"There was two of 'em in it," continued Blathers, "and they had a boy with 'em. That's plain from the size of the window. That's all to be said at present. We'll see this lad that you've got upstairs at once, if you please."

"Perhaps they will take something to drink first, Mrs. Maylie?" said the doctor, his face brightening, as if some new thought had occurred to him.

"Oh, to be sure!" exclaimed Rose, eagerly. "You shall have it immediately, if you will."

"Why, thank you, miss!" said Blathers, drawing his coat sleeve across his mouth. "It's dry work, this sort of duty. Anythink that's handy, miss. Don't put yourself out of the way, on our accounts."

"What shall it be?" asked the doctor, following the young lady to the sideboard.

"A little drop of spirits, master, if it's all the same," replied Blathers. "Ah! I have seen a good many pieces of business like this, in my time, ladies."

"That crack down in the back lane at Edmonton, Blathers," said Mr. Duff, assisting his colleague's memory.

"That was something in this way, warn't it?" rejoined Mr. Blathers, as the doctor slipped out of the room. "That was done by Conkey Chickweed, that was."

"You always gave that to him," replied Duff. "It was the Family Pet, I tell you. Conkey hadn't any more to do with it than I had."

"Get out!" retorted Mr. Blathers. "I know better. Do you mind that time when Conkey was robbed of his money, though? What a start that was! Better than any novel book *I* ever see!"

"What was that?" inquired Rose, anxious to encourage any symptoms of good-humor in the unwelcome visitors.

"It was a robbery, miss, that hardly anybody would have been down upon," said Blathers. "This here Conkey Chickweed—"

"Conkey means Nosey, ma'am," interposed Duff.

"Of course the lady knows that, don't she?" demanded Mr. Blathers. "Always interrupting, you are, partner!" The officer then proceeded to tell the lengthy story of how Conkey had come to be robbed, during the telling of which the doctor returned to the room.

"Now, if you please, you can walk upstairs," said the doctor.

Closely following Mr. Losberne, the two officers ascended to Oliver's bedroom, Mr. Giles preceding the party, with a lighted candle.

Oliver looked worse, and was more feverish than he had appeared yet. Being assisted by the doctor, he managed to sit up in bed for a minute or so, and looked at the strangers without at all understanding what was going forward—in fact, without seeming to recollect where he was, or what had been passing.

"This," said Mr. Losberne, speaking softly, but with great vehemence notwithstanding, "this is the lad, who, being accidentally wounded by a spring-gun in some boyish trespass on Mr. What-d'ye-call-him's grounds, at the back here, comes to the house for assistance this morning, and is immediately laid hold of and maltreated, by that gentleman with the candle in his hand, who has placed his life in considerable danger, as I can professionally certify."

Messrs. Blathers and Duff looked at Mr. Giles. The bewildered butler gazed from them towards Oliver, and from Oliver towards Mr. Losberne, with a most ludicrous mixture of fear and perplexity.

"You don't mean to deny that, I suppose?" said the doctor, laying Oliver gently down again.

"It was all done for the best, sir," answered Giles. "I am sure I thought it was the boy, or I wouldn't have meddled with him. I am not of an inhuman disposition, sir."

"Thought it was what boy?" inquired the senior officer.

"The housebreaker's boy, sir!" replied Giles. "They—they certainly had a boy."

"Well? Do you think so now?" inquired Blathers.

"Think what, now?" replied Giles, looking vacantly at his questioner.

"Think it's the same boy, Stupid-head?" rejoined Blathers, impatiently.

"I don't know. I really don't know," said Giles. "I couldn't swear to him."

"What do you think?" asked Mr. Blathers.

"I don't know what to think," replied poor Giles. "I don't think it is the boy. Indeed, I'm almost certain that it isn't. You know it can't be."

"What a precious muddle-headed chap you are!" said Duff, addressing Mr. Giles, with supreme contempt.

Mr. Losberne now rose from the chair by the bedside, and remarked, that if the officers had any doubts upon the subject, they would perhaps like to step into the next room, and have Brittles before them.

They adjourned to a neighboring apartment, where Mr. Brittles, being called in, involved himself and his superior in such a wonderful maze of fresh contradictions and impossibilities, as tended to throw no particular light on anything. Indeed, he declared that he shouldn't know the real boy, if he were put before him that instant; that he had only taken Oliver to be he, because Mr. Giles had said he was; and that Mr. Giles had, five minutes previously, admitted in the kitchen that he began to be afraid he had been a little too hasty.

The question was then raised whether Mr. Giles had really hit anybody. Upon examination of the fellow pistol to that which he had fired, it turned out to have no more destructive loading than gunpowder and brown paper, a discovery that made a considerable impression on everybody but the doctor, who had drawn the ball about ten minutes before.

After some more examination, and a great deal more conversation, a neighboring magistrate was readily induced to take the joint bail of Mrs. Maylie and Mr. Losberne for Oliver's appearance if he should ever be called upon. Blathers and Duff, being rewarded with a couple of guineas, returned to town with divided opinions. The latter gentleman believed that the burglarious attempt had originated with the Family Pet; the former attributed it to the great Mr. Conkey Chickweed.

Meanwhile, Oliver gradually improved under the united care of Mrs. Maylie, Rose, and the kindhearted Mr. Losberne. If fervent prayers be heard in heaven, the blessings that the orphan child called down upon them sank into their souls, diffusing peace and happiness.

CHAPTER 31

Oliver's ailings were neither slight nor few. In addition to the pain of a broken limb, a fever hung about him for many weeks. But, at length, he began to get better, and to be able to say sometimes, in a few tearful words, how deeply he felt the goodness of the two sweet ladies, and how ardently he hoped that when he grew strong and well again, he could do something to show his gratitude.

"Poor fellow!" said Rose, when Oliver had been one day feebly trying to utter words of thankfulness. "You shall have many opportunities of serving us, if you will. We are going into the country, and you shall accompany us. The quiet place, the pure air, and all the beauties of spring will restore you in a few days. We will employ you in a hundred ways, when you can bear the trouble."

"The trouble!" cried Oliver. "Oh, dear lady, if I could only give you pleasure by watering your flowers, or watching your birds, or running up and down the whole day long, to make you happy. What would I give to do it!"

"You shall give nothing at all," said Miss Maylie, smiling, "To think that my dear good aunt should have rescued anyone from such sad misery as you have described to us, would be an unspeakable pleasure to me. But to know that the object of her compassion was sincerely grateful and attached, in consequence, would delight me, more than you can well imagine. Do you understand me?" she inquired, watching

Oliver's thoughtful face.

"Oh yes, ma'am, yes!" replied Oliver eagerly. "But I was thinking that I am ungrateful now."

"To whom?" inquired the young lady.

"To the kind gentleman, and the dear old nurse, who took so much care of me before," rejoined Oliver. "If they knew how happy I am, they would be pleased, I am sure."

"I am sure they would," rejoined Oliver's benefactress, "and Mr. Losberne has already promised that when you are well enough to bear the journey, he will carry you to see them."

"Has he, ma'am?" cried Oliver, his face brightening with pleasure. "I don't know what I shall do for joy when I see their kind faces once again!"

In a short time Oliver was sufficiently recovered to undergo this expedition. One morning he and Mr. Losberne set out in a little carriage. When they came to Chertsey Bridge, Oliver turned pale, and uttered a loud exclamation.

"What's the matter with the boy?" cried the doctor. "Do you see anything—hear anything—feel anything—eh?"

"That, sir," cried Oliver, pointing out of the carriage window. "That house!"

"Yes, well, what of it? Stop coachman," cried the doctor. "What of the house, my man, eh?"

"The thieves—the house they took me to!" whispered Oliver.

"The devil it is!" cried the doctor. "Hallo, there! Let me out!"

But, before the coachman could dismount from his box, the doctor had tumbled out of the coach, and, running down to the deserted house, began kicking at the door like a madman.

"Hallo?" said a little ugly hump-backed man, opening the door so suddenly, that the doctor, from the force of his last kick, nearly fell forward into the passage. "What's the matter here?"

"Matter!" exclaimed the other, collaring him. "A good deal. Robbery is the matter."

"There'll be murder the matter, too," replied the hump-backed man, coolly, "if you don't take your hands off. Do you hear me?"

"I hear you," said the doctor, giving his captive a hearty shake. "Where's—confound the fellow, what's his rascally name—Sikes, that's it. Where's Sikes, you thief?"

The hump-backed man stared in indignation. Then, twisting himself from the doctor's grasp, growled forth a volley of horrid oaths. Before he could shut the door, however, the doctor had passed into the parlor.

He looked anxiously round. Not an article of furniture, not anything, not even the position of the cupboards, answered Oliver's description!

"Now!" said the hump-backed man, who had watched him keenly, "what do you mean by coming into my house, in this violent way? Do you want to rob me, or to murder me?"

"Did you ever know a man come out to do either, in a chariot and pair, you ridiculous old vampire?" said the irritable doctor.

"What do you want, then?" demanded the hunchback. "Will you take yourself off, before I do you a mischief? Curse you!"

"As soon as I think proper," said Mr. Losberne, looking into the other parlor, which, like the first, bore no resemblance whatever to Oliver's account of it. "I shall find you out, some day, my friend."

"Will you?" sneered the cripple. "If you ever want me, I'm here. I haven't lived here mad and all alone, for five-and-twenty years, to be scared by you. You shall pay for this." The misshapen little demon set up a yell, and danced upon the ground, as if wild with rage.

"The boy must have made a mistake," muttered the doctor to himself. "Here! Put that in your pocket, and shut yourself up again." With these words he flung the hunchback a piece of money, and returned to the carriage.

The man followed him to the door, uttering the wildest curses all the way. As Mr. Losberne turned to speak to the driver, the little man looked into the carriage, and eyed Oliver for an instant with a glance so fierce, furious and vindictive, that, waking or sleeping, the boy could not forget it for months afterwards. When they were once more on their way, they could see him some distance behind, beating his feet upon the ground, and tearing his hair, in transports of real or pretended rage.

"I am an ass!" said the doctor, after a long silence. "Even if it had been the right place, and the right fellows had been there, what could I have done, single-handed? And if I had had assistance, I see no good that I should have done, except expose the manner in which I have hushed up this business. That would have served me right, though. I am always involving myself in some scrape or other, by acting on impulse. It might have done me good."

If the truth must be told, he was also a little out of temper at not procuring any evidence of Oliver's story at the very first chance of doing so. But finding that Oliver's replies to his questions were still as straightforward and consistent as they had ever been, he made up his mind to fully believe them, from that time forth.

When the coach turned into the street where Mr. Brownlow lived, Oliver's heart beat so violently, that he could scarcely draw his breath.

"Now, my boy, which house is it?" inquired Mr. Losberne.

"That!" replied Oliver, pointing eagerly out of the window. "The white house. Oh! Make haste! I feel as if I should die, it makes me tremble so."

"Come, come!" said the good doctor, patting him on the shoulder. "You will see them directly, and they will be overjoyed to find you safe and well."

"Oh! I hope so!" cried Oliver. "They were so very, very good to me."

The coach stopped. Oliver looked up at the windows, with tears of happy expectation coursing down his face.

Alas! The white house was empty, and there was a bill in the window. "To Let."

"Knock at the next door," cried Mr. Losberne, taking Oliver's arm in his. "What has become of Mr. Brownlow, who used to live in the adjoining house, do you know?"

The servant said that Mr. Brownlow had sold off his goods, and gone to the West Indies, six weeks before. Oliver clasped his hands, and sank feebly backward.

"Has his housekeeper gone too?" inquired Mr. Losberne, after a moment's pause.

"Yes, sir," replied the servant. "The old

gentleman, the housekeeper, and a gentleman who was a friend of Mr. Brownlow's all went together."

"Then turn towards home again," said Mr. Losberne to the driver, "and don't stop till you get out of this confounded London!"

"The bookstall keeper, sir?" said Oliver. "I know the way there. See him, pray, sir! Do see him!"

"My poor boy, this is disappointment enough for one day," said the doctor. "Quite enough for both of us. If we go to the bookstall keeper's, we shall certainly find that he is dead, or has set his house on fire, or run away. No—straight home again!"

This bitter disappointment caused Oliver much sorrow and grief, even in the midst of his happiness. Many times during his illness, he thought of all that Mr. Brownlow and Mrs. Bedwin would say to him. The hope of eventually clearing himself with them, too, and explaining how he had been forced away, had sustained him, under many of his recent trials. Now, the idea that they should have gone so far, and carried with them the belief that he was an impostor and a robber was almost more than he could bear.

The situation did not change the behavior of his benefactors, however. After another fortnight, when the fine warm weather had fairly begun, and every tree and flower was putting forth its young leaves and rich blossoms, they made preparations for leaving the house at Chertsey, for some months.

Sending the silver to the banker's, and leaving Giles and another servant in care of the house, they departed to a cottage in the country, and took Oliver with them.

It was a lovely spot to which they repaired. Oliver, whose days had been spent among squalid crowds, seemed to enter a new existence there. The rose and honeysuckle clung to the cottage walls; the ivy crept round the trunks of the trees; and the garden flowers perfumed the air. Nearby was a little churchyard, covered with fresh turf and moss, beneath which the old people of the village lay at rest. Oliver often wandered here, and, thinking of the wretched grave in which his mother lay, would sometimes sit him down and sob unseen. But, when he raised his eyes to the sky, he would cease to think of her as lying in the ground, and would weep for her, sadly, but without pain.

Every morning he went to a white-headed old gentleman, who taught him to read better, and to write. He spoke so kindly, and took such pains, that Oliver could never try enough to please him. Then, he would walk with Mrs. Maylie and Rose, and hear them talk of books, or sit near them, in some shady place, and listen whilst the young lady read, which he could have done until it grew too dark to see the letters. Then, he had his own lesson for the next day to prepare. He would work hard, in a little room that looked into the garden, till evening came slowly on, when he and the ladies would walk out again. When it became quite dark, and they returned home, the young lady would sit down to the piano, and play some pleasant air, or sing, in a low and gentle voice, some old song that it pleased her aunt to hear. Oliver would sit by one of the windows, listening to the sweet music, in a perfect rapture.

And when Sunday came, they went to the little church in the morning, with the green leaves fluttering at the windows and the birds singing outside. The poor people were so neat and clean, and knelt so reverently in prayer, that it seemed a pleasure, not a tedious duty, their assembling there together. Then, there were the walks as usual, and many calls at the clean houses of the laboring men. At night, Oliver read a chapter or two from the Bible, which he had been studying all week. Performing this duty, he felt more proud and pleased than if he had been the clergyman himself.

In the morning, Oliver would be up by six o'clock, roaming the fields for nosegays of wild flowers. Then he took great care to arrange them on the breakfast table. There was fresh groundsel, too, for Miss Maylie's birds, with which Oliver would decorate the cages. When the birds were made all spruce and smart for the day, there was usually some little charity to perform in the village; or there was cricket-playing, sometimes, on the green; or there was always something to do in the garden, or about the plants, to which Oliver, who was studying this science under the village clerk, who was a gardener by trade, applied himself with hearty good will. When Miss Rose made her appearance, she would bestow a thousand praises on all he had done.

It is no wonder that, by the end of three months, Oliver Twist had become completely domesticated with the old lady and her niece, and that the fervent attachment of his young and sensitive heart was repaid by their pride in, and attachment to, himself.

CHAPTER 32

One beautiful night, after they had returned from a walk, Rose sat down to the piano as usual. After running abstractedly over the keys for a few minutes, she fell into a low and solemn air, and as she played it, they heard a sound as if she were weeping.

"Rose, my love!" cried Mrs. Maylie, rising hastily, and bending over her. "What is this? In tears! My dear child, what distresses you?"

"Nothing, Aunt," replied the young lady. "I don't know what it is, but I feel—"

"Not ill, my love?" interposed Mrs. Maylie.

"No! Oh, not ill!" replied Rose. "I shall be better presently. Close the window, pray!"

Oliver hastened to comply with her request. The young lady, making an effort to recover her cheerfulness, strove to play some livelier tune. But her fingers dropped powerless over the keys. Covering her face with her hands, she sank upon a sofa, and gave vent to tears.

"My child!" said the elderly lady, folding her arms about her, "I never saw you so before."

"I would not alarm you if I could avoid it," rejoined Rose. "I fear I *am* ill, Aunt."

She was, indeed. When candles were brought, they saw that in the short time that had elapsed since their return home, the color of her face had changed to a marble whiteness. Another minute, and it was flushed, and a heavy wildness came over her soft blue eyes. Again this disappeared, like the shadow thrown by a passing cloud, and she was once more deadly pale.

Oliver, who watched the old lady anxiously, observed that she was alarmed, and so was he. But seeing that she affected to make light of the situation, he endeavored to do the same. They so far succeeded, that when Rose was persuaded by her aunt to retire for the night, she was in better spirits. She assured them that she felt certain she should rise in the morning, quite well.

"I hope," said Oliver, when Rose had gone, "that nothing is the matter? She don't look well tonight, but—"

The old lady motioned to him not to speak. At length, she said, in a trembling voice, "I hope not, Oliver. I have been very happy with her for some years, too happy, perhaps. It may be time that I should meet with some misfortune. But I hope it is not this."

"What?" inquired Oliver.

"The heavy blow," said the old lady, "of losing the dear girl who has so long been my comfort and happiness."

"Oh! God forbid!" exclaimed Oliver, hastily.

"Amen to that, my child!" said the old lady, wringing her hands. "But she is very ill, and will be worse, I am sure. My dear, dear Rose! Oh, what shall I do without her!"

She gave way to such great grief, that Oliver, suppressing his own emotion, ventured to beg that, for the sake of the dear young lady herself, she would be more calm.

"And consider, ma'am," said Oliver, as the tears forced themselves into his eyes, "how young and good she is, and what pleasure and comfort she gives to all about her. I am sure that, for your sake, who are so good yourself, and for her own, and for the sake of all she makes so happy, she will not die. Heaven will never let her die so young."

"Hush!" said Mrs. Maylie, laying her hand on Oliver's head. "You think like a child, poor boy. I have seen enough to know that it is not always the youngest and best who are spared. But this should give us comfort in our sorrow, for such things teach us that there is a brighter world than this, and that the passage to it is speedy. God's will be done! I love her, and He knows how well!"

Oliver was surprised to see that as Mrs. Maylie said these words, she became composed and firm. He was still more astonished to find that this firmness lasted, and that Mrs. Maylie was ever ready and collected, performing cheerfully all the duties that fell to her. But he was young, and did not know what strong minds are capable of, under trying circumstances.

An anxious night ensued. When morning came, Mrs. Maylie's predictions were verified. Rose was in the first stage of a dangerous fever.

"We must be active, Oliver, and not give way to useless grief," said Mrs. Maylie, as she looked steadily into his face. "This letter must be sent to Mr. Losberne. It must be carried to the market-town, by the footpath across the field, and dispatched, by an express on horseback, straight to Chertsey. The people at the inn will do this, and I can trust to you to see it done, I know."

Oliver could make no reply, but his anxiety seemed to be gone at once.

"Here is another letter," said Mrs. Maylie, pausing to reflect, "but whether to send it now, or wait until I see how Rose goes on, I scarcely know. I would not forward it, unless I feared the worst."

"Is it for Chertsey, too, ma'am?" inquired Oliver, holding out his hand for the letter.

"No," replied the old lady, giving it to him. Oliver glanced at it, and saw that it was directed to Harry Maylie, Esquire, at some great lord's house in the country—where, he could not make out.

"Shall it go, ma'am?" asked Oliver, looking up, impatiently.

"I think not," replied Mrs. Maylie, taking it back. "I will wait until tomorrow."

With these words, she gave Oliver her purse, and he started off at the greatest speed he could muster.

Swiftly he ran across the fields, and down the little lanes that sometimes divided them. Nor did he stop once, until he came, covered with dust, on the little marketplace of the market-town. He hastened to a large house, with all the wood about it painted green, bearing the sign of "The George."

He spoke to the landlord, who walked with much deliberation into the bar to make out the bill, which took a long time making out. After it was ready, and paid, a horse had to be saddled, and a man to be dressed, which took up ten minutes more. Meanwhile Oliver was in such a desperate state of impatience and anxiety, that he felt as if he could have jumped upon the horse himself, and galloped away. At length, all was ready, and the man set spurs to his horse, and rattling over the uneven paving of the marketplace, was out of the town in a couple of minutes.

Oliver hurried up the inn-yard, with a somewhat lighter heart. He was turning out of the gateway when he accidentally stumbled against a tall man wrapped in a cloak, who was at that moment coming out of the inn door.

"Hah!" cried the man, fixing his eyes on Oliver, and suddenly recoiling. "What the devil's this?"

"I beg your pardon, sir," said Oliver. "I was in a great hurry to get home, and didn't see you were coming."

"Death!" muttered the man to himself, glaring at the boy with his large dark eyes. "Who would have thought it! Grind him to ashes! He'd start up from a stone coffin, to come in my way!"

"I am sorry," stammered Oliver, confused by the strange man's wild look. "I hope I have not hurt you!"

"Rot you!" murmured the man, between his clenched teeth. "If I had only had the courage to say the word, I might have been free of you in a night. Curses on your head, and black death on your heart, you imp! What are you doing here?"

The man shook his fist, as he uttered these words incoherently. He advanced towards Oliver, as if with the intention of aiming a blow at him, but fell violently on the ground, writhing and foaming, in a fit.

Oliver gazed at the struggles of the madman (for such he supposed him to be), and then darted into the house for help. Having seen him safely carried into the hotel, he turned his face homeward, running as fast as he could, and recalling with a great deal of astonishment and some fear, the extraordinary behavior of the man.

It did not dwell in his mind long, however. When he reached the cottage, he found that Rose Maylie had rapidly grown worse, and before midnight she was delirious. A medical practitioner, who resided nearby, attended her. After first seeing the patient, he had taken Mrs. Maylie aside, and pronounced her disorder to be one of a most alarming nature. "In fact," he said, "it would be little short of a miracle, if she recovered."

How often did Oliver start from his bed that night, and stealing out to the staircase, listen for the slightest sound from the sick chamber! How often did a tremble shake his frame, and cold drops of terror start upon his brow, when a sudden trampling of feet caused him to fear that something too dreadful to think of had occurred!

Morning came, and the little cottage was lonely and still. All the livelong day, and for hours after it had grown dark, Oliver paced softly up and down the garden, raising his eyes every instant to the sick chamber. Late that night, Mr. Losberne arrived. "It is hard," said the good doctor. "So young, so much beloved. But there is little hope."

Another morning. The sun shone as brightly as if it looked upon no misery or care. With every leaf and flower in full bloom about her, the fair young creature lay, wasting fast. Oliver crept away to the old churchyard, and sitting down on one of the green mounds, wept and prayed for her.

There was such peace and beauty in the churchyard, that, when the boy raised his aching eyes, and looked about, the thought instinctively occurred to him, that this was not a time for death. Rose could surely never die when humbler things were all so glad. Oliver turned homeward, thinking on the many kindnesses he had received from the young lady, and wishing that he might never cease showing her how grateful and attached he was.

When he reached home Mrs. Maylie was sitting in the little parlor. Oliver's heart sank at sight of her, for she had never left the bedside of her niece. He trembled to think what change could have driven her away. He learnt that she had fallen into a deep sleep, from which she would waken, either to recovery and life, or to bid them farewell, and die.

They sat, listening, and afraid to speak, for hours. The untasted meal was removed, and they watched the sun sink lower and lower. Their quick ears caught the sound of an approaching footstep. They both involuntarily darted to the door, as Mr. Losberne entered.

"What of Rose?" cried the old lady. "Tell me at once! I can bear it—anything but suspense!"

"You must compose yourself," said the doctor supporting her. "Be calm, my dear ma'am, pray."

"Let me go, in God's name! My dear child! She is dead! She is dying!"

"No!" cried the doctor, passionately. "As He is good and merciful, she will live to bless us all, for years to come."

The lady fell upon her knees, and sank into the friendly arms that were extended to receive her.

CHAPTER 33

It was almost too much happiness to bear. Oliver could not weep, or speak, or rest. He could scarcely understand what had passed, until, after a long ramble in the quiet evening air, a burst of tears came, and he seemed to awaken to a full sense of the joyful change that had occurred.

The night was fast closing in when he returned homeward, laden with flowers that he had picked for the sick chamber. As he walked briskly along the road, he heard behind him the noise of some vehicle, approaching at a furious pace. Looking round, he saw that it was a post chaise, driven at great speed. He stood leaning against a gate until it should pass him.

As it dashed on, Oliver caught a glimpse of a man in a white nightcap. In another second or two, a stentorian voice bellowed to the driver to stop.

"Here!" cried the voice. "Oliver, what's the news? Miss Rose! Master O-li-ver!"

"Is it you, Giles?" cried Oliver, running up to the chaise door.

Giles was suddenly pulled back by a young gentleman who occupied the other corner of the chaise, and who eagerly demanded what was the news.

"Better—much better!" replied Oliver, hastily. "Mr. Losberne says that all danger is at an end."

The gentleman said not another word, but, opening the chaise door, leaped out, and taking Oliver hurriedly by the arm, led him aside.

"You are quite certain? There is no possibility of

any mistake on your part, my boy, is there?" demanded the gentleman in a tremulous voice. "Do not deceive me, by awakening hopes that are not to be fulfilled."

"I would not for the world, sir," replied Oliver. "Mr. Losberne's words were that she would live to bless us all for many years to come. I heard him say so."

The gentleman turned his face away, and remained silent, for some minutes. Oliver thought he heard him sob, more than once.

All this time, Mr. Giles, with the white nightcap on, had been sitting on the steps of the chaise, wiping his eyes with a blue cotton pocket-handkerchief.

"I think you had better go on to my mother's in the chaise, Giles," said he. "I would rather walk slowly on, so as to gain a little time before I see her. You can say I am coming."

"I beg your pardon, Mr. Harry," said Giles, "but if you would leave the post boy to say that, I should be much obliged to you. It wouldn't be proper for the maids to see me in this state, sir. I should never have any more authority with them if they did."

"Well," rejoined Harry Maylie, smiling, "you can do as you like. Let him go on with the luggage, and you follow with us. Only first exchange that nightcap for some more appropriate covering, or we shall be taken for madmen."

Mr. Giles snatched off and pocketed his nightcap, and substituted a hat. This done, the post boy drove off, and Giles, Mr. Maylie, and Oliver followed at their leisure.

As they walked along, Oliver glanced from time to time with much interest at the new comer. He seemed about twenty-five years of age. His face was frank and handsome, and his demeanor easy and confident.

Mrs. Maylie was anxiously waiting to receive her son when he reached the cottage.

"Mother!" whispered the young man, "why did you not write before?"

"I did," replied Mrs. Maylie, "but, on reflection, I decided to keep back the letter until I had heard Mr. Losberne's opinion."

"But why," said the young man, "why run the chance of that occurring that so nearly happened? If Rose had—I cannot utter that word now—if this illness had terminated differently, how could you ever have forgiven yourself! How could I ever have known happiness again!"

"If that *had* been the case, Harry," said Mrs. Maylie, "I fear your happiness would have been effectually blighted, and that your arrival here, a day sooner or a day later, would have been of little import." After a pause, the older woman continued. "She deserves the best and purest love the heart of man can offer. If I did not feel this, and know, besides, that a changed behavior in one she loved would break her heart, I should not feel my task so difficult, when I take what seems to me to be the strict line of duty."

"This is unkind, Mother," said Harry. "Do you still suppose that I am a boy ignorant of my own mind, and mistaking the impulses of my own soul?"

"I think, my dear son," returned Mrs. Maylie, laying her hand upon his shoulder, "that youth has many generous impulses that do not last. Above all, I think that if an enthusiastic, ardent, and ambitious man marry a wife on whose name there is a stain, which, though it originate in no fault of hers, may be visited by cold and sordid people upon her, and upon his children also, he may, no matter how generous and good his nature, one day regret the marriage. And she may have the pain of knowing that he does so."

"Mother," said the young man, impatiently, "my passion, as you well know, is not one of yesterday, nor one I have lightly formed. On Rose, sweet, gentle girl! my heart is set, as firmly as ever heart of man was set on woman. I have no hope in life beyond her. If you oppose me, you take my peace and happiness in your hands, and cast them to the wind. Mother, think better of this, and of me, and do not disregard the happiness of which you seem to think so little."

"Harry," said Mrs. Maylie, "it is because I think so much of warm and sensitive hearts, that I would spare them from being wounded. But we have said more than enough on this matter, just now."

"Let it rest with Rose, then," interposed Harry. "You will not press these overstrained opinions of yours so far as to throw any obstacle in my way?"

"I will not," rejoined Mrs. Maylie, "but I would have you consider—"

"Mother, I have considered, years and years. My feelings remain unchanged, as they ever will, and why should I delay expressing them? No! Before I leave this place, Rose shall hear me."

"She shall," said Mrs. Maylie.

"There is something in your manner, which would almost imply that she will hear me coldly, Mother," said the young man.

"Not coldly," rejoined the old lady, "far from it."

"How then?" urged the young man. "She has

formed no other attachment?"

"No, indeed," replied his mother, "you have too strong a hold on her affections already. What I would say is this. Before you stake all on this chance, reflect for a few moments, my dear child, on Rose's history, and consider what effect the knowledge of her doubtful birth may have on her decision, devoted as she is to us, with all the intensity of her noble mind, and with that perfect sacrifice of self, which has always been her characteristic."

"What do you mean?"

"That I leave you to discover," replied Mrs. Maylie. "I must go back to her. God bless you!"

"I shall see you again tonight?" said the young man, eagerly.

"By and by," replied the lady, "when I leave Rose."

"You will tell her I am here?" said Harry.

"Of course," replied Mrs. Maylie.

"And how anxious I have been, and how I long to see her. You will not refuse to do this, Mother?"

"No," said the old lady, "I will tell her all." And pressing her son's hand, affectionately, she hastened from the room.

Mr. Losberne and Oliver had remained at another end of the apartment while this hurried conversation was proceeding. The former now held out his hand to Harry Maylie, and hearty salutations were exchanged between them. The doctor then communicated a precise account of his patient's situation, while Mr. Giles, who pretended to be busy about the luggage, listened with greedy ears.

"Have you shot anything particular, lately, Giles?" inquired the doctor, when he had concluded.

"Nothing particular, sir," replied Mr. Giles, coloring up to the eyes.

"Nor catching any thieves, nor identifying any housebreakers?" said the doctor.

"None at all, sir," replied Mr. Giles, with much gravity.

"Well," said the doctor, "I am sorry to hear it, because you do that sort of thing admirably. Seeing you here reminds me, Mr. Giles, that I have executed, at the request of your good mistress, a small commission in your favor. Just step into this corner a moment, will you?"

Mr. Giles walked into the corner with some wonder, and was honored with a short whispering conference with the doctor, at the end of which, he made a great many bows. Then he walked straight into the kitchen, and having called for a mug of ale, announced, with an air of majesty, that it had pleased his mistress, in consideration of his gallant behavior on the occasion of that attempted robbery, to deposit, in the local savings bank, the sum of five-and-twenty pounds, for his sole use and benefit.

Above stairs, the remainder of the evening passed cheerfully away, for the doctor was in high spirits, which resulted in an abundance of small jokes, which struck Oliver as being the funniest things he had ever heard, to the evident satisfaction of the doctor, who laughed immoderately at himself, and made Harry laugh almost as heartily. It was late before they retired, with light and thankful hearts.

Oliver rose next morning, and went about his usual occupations with more hope and pleasure than he had known for many days. The birds once more sang in their old places, and the sweetest wild flowers that could be found were once more gathered to gladden Rose with their beauty.

Oliver's morning expeditions were no longer made alone. Harry Maylie, after the first morning when he met Oliver coming laden home, was seized with such a passion for flowers, and displayed such a taste in their arrangement, as left his young companion far behind. Yet Oliver knew where the best were to be found. Morning after morning they scoured the country together, and brought home the fairest that blossomed.

The window of the young lady's chamber was opened now, for she loved to feel the rich summer air stream in. There always stood in water, just inside the window frame, one particular little bunch of flowers, which was made up with great care, every morning. Oliver could not help noticing that the withered flowers were never thrown away, although the little vase was regularly replenished. Nor could he help observing that whenever the doctor came into the garden, he invariably cast his eyes up to that particular corner, and nodded his head most expressively, as he set forth on his morning's walk.

The days were flying by, and Rose was rapidly recovering. Oliver applied himself diligently to the instructions of the white-headed old gentleman, and labored so hard that his quick progress surprised even himself. It was while he was engaged in this pursuit, that he was greatly startled and distressed by a most unexpected occurrence.

The little room in which he was accustomed to sit, when busy at his books, was on the ground floor, at the back of the house. It had a lattice window, around which were clusters of jasmine and honeysuckle that crept over the casement, and filled the place with their delicious perfume. It looked into a garden, where a wicket gate opened into a small paddock. Beyond was fine meadowland and wood. There was no other dwelling near, and the view it commanded was extensive.

One evening at twilight, Oliver sat at this window, intent upon his books. He had been poring over them for some time, and as the day had been uncommonly sultry, and he had exerted himself a great deal, by slow degrees he fell asleep.

As he slept, Oliver knew that he was in his own little room, that his books were lying on the table before him, that the sweet air was stirring among the creeping plants outside. And yet he was asleep. Suddenly, the air became close and confined, and he thought, with a glow of terror, that he was in the Jew's house again. There sat the hideous old man, in his accustomed corner, pointing at him, and whispering to another man, with his face averted, who sat beside him.

"Hush, my dear!" he thought he heard the Jew say. "It is he, sure enough. Come away."

"He!" the other man seemed to answer. "Could I mistake him? If a crowd of ghosts were to put themselves into his exact shape, and he stood amongst them, there is something that would tell me how to point him out. If you buried him fifty feet deep, and took me across his grave, I fancy I should know, if there wasn't a mark above it, that he lay buried there!"

The man seemed to say this with such dreadful hatred that Oliver awoke from the fear, and started up.

Good Heaven! What was that, which sent the

blood tingling to his heart, and deprived him of his voice, and of power to move? There—there—at the window—close before him—so close, that he could have almost touched him, with his eyes peering into the room, and meeting his, stood the Jew! And beside him, white with rage or fear, or both, were the scowling features of the man who had accosted him in the inn-yard.

It was but a flash before his eyes, and they were gone. But they had recognized him, and he them. He stood transfixed for a moment. Then, leaping from the window into the garden, he called loudly for help.

CHAPTER 34

The inmates of the house, attracted by Oliver's cries, found him, pale and agitated, pointing in the direction of the meadows behind the house, and scarcely able to articulate the words, "The Jew! The Jew!"

Harry Maylie, who had heard Oliver's history from his mother, understood it at once.

"What direction did he take?" he asked, catching up a heavy stick standing in a corner.

Oliver pointed out the course the man had taken. "I missed them in an instant."

"Then, they are in the ditch!" said Harry. "Follow! And keep as near me as you can." He sprang over the hedge, and darted off with a speed difficult for the others to match.

Mr. Losberne, who had just returned from a walk, tumbled over the hedge after them, shouting all the while to know what was the matter.

On they went until the leader, striking off at the angle indicated by Oliver, began to search the nearby ditch and hedge, while the remainder of the party caught up.

The search was all in vain. There were not even the traces of recent footsteps to be seen. They stood now, on the summit of a little hill, commanding the open fields in every direction for three or four miles. There was the village in the hollow on the left; but, in order to gain that, the men must have made a circuit of open ground, which they could not have done in so short a time. A thick wood skirted the meadow in another direction, but they could not have gained that position for same reason.

"It must have been a dream, Oliver," said Harry Maylie.

"Oh no, indeed, sir," replied Oliver, shuddering at the memory of the old wretch's face. "I saw him too plainly for that."

"Who was the other?" inquired Mr. Losberne.

"The same man I told you of, who came so suddenly upon me at the inn," said Oliver.

"They took this way?" demanded Harry. "Are you sure?"

"As I am that the men were at the window," replied Oliver, pointing down to the hedge that divided the cottage garden from the meadow. "The tall man leaped over, just there, and the Jew, running a few paces to the right, crept through that gap."

The two gentlemen seemed to feel satisfied of the accuracy of what he said. Still, there was no sign of the trampling of men in hurried flight.

"This is strange!" said Harry.

"Strange?" echoed the doctor. "Blathers and Duff themselves could make nothing of it."

Nevertheless, they did not give up their search until nightfall. Giles went to the different ale houses in the village, furnished with the best description Oliver could give of the strangers. But he returned without any news.

On the next day, a fresh search was made, but with no better success. On the day following, Oliver and Mr. Maylie went to the market-town, in the hope of seeing or hearing something of the men there, but this effort was equally fruitless. After a few days, the affair began to be forgotten.

Meanwhile, Rose was rapidly recovering. She was able to go out, and, mixing once more with the family, she carried joy into the hearts of all.

But, although cheerful voices and merry laughter were once more heard in the cottage, there was at times a restrained feeling, even upon Rose herself, which Oliver could not help but notice. Mrs. Maylie and her son were often closeted together for a long time, and more than once Rose appeared with traces of tears upon her face. After Mr. Losberne had fixed a day for his departure to Chertsey, these symptoms increased, and it became evident that something affected the peace of the young lady, and of somebody else besides.

One morning, when Rose was alone in the breakfast parlor, Harry Maylie entered, and begged permission to speak with her for a few moments.

The young man drew his chair towards her. "What I shall have to say has already presented itself to your mind. The most cherished hopes of my heart are not unknown to you, though from my lips you have not heard them stated."

Rose had been pale from the moment of his entrance, but that might have been the effect of her recent illness. She merely bowed, and waited in silence for him to proceed.

"I—I—ought to have left here before," said Harry.

"You should, indeed," replied Rose. "Forgive me for saying so, but I wish you had."

"I was brought here by the most dreadful of all fears," said the young man, "the fear of losing the one dear being on whom my every wish and hope are fixed. We know, Heaven help us! that the best and fairest too often fade in blooming."

There were tears in the eyes of the gentle girl, as these words were spoken.

"A creature," continued the young man, passionately, "as fair and innocent as one of God's own angels fluttered between life and death. Rose, Rose, to know that you were passing away like some soft shadow, and yet to pray that you might be restored to those who loved you—these were distractions almost too great to bear. With them came such a rushing torrent of fears, and selfish regrets, lest you should die, and never know how devotedly I loved you. Then you recovered. Day by day, and almost hour by hour, I have watched you change almost from death to life. Do not tell me that you wish I had lost this, for it has softened my heart to all mankind."

"I did not mean that," said Rose, weeping. "I only wish that you might have turned to high and noble pursuits again, pursuits well worthy of you."

"There is no pursuit more worthy of me than the struggle to win such a heart as yours," said the young man, taking her hand. "Rose, my own dear Rose! For years I have loved you, hoping to win my way to fame, and then come proudly home and tell you it had been pursued only for you to share. That time has not arrived, but here, with fame not won, I offer you the heart so long your own."

"Your behavior has ever been kind and noble," said Rose. "And knowing that I am not insensible or ungrateful, so hear my answer."

"Is it that I may endeavor to deserve you, dear Rose?"

"It is," replied Rose, "that you must endeavor to

forget me—not as your old and dearly-attached friend, for that would wound me deeply, but, as the object of your love. Look into the world—think how many hearts you would be proud to gain. Confide some other passion to me, if you will. I will be the truest, warmest, and most faithful friend you have."

There was a pause, during which Rose, who had covered her face with one hand, gave free vent to her tears. Harry still retained the other.

"And your reasons, Rose," he said, in a low voice, "for this decision?"

"You have a right to know them," rejoined Rose. "It is a duty that I must perform. I owe it, alike to others, and to myself. I owe it to myself, that I, a friendless girl, with a blight upon my name, should not give your friends reason to suspect that I had fastened myself, a clog, on all your hopes and projects. I owe it to you and yours to prevent you from placing an obstacle to your progress in the world."

"If your inclinations chime with your sense of duty—" Harry began.

"They do not," replied Rose, coloring deeply.

"Then you return my love?" said Harry. "Do not conceal that from me, at least, Rose."

"I will not conceal it," said Rose. "But," she added, disengaging her hand, "why should we prolong this painful interview? Most painful to me, and yet it *will* be happiness to know that I once held the high place in your regard that I now occupy."

"Another word, Rose," said Harry. "Your reason in your own words. From your own lips, let me hear it!"

"The prospect before you," answered Rose, firmly, "is a brilliant one. All the honors which great

talents and powerful connections can bring men are
in store for you. But I will neither mingle with people who might scorn the mother who gave me life,
nor bring disgrace on the son of the woman who has
so well taken that mother's place. In a word," said
the young lady, turning away, "there is a stain upon
my name, which the world visits on innocent heads.
I will carry it into no blood but my own."

"Dearest Rose!" cried Harry, throwing himself
before her. "If I had been less fortunate, if some
obscure and peaceful life had been my destiny—if I
had been poor, sick, helpless—would you have
turned from me then?"

"Do not press me to reply," answered Rose.
"The question does not arise, and never will. It is
unfair, almost unkind, to urge it."

"If your answer be what I hope it is," retorted
Harry, "it will shed a gleam of happiness upon my
lonely way, and light the path before me. Oh, Rose,
in the name of my enduring love, answer me this one
question!"

"Then, if your lot had been differently cast,"
rejoined Rose, "if I could have been a help and comfort to you, and not a drawback, I should have been
spared this trial. I have every reason to be happy
now. But then, Harry, I think I would have been
happier."

Old hopes crowded into her mind, but they
brought tears with them, as old hopes will when they
come back withered.

Rose extended her hand. "I must leave you
now."

"I ask one promise," said Harry. "Say within a
year, but it may be much sooner—I may speak to you

again on this subject, for the last time."

"Not to press me to alter my decision," replied Rose, with a melancholy smile.

"No," said Harry, "to hear you repeat it, if you will! I will lay at your feet whatever fortune I may possess, and if you still adhere to your decision, I will not seek to change it."

"Then let it be so," rejoined Rose. "By that time I may be able to bear it better."

She extended her hand again. But the young man caught her to his chest, and imprinting one kiss on her beautiful forehead, hurried from the room.

CHAPTER 35

"And so you are resolved to be my traveling companion this morning?" said the doctor, as Harry Maylie joined him and Oliver at the breakfast table. "Why, you seem to change your mind every half-hour!"

"You will tell me a different tale one of these days," said Harry, coloring.

"I hope I may have good cause to do so," replied Mr. Losberne, "though I confess I don't think I shall. But yesterday morning you had made up your mind, in a great hurry, to stay here, and to accompany your mother, like a dutiful son, to the seaside. Before noon, you announce that you are going to do me the honor of accompanying me as far as I go, on your road to London. And at night, you urge me, with great mystery, to start before the ladies are stirring. So young Oliver here is pinned down to his breakfast when he ought to be ranging the meadows after botanical phenomena of all kinds. Too bad, isn't it, Oliver?"

"I would have been very sorry not to have been at home when you and Mr. Maylie went away, sir," rejoined Oliver.

"That's a fine fellow," said the doctor. "You shall come and see me when you return. But, to speak seriously, Harry—has any news from your uncle made you suddenly anxious to be gone?"

"No," replied Harry, "he has not communicated with me at all, since I have been here. Nor, at this time of the year, is it likely that I would need to be among him and his colleagues."

"Well," said the doctor, "you are a queer fellow. But of course they will get you into parliament at the election before Christmas, and these sudden changes are no bad preparation for political life. Good training is always desirable, whether the race be for place, cup, or sweepstakes."

Harry Maylie looked as if he could have made one or two remarks that would have staggered the doctor. But he contented himself with saying, "We shall see," and pursued the subject no further. The post chaise drove up to the door shortly afterwards, and the good doctor bustled out, to see it packed.

"Oliver," said Harry Maylie, in a low voice, "let me speak a word with you."

Oliver went to the spot where Harry beckoned him.

"You can write well now?" said Harry, laying his hand upon his arm.

"I hope so, sir," replied Oliver.

"I shall not be at home again, perhaps for some time. I wish you would write to me—say once every two weeks, every alternate Monday, to the General Post Office in London. Will you?"

"Oh, certainly, sir. I shall be proud to do it," exclaimed Oliver, greatly delighted with the commission.

"I should like to know how my mother and Miss Maylie are," said the young man, "and you can fill up a sheet by telling me what walks you take, and what you talk about, and whether she—they, I mean—seem happy and quite well. You understand me?"

"Oh! quite, sir," replied Oliver.

"I would rather you did not mention it to them," said Harry, "because it might make my mother anxious to write to me oftener, and it is a worry to her. Let it be a secret between you and me, and mind you tell me everything! I depend upon you."

Oliver, quite elated and honored by a sense of his importance, faithfully promised to be secret and explicit in his communications. Mr. Maylie took leave of him, with many assurances of his regard and protection.

The doctor was in the chaise, and Giles held the door open. Harry cast one glance at the latticed window, and jumped into the carriage.

Jingling and clattering, the vehicle wound its way along the road. There was one looker-on who remained with eyes fixed upon the spot where the carriage had disappeared, long after it was many miles away. Behind the white curtain that had shrouded her from view when Harry raised his eyes towards the window sat Rose herself.

"He seems in high spirits and happy," she said, at length. "I feared for a time he might be otherwise. I was mistaken. I am very glad."

Tears are signs of gladness as well as grief, but those that coursed down Rose's face seemed to tell more of sorrow than of joy.

CHAPTER 36

Mr. Bumble sat in the workhouse parlor, with his eyes moodily fixed on the cheerless grate. His appearance announced that a great change had taken place in his affairs. The laced coat, and the cocked hat were gone. He still wore knee breeches, but they were not *the* breeches. The coat was wide-skirted, and in that respect like *the* coat, but, oh how different! The mighty cocked hat was replaced by a modest round one. Mr. Bumble was no longer a beadle.

He had married Mrs. Corney, and was master of the workhouse. Another beadle had come into power. To him the cocked hat, gold-laced coat, and cane now belonged.

"And tomorrow two months it was done!" said Mr. Bumble, with a sigh. "It seems an age."

Mr. Bumble might have meant that he had concentrated a great amount of happiness into the short space of eight weeks, but there was a vast deal of meaning in the sigh.

"I sold myself," said Mr. Bumble, "for six teaspoons, a pair of sugar tongs, and a milk pot, with a small quantity of second-hand furniture, and twenty pound in money. I went very reasonable. Cheap, dirt cheap!"

"Cheap!" cried a shrill voice in Mr. Bumble's ear, "you would have been dear at any price, and dear enough I paid for you!"

Mr. Bumble turned, and encountered the face of his interesting consort. "Have the goodness to look at me," said Mr. Bumble, fixing his eyes upon her. "(If she stands such a look as that," thought Mr. Bumble to himself, "she can stand anything. It is a look I never knew to fail with paupers. If it fails with her, my power is gone.")

The matron was in no way overpowered by Mr. Bumble's scowl, but, on the contrary, treated it with great disdain, and even raised a laugh.

On hearing this most unexpected sound, Mr. Bumble looked, first incredulous, and afterwards amazed. He then relapsed into his former state.

"Are you going to sit snoring there, all day?" inquired Mrs. Bumble.

"I am going to sit here as long as I think proper, ma'am," rejoined Mr. Bumble, "and although I was *not* snoring, I shall snore, sneeze, laugh, or cry, as the humor strikes me, such being my prerogative."

"*Your* prerogative!" sneered Mrs. Bumble.

"I said the word, ma'am," said Mr. Bumble. "The prerogative of a man is to command."

"And what's the prerogative of a woman, in the name of Goodness?" she cried.

"To obey, ma'am," thundered Mr. Bumble. "Your late unfortunate husband should have taught it you. Then, perhaps, he might have been alive now. I wish he was, poor man!"

Mrs. Bumble no sooner heard this allusion to the dead and gone, than she dropped into a chair, and with a loud scream that Mr. Bumble was a hard-hearted brute, fell into a paroxysm of tears.

But Mr. Bumble's heart was waterproof. Being tokens of weakness, and admissions of his own power, tears pleased and exalted him. He gave a look of great satisfaction, and begged, in an encouraging manner, that she should cry her hardest.

"It opens the lungs, washes the face, exercises the eyes, and softens the temper," said Mr. Bumble. "So cry away."

He then took his hat from a peg, and putting it on, rather rakishly on one side, thrust his hands into his pockets, and sauntered towards the door, with much ease and waggishness.

Now, Mrs. Bumble had tried the tears because they were less troublesome than a manual assault. But she was quite prepared to try the latter tactic.

Mr. Bumble first experienced the sudden flying off of his hat to the opposite end of the room. Then the expert lady, clasping him tightly round the throat with one hand, inflicted a shower of blows upon his head with the other. This done, she created a little variety by scratching his face, and tearing his hair, and then she pushed him over a chair, and defied him to talk about his prerogative again, if he dared.

"Get up!" said Mrs. Bumble, in a voice of command. "And take yourself away from here, unless you want me to do something desperate."

Mr. Bumble rose with a rueful expression, wondering what something desperate might be. Picking up his hat, he looked towards the door.

"Are you going?" demanded Mrs. Bumble.

"Certainly, my dear, certainly," rejoined Mr. Bumble, making a quicker motion towards the door. "I'm going, my dear! You are so violent, that really I—"

At this instant, Mrs. Bumble stepped hastily forward to replace the carpet, which had been kicked up in the scuffle. Mr. Bumble immediately darted out of the room, leaving the late Mrs. Corney in full possession of the field.

Mr. Bumble was fairly taken by surprise, and fairly beaten. He left the workhouse, and walked up one street, and down another, until his grief had abated, and then he felt thirsty. He paused before a public house in a byway, whose parlor, as he gathered from a hasty peep over the blinds, was deserted, save by one solitary customer. It began to rain, heavily, at the moment. Mr. Bumble stepped in, and ordered something to drink.

The man who was seated there was tall and dark, and wore a large cloak. He seemed, by a certain haggardness in his look, as well as by the dusty soils on his dress, to have traveled some distance. He eyed Bumble sideways, as he entered, but scarcely acknowledged his greeting.

Mr. Bumble had quite dignity enough for two, so he drank his gin and water in silence, and read the paper with great show of pomp and circumstance.

He felt, every now and then, a powerful urge to steal a look at the stranger. Whenever he did so, he withdrew his eyes, in some confusion, to find that the stranger was at that moment stealing a look at him. Mr. Bumble's awkwardness was enhanced by the stranger's scowl of distrust and suspicion, unlike anything he had ever observed before, and repulsive to behold.

When they had encountered each other's glance several times in this way, the stranger, in a harsh, deep voice, broke silence.

"Were you looking for me," he said, "when you peered in at the window?"

"Not that I am aware of, unless you're Mr. —" Here Mr. Bumble stopped short, for he was curious to know the stranger's name, and thought he might supply the blank.

"I see you were not," said the stranger; an expression of quiet sarcasm playing about his mouth, "or you would have known my name. I would recommend you not to ask for it."

"I meant no harm, young man," observed Mr. Bumble, majestically.

"And have done none," said the stranger. "I have seen you before. You were differently dressed at that time. You were beadle here, once, were you not?"

"I was," said Mr. Bumble, in some surprise, "porochial beadle."

"Just so," rejoined the other, nodding his head. "What are you now?"

"Master of the workhouse," rejoined Mr. Bumble, slowly and impressively.

"You have the same eye for your own interest, that you always had, I doubt not?" resumed the stranger, looking keenly into Mr. Bumble's eyes, as he raised them in astonishment at the question.

"I suppose, a married man," replied Mr. Bumble, "is not more averse to turning an honest penny when he can, than a single one. Porochial officers are not so well paid that they can afford to refuse any little extra fee, when it comes to them in a civil and proper manner."

The stranger smiled, and nodded his head again, then rang the bell.

"Fill this glass again," he said, handing Mr. Bumble's empty tumbler to the landlord. "Let it be strong and hot. You like it so, I suppose?"

"Not too strong," replied Mr. Bumble, with a delicate cough.

"You understand what that means, landlord!" said the stranger, dryly.

The host smiled, disappeared, and shortly afterwards returned with a steaming drink, of which the first gulp brought tears into Mr. Bumble's eyes.

"Now listen to me," said the stranger, after closing the door and window. "I came down to this place today to find you, and, by one of those chances that the devil throws in the way of his friends sometimes, you walked into the very room I was sitting in, while you were uppermost in my mind. I want some information from you. I don't ask you to give it for nothing, slight as it is. Take that, to begin with."

As he spoke, he pushed a couple of sovereigns across the table to his companion, carefully, as though unwilling that the clinking of money should be heard outside. When Mr. Bumble had put them away, with much satisfaction, in his waistcoat pocket, he went on, "Carry your memory back—let me see—twelve years, last winter."

"It's a long time," said Mr. Bumble. "Very good. I've done it."

"The scene, the workhouse at night."

"Yes."

"And the place, wherever it was, in which miserable drabs gave birth to children for the parish to rear, and hid their shame, rot 'em in the grave!"

"The lying-in room, I suppose?" said Mr. Bumble, not quite following the stranger's excited description.

"Yes," said the stranger. "A boy was born there."

"Many boys," observed Mr. Bumble, shaking his head, despondently.

"I speak of one, a meek-looking, pale-faced boy, who was apprenticed down here, to a coffin-maker— I wish he had made his coffin, and screwed his body in it—and who afterwards ran away to London, as it was supposed."

"Why, you mean Oliver Twist!" said Mr. Bumble. "I remember him, of course. There wasn't a more obstinate young rascal—"

"It's not of him I want to hear—I've heard enough of him," said the stranger. "It's of a woman—the hag that nursed his mother. Where is she?"

"Where is she?" said Mr. Bumble. "She died last winter."

The man looked fixedly at him. For some time, he appeared doubtful whether he ought to be relieved or disappointed by the news. But at length he breathed more freely, and observed that it was no great matter. With that he rose, as if to depart.

But Mr. Bumble at once saw that an opportunity was opened for the lucrative disposal of some secret in the possession of his better half. He well remembered the night of old Sally's death. Although his wife had never confided to him what had happened, he had heard enough to know that it related to the young mother of Oliver Twist. He informed the stranger, with an air of mystery, that one woman had been closeted with the old harridan shortly before she died, and that she could throw some light on the subject of his inquiry.

"How can I find her?" said the stranger, thrown off his guard.

"Only through me," rejoined Mr. Bumble.

"When?" cried the stranger, hastily.

"Tomorrow," rejoined Bumble.

"At nine in the evening," said the stranger, producing a scrap of paper, and writing down an obscure address by the waterside. "Bring her to me there. I needn't tell you to be secret. It's in your interest."

With these words, he led the way to the door, after stopping to pay for the liquor that had been drunk. Then he departed.

On glancing at the address, Mr. Bumble observed that it contained no name. The stranger had not gone far, so he made after him to ask it.

"What do you want?" cried the man, turning quickly round, as Bumble touched him on the arm. "Following me?"

"Only to ask a question," said the other, pointing to the scrap of paper. "What name am I to ask for?"

"Monks!" rejoined the man, and strode hastily away.

CHAPTER 37

The clouds threatened a violent thunderstorm, when Mr. and Mrs. Bumble walked towards a scattered little colony of ruinous houses, bordering upon the river. They were both wrapped in old and shabby outer garments, which might, perhaps, serve the double purpose of protecting them from the rain, and sheltering them from observation. The husband carried an unlit lantern, and trudged on, a few paces in front.

In the heart of this cluster of huts stood a large building that had gone to ruin. A considerable portion of the building had already sunk down into the water while the remainder tottered over it.

It was before this ruinous building that the couple paused, as the first peal of distant thunder reverberated in the air, and the rain commenced pouring violently down.

"Hallo there!" cried a voice from above.

Following the sound, Mr. Bumble raised his head and saw a man looking out of a door on the second story.

"Stand still, a minute," cried the voice. "I'll be with you directly."

"Mind what I told you," said the matron to Mr. Bumble, "and be careful to say as little as you can, or you'll betray us at once."

Mr. Bumble was apparently about to express some doubts about proceeding any further with the enterprise, when Monks opened a small door near which they stood, and beckoned them inside.

The woman, who had hesitated at first, walked boldly in, without any other invitation. Mr. Bumble followed, obviously ill at ease.

Once inside, Monks turned short upon the matron, and bent his gaze upon her, till even she, who was not easily cowed, looked away.

"This is the woman, is it?" demanded Monks.

"That is the woman," replied Mr. Bumble, mindful of his wife's caution.

Bestowing something halfway between a smile and a frown upon his two companions, and again beckoning them to follow him, the man hastened across the apartment. He led the way up a steep ladder, and hastily closing the window shutter of the room into which it led, lowered a lantern, which cast a dim light upon an old table and three chairs that were placed beneath it.

"Now," said Monks, when they had all three seated themselves, "the sooner we come to our business, the better for all. The woman knows what it is, does she?"

The question was addressed to Bumble, but his wife said that she was perfectly acquainted with it.

"He is right in saying that you were with this hag the night she died, and that she told you something—"

"About the mother of the boy you named," replied the matron interrupting him. "Yes."

"The first question is, of what nature was her communication?" said Monks.

"That's the second," observed the woman with much deliberation. "The first is, what may the communication be worth?"

"Who the devil can tell that, without knowing of

what kind it is?" asked Monks.

"Nobody better than you, I am persuaded," answered Mrs. Bumble.

"Something that was taken from her," said Monks. "Something that she wore. Something that—"

"You had better bid," interrupted Mrs. Bumble. "I have heard enough, already, to assure me that you are the man I ought to talk to."

Monks then sternly demanded what sum was required for the disclosure.

"What's it worth to you?" asked the woman, as collectedly as before.

"It may be nothing, or it may be twenty pounds," replied Monks. "Speak out, and let me know which."

"Give me twenty-five pounds in gold," said the woman, "and I'll tell you all I know. Not before."

"Twenty-five pounds!" exclaimed Monks, drawing back.

"I spoke as plainly as I could," replied Mrs. Bumble. "It's not a large sum, either."

"Not a large sum for a paltry secret that may be nothing when it's told!" cried Monks impatiently, "and which has been lying dead for twelve years past or more!"

"Such matters keep well, and, like good wine, often double their value in course of time," answered the matron.

"What if I pay it for nothing?" asked Monks, hesitating.

"You can easily take it away again," replied the matron. "I am but a woman alone here, and unprotected."

"Not alone, my dear, nor unprotected, neither," submitted Mr. Bumble, in a voice tremulous with fear. "I am here, my dear. And besides, Mr. Monks is too much of a gentleman to attempt any violence on porochial persons. Mr. Monks is aware that I am a determined officer, with very uncommon strength, if I'm once roused."

"You are a fool," said Mrs. Bumble, in reply, "and had better hold your tongue."

"He had better have cut it out if he can't speak in a lower tone," said Monks, grimly. "So! He's your husband, eh?"

"He's my husband!" tittered the matron, parrying the question.

"I thought as much, when you came in," rejoined Monks, marking the angry glance that the lady darted at her spouse as she spoke. "So much the better. I have less hesitation in dealing with two people, when I find that there's only one will between them. I'm in earnest. See here!"

He produced a canvas bag, took out twenty-five sovereigns on the table, and pushed them over to the woman.

"Now," he said, "let's hear your story."

The faces of the three nearly touched, as the two men leaned over the small table in their eagerness to hear, and the woman also leaned forward to make her whisper heard.

"When old Sally died," the matron began, "she and I were alone."

"Was there no one by?" asked Monks, in a hollow whisper. "No one who could hear, and might understand?"

"Not a soul," replied the woman.

"Good," said Monks, regarding her attentively. "Go on."

"She spoke of a young creature," resumed the matron, "who had brought a child into the world some years before, in the same bed in which she then lay dying."

"Ay?" said Monks, with quivering lip, and glancing over his shoulder, "Blood! How things come about!"

"The child was the one you named to him last night," said the matron, nodding towards her husband, "the mother this nurse had robbed."

"In life?" asked Monks.

"In death," replied the woman, with something like a shudder. "She stole from the corpse that which the dead mother had asked her, with her last breath, to keep for the infant's sake."

"She sold it," cried Monks, with desperate eagerness. "Did she sell it? Where? When? To whom? How long before?"

"As she told me, with great difficulty, that she had done this," said the matron, "she fell back and died."

"Without saying more?" cried Monks. "It's a lie! I'll not be played with. She said more. I'll tear the life out of you both, but I'll know what it was."

"She didn't utter another word," said the woman, unmoved by the strange man's violence, "but she clutched my gown, violently, with one hand, which was partly closed. When I saw that she was dead, and so removed the hand by force, I found it clasped a scrap of dirty paper."

"Which contained—" interposed Monks, stretching forward.

"Nothing," replied the woman, "it was a pawn-broker's duplicate."

"For what?" demanded Monks.

"In good time I'll tell you," said the woman. "I judge that she had pawned the trinket and had scraped together money to pay the pawnbroker's interest year by year, and prevent its running out, so that if anything came of it, it could still be redeemed. Nothing had come of it, and, as I tell you, she died with the scrap of paper, all worn and tattered, in her hand. The time was out in two days. I thought something might one day come of it too, and so redeemed the pledge."

"Where is it now?" asked Monks quickly.

"There," replied the woman. And, as if glad to be relieved of it, she hastily threw upon the table a small bag scarcely large enough for a watch, which Monks tore open with trembling hands. It contained a little gold locket, in which were two locks of hair, and a plain gold wedding ring.

"It has the word 'Agnes' engraved on the inside," said the woman.

"There is a blank left for the surname; and then follows the date, which is within a year before the child was born. I found out that."

"And this is all?" said Monks, after a close and eager scrutiny of the contents of the little packet.

"All," replied the woman.

Mr. Bumble drew a long breath, as if he were glad to find that the story was over, and no mention made of taking the twenty-five pounds back again.

"I know nothing of the story, beyond what I can guess at," said his wife addressing Monks, after a short silence, "and I want to know nothing. But I may ask you two questions, may I?"

"You may ask," said Monks, with some show of surprise, "but whether I answer or not is another question."

"Is that what you expected to get from me?" demanded the matron.

"It is," replied Monks. "The other question?"

"What do you propose to do with it? Can it be used against me?"

"Never," rejoined Monks, "nor against me either. See here! But don't move a step forward, or your life is not worth a bulrush."

With these words, he suddenly wheeled the table aside, and pulling an iron ring in the boarding, threw back a large trapdoor that opened close to Mr. Bumble's feet, and caused that gentleman move several steps backward.

"Look down," said Monks, lowering the lantern into the gulf. "Don't fear me. I could have let you down, quietly enough, when you were seated over it, if that had been my game."

Thus encouraged, the matron drew near to the brink, and even Mr. Bumble himself ventured to do the same. The turbid water, swollen by the heavy rain, was rushing rapidly on below, and all other sounds were lost in the noise of its splashing against the green and slimy piles. There had once been a watermill beneath, and there were still a few rotten stakes and fragments of machinery in the water.

"If you flung a man's body down there, where would it be tomorrow morning?" said Monks, swinging the lantern to and fro in the dark well.

"Twelve miles down the river, and cut to pieces besides," replied Bumble, recoiling at the thought.

Monks drew the little packet from his breast, and tying it to a leaden weight, dropped it into the stream. It fell straight, hitting the water with a scarcely audible splash, and was gone.

The three, looking into each other's faces, seemed to breathe more freely.

"There!" said Monks, closing the trapdoor. "If the sea ever gives up its dead, as books say it will, it will keep its gold and silver to itself, and that trash among it. We have nothing more to say, and may break up our pleasant party."

"By all means," observed Mr. Bumble.

"You'll keep a quiet tongue in your head, will you?" said Monks, with a threatening look. "I am not afraid of your wife."

"You may depend upon me, young man," answered Mr. Bumble, bowing himself gradually towards the ladder, with excessive politeness. "On everybody's account, Mr. Monks."

"I am glad, for your sake, to hear it," remarked Monks. "Light your lantern! And get away from here as fast as you can."

Mr. Bumble lighted his lantern and descended in silence, followed by his wife. Monks brought up the rear, after pausing on the steps to satisfy himself that there were no other sounds to be heard than the beating of the rain without, and the rushing of the water.

They traversed the lower room with caution, for Monks started at every shadow, and Mr. Bumble, holding his lantern a foot above the ground, looked nervously about him for hidden trapdoors. The gate at which they had entered was softly unfastened and opened by Monks. Merely exchanging a nod with their mysterious acquaintance, the married couple emerged into the wet and darkness outside.

They were no sooner gone, than Monks, who appeared to detest being left alone, called to a boy who had been hidden somewhere below. Bidding him go first, and bear the light, he returned to the chamber he had just quit.

CHAPTER 38

The following evening, Mr. William Sikes, awoke from a nap. He was lying on the bed, wrapped in his white greatcoat, his face wearing the color of illness, and a stiff, black beard of a week's growth. The dog sat at the bedside, and seated by the window, busily engaged in patching an old waistcoat, was a woman so pale and tired that it was difficult to recognize her as Nancy, but for her voice.

"How do you feel tonight, Bill?"

"As weak as water," replied Mr. Sikes. "Lend us a hand, and let me get off this thundering bed anyhow."

Illness had not improved Mr. Sikes's temper, for, as the girl raised him up and led him to a chair, he muttered various curses on her awkwardness, and struck her.

"Whining are you?" said Sikes. "Don't stand snivelling there. If you can't do anything better than that, cut off altogether. D'ye hear me?"

"I hear you," replied the girl, turning her face aside, and forcing a laugh.

"Oh! You've thought better of it, have you?" growled Sikes, marking the tear that trembled in her eye. "All the better for you."

"Such a number of nights," said the girl, with a touch of woman's tenderness, "such a number of nights I've been patient with you, nursing and caring for you, as if you had been a child, and this the first that I've seen you like yourself. You wouldn't have served me as you did just now, if you'd thought of that, would you? Come, come—say you wouldn't."

"Well, then," rejoined Mr. Sikes, "I wouldn't. Why, damn now, the girl's whining again!"

"It's nothing," said the girl, throwing herself into a chair. "Don't mind me. It'll soon be over."

"What'll be over?" demanded Mr. Sikes in a savage voice. "What foolery are you up to, now, again? Get up and bustle about, and don't come to me with your woman's nonsense."

The girl, being weak and exhausted, dropped her head over the back of the chair, and fainted. Not knowing what to do in this uncommon emergency, Mr. Sikes tried a little blasphemy, and finding it wholly ineffectual, called for assistance.

"What's the matter here, my dear?" said Fagin, looking in.

"Lend a hand to the girl, can't you?" replied Sikes impatiently. "Don't stand chattering and grinning at me!"

With an exclamation of surprise, Fagin hastened to the girl's assistance, while the Artful Dodger hastily deposited a bundle on the floor, and, snatching a bottle from the grasp of Master Charles Bates who came close at his heels, uncorked it in a twinkling with his teeth, and poured a portion of its contents down the patient's throat.

The girl gradually recovered her senses, and, staggering to a chair by the bedside, hid her face upon the pillow, leaving Mr. Sikes to confront the newcomers, in some astonishment.

"Why, what evil wind has blowed you here?" he asked Fagin.

"No evil wind at all, my dear. I've brought

something good with me, that you'll be glad to see. Dodger, my dear, open the bundle, and give Bill the little trifles that we spent all our money on this morning."

The Artful untied this bundle, and handed the articles it contained, one by one, to Charley Bates, who placed them on the table.

"A rabbit pie, Bill," exclaimed that young gentleman, "a pound and a half of moist sugar; two half-quartern loaves; piece of double Glo'ster cheese; and some of the richest sort you ever lushed!"

Master Bates produced a full-sized wine bottle, carefully corked, while Mr. Dawkins poured out a wineglass full of raw spirits from the bottle he carried, which the invalid tossed down his throat without a moment's hesitation.

"Ah!" said Fagin, rubbing his hands with great satisfaction. "You'll do now, Bill."

"Do!" exclaimed Mr. Sikes. "I might have been done for, twenty times over, afore you'd have done anything to help me. What do you mean by leaving a man in this state, three weeks and more, you false-hearted wagabond?"

"Only hear him, boys!" said Fagin, shrugging his shoulders. "And us come to bring him all these beautiful things."

"The things is well enough in their way," observed Mr. Sikes, a little soothed as he glanced over the table, "but what have you got to say for yourself, why you should leave me here, down in the mouth, and everything else, and take no more notice of me, all this mortal time, than if I was that 'ere dog. What have you got to say for yourself, you withered old fence, eh?"

"I was away from London, a week and more on a plant," replied the Jew.

"What about the other two weeks that you've left me lying here, like a sick rat in his hole?" demanded Sikes.

"I can't go into a long explanation before company. But I couldn't help it, upon my honor."

"Upon your what?" growled Sikes, with excessive disgust. "Here! Cut me off a piece of that pie, one of you boys, to take the taste of that out of my mouth, or it'll choke me dead."

"Don't be out of temper, my dear," urged Fagin, submissively. "I have never forgot you, Bill, never once."

"No! I'll pound it that you han't," replied Sikes, with a bitter grin. "You've been scheming and plotting away, every hour that I have laid shivering and burning here. Bill was to do this and that, and do it all, dirt cheap, as soon as he got well, and was quite poor enough for your work. If it hadn't been for the girl, I might have died."

"There now, Bill," remonstrated Fagin. "If it hadn't been for the girl! Who but poor ould Fagin supplied such a handy girl about you?"

"He says true enough there!" said Nancy, coming hastily forward. "Let him be."

Nancy's appearance gave a new turn to the conversation, for the boys, receiving a sly wink from the wary old Jew, began to ply her with liquor, of which, however, she took very sparingly. Fagin gradually brought Mr. Sikes into a better temper, by pretending to regard his threats as a little pleasant banter, and, moreover, by laughing heartily at one or two rough jokes.

"It's all very well," said Mr. Sikes, "but I must have some blunt from you tonight."

"I haven't a piece of coin about me," replied the Jew.

"Then you've got lots at home," retorted Sikes, "and I must have some from there."

"Lots!" cried Fagin, holding up his hands. "I haven't so much as would—"

"I don't know how much you've got, and I dare say you hardly know yourself, as it would take a pretty long time to count it," said Sikes. "But I must have some tonight, and that's flat. Nancy shall go to the ken and fetch it, and I'll lie down and have a snooze while she's gone."

After a great deal of haggling, Fagin beat down the amount of the required advance from five pounds to three pounds four and sixpence. Then, taking leave of his affectionate friend, the Jew returned homeward, attended by Nancy and the boys.

In due course, they arrived at Fagin's abode, where they found Toby Crackit and Mr. Chitling intent upon their fifteenth game at cribbage. Mr. Crackit, apparently somewhat ashamed at being found relaxing himself with a gentleman so much his inferior, yawned, and after inquiring after Sikes, took up his hat to go.

"Has nobody been, Toby?" asked Fagin.

"Not a living leg," answered Mr. Crackit, "it's been as dull as swipes. You ought to pay something handsome, Fagin, to recompense me for keeping house so long."

Mr. Toby Crackit swept up his winnings, and crammed them into his waistcoat pocket with a haughty air. This done, he swaggered out of the room.

"Dodger! Charley! Come! It's near ten, and nothing done yet," cried Fagin.

In obedience to this hint, the boys, nodding to Nancy, took up their hats, and left the room.

"Now," said Fagin, "I'll go and get you that cash, Nancy. This is only the key of a little cupboard where I keep a few odd things the boys get, my dear. I never lock up my money, for I've got none to lock up, my dear—ha! ha! ha! It's a poor trade, Nancy, and no thanks, but I'm fond of seeing the young people about me. Hush!" he said, hastily concealing the key, "who's that? Listen!"

The girl, who was sitting at the table with her arms folded, appeared in no way interested in the arrival, until the murmur of a man's voice reached her ears. The instant she caught the sound, she tore off her bonnet and shawl, with the rapidity of lightning, and thrust them under the table, unseen by Fagin.

"Bah!" he whispered, as though nettled by the interruption, "it's the man I expected before. He's coming downstairs. Not a word about the money while he's here, Nance. He won't stop long. Not ten minutes, my dear."

Laying his skinny forefinger upon his lip, the Jew carried a candle to the door, as a man's step was heard upon the stairs. He reached it, at the same moment as the visitor, who came hastily into the room.

It was Monks.

"Only one of my young people," said Fagin, observing that Monks drew back on beholding a stranger. "Don't move, Nancy."

The girl drew closer to the table, and glancing at Monks with an air of careless levity, withdrew her eyes. But as he turned towards Fagin, she stole another look so keen and searching that if there had been any bystander to observe the change, he could hardly have believed the two looks to have been from the same person.

"Any news?" inquired Fagin.

"Great."

"And—and—good?" asked Fagin.

"Not bad, any way," replied Monks with a smile. "I have been prompt enough this time. Let me have a word with you."

The girl drew closer to the table, and made no offer to leave the room. The Jew pointed upwards, and took Monks out of the room to the second story.

Before the sound of their footsteps had ceased to echo through the house, the girl had slipped off her shoes, and drawing her gown loosely over her head, and muffling her arms in it, stood at the door, listening with breathless interest. The moment the noise ceased, she glided from the room, ascended the stairs with incredible softness and silence, and was lost in the gloom above.

The room remained deserted for a quarter of an hour or more, and then the girl glided back with the same unearthly tread. Immediately afterwards, the two men were heard descending. Monks went at once into the street, and the Jew went upstairs again for the money. When he returned, the girl was adjusting her shawl and bonnet, as if preparing to be gone.

"Why, Nance!" exclaimed the Jew, starting back as he put down the candle, "how pale you are! What have you been doing to yourself?"

"Nothing that I know of, except sitting in this close place for I don't know how long," replied the girl carelessly. "Come! Let me get back, that's a dear."

With a sigh for every piece of money, Fagin counted the amount into her hand. They parted without more conversation, merely exchanging a "good night."

When the girl got into the open street, she sat down upon a doorstep, and seemed, for a few moments, wholly bewildered. Suddenly she arose, and hurrying on, in a direction quite opposite to that in which Sikes was awaiting her return, quickened her pace into a violent run. After completely exhausting herself, she stopped to take breath, wrung her hands, and burst into tears.

It might be that her tears relieved her, or that she felt the full hopelessness of her condition. But she turned back, and hurrying in the contrary direction, she soon reached the dwelling where she had left the housebreaker.

If she betrayed any agitation, when she presented herself to Mr. Sikes, he did not observe it. He uttered a growl of satisfaction about the money, and replacing his head upon the pillow, resumed his slumber.

As that day closed in, the girl's excitement increased, and, when night came on, and she sat by, watching until the housebreaker should drink himself asleep, there was an unusual paleness in her cheek, and a fire in her eye.

Mr. Sikes was lying in bed, taking hot water with his gin, and he had pushed his glass towards Nancy to be replenished for the third or fourth time, when her symptoms first struck him.

"Why, burn my body!" said the man, raising himself on his hands as he stared the girl in the face. "You look like a corpse come to life again. What's the matter?"

"Matter!" replied the girl. "Nothing. What do you look at me so hard for?"

"What foolery is this?" demanded Sikes, grasping her by the arm, and shaking her roughly. "What is it? What are you thinking of?"

"Of many things, Bill," replied the girl, shivering, and as she did so, pressing her hands upon her eyes. "But, Lord! What odds in that?"

The tone of forced gaiety in which the last words were spoken produced a deep impression on Sikes.

"I tell you wot it is," said Sikes, "if you haven't caught the fever, and got it comin' on, now, there's something more than usual in the wind, and something dangerous too. You're not a-going to—No, damn! you wouldn't do that!"

"Do what?" asked the girl.

"There ain't," said Sikes, fixing his eyes upon her, "there ain't a stauncher-hearted gal going, or I'd have cut her throat three months ago. She's got the fever coming on, that's it."

Fortifying himself with this assurance, Sikes drained the glass to the bottom, and then, with many grumbling oaths, called for his medicine. The girl jumped up, poured it quickly out, but with her back towards him, and held the vessel to his lips, while he drank off the contents.

"Now," said the robber, "come and sit beside me, and put on your own face, or I'll alter it so, that you won't know it agin when you do want it."

The girl obeyed. Sikes, locking her hand in his,

fell back upon the pillow, turning his eyes upon her face. They closed; opened again; closed once more; again opened. He shifted his position restlessly, and, after dozing again, for two or three minutes, and springing up with a look of terror, and gazing vacantly about him, he was suddenly stricken into a heavy sleep. The grasp of his hand relaxed and he lay like one in a profound trance.

"The laudanum has taken effect at last," murmured the girl, as she rose from the bedside. "I may be too late, even now."

She hastily put on her bonnet and shawl. Then, stooping softly over the bed, she kissed the robber's lips and hurried from the house.

Many of the shops were already closing in the back lanes and avenues through which she tracked her way, in making from Spitalfields towards the West End of London. The clock struck ten, increasing her impatience. She tore along the narrow pavement, elbowing the passengers from side to side, and, darting almost under the horses' heads, she crossed crowded streets.

"The woman is mad!" said the people, turning to look after her as she rushed away.

When she reached the more wealthy quarter of the town, the streets were comparatively deserted. When she neared her place of destination, she was alone.

It was a family hotel in a quiet but handsome street near Hyde Park. The clock struck eleven, and she stepped into the hall. The porter's seat was vacant. She looked round and advanced towards the stairs.

"Now, young woman!" said a smartly-dressed female, looking out from a door behind her, "who do you want here?"

"A lady who is staying in this house," answered the girl.

"A lady!" was the reply, accompanied with a scornful look. "What lady?"

"Miss Maylie," said Nancy.

The young woman, who had by this time noted her appearance, replied only by a look of virtuous disdain, and summoned a man to answer her. To him, Nancy repeated her request.

"What name am I to say?" asked the waiter.

"It's of no use saying any," replied Nancy.

"Nor business?" said the man.

"No, nor that neither," rejoined the girl. "I must see the lady."

"Come!" said the man, pushing her towards the door. "None of this. Take yourself off."

"I shall be carried out if I go!" said the girl violently, "and I can make that a job that two of you won't like to do. Isn't there anybody here," she said, looking round, "that will see a simple message carried for a poor wretch like me?"

This appeal produced an effect on a good-tempered cook, who with some of the other servants was looking on, and who stepped forward to interfere.

"Take it up for her, Joe, can't you?" said the man.

"What's the good?" replied the man. "You don't suppose the young lady will see such as her, do you?"

This allusion to Nancy's doubtful character raised a vast quantity of chaste wrath in the bosoms of four housemaids, who remarked that the creature was a disgrace to her sex, and strongly advocated her being thrown into the street.

"Do what you like with me," said the girl, turning to the men again, "but do what I ask you first, and I ask you to give this message for God Almighty's sake."

"What's it to be?" said the man, with one foot on the stairs.

"That a young woman earnestly asks to speak to Miss Maylie alone," said Nancy, "and that if the lady will only hear the first word she has to say, she will know whether to hear her business, or to have her turned out of doors as an impostor. You give the message, and let me hear the answer."

The man ran upstairs. Nancy remained, pale and almost breathless, listening with quivering lip to the audible expressions of scorn from the housemaids. The man returned, and said the young woman was to walk upstairs. Nancy followed the man, with trembling limbs, to a small antechamber, lighted by a lamp from the ceiling. Here he left her, and retired.

CHAPTER 39

When Nancy heard a light step approaching the door opposite, and thought of the wide contrast to herself that the small room would in another moment contain, she felt burdened with deep shame, and shrunk as though she could scarcely bear the presence of the woman with whom she had sought this interview.

She saw that the person who entered was a slight and beautiful girl. Nancy tossed her head with affected carelessness as she said, "It's a hard matter to get to see you, lady. If I had taken offense, and gone away, as many would have done, you'd have been sorry for it one day, and not without reason either."

"I am very sorry if any one has behaved harshly to you," replied Rose. "Do not think of that. Tell me why you wished to see me."

The kind tone of this answer took the girl completely by surprise, and she burst into tears.

"Oh, lady!" she said, clasping her hands passionately before her face, "if there was more like you, there would be fewer like me!"

"Sit down," said Rose, earnestly. "If you are in poverty or affliction I shall be truly glad to relieve you if I can."

"Let me stand, lady," said the girl, still weeping, "and do not speak to me so kindly till you know me better. I am the girl that dragged little Oliver back to old Fagin's on the night he went out from the house in Pentonville."

"You!" said Rose Maylie.

"I, lady!" replied the girl. "I am the infamous creature you have heard of, that lives among the thieves, and that never have known any better life, or kinder words than the streets of London have given me, so help me God! Do not mind shrinking openly from me, lady. The poorest women fall back, as I make my way along the crowded pavement."

"What dreadful things are these!" said Rose.

"Thank Heaven upon your knees, dear lady," cried the girl, "that you had friends to care for and keep you in your childhood, and that you were never in the midst of cold and hunger, and riot and drunkenness, as I have been from my cradle. I may use the word, for the alley and the gutter were mine, as they will be my deathbed."

"It wrings my heart to hear you!" said Rose, in a broken voice.

"Heaven bless you for your goodness!" rejoined the girl. "But I have stolen away from those who would surely murder me, if they knew I had been here, to tell you what I have overheard. Do you know a man named Monks?"

"No," said Rose.

"He knows you," replied the girl, "and knew you were here, for it was by hearing him tell the place that I found you out."

"I never heard the name," said Rose.

"Then he goes by some other amongst us," rejoined the girl. "Soon after Oliver was put into your house on the night of the robbery, I—suspecting this man—listened to a conversation held between him and Fagin in the dark. I found out that Monks had seen him accidentally with two of our boys on the day we first lost him, and had recognized him to be the same child that he was watching for, though I couldn't make out why. A bargain was struck with Fagin, that if Oliver was got back he should have a certain sum, and he was to have more for making him a thief."

"For what purpose?" asked Rose.

"He caught sight of my shadow on the wall as I listened, in the hope of finding out," said the girl, "and there are not many people besides me that could have got out of their way in time to escape discovery. But I did, and I saw him no more till last night."

"And what occurred then?"

"I'll tell you, lady. Last night he came again. Again they went upstairs, and I again listened at the door. The first words I heard Monks say were these: "So the only proofs of the boy's identity lie at the bottom of the river, and the old hag that received them from the mother is rotting in her coffin." They laughed, and talked of his success in doing this. Monks, talking on about the boy, and getting very wild, said that though he had got the young devil's money safely now, he'd rather have had it the other way. What a game it would have been to have brought down the father, by driving the boy through every jail in town, and then hauling him up for some capital felony that Fagin could easily manage, after having made a good profit of him besides."

"What is all this!" said Rose.

"The truth, lady, though it comes from my lips," replied the girl. "Then, he said that if he could gratify his hatred by taking the boy's life without bringing his own neck in danger, he would. But, as he couldn't, he'd be upon the watch to meet him at every turn in life, and if he took advantage of his birth and history, he might harm him yet. "In short, Fagin," he says, "Jew as you are, you never laid such snares as I'll contrive for my young brother, Oliver."

"His brother!" exclaimed Rose.

"Those were his words," said Nancy. "When he spoke of you and the other lady, and said it seemed contrived by Heaven against him, that Oliver should come into your hands, he laughed, and said there was some comfort in that too, for how many hundreds of thousands of pounds would you not give, if you had them, to know who your two-legged spaniel was."

"You do not mean," said Rose, turning pale, "to tell me that this was said in earnest?"

"He spoke in hard and angry earnest, if a man ever did," replied the girl, shaking her head. "It is growing late, and I have to reach home without suspicion of having been on such an errand as this. I must get back quickly."

"But what can I do?" said Rose. "To what use can I turn this communication without you? Back! Why do you wish to return to companions you paint in such terrible colors? If you repeat this information to a gentleman whom I can summon in an instant from the next room, you can be consigned to some place of safety without half an hour's delay."

"I wish to go back," said the girl. "because among the men I have told you of, there is one, the most desperate among them all, that I can't leave. No, not even to be saved from the life I am leading now."

"Your having interfered in this dear boy's behalf

before," said Rose, "your coming here, at so great a risk, to tell me what you have heard; your evident regret, and sense of shame; all lead me to believe that you might yet be redeemed. Do hear my words, and let me save you yet, for better things."

"Lady," cried the girl, sinking on her knees, "it is too late, it is too late!"

"It is never too late," said Rose, "for penitence and atonement."

"It is," cried the girl, writhing in agony, "I cannot leave him now! I could not be his death."

"Why should you be?" asked Rose.

"Nothing could save him," cried the girl. "If I told others what I have told you, and led to their being taken, he would be sure to die. He is the boldest, and has been so cruel!"

"Is it possible," cried Rose, "that for such a man as this, you can resign every future hope, and the certainty of immediate rescue? It is madness."

"I don't know what it is," answered the girl. "I only know that it is so. I am drawn back to him through every suffering and ill usage. I should be, I believe, if I knew that I was to die by his hand at last."

"What am I to do?" said Rose. "I should not let you depart from me thus."

"You should, lady, and I know you will," rejoined the girl, rising. "You will not stop my going because I have trusted in your goodness, and forced no promise from you, as I might have done."

"Of what use, then, is the communication you have made?" said Rose. "How will its disclosure benefit Oliver, whom you are anxious to serve?"

"You must have some kind gentleman about you that will hear it as a secret, and advise you what to do," rejoined the girl.

"But where can I find you again when it is necessary?" asked Rose.

"Will you promise me that you will have my secret strictly kept, and come alone, or with the only other person that knows it, and that I shall not be watched or followed?" asked the girl.

"I promise you solemnly," answered Rose.

"Every Sunday night, from eleven until the clock strikes twelve," said the girl, "I will walk on London Bridge if I am alive."

"You will," said Rose, after a pause, "take some money from me, which may enable you to live without dishonesty—at all events until we meet again?"

"Not a penny," replied the girl, waving her hand.

"Do not close your heart against all my efforts to help you," said Rose, stepping gently forward. "I wish to serve you indeed."

"You would serve me best, lady," replied the girl, wringing her hands, "if you could take my life at once, for I have felt more grief to think of what I am, tonight, than I ever did before, and it would be something not to die in the hell in which I have lived. God bless you, sweet lady, and send as much happiness on your head as I have brought shame on mine!"

Thus speaking, and sobbing aloud, the unhappy creature turned away, while Rose Maylie, overpowered by this extraordinary interview, sank into a chair, and endeavored to collect her thoughts.

CHAPTER 40

They intended remaining in London only three days, prior to going for some weeks to a distant part of the coast. It was now midnight of the first day. What course of action could Rose take, which could be adopted in forty-eight hours? Or how could she postpone the journey without exciting suspicion?

Mr. Losberne was with them, and would be for the next two days. Rose foresaw too clearly the wrath with which he would regard the person responsible for Oliver's recapture, to trust him with the secret. If she spoke to Mrs. Maylie on the subject, her first impulse would be to hold a conference with the worthy doctor.

Rose passed a sleepless and anxious night. After more debating with herself next day, she arrived at the desperate conclusion of consulting Harry. She had taken up a pen and laid it down again fifty times without writing a word, when Oliver, who had been walking in the streets with Mr. Giles for a bodyguard, entered the room in breathless haste and violent agitation.

"I have seen the gentleman who was so good to me," said Oliver, scarcely able to articulate, "—Mr. Brownlow, that we have so often talked about."

"Where?" asked Rose.

"Getting out of a coach," replied Oliver, shedding tears of delight, "and going into a house. I couldn't speak to him, for he didn't see me, and I trembled so, that I was not able to go up to him. But

Giles asked for me whether he lived there, and they said he did. Look here," said Oliver, opening a scrap of paper, "here's where he lives—I'm going there directly!"

Rose read the address, which was Craven Street, in the Strand.

"Quick!" she said. "I will take you there directly, without a minute's loss of time. I will only tell my aunt that we are going out for an hour."

In little more than five minutes they were on their way to Craven Street. When they arrived there, Rose left Oliver in the coach, under pretense of preparing the old gentleman to receive him. Sending up her card by the servant, she requested to see Mr. Brownlow on pressing business. The servant soon returned, to beg that she would walk upstairs. Following him into an upper room, Miss Maylie was presented to an elderly gentleman of benevolent appearance, in a bottle-green coat. At no great distance from him was seated another old gentleman, who did not look particularly benevolent, and who was sitting with his hands clasped on the top of a thick stick.

"Dear me," said the gentleman, in the bottle-green coat, hastily rising with great politeness, "I beg your pardon, young lady—I imagined it was some other person who—I beg you will excuse me. Be seated, pray."

"Mr. Brownlow, I believe, sir?" said Rose, glancing from the other gentleman to the one who had spoken.

"That is my name," said the old gentleman. "This is my friend, Mr. Grimwig. Grimwig, will you leave us for a few minutes?"

"I believe," interposed Miss Maylie, "that I need not give that gentleman the trouble of going away. If I am correctly informed, he is familiar with the business on which I wish to speak to you."

Mr. Brownlow inclined his head. Mr. Grimwig, who had made one stiff bow, and risen from his chair, made another stiff bow, and dropped into it again.

"I shall surprise you very much, I have no doubt," said Rose, naturally embarrassed, "but you once showed great benevolence and goodness to a very dear young friend of mine, and I am sure you will take an interest in hearing of him again."

"Indeed!" said Mr. Brownlow.

"Oliver Twist you knew him as," replied Rose.

The words no sooner escaped her lips, than Mr. Grimwig, who had been affecting to look at a large book that lay on the table, upset it with a great crash, and falling back in his chair, gave a stare of absolute wonder.

Mr. Brownlow was no less surprised, although his astonishment was not expressed in the same eccentric manner. He drew his chair nearer to Miss Maylie's, and said, "If you have it in your power to produce any evidence that will alter the unfavorable opinion I was once induced to entertain of that poor child, in Heaven's name put me in possession of it."

"A bad one! I'll eat my head if he is not a bad one," growled Mr. Grimwig.

"He is a child of a noble nature and a warm heart," said Rose, coloring, "with affections and feelings that would do honor to many who have numbered his days six times over."

"I'm only sixty-one," said Mr. Grimwig, with a rigid face. "And, as this Oliver is not twelve years old, I don't see the application of that remark."

"Do not heed my friend, Miss Maylie," said Mr. Brownlow, "he does not mean what he says."

"He'll eat his head, if he doesn't," growled Mr. Grimwig.

"He would deserve to have it knocked off, if he does," said Mr. Brownlow.

"And he'd uncommonly like to see any man offer to do it," responded Mr. Grimwig, knocking his stick upon the floor.

Having gone thus far, the two old gentlemen shook hands, according to their usual custom.

"Now, Miss Maylie," said Mr. Brownlow, "will you let me know what information you have of this poor child? I promise that I exhausted every means in my power of discovering any."

Rose at once related, in a few natural words, all that had befallen Oliver since he left Mr. Brownlow's house, reserving Nancy's information for that gentleman's private ear, and concluding with the assurance that his only sorrow, for some months past, had been not being able to meet with his former benefactor and friend.

"Thank God!" said the old gentleman. "This is great happiness to me. But you have not told me where he is now, Miss Maylie. Why not have brought him?"

"He is waiting in a coach at the door," replied Rose.

"At this door!" cried the old gentleman. He hurried out of the room, down the stairs, up the coach steps, and into the coach, without another word.

When the room door closed behind him, Mr. Grimwig rose and limped as fast as he could up and down the room at least a dozen times, and then stopping suddenly before Rose, kissed her without the slightest warning.

"Hush!" he said, as the young lady rose in some alarm at this unusual proceeding. "Don't be afraid. I'm old enough to be your grandfather. You're a sweet girl. I like you. Here they are!"

As he threw himself into his former seat, Mr. Brownlow returned, accompanied by Oliver, whom Mr. Grimwig received graciously.

"There is somebody else who should not be forgotten," said Mr. Brownlow, ringing the bell. "Send Mrs. Bedwin here, if you please."

The old housekeeper answered the summons, and dropping a curtsy at the door, waited for orders.

"Why, you get blinder every day, Bedwin," said Mr. Brownlow, rather testily.

"Well, that I do, sir," replied the old lady. "People's eyes, at my time of life, don't improve with age, sir."

"I could have told you that," rejoined Mr. Brownlow, "but put on your glasses, and see if you can't find out what you were wanted for, will you?"

The old lady began to rummage in her pocket for her spectacles. But Oliver's patience could not stand it, and so he sprang into her arms.

"God be good to me!" cried the old lady, embracing him, "it is my innocent boy!"

"My dear old nurse!" cried Oliver.

"He would come back—I knew he would," said the old lady, holding him in her arms. "How well he looks! Where have you been, this long, long while? Ah! The same sweet face, but not so pale; the same soft eyes, but not so sad. I have never forgotten them or his quiet smile." Running on thus, and now holding Oliver from her to mark how he had grown, now clasping him to her and passing her fingers fondly through his hair, the good soul laughed and wept upon him.

Leaving her and Oliver to compare notes, Mr. Brownlow led the way into another room. There, he heard from Rose a full narration of her interview with Nancy. Rose also explained her reasons for not confiding in her friend Mr. Losberne. The old gentleman said that she had acted prudently, and volunteered to hold a conference with the worthy doctor himself. It was arranged that he should call at the hotel at eight o'clock that evening, and that in the meantime Mrs. Maylie should be cautiously informed of all that had occurred. These plans made, Rose and Oliver returned home.

Rose had by no means overrated the good doctor's wrath. Nancy's history was no sooner unfolded to him, than he poured forth a shower of mingled threats. But he was restrained by corresponding violence on the side of Mr. Brownlow, who was himself of a stubborn temperament.

"Then what the devil is to be done?" said the impetuous doctor, when they had rejoined the two ladies. "Are we to pass a vote of thanks to all these vagabonds, male and female, and beg them to accept a hundred pounds apiece, as a trifling mark of our esteem, and some slight acknowledgment of their kindness to Oliver?"

"Not exactly that," rejoined Mr. Brownlow, laughing, "but we must proceed gently and with great care."

"Gentleness and care," exclaimed the doctor.

"I'd send them one and all to—"

"Never mind where," interrupted Mr. Brownlow. "But reflect whether sending them anywhere is likely to serve our purpose."

"What purpose?" asked the doctor.

"Simply, the discovery of Oliver's parentage, and regaining for him the inheritance of which he has been fraudulently deprived."

"Ah!" said Mr. Losberne, cooling himself with his pocket handkerchief, "I almost forgot that."

"You see," pursued Mr. Brownlow, "supposing it were possible to bring these scoundrels to justice without compromising the girl's safety, what good should we bring about?"

"Hanging a few of them at least," suggested the doctor.

"Very good," replied Mr. Brownlow, smiling, "but no doubt they will bring that about for themselves eventually, and if we step in, it seems to me that we shall be acting in direct opposition to our own interest—or at least to Oliver's, which is the same thing."

"How?" inquired the doctor.

"It is quite clear that we cannot get to the bottom of this mystery, unless we can bring this man, Monks, upon his knees. That can only be done by catching him when he is not surrounded by these people. For, suppose he were apprehended, we have no proof against him. It is unlikely that he could receive any further punishment than being committed to prison as a vagabond, and then his mouth would be so obstinately closed that he might as well, for our purposes, be deaf, dumb, blind, and an idiot."

Mr. Brownlow continued. "We must see the girl,

to find out whether she will point out this Monks, on the understanding that he is to be dealt with by us, and not by the law. She cannot be seen until next Sunday night. This is Tuesday. I would suggest that in the meantime, we remain perfectly quiet, and keep these matters secret even from Oliver himself."

Although Mr. Losberne did not like a delay of five whole days, he had to admit that no better plan occurred to him just then. And as both Rose and Mrs. Maylie sided strongly with Mr. Brownlow, that gentleman's proposition was agreed to by all.

"I should like," he said, "to call in the aid of my friend Grimwig. He is a strange creature, but a shrewd one, and might prove useful to us. He was trained as a lawyer."

"I have no objection to your calling in your friend if I may call in mine," said the doctor.

"We must put it to the vote," replied Mr. Brownlow, "who may he be?"

"That lady's son, and this young lady's—old friend," said the doctor, motioning towards Mrs. Maylie, and concluding with an expressive glance at her niece.

Rose blushed deeply, but she did not make any audible objection to this motion, and Harry Maylie and Mr. Grimwig were accordingly added to the committee.

"We stay in town, of course," said Mrs. Maylie. "I will spare neither trouble nor expense, and I am content to remain here, if it be for twelve months, so long as you assure me that any hope remains."

"Good!" rejoined Mr. Brownlow. "Come! Supper has been announced, and young Oliver, who is all alone in the next room, will have begun to think that we have wearied of his company, and entered into some dark conspiracy to thrust him forth upon the world."

With these words, the old gentleman gave his hand to Mrs. Maylie, and escorted her into the supper room. Mr. Losberne followed, leading Rose, and the council was, for the present, effectually broken up.

CHAPTER 41

Upon the night that Nancy hurried on her mission to Rose Maylie, there advanced towards London two persons, male and female. They had toiled along the dusty road, taking little heed of any object within sight, until they passed through Highgate archway. Then the foremost traveler stopped and called impatiently to his companion, "What a lazybones yer are, Charlotte."

"It's a heavy load, I can tell you," said the female, coming up, almost breathless with fatigue.

"Heavy! What are yer talking about?" rejoined the male traveler, changing his own little bundle as he spoke, to the other shoulder. "Well, if yer ain't enough to tire anybody's patience out, I don't know what is!"

"Is it much farther?" asked the woman, resting herself against a bank, and looking up with the perspiration streaming from her face.

"Much farther! Yer as good as there," said the long-legged tramper, pointing out before him. "Look there! Those are the lights of London."

"They're a good two mile off, at least," said the woman despondently.

"Never mind whether they're two mile off, or twenty," said Noah Claypole, "but get up and come on, or I'll kick yer, and so I give yer notice."

The woman rose without any further remark, and trudged onward by his side.

"Where do you mean to stop for the night,

Noah?" she asked, after they had walked a few hundred yards.

"How should I know?" replied Noah, whose temper had been considerably impaired by walking.

"Near, I hope," said Charlotte.

"No, not near," replied Mr. Claypole. "A pretty thing it would be, to go and stop at the very first public house outside the town, so that Sowerberry might poke in his old nose, and have us taken back in a cart with handcuffs on," said Mr. Claypole in a jeering tone. "No! I shall not stop till we come to the very out-of-the-wayest house I can set eyes on. Yer may thanks yer stars I've got a head, for if we hadn't gone, at first, the wrong road a purpose, and come back across country, yer'd have been locked up hard and fast a week ago, my lady. And serve yer right for being a fool."

"I know I ain't as cunning as you are," replied Charlotte, "but don't put all the blame on me, and say I should have been locked up. You would have been if I had been, anyway."

"Yer took the money from the till, yer know yer did," said Mr. Claypole.

"I took it for you, Noah, dear," rejoined Charlotte.

"Did I keep it?" asked Mr. Claypole.

"No, you trusted in me, and let me carry it like a dear, and so you are," said the lady, chucking him under the chin, and drawing her arm through his.

It should be observed that he had trusted Charlotte to this extent, in order that, if they were pursued, the money might be found on her. Of course, he gave no explanation of his motives, and they walked on lovingly together.

When they arrived at the Angel at Islington, Noah wisely judged, from the crowd of passengers and numbers of vehicles, that London began in earnest. He crossed into Saint John's Road, and was soon deep in intricate and dirty ways that were some of the lowest and worst of London.

At length, he stopped in front of a public house, more humble in appearance and more dirty than any he had yet seen. He graciously announced his intention of putting up there, for the night.

"So give us the bundle," said Noah, "and don't yer speak, except when yer spoke to. What's the name of the house—t-h-r—three what?"

"Cripples," said Charlotte.

"Three Cripples," repeated Noah, "and a good sign too. Now, then! Keep close at my heels, and come along." He pushed the rattling door with his shoulder, and entered the house, followed by his companion.

There was nobody in the bar but a young Jew. He stared hard at Noah, and Noah stared hard at him.

"Is this the Three Cripples?" asked Noah.

"That is the dabe of this 'ouse," replied the Jew.

"We want to sleep here tonight." said Noah.

"I'b dot certaid you cad," said Barney, who was the attendant, "but I'll idquire."

"Show us the tap, and give us a bit of cold meat and a drop of beer while yer inquiring, will yer?" said Noah.

Barney complied by ushering them into a small backroom, and setting the required items before them. Having done so, he informed the travelers that they could be lodged that night, and left the amiable couple to their refreshment.

Now, this backroom was immediately behind the bar, and some steps lower, so that any person connected with the house, undrawing a small curtain that concealed a single pane of glass, could not only look down upon any guests in the backroom without being observed, but could also listen to their conversation.

Barney had only just returned from the room, when Fagin, in the course of his evening's business, came into the bar to inquire after some of his young pupils.

"Hush!" said Barney, "stradegers id the next roob."

"Strangers!" repeated the old man in a whisper.

"Frob the cuttry," added Barney, "but subthig in your way, or I'b bistaked."

Fagin appeared to receive this communication with great interest.

Mounting a stool, he cautiously applied his eye to the pane of glass. He could see Mr. Claypole taking cold beef from the dish, and porter from the pot, and administering tiny doses of both to Charlotte, who sat patiently by, eating and drinking at his pleasure.

"Aha!" he whispered, looking round to Barney, "I like that fellow's looks. He'd be of use to us. He knows how to train the girl already."

Turning his ear to the partition, he listened attentively.

"So I mean to be a gentleman," said Mr. Claypole, kicking out his legs. "No more jolly old coffins, Charlotte, but a gentleman's life for me, and, if yer like, yer shall be a lady."

"I should like that well enough, dear," replied

Charlotte, "but tills ain't to be emptied every day, and people to get clear off after it."

"Tills be blowed!" said Mr. Claypole, "there's more things besides tills to be emptied."

"What do you mean?" asked his companion.

"Pockets, houses, mail coaches, banks!" said Mr. Claypole.

"But you can't do all that, dear," said Charlotte.

"I shall get into company with them as can," replied Noah. "They'll be able to make us useful some way or another. Why, you yourself are worth fifty women. I never seen such a precious sly and deceitful creetur as yer can be when I let yer."

"I should like to be the captain of some band, and have the whopping of 'em, and follering 'em about, unbeknown to themselves. That would suit me, if there was good profit. If we could only get in with some gentleman of this sort, I say it would be cheap at that twenty-pound note you've got—especially as we don't very well know how to get rid of it ourselves."

After expressing this opinion, Mr. Claypole took a drink, after which he appeared greatly refreshed. He was taking another, when the appearance of a stranger interrupted him.

The stranger was Mr. Fagin. And very low bow he made, as he advanced, and setting himself down at the nearest table, ordered something to drink of the grinning Barney.

"A pleasant night, sir, but cool for the time of year," said Fagin, rubbing his hands. "From the country, I see, sir?"

"How do yer see that?" asked Noah Claypole.

"We have not so much dust as that in London,"

replied Fagin, pointing from Noah's shoes to those of his companion, and from them to the two bundles.

"Yer a sharp feller," said Noah.

"Why, one need be sharp in this town, my dear," replied the Jew, sinking his voice to a confidential whisper, "and that's the truth."

Fagin followed up this remark by sharing the liquor Barney brought in a friendly manner.

"Good stuff that," observed Mr. Claypole, smacking his lips.

"Dear!" said Fagin. "A man need be always emptying a till, or a pocket, or a house, or a mail coach, or a bank, if he drinks it regularly."

Mr. Claypole no sooner heard this sample from his own remarks than he fell back in his chair, and looked from the Jew to Charlotte with an expression of excessive terror.

"Don't mind me, my dear," said Fagin, drawing his chair closer. "Ha! Ha! It was lucky it was only me that heard you by chance."

"I didn't take it," stammered Noah. "It was all her doing. Yer've got it now, Charlotte, yer know yer have."

"No matter who's got it, or who did it, my dear," replied Fagin. "I'm in that way myself, and I like you for it."

"In what way?" asked Mr. Claypole, a little recovering.

"In that way of business," rejoined Fagin, "and so are the people of the house. There is not a safer place in all this town than is the Cripples—that is, when I like to make it so. And I have taken a fancy to you and the young woman. So I've said the word, and you may make your minds easy."

"I'll tell you more," said Fagin, "I have got a friend that I think can put you in the right way, where you can take whatever department of the business you think will suit you best at first, and be taught all the others. Here! Let me have a word with you outside."

"There's no occasion to trouble ourselves to move," said Noah. "She'll take the luggage upstairs. Charlotte, see to them bundles."

Charlotte made her way off with the packages while Noah held the door open and watched her out.

"She's kept tolerably well under, ain't she?" he asked as he resumed his seat, in the tone of a keeper who had tamed some wild animal.

"Quite perfect," rejoined Fagin, clapping him on the shoulder. "You're a genius, my dear."

"Why, I suppose if I wasn't, I shouldn't be here," replied Noah. "But, I say, she'll be back if yer lose time."

"Now, what do you think?" said Fagin. "If you was to like my friend, could you do better than join him?"

"Is he in a good way of business?" responded Noah.

"The top of the tree; employs a power of hands; has the best society in the profession," replied Fagin.

"When could I see him?" asked Noah doubtfully.

"Tomorrow morning."

"Where?"

"Here."

"Um!" said Noah. "What's the wages?"

"Live like a gentleman—board and lodging, pipes and spirits free—half of all you earn, and half of all the young woman earns," replied Mr. Fagin.

Since Noah realized that, in the event of his refusal, his new acquaintance could give him up to justice immediately, he gradually relented to the terms, and said he thought that would suit him.

"But, yer see," observed Noah, "as she will be able to do a good deal, I should like to take something light. What do you think would suit me now? Something not too trying for the strength, and not very dangerous, you know. That's the sort of thing!"

"I heard you talk of something in the spy way upon the others, my dear," said Fagin. "My friend wants somebody who would do that well, very much."

"Why, I shouldn't mind turning my hand to it sometimes," rejoined Mr. Claypole slowly, "but it wouldn't pay by itself, you know."

"That's true!" observed the Jew. "No, it might not."

"What do you think, then?" asked Noah, anxiously regarding him. "Something in the sneaking way, where it was pretty sure work, and not much more risk than being at home."

"Stop!" said Fagin, laying his hand on Noah's knee. "The kinchin lay."

"What's that?" demanded Mr. Claypole.

"The kinchins, my dear," said Fagin, "is the young children that's sent on errands by their mothers, with sixpences and shillings. The lay is just to take their money away—they've always got it ready in their hands—then knock 'em into the gutter, and walk off slow, as if there were nothing else the matter but a child fallen down and hurt itself. Ha! ha! ha!"

"Ha! ha!" roared Mr. Claypole, kicking up his legs in an ecstasy. "Lord, that's the very thing!"

"To be sure it is," replied Fagin, "and you can have a few good beats chalked out in Camden Town, and Battle Bridge, and neighborhoods like that, where they're always going errands. You can upset as many kinchins as you want, any hour in the day. Ha! ha! ha!"

"Well, that's all right!" said Noah, when he had recovered himself, and Charlotte had returned. "What time tomorrow shall we say?"

"Will ten do?" asked Fagin, adding, as Mr. Claypole nodded assent, "What name shall I tell my good friend?"

"Mr. Morris Bolter," replied Noah, who had prepared himself for such emergency. "This is Mrs. Bolter."

"Mrs. Bolter's humble servant," said Fagin, bowing with grotesque politeness. "I hope I shall know her better shortly."

"Do you hear the gentleman, Charlotte?" thundered Mr. Claypole.

"Yes, Noah, dear!" replied Mrs. Bolter, extending her hand.

"She calls me Noah, as a sort of fond way of talking," said Mr. Morris Bolter, turning to Fagin. "You understand?"

"Oh yes, I understand—perfectly," replied Fagin, telling the truth for once. "Good night!"

With many adieus and good wishes, Mr. Fagin went his way, while Noah Claypole proceeded to enlighten Charlotte about the arrangement he had made.

CHAPTER 42

"And so it was you that was your own friend, was it?" asked Mr. Claypole, otherwise Bolter, when he arrived next day to Fagin's house.

"Every man's his own friend, my dear," replied Fagin. "He hasn't as good a one as himself anywhere. Some conjurers say that number three is the magic number, and some say number seven. It's neither, my friend. It's number one."

"Ha! ha!" cried Mr. Bolter. "Number one forever."

"In a little community like ours, my dear," said Fagin, "we have a general rule. For instance, it's your object to take care of number one—meaning yourself."

"Certainly," replied Mr. Bolter. "Yer about right there."

"Well! You can't take care of yourself, number one, without taking care of me, number one."

"Number two, you mean," said Mr. Bolter.

"No, I don't!" retorted Fagin. "I'm of the same importance to you, as you are to yourself."

"I say," interrupted Mr. Bolter, "yer a nice man, and I'm fond of yer. But we ain't that thick together."

"Only think," said Fagin, shrugging his shoulders, and stretching out his hands, "you've done what's a very pretty thing, and what I love you for doing. But at the same time, it would put the noose round your throat, that's so very easily tied and so very difficult to unloose!"

Mr. Bolter put his hand to his neckerchief, as if

he felt it inconveniently tight.

"The gallows," continued Fagin, "has stopped many a bold fellow's career on the broad highway. To keep on the easy road is object number one with you. To be able to do that, you depend upon me. To keep my little business all snug, I depend upon you. The first is your number one, the second my number one. The more you value your number one, the more careful you must be of mine. So we come at last to our general rule—that a regard for number one holds us all together, and must do so, unless we would all go to pieces in company."

"That's true," rejoined Mr. Bolter, thoughtfully. "Yer a cunning old codger!"

Mr. Fagin saw with delight that he had impressed his recruit with a sense of his wily genius. He followed up by acquainting him with the nature of his operations, blending truth and fiction as best served his purpose. Mr. Bolter's respect visibly increased, and became tempered, at the same time, with a degree of wholesome fear, which it was highly desirable to awaken.

"It's this mutual trust we have in each other that consoles me under heavy losses," said Fagin. "My best hand was taken from me, yesterday morning."

"You don't mean to say he died?" cried Mr. Bolter.

"No," replied Fagin, "not so bad as that. He was charged with attempting to pick a pocket, and they found a silver snuffbox on him. They remanded him till today, for they thought they knew the owner. Ah! he was worth fifty boxes, and I'd give the price of as many to have him back. You should have known the Dodger."

"Well, but I shall know him, I hope. Don't yer think so?" said Mr. Bolter.

"I'm doubtful about it," replied Fagin, with a sigh. "If they don't get any fresh evidence, it'll only be a summary conviction, and we shall have him back again after six weeks or so. But, if they do, he'll be a lifer."

Master Bates entered, with his face twisted into a look of woe. "It's all up, Fagin," he said, when he and his new companion had been made known to each other. "They've found the gentleman as owns the box. Two or three more's a coming to ''dentify him, and the Artful's booked for a passage out. To think of Jack Dawkins going abroad for a common twopenny-halfpenny sneeze-box! Oh, why didn't he rob some rich old gentleman of all his walables, and go out as a gentleman, and not like a common prig, without no honor nor glory!"

Master Bates sat himself on the nearest chair with an air of despondency.

"What do you talk about his having neither honor nor glory for!" exclaimed Fagin, darting an angry look at his pupil. "Wasn't he always the top one among you all! Eh?"

"Yes," replied Master Bates, in a voice rendered husky by regret.

"Then what are you blubbering for?" replied Fagin angrily.

"'Cause it isn't on the record, is it?" said Charley. "'Cause nobody will never know half of what he was. How will he stand in the newspaper? P'raps not be there at all. Oh, my eye, wot a blow it is!"

"Ha! ha!" cried Fagin, turning to Mr. Bolter in a fit of chuckling, "see what a pride they take in their profession, my dear. Ain't it beautiful?"

Mr. Bolter nodded, and Fagin stepped up to Charley and patted him on the shoulder.

"Never mind, Charley," said Fagin soothingly, "it'll be sure to come out. They'll all know what a clever fellow he was. He'll show it himself, and not disgrace his old pals and teachers. Think how young he is too! What a distinction, Charley, to be lagged at his time of life!"

"Well, it is an honor!" said Charley, a little consoled.

"He shall have all he wants," continued the Jew. "He shall be kept like a gentleman. With his beer every day, and money in his pocket to pitch and toss with, if he can't spend it. We'll have a bigwig, Charley, one that's got the greatest gift of the gab, to carry on his defense. He shall make a speech for himself, too, if he likes, and we'll read it all in the papers—'Artful Dodger'—shrieks of laughter—here the court was convulsed"—eh, Charley?"

"Ha! ha!" laughed Master Bates, "what a lark that would be, wouldn't it, Fagin? I see it all afore me, Fagin. What a game! All the bigwigs trying to look solemn, and Jack Dawkins addressing 'em as intimate and comfortable as if he was the judge's own son making a speech arter dinner—ha! ha!"

"We must know how he gets on today, by some handy means or other," said Fagin.

"Shall I go?" asked Charley.

"Not for the world," replied Fagin. "Are you stark mad, my dear, that you'd walk into the very place where—no, Charley, no. One is enough to lose at a time."

"Then why don't you send this new cove?"

asked Master Bates, laying his hand on Noah's arm. "Nobody knows him."

"Why, if he didn't mind—" observed Fagin.

"Mind!" interposed Charley. "What should he have to mind?"

"Really nothing, my dear," said Fagin, turning to Mr. Bolter.

"No, no—none of that. It's not in my department, that ain't," observed Noah, backing towards the door, and shaking his head with a kind of sober alarm.

"Wot department has he got, Fagin?" inquired Master Bates, surveying Noah's lank form with much disgust. "The cutting away when there's anything wrong, and the eating all the wittles when there's everything right—is that his branch?"

"Never mind," retorted Mr. Bolter, "and don't yer take liberties with yer superiors, little boy, or yer'll find yerself in the wrong shop."

Master Bates laughed so vehemently at this magnificent threat, that it was some time before Fagin could explain to Mr. Bolter that he faced no possible danger in visiting the police office. If he were properly disguised, it would be as safe a spot for him to visit as any in London, since it would be the last place to which he could be supposed to go of his own free will.

Persuaded by these ideas and his fear of Fagin, Mr. Bolter at length consented to make the trip. He put on a waggoner's shirt, velveteen breeches, and leather leggings. He was also furnished with a felt hat well garnished with turnpike tickets. Thus equipped, he was to saunter into the office, as some country fellow from Covent Garden market might do out of curiosity. As he was an awkward, ungainly, and raw-boned a fellow, he would look the part to perfection.

He was informed of how to recognize the Artful Dodger, and was taken by Master Bates through dark and winding ways to within a short distance of Bow Street. Charley Bates bade him hurry on alone, and promised to await his return on the spot of their parting.

Noah punctually followed the directions he had received. He found himself jostled among a crowd of people, chiefly women, who were huddled together in a dirty room, at the upper end of which was a raised platform railed off from the rest, with a dock for the prisoners on the left hand against the wall, a box for the witnesses in the middle, and a screened-off desk for the magistrates on the right.

There were only a couple of women in the dock, who were nodding to their admiring friends, while the clerk read some depositions to a couple of police-men and a man in plain clothes who leaned over the table. A jailer stood reclining against the dockrail, tapping his nose listlessly with a large key.

Nobody answering the description of Mr. Dawkins was to be seen. Noah waited in a state of much uncertainty until the women, being committed for trial, went flaunting out. Then he was quickly relieved by the appearance of another prisoner who he felt at once could be no other than the Dodger.

It was indeed Mr. Dawkins. He shuffled into the office with the big coat sleeves tucked up as usual, his hat in his right hand, and, taking his place in the dock, requested to know what he was placed in that disgraceful sitivation for.

"Hold your tongue, will you?" said the jailer.

"I'm an Englishman, ain't I?" rejoined the Dodger. "Where are my priwileges?"

"You'll get your privileges soon enough," retorted the jailer, "and pepper with 'em."

"We'll see wot the Secretary of State for the Home Affairs has got to say to the beaks, if I don't," replied Mr. Dawkins. "Wot is this here business? I shall thank the madg'strates to dispose of this here little affair, and not to keep me while they read the paper, for I've got an appointment with a genelman in the city, and as I am a man of my word and wery punctual in business matters, he'll go away if I ain't there to my time, and then pr'aps ther won't be an action for damage against them as kep me away."

"Silence there!" cried the jailer.

"What is this?" inquired one of the magistrates.

"A pickpocketing case, Your Worship."

"Has the boy ever been here before?"

"He ought to have been, many times," replied the jailer. "He has been pretty well everywhere else. I know him well, Your Worship."

"Oh! you know me, do you?" cried the Artful. "Wery good. That's a case of deformation of character, anyway."

Here there was another laugh, and another cry of silence.

"Now then, where are the witnesses?" said the clerk.

"Ah! That's right," added the Dodger. "Where are they? I should like to see 'em."

A policeman stepped forward who had seen the prisoner attempt the pocket of an unknown gentleman in a crowd, and indeed take a handkerchief therefrom, which, being a old one, he deliberately put back again. For this reason, he took the Dodger into custody, and the said Dodger, being searched, had upon his person a silver snuffbox, with the owner's name engraved upon the lid. Being then and there present in the court, the owner swore that the snuffbox was his, and that he had missed it on the previous day.

"Have you anything to say, boy?" said the magistrate.

"I beg your pardon," said the Dodger, looking up with an air of abstraction. "Did you address yourself to me, my man?"

"I never seen such an out-and-out young wagabond, Your Worship," observed the jailer with a grin. "Do you mean to say anything, you young shaver?"

"No," replied the Dodger, "for this ain't the shop for justice. Besides which, my attorney is a-breakfasting this morning with the Wice President of the House of Commons. But I shall have something to say elsewhere, and so will he. I'll—"

"Take him away!" interrupted the clerk.

"Come on," said the jailer.

"I'll come on," replied the Dodger, brushing his hat with the palm of his hand. "Ah! (to the Bench) it's no use your looking frightened. I won't show you no mercy. You'll pay for this, my fine fellers. I wouldn't go free, now, if you was to fall down on your knees and ask me. Here, carry me off to prison!"

The Dodger let himself be led off by the collar, threatening, till he got into the yard, to make a parliamentary business of it, and then grinning in the officer's face, with great glee.

Having seen him locked up in a little cell, Noah made his way back to where he had left Master Bates. The two hastened back together, to bring Mr. Fagin the news that the Dodger was doing full justice to his upbringing, and establishing for himself a glorious reputation.

CHAPTER 43

There were times when Nancy felt some regret about what she had done. Her mental struggles forced themselves upon her, again and again, and left their traces. She grew pale and thin. At times, she took no heed of what was passing before her, or no part in conversations. At other times, she laughed without merriment, and a moment afterwards, she sat silent and dejected.

It was Sunday night, and the bell of the nearest church struck the hour. Eleven.

"An hour this side of midnight," said Sikes, raising the blind to look out. "Dark and heavy it is too. A good night for business."

"Ah!" replied Fagin. "What a pity, Bill, that there's none quite ready to be done."

"You're right for once," replied Sikes gruffly. "It is a pity, for I'm in the humor too. We must make up for lost time."

"That's the way to talk, my dear," replied Fagin, venturing to pat him on the shoulder. "You're like yourself tonight, Bill."

"I don't feel like myself when you lay that withered old claw on my shoulder, so take it away," said Sikes, casting off the Jew's hand.

"It make you nervous, Bill—reminds you of being nabbed, does it?" said Fagin, determined not to be offended.

"Reminds me of being nabbed by the devil," returned Sikes.

Fagin offered no reply to this compliment, but pointed his finger towards Nancy, who had put on her bonnet.

"Hallo!" cried Sikes. "Where's the gal going to at this time of night?"

"I don't know where," replied the girl.

"Then I do," said Sikes. "Nowhere. Sit down."

"I'm not well," rejoined the girl. "I want a breath of air."

"Put your head out of the winder," replied Sikes.

"There's not enough there," said the girl. "I want it in the street."

"Then you won't have it," replied Sikes. He rose, locked the door, took the key out, and pulling her bonnet from her head, flung it up to the top of an old rafter.

"It's not such a matter as a bonnet would keep me," said the girl turning pale. "What do you mean, Bill? Do you know what you're doing?"

"Know what I'm—Oh!" cried Sikes, turning to Fagin, "she's out of her senses, or she daren't talk to me in that way."

"You'll drive me to something desperate," muttered the girl. "Tell him to let me go, Fagin. He had better. Do you hear me?" cried Nancy, stamping her foot upon the ground.

"Hear you!" repeated Sikes. "Aye! And if I hear you for half a minute longer, the dog shall have such a grip on your throat as'll tear some of that screaming voice out!"

"Let me go," said the girl with great earnestness. Then sitting herself down on the floor, before the door, she said, "Bill, let me go. For only one hour—do—do!"

"Cut my limbs off one by one!" cried Sikes, seizing her roughly by the arm, "If I don't think the gal's stark raving mad. Get up."

"Not till you let me go—Never—never!" screamed the girl. Pinioning her hands, Sikes dragged her, struggling with him all the way, into a small room, where he pushed her into a chair and held her down by force. She struggled and implored by turns until twelve o'clock had struck, and then, exhausted, ceased to contest the point any further. With a caution, backed by many oaths, to make no more efforts to go out that night, Sikes left her and rejoined Fagin.

"Whew!" said the housebreaker wiping the perspiration from his face. "Wot did she take it into her head to go out tonight for, do you think? You should know her better than me. Wot does it mean?"

"Woman's obstinacy, I suppose, my dear."

"Well, I suppose it is," growled Sikes. "I thought I had tamed her, but she's as bad as ever."

"Worse," said Fagin thoughtfully. "I never knew her like this, for such a little cause."

"Nor I," said Sikes. "I think she's got a touch of that fever in her blood yet, and it won't come out."

"That's it, my dear," replied the Jew in a whisper. "Hush!"

The girl appeared and resumed her former seat. She rocked herself to and fro, tossed her head, and, after a little time, burst out laughing.

"Why, now she's on the other tack!" exclaimed Sikes, with a look of excessive surprise.

In a few minutes, the girl subsided into her usual demeanor. Fagin took up his hat and bade Sikes good night. He paused when he reached the room door, and looking round, asked if somebody would light him down the dark stairs.

"Light him down," said Sikes, who was filling his pipe.

Nancy followed the old man downstairs with a candle. When they reached the passage, he drew close to the girl, and said, in a whisper, "What is it, Nancy, dear?"

"What do you mean?" replied the girl, in the same tone.

"The reason of all this," replied Fagin. "If *he* is so hard with you, why don't you—"

"Well?" said the girl, as Fagin paused, his eyes looking into hers.

"No matter just now. We'll talk of this again. You have a friend in me, Nance. If you want revenge on those that treat you like a dog—worse than his dog—come to me. You know me of old, Nance."

"I know you well," replied the girl, without showing the least emotion. "Good night."

She shrank back, as Fagin offered to lay his hand on hers, but said good night again, in a steady voice, and, answering his parting look with a nod of intelligence, closed the door between them.

Fagin walked towards his home. He decided that Nancy, wearied of the housebreaker's brutality, had developed an attachment for some new friend. Her altered manner, her repeated absences from home alone, her comparative indifference to the gang for which she had once been so zealous, and her desperate impatience to leave home that night at a particular hour, all pointed to it. The object of this new liking was not among his gang. He would be a valuable acquisition with such an assistant as Nancy, and must be secured without delay.

There was another, darker object to be gained. Sikes knew too much, and his ruffian taunts were wearing on Fagin. The girl must know that if she shook him off, she could never be safe from his fury, and that it would surely mean the maiming of limbs, or perhaps the loss of life, for the recent object of her fancy.

"With a little persuasion," thought Fagin, "would she consent to poison him? The dangerous villain, the man I hate, would be gone, another secured in his place, and my influence over the girl, with a knowledge of this crime to back it, unlimited."

When he had given the girl broken hints at their recent parting, she showed no expression of surprise. The girl clearly comprehended his meaning. But perhaps she would recoil from a plot to take the life of Sikes. "How," thought Fagin, as he crept homeward, "can I increase my influence with her?"

If he discovered the new object of her regard, and threatened to reveal the whole history to Sikes unless she entered into his plan, would she comply?

"She could not refuse me then," said Fagin aloud. "Not for her life! The means are ready, and shall be set to work. I shall have you yet!"

He cast back a dark look, and a threatening motion of the hand, towards the spot where he had left the bolder villain, and went on his way.

CHAPTER 44

The next morning, Fagin drew up a chair at breakfast, seating himself opposite Noah.

"I want you, Bolter," said Fagin, leaning over the table, "to do a piece of work for me that needs great care and caution."

"I say," rejoined Bolter, "don't yer go shoving me into danger, or sending me any more o' yer police offices."

"There's not the smallest danger in it," said the Jew. "It's only to dodge a woman. Not to do anything, but to tell me where she goes, who she sees, and, if possible, what she says, and to bring me back all the information you can."

"What'll yer give me?" asked Noah.

"If you do it well, a pound, my dear," said Fagin, wishing to interest him in the scent as much as possible.

"Who is she?" inquired Noah.

"One of us."

"Oh Lor!" cried Noah, curling up his nose. "Yer doubtful of her, are yer?"

"She has found some new friends, and I must know who they are," replied Fagin.

"I'm your man," said Noah.

"I knew you would be," cried Fagin.

"Where is she? Where am I to wait for her?"

"I'll point her out at the proper time," said Fagin. "You keep ready, and leave the rest to me."

Six nights passed, and on each, Fagin came

home with a disappointed face, and briefly said that it was not yet time. On the seventh, he returned earlier, with an exultation he could not conceal. It was Sunday.

"She goes abroad tonight," said Fagin to Noah, "and on the right errand, I'm sure, the man she is afraid of will not be back much before daybreak. Come with me. Quick!"

They left the house stealthily, and hurrying through a labyrinth of streets, arrived at length before the Three Cripples.

It was past eleven o'clock, and the door was closed. It opened softly on its hinges as Fagin gave a low whistle. They entered, without noise, and the door was closed behind them.

Scarcely venturing to whisper, Fagin, and the young Jew who had admitted them, signed to Noah to climb up to a window and observe the person in the adjoining room.

"I can't see her face well," whispered Noah. "She is looking down, and the candle is behind her."

"Stay there," whispered Fagin. He signed to Barney, who withdrew. In an instant, the lad entered the room adjoining, and, under pretense of snuffing the candle, moved it in the required position, and, speaking to the girl, caused her to raise her face.

"I see her now," cried the spy.

"Plainly?"

"I should know her among a thousand."

He hastily descended, as the room door opened, and the girl came out. Fagin drew him behind a small partition, and they held their breaths as she passed within a few feet of them, and exited by the door at which they had entered.

"Hist!" cried the lad who held the door. "Dow."

Noah exchanged a look with Fagin, and darted out.

"To the left," whispered the lad, "and keep od the other side."

He did so, and, by the light of the lamps, saw the girl's retreating figure, already at some distance before him. He advanced as near as he considered prudent. She looked nervously round, twice or thrice, and once stopped to let two men who were following close behind her pass on. She seemed to gather courage as she advanced, and to walk with a steadier and firmer step. The spy preserved the same relative distance between them, and followed with his eye upon her.

CHAPTER 45

Two minutes after midnight, a young lady, accompanied by a gray-haired gentleman, alighted from a carriage within a short distance of London Bridge, and, having dismissed the vehicle, walked straight towards it. They had scarcely set foot upon its pavement, when the girl standing on the bridge immediately made towards them.

The couple walked onward, looking about them with little expectation, when they were suddenly joined by this new associate. They halted with an exclamation of surprise, but suppressed it immediately, for a man in the garments of a countryman brushed against them, at that precise moment.

"Not here," said Nancy hurriedly, "Come away—out of the public road—down the steps!"

As she indicated, with her hand, the direction in which she wished them to proceed, the countryman looked round, and roughly asking what they took up the whole pavement for, passed on.

The steps to which the girl had pointed formed a landing stairs from the river. To this spot, the countryman hastened unobserved and began to descend.

These stairs were a part of the bridge and consisted of three flights. Just below the end of the second, going down, the stone wall on the left terminated in an ornamental pilaster facing towards the Thames. At this point the lower steps widened, so that a person turning there was necessarily unseen by any others on the stairs above him. The countryman looked hastily round when he reached this point and slipped aside, and there waited.

He heard the sound of footsteps and directly afterwards voices close by. Scarcely breathing, he listened attentively.

"This is far enough," said the gentleman. "Why not have let me speak to you above, where it is light, and there is something stirring, instead of bringing us to this dark and dismal hole?"

"I was afraid to speak to you there," replied Nancy. "I don't know why it is, but I have such a dread upon me tonight that I can hardly stand." She shuddered.

"A fear of what?" asked the gentleman, who seemed to pity her.

"I scarcely know of what," replied the girl. "Horrible thoughts of death, and shrouds with blood upon them, and a fear that has made me burn as if I was on fire, have been upon me all day."

There was something so uncommon in her manner, that the flesh of the concealed listener crept as he heard the girl utter these words, and the blood chilled within him. He had never experienced a greater relief than in hearing the sweet voice of the young lady as she begged her to be calm, and not allow herself to become the prey of such fearful fancies.

"Speak to her kindly," said the young lady to her companion. "Poor creature! She seems to need it."

These words afforded Nancy time to recover herself. The gentleman, shortly afterwards, addressed himself to her.

"You were not here last Sunday night," he said.

"I couldn't come," replied Nancy. "I was kept by force."

"By whom?"

"Him that I told the young lady of before."

"He did not suspect you, I hope?" asked the old gentleman.

"No," replied the girl, shaking her head. "It's not very easy for me to leave him unless he knows why. I couldn't give him a drink of laudanum last Sunday."

"Did he awake before you returned from seeing Miss Maylie?" inquired the gentleman.

"No, and neither he nor any of them suspect me."

"Good," said the gentleman. "Now listen to me. This young lady has communicated to me, and to some other friends who can be safely trusted, what you told her nearly two weeks ago. I confess to you that I had doubts, at first, whether you were to be relied upon, but now I firmly believe you are."

"I am," said the girl earnestly.

"I repeat that I firmly believe it. To prove to you that I am disposed to trust you, I tell you that we propose to extort the secret, whatever it may be, from this man Monks. But if—if—" said the gentleman, "he cannot be secured, or, if secured, cannot be acted upon as we wish, you must deliver up the Jew."

"Fagin," cried the girl, recoiling. "I will not do it! I will never do it! Devil that he is, and worse than devil as he has been to me, I will never do that."

"You will not?" said the gentleman, who seemed fully prepared for this answer.

"Never!" returned the girl.

"Tell me why?"

"For one reason," rejoined the girl firmly, "that the lady knows and will stand by me in, for I have her promise. And for this other reason, besides that, bad life as he has led, I have led a bad life too. There are many of us who have kept the same path together, and I'll not turn upon them, who might have turned upon me, but didn't, bad as they are."

"Then," said the gentleman, quickly, "put Monks into my hands, and leave him to me to deal with."

"What if he turns against the others?"

"I promise you that in that case, if the truth is forced from him, there the matter will rest. There must be circumstances in Oliver's little history that it would be painful to drag before the public eye, and if the truth is once elicited, they shall go scot-free."

"And if it is not?" suggested the girl.

"Then," pursued the gentleman, "this Fagin shall not be brought to justice without your consent. In such a case I could show you reasons, I think, which would induce you to yield it."

"Have I the lady's promise for that?" asked the girl.

"You have," replied Rose. "My true and faithful pledge."

"Monks would never learn how you knew what you do?" said the girl, after a short pause.

"Never," replied the gentleman. "He could never even guess."

"I have been a liar, and among liars from a little child," said the girl, "but I will take your word."

After receiving an assurance from both that she might safely do so, she proceeded in a low voice to describe the public house whence she had been followed that night. From the manner in which she occasionally paused, it appeared as if the gentleman were making some hasty notes of the information. She thoroughly explained the localities of the place, the best position from which to watch it without exciting observation, and the night and hour on which Monks was most in the habit of frequenting it.

"He is tall," said the girl, "and a strongly made man, but not stout. He has a lurking walk, and as he walks, constantly looks over his shoulder, first on one side, and then on the other. Don't forget that, for his eyes are sunk in his head so much deeper than any other man's, that you might almost tell him by that alone. His face is dark, like his hair and eyes, and, although he can't be more than twenty-eight, withered and haggard. His lips are often discolored and disfigured with the marks of teeth, for he has desperate fits, and sometimes even bites his hands and covers them with wounds—why did you start?" said the girl, stopping suddenly.

The gentleman replied, in a hurried manner, that he was not conscious of having done so, and begged her to proceed.

"Part of this," said the girl, "I have drawn out from other people at the house I tell you of, for I have only seen him twice, and both times he was covered up in a large cloak. I think that's all I can give you to know him by. Wait, though," she added. "Upon his throat, so high that you can see a part of it below his neckerchief when he turns his face, there is—"

"A broad red mark, like a burn or scald?" cried the gentleman.

"How's this?" said the girl. "You know him!"

The young lady uttered a cry of surprise, and for a few moments they were so still that the listener could distinctly hear them breathe.

"I think I do," said the gentleman, breaking silence. "We shall see. Many people are singularly like each other. It may not be the same. Now, you have given us most valuable assistance, young woman, and I wish you to be the better for it. What can I do to serve you?"

"Nothing, sir," rejoined the girl, weeping. "You can do nothing to help me. I am past all hope, indeed."

"You are not beyond it," said the gentleman. "The past has been a dreary waste with you, of youthful energies misspent, but, for the future, you may hope. I do not say that it is in our power to offer you peace of heart and mind, for that must come as you seek it. But a quiet retreat, either in England, or, if you fear to remain here, in some foreign country, is not only within our ability but our most anxious wish to secure you. Before the dawn, you shall be placed as entirely beyond the reach of your former associates, and leave no trace behind you, as if you were to disappear from the earth this moment. Come! Quit them all, while there is time and opportunity!"

"She will be persuaded now," cried the young lady. "She hesitates, I am sure."

"I fear not, my dear," said the gentleman.

"No sir, I do not," replied the girl, after a short struggle. "I am chained to my old life. I loathe and hate it now, but I cannot leave it. I must have gone too far to turn back. But," she said, looking hastily round, "this fear comes over me again. I must go home."

"Home!" repeated the young lady, with great stress upon the word.

"Home, lady," rejoined the girl. "To such a home as I have made for myself with the work of my whole life. Let us part. I shall be watched or seen. Go! If I have done you any service all I ask is that you leave me, and let me go my way alone."

"It is useless," said the gentleman, with a sigh. "We compromise her safety, perhaps, by staying here."

"What," cried the young lady, "can be the end of this poor creature's life!"

"Look before you, lady. Look at that dark water. How many times do you read of such as I who spring into the tide, and leave no living thing to care for, or bewail them. I shall come to that at last."

"Do not speak thus, please," returned the young lady, sobbing.

"It will never reach your ears, dear lady, and God forbid such horrors should!" replied the girl. "Good night!"

"This purse," cried the young lady. "Take it for my sake, that you may have some resource in an hour of need and trouble."

"No!" replied the girl. "I have not done this for money. Let me have that to think of. And yet—give me something that you have worn. I should like to have something—no, no, not a ring—your gloves or handkerchief—anything that I can keep, as having belonged to you, sweet lady. There. God bless you. Good night!"

The sound of retreating footsteps was audible and the voices ceased.

The two figures of the young lady and her companion soon afterwards appeared upon the bridge. They stopped at the summit of the stairs.

"Hark!" cried the young lady, listening. "Did she call! I thought I heard her voice."

"No, my love," replied Mr. Brownlow, looking sadly back. "She has not moved, and will not till we are gone."

Rose Maylie lingered, but the old gentleman led her, with gentle force, away. As they disappeared, the girl sank down upon one of the stone stairs, and vented the anguish of her heart in bitter tears.

After a time she arose, and with feeble steps ascended the street. The astonished listener remained motionless for some minutes afterwards. Then he crept slowly from his hiding place, and returned, stealthily, in the same manner as he had descended.

Peeping out, more than once, when he reached the top, to make sure that he was unobserved, Noah Claypole made for the Jew's house as fast as his legs would carry him.

CHAPTER 46

I t was nearly two hours before daybreak. Fagin sat
in his old lair, with face so distorted and pale, and
eyes so red and bloodshot, that he looked less like a
man, than like some hideous phantom, moist from
the grave.

Stretched upon a mattress on the floor lay Noah
Claypole, fast asleep. Towards him the old man
sometimes looked. But his thoughts were busy elsewhere—hatred of the girl who had dared to conspire
with strangers; utter distrust of the sincerity of her
refusal to turn him in; bitter disappointment at the
loss of his revenge on Sikes; the fear of detection,
and ruin, and death; and a fierce and deadly rage kindled by all.

He sat without appearing to take the smallest
heed of time, until his quick ear heard a footstep in
the street.

"At last," he muttered, wiping his dry and
fevered mouth.

He crept upstairs to the door, and returned
accompanied by Sikes, who carried a bundle under
one arm.

"There!" he said, laying the bundle on the table.
"Do the most you can with it. It's been trouble
enough to get. I thought I should have been here
three hours ago."

Fagin locked the bundle in the cupboard, and
sat down again without speaking. Now that they sat
face to face, he looked fixedly at Sikes, with his lips

quivering so violently, and his face so altered by the emotions which had mastered him, that the house-breaker involuntarily drew back his chair, and surveyed him with a look of real fright.

"Wot do you look at a man so for?" cried Sikes.

"I've got something to tell you, Bill," said Fagin, drawing his chair nearer, "that will make you worse than me."

"Aye?" returned the robber with an incredulous air. "Tell away!"

"Suppose that lad that's laying there—" Fagin began, "—was to peach—to blow upon us all—first seeking out the right folks for the purpose, and then having a meeting with 'em in the street to describe every mark that they might know us by, and the crib where we might be most easily taken. Suppose he was to do all this of his own free will, not grabbed, trapped, tried; stealing out at nights to find those most interested against us, and peaching to them. Do you hear me?" cried the Jew, his eyes flashing with rage. "Suppose he did all this, what then?"

"What then!" replied Sikes. "If he was left alive till I came, I'd grind his skull under the iron heel of my boot into as many grains as there are hairs upon his head."

"What if I did it!" cried Fagin almost in a yell. "I, that knows so much, and could hang so many besides myself!"

Sikes clenched his teeth and turned white at the mere suggestion. "If I was tried along with you, I'd fall upon you in the open court, and beat your brains out afore the people. I would smash your head as if a loaded wagon had gone over it."

"If it was Charley, or the Dodger, or Bet, or—"

"I don't care who," replied Sikes impatiently. "Whoever it was, I'd serve them the same."

Fagin looked hard at the robber, and, motioning him to be silent, stooped over the bed upon the floor, and shook the sleeper to rouse him.

When his assumed name had been repeated several times, Noah rubbed his eyes, and, giving a heavy yawn, looked sleepily about him.

"Tell me that again about—*Nancy*—once again, just for him to hear," said Fagin, clutching Sikes by the wrist, as if to prevent his leaving the house before he had heard enough. "You followed her?"

"Yes."

"To London Bridge?"

"Yes."

"Where she met two people."

"So she did."

"A gentleman and a lady that she had gone to of her own accord before, who asked her to give up all her pals, and Monks first, which she did—and to describe him, which she did—and to tell her what house it was that we meet at, which she did—and where it could be best watched from, which she did—and what time the people went there, which she did. She told it all every word without a threat, she did— did she not?" cried Fagin, half-mad with fury.

"All right," replied Noah, scratching his head. "That's just what it was!"

"What did they say about last Sunday?"

"About last Sunday!" replied Noah, considering. "They asked her why she didn't come, last Sunday, as she promised. She said she couldn't."

"Why? Tell him that."

"Because she was forcibly kept at home by Bill,

the man she had told them of before," replied Noah.

"What more of him?" cried Fagin.

"Why, that she couldn't easily get out of doors unless he knew where she was going to," said Noah, "and so the first time she went to see the lady, she gave him a drink of laudanum."

"Hell's fire!" cried Sikes, breaking fiercely from the Jew. "Let me go!"

Flinging the old man from him, he rushed from the room, and darted, wildly and furiously, up the stairs. He pulled open the door, and dashed into the silent streets.

His teeth so tightly compressed that the strained jaw seemed starting through his skin, the robber held on his headlong course until he reached his own door. He opened it, softly, with a key, strode lightly up the stairs, and, entering his own room, double-locked the door. Then he drew back the curtain of the bed.

The girl was lying, half-dressed, upon it. He had woken her, for she raised herself with a startled look.

"Get up!" said the man.

"It is you, Bill!" said the girl, with an expression of pleasure at his return.

"It is," was the reply. "Get up."

Seeing the faint light of early day outside, the girl rose to undraw the curtain.

"Let it be," said Sikes. "There's enough light for wot I've got to do."

"Bill," said the girl, in the low voice of alarm, "why do you look like that at me!"

The robber sat regarding her, for a few seconds, with dilated nostrils and heaving chest. Then, grasp-ing her by the head and throat, dragged her into the middle of the room, and looking once towards the door, placed his heavy hand upon her mouth.

"Bill!" gasped the girl, wrestling with the strength of mortal fear—"I—I won't scream or cry—not once—hear me—speak to me—tell me what I have done!"

"You know, you she-devil!" returned the robber. "You were watched tonight. Every word you said was heard."

"Then spare my life for the love of Heaven, as I spared yours," rejoined the girl, clinging to him. "Bill, dear Bill, you cannot have the heart to kill me. Oh, think of all I have given up, only this one night, for you. Bill, Bill, for dear God's sake, for your own, for mine, stop before you spill my blood! I have been true to you, upon my guilty soul I have!"

The man struggled violently, to release his arms, but those of the girl were clasped round his, and fight her as he would, he could not tear them away.

"Bill," cried the girl, striving to lay her head upon his breast, "the gentleman and that dear lady told me tonight of a home in some foreign country where I could end my days in solitude and peace. Let me see them again, and beg them, on my knees, to show the same mercy and goodness to you. Let us both leave this dreadful place, and far apart lead better lives, and forget how we have lived, except in prayers, and never see each other more. It is never too late to repent. They told me so—I feel it now—but we must have time—a little, little time!"

The housebreaker freed one arm, and grasped his pistol. He beat it twice with all the force he could summon upon the upturned face that almost touched his own.

She staggered and fell, nearly blinded with the blood that rained down from a deep gash in her forehead. But raising herself, with difficulty, on her knees, she drew from her bosom a white handkerchief—Rose Maylie's own—and holding it up, in her folded hands, as high towards Heaven as her feeble strength would allow, breathed one prayer for mercy to her Maker.

It was a ghastly sight to look upon. The murderer staggered backward to the wall, and shutting out the sight with his hand, seized a heavy club and struck her down.

CHAPTER 47

The sun burst upon the crowded city, and lit up the room where the murdered woman lay. If the sight had been a ghastly one in the dull morning, what was it, now, in all that brilliant light!

There had been a moan and motion of the hand, and, with terror added to rage, he had struck and struck again. Once he threw a rug over it, but it was worse to imagine the eyes moving towards him, than to see them glaring upwards. He had plucked it off again. And there was the body, and so much blood!

He kindled a fire, and thrust the club into it. He held the weapon till it broke, and then piled it on the coals to burn away, and smolder into ashes. He washed himself, and rubbed his clothes. There were spots that would not be removed, but he cut the pieces out, and burnt them. How those stains were dispersed about the room! The very feet of the dog were bloody.

All this time he had never once turned his back upon the corpse. Such preparations completed, he moved, backward, towards the door, dragging the dog with him. He shut the door softly, locked it, took the key, and left the house.

He crossed over, and glanced up at the window, to be sure that nothing was visible from the outside. There was the curtain still drawn, which she would have opened to admit the light she never saw again. It was a relief to have got free of the room. He whistled at the dog, and walked rapidly away.

He went through Islington; strode up the hill at Highgate, uncertain where to go; struck off to the right again, and, taking the footpath across the fields, skirted Caen Wood, and so came on Hampstead Heath. Then he made to the fields at North End, in one of which he laid himself down under a hedge, and slept.

Soon he was up again, and away, back towards London by the high road—then back again into the country, wandering up and down in fields, and lying on hills to rest, and starting up to make for some other spot, and do the same, and ramble on again.

He shaped his course for Hatfield. It was nine o'clock at night, when, quite tired out, he and the dog turned down the hill by the church of the quiet village, and plodding along the little street, crept into a small public house. There was a fire in the tap room, and some country laborers were drinking before it.

He sat down in the furthest corner, and ate and drank alone, or rather with his dog, to whom he cast a morsel of food from time to time.

After paying his bill, the robber sat silent and unnoticed in his corner, and had almost dropped asleep, when he was half wakened by the noisy entrance of a newcomer.

This was an animated fellow, half-peddler and half-conman, who traveled about the country on foot to sell razors, washballs, harness paste, medicine for dogs and horses, cheap perfumery, cosmetics, and other such wares, which he carried in a case slung to his back. After he had eaten his supper, he opened his box of treasures.

"And what be that stoof? Good to eat, Harry?"

asked a grinning countryman, pointing to some cakes in one corner.

"This," said the fellow, producing one, "is the infallible and invaluable composition for removing all sorts of stain, rust, dirt, mildew, spick, speck, spot, or spatter, from silk, satin, linen, cloth, crepe, carpet, merino, muslin, or wool. Wine stains, fruit stains, beer stains, water stains, paint stains, any stains, all come out at one rub with the infallible and invaluable composition. If a lady stains her honor, she has only need to swallow one cake and she's cured at once—for it's poison. With all these virtues, one penny a square!"

There were two buyers directly, but more of the listeners plainly hesitated. The vendor observing this continued to talk.

"Here is a stain upon the hat of a gentleman in company, that I'll take clean out, before he can order me a pint of ale."

"Hah!" cried Sikes starting up. "Give that back."

"I'll take it clean out, sir," replied the man, winking to the company, "before you can come across the room to get it. Gentlemen all, observe the dark stain upon this gentleman's hat, no wider than a shilling, but thicker than a half-crown. Whether it is a wine stain, fruit stain, beer stain, water stain, paint stain, pitch stain, mud stain, or blood stain—"

The man got no further, for Sikes overthrew the table, and tearing the hat from him, burst out of the house.

The murderer, finding that he was not followed, and that they most probably considered him some drunken sullen fellow, turned back into the town, and getting out of the glare of the lamps of a stagecoach that was standing in the street, was walking past, when he recognized the mail from London, and saw that it was standing at the little post office. He crossed over, and listened.

The guard was standing at the door, waiting for the letter bag. A man, dressed like a gamekeeper, came up at the moment.

"Anything new up in town, Ben?" asked the gamekeeper.

"No, nothing that I knows of," replied the man, pulling on his gloves. "Corn's up a little. I heerd talk of a murder, too, down Spitalfields way, but I don't reckon much upon it."

"Oh, that's quite true," said a gentleman inside, who was looking out of the window. "And a dreadful murder it was."

"Was it, sir?" rejoined the guard, touching his hat. "Man or woman, pray, sir?"

"A woman," replied the gentleman. "It is supposed—"

"Now, Ben," replied the coachman impatiently.

"Damn that 'ere bag," said the guard, "are you gone to sleep in there?"

"Coming!" cried the office keeper, running out.

The horn sounded a few cheerful notes, and the coach was gone.

Sikes remained standing in the street, apparently unmoved by what he had just heard, and agitated by no stronger feeling than a doubt where to go. At length he went back again, and took the road that leads from Hatfield to St. Albans.

As he plunged into the solitude and darkness of the road, he felt a dread creeping upon him that shook him to the core. Every object before him, substance or shadow, looked like some fearful thing. But these fears were nothing compared to the sense that haunted him of that morning's ghastly figure following at his heels. He could hear its garments rustling in the leaves, and every breath of wind came laden with that last low cry. If he stopped it did the same. If he ran, it followed.

At times, he turned, resolved to beat this phantom off. But the hair rose on his head, and his blood stood still, for it had turned with him and was behind him then. He had kept it before him that morning, but it was behind now—always. He leaned his back against a bank, and felt that it stood above him, visibly out against the cold night sky. He threw himself upon the road, on his back. At his head it stood, silent, erect, and still—a living gravestone.

There was a shed in a field he passed, which offered shelter for the night. Before the door were three tall poplar trees, which made it very dark within, and the wind moaned through them. Here he stretched himself close to the wall—to undergo new torture.

Now, a vision came before him, more terrible than that from which he had escaped. Those widely staring eyes, so glassy, appeared in the midst of the darkness. There were but two, but they were everywhere. If he shut out the sight, there came the room with every well-known object, each in its accustomed place. The body was in *its* place, and its eyes were as he saw them when he stole away. He got up, and rushed into the field. The figure was behind him. He re-entered the shed, and shrunk down once more. The eyes were there, before he had laid himself down.

And here he remained in terror, trembling in

every limb, and the cold sweat starting from every pore, when suddenly there came the noise of distant shouting, and the roar of voices mingled in alarm and wonder. Springing to his feet, he rushed into the open air.

The broad sky seemed on fire. Rising into the air with showers of sparks were sheets of flame, lighting the atmosphere for miles round, and driving clouds of smoke in the direction where he stood. He could hear the cry of Fire! mingled with the ringing of an alarm bell, the fall of heavy bodies, and the crackling of flames. There were people there, light and bustle. It was like new life to him. He darted onward, leaping gate and fence as madly as his dog.

He came upon the spot. There were half-dressed figures tearing to and fro, some trying to drag the frightened horses from the stables, others driving the cattle from the yard and outhouses, and others coming laden from the burning pile, amidst a shower of falling sparks, and the tumbling down of red-hot beams. The openings, where doors and windows stood an hour ago, disclosed a mass of raging fire; walls rocked and crumbled into the burning well. Women and children shrieked, and men encouraged each other with noisy shouts and cheers. The clanking of the engine pumps, and hissing of the water as it fell upon the blazing wood, added to the tremendous roar. He shouted, too, till he was hoarse; and flying from memory and himself, plunged into the thickest of the throng.

Hither and thither he dived that night, now working at the pumps, and now hurrying through the smoke and flame. Up and down the ladders, upon the roofs of buildings, over floors that quaked and trembled with his weight, under the path of falling bricks and stones, in every part of that great fire was he. But he bore a charmed life, and had neither scratch nor bruise, nor weariness nor thought, till morning dawned again, and only smoke and blackened ruins remained.

This mad excitement over, there returned, with ten-fold force, the dreadful consciousness of his crime. He looked suspiciously about him, for the men were conversing in groups, and he feared to be the subject of their talk. He and the dog went off, stealthily, together. He passed near an engine where some men were seated, and they called to him to share in their refreshment. He took some bread and meat; and as he took a drink of beer, heard the firemen, who were from London, talking about the murder. "He has gone to Birmingham, they say," said one, "but they'll have him yet, for the scouts are out."

He hurried off, and walked till he almost dropped upon the ground. Then he lay down in a lane, and had a long, but broken and uneasy sleep. He wandered on again, fearful of another solitary night.

Suddenly, he decided on going back to London.

"There's somebody to speak to there, at all events," he thought. "A good hiding place, too. They'll never expect to nab me there. Why can't I lie low for a week or so, and, forcing money from Fagin, get abroad to France? Damn, I'll risk it."

The dog, though. It would not be forgotten that the dog was missing, and had probably gone with him. This might lead to his apprehension as he passed along the streets. He decided to drown him, and walked on, looking about for a pond. He picked up a heavy stone and tied it to his handkerchief as he went.

The animal looked up into his master's face during these preparations, and he lagged a little farther back than usual. When his master halted at the brink of a pool, and looked round to call him, he stopped outright.

"Do you hear me call? Come here!" cried Sikes.

The animal came up from the force of habit. But as Sikes stooped to attach the handkerchief to his throat, he uttered a low growl and started back.

"Come back!" said the robber.

The dog wagged his tail, but moved not. Sikes called him again.

The dog advanced, retreated, paused an instant, and darted away at his hardest speed.

The man whistled again and again, and sat down and waited in the expectation that he would return. But no dog appeared, and at length he resumed his journey.

CHAPTER 48

The twilight was beginning to close in, when Mr. Brownlow alighted from a coach at his own door, and knocked softly. The door being opened, a sturdy man got out of the coach and stationed himself on one side of the steps, while another man, who had been seated on the box, dismounted too, and stood upon the other side. At a sign from Mr. Brownlow, they helped out a third man, and taking him between them, hurried him into the house. This man was Monks.

Mr. Brownlow led the way into a backroom. At the door of this apartment, Monks, who had ascended with evident reluctance, stopped. The two men looked at the old gentleman as if for instructions.

"He knows the alternative," said Mr. Brownlow. "If he hesitates or moves a finger except as you bid him, drag him into the street, call for the aid of the police, and impeach him as a felon in my name."

"How dare you say this of me?" asked Monks.

"How dare you urge me to it, young man?" replied Mr. Brownlow, confronting him with a steady look. "Are you mad enough to leave this house? Unhand him. There, sir. You are free to go, and we to follow. But I warn you, by all I hold most sacred, that instant will have you apprehended on a charge of fraud and robbery. I am resolute. If you are determined to be the same, your blood will be upon your own head!"

Monks was plainly disconcerted, and alarmed besides. He hesitated.

"You will decide quickly," said Mr. Brownlow, with perfect composure. "If you wish me to make my charges publicly, and consign you to a punishment that I cannot control, then you know the way. If not, and you appeal to my caution, and the mercy of those you have deeply injured, seat yourself in that chair."

"Is there—" demanded Monks—"is there—no middle course?"

"None."

Monks, reading in the gentleman's face nothing but severity and determination, walked into the room, and, shrugging his shoulders, sat down.

"Lock the door on the outside," said Mr. Brownlow to the attendants, "and come when I ring."

The two were left alone together.

"This is nice treatment, sir," said Monks, throwing down his hat and cloak, "from my father's oldest friend."

"It is because I was your father's oldest friend, young man," returned Mr. Brownlow. "It is because he knelt with me beside his only sister's deathbed when he was yet a boy, on the morning that would have made her my young wife. It is because my seared heart clung to him, from that time forth, through all his trials and errors, till he died. It is because old recollections filled my heart, and even the sight of you brings old thoughts of him. It is because of all these things that I am moved to treat you gently now—yes, Edward Leeford, even now—and blush for your unworthiness to bear the name."

"What is the name to me?" asked the other.

"Nothing," replied Mr. Brownlow, "nothing to

you. But it was *hers*. I am glad you have changed it—very."

"This is all mighty fine," said Monks, after a long silence, during which he had jerked himself in sullen defiance to and fro. "But what do you want with me?"

"You have a brother," said Mr. Brownlow.

"I have no brother," replied Monks. "You know I was an only child. Why do you talk to me of brothers?"

"I shall interest you by and by," said Mr. Brownlow. "I know that from the wretched marriage, into which family pride, and the most sordid of all ambition, forced your unhappy father when a mere boy, you were the only and most unnatural offspring."

"I don't care for hard names," interrupted Monks with a jeering laugh.

"But I also know," pursued the old gentleman, "the slow torture, of that union. I know how indifference gave way to dislike, dislike to hate, and hate to loathing, until at last they wrenched the bond asunder, and retiring a wide space apart, carried each a painful fragment, to hide it beneath the happiest faces they could assume. Your mother succeeded; she forgot it soon. But it rusted and cankered at your father's heart for years."

"Well, they were separated," said Monks, "and what of that?"

"When they had been separated for some time," returned Mr. Brownlow, "and your mother had utterly forgotten the young husband ten good years her junior, who, with prospects ruined, lingered on at home, he fell among new friends. I speak of fifteen years ago, when you were not more than eleven years old, and your father but thirty-one. These new friends were a naval officer retired from active service, whose wife had died some half-a-year before, and left him with two children. They were both daughters— one a beautiful creature of nineteen, and the other a mere child of two or three years old."

"What's this to me?" asked Monks.

"Acquaintance, intimacy, friendship, fast followed on each other," said Mr. Brownlow. "Your father was gifted as few men are, and he had his sister's soul. As the old officer knew him more and more, he grew to love him. His daughter did the same."

The old gentleman paused. Monks was biting his lips, with his eyes fixed upon the floor.

"The end of a year found him promised to that daughter—he was the object of the first, true, and only passion of a naive girl. At length one of those rich relations, for whose interest and importance your father had been sacrificed, died, and left him his cure for all griefs—money. He had to go immediately to Rome, where this man had died, leaving his affairs in great confusion. He went and was seized with mortal illness there. He was followed, the moment the news reached Paris, by your mother, who carried you with her. He died the day after her arrival, leaving no will—so that the whole property fell to her and you."

At this part of the recital Monks held his breath, and wiped his hot face and hands.

"Before he went abroad," said Mr. Brownlow, slowly, and fixing his eyes upon the other's face, "he came to me."

"I never heard of that," interrupted Monks in a

tone of disagreeable surprise.

"He left with me, among some other things, a portrait painted by himself—a likeness of this poor girl—which he did not wish to leave behind, and could not carry on his hasty journey. He was worn by anxiety and remorse almost to a shadow. He talked in a wild, distracted way, of ruin and dishonor worked by himself. He confided to me his intention to convert his whole property, at any loss, into money, and, having settled on his wife and you a portion of his recent inheritance, to flee the country—I guessed too well he would not fly alone—and never see it more. Even from me, his old friend, he withheld any more information, promising to write and tell me all, and after that to see me once again, for the last time on earth. Alas! *That* was the last time. I had no letter, and I never saw him more."

"I went," said Mr. Brownlow, after a short pause, "when all was over, to the scene of his guilty love, resolved that if my fears were realized that the girl should find a home to shelter and care for her. The family had left a week before by night. Why, or whither, none can tell."

Monks drew his breath yet more freely, and looked round with a smile of triumph.

"When your brother," said Mr. Brownlow, drawing nearer to the other's chair, "a feeble, ragged, neglected child, was cast in my way by a stronger hand than chance, and rescued by me from a life of vice and infamy—"

"What?" cried Monks.

"By me," said Mr. Brownlow. "I told you I should interest you before long. When he was rescued by me, then, and lay recovering from sickness in my house, his strong resemblance to this picture I have spoken of, struck me with astonishment. Even when I first saw him in all his dirt and misery, there was a lingering expression in his face that seemed like a glimpse of some old friend. I need not tell you he was snared away before I knew his history—"

"Why not?" asked Monks hastily.

"Because you know it well."

"I!"

"Denial to me is vain," replied Mr. Brownlow. "I shall show you that I know more than that."

"You—you—can't prove anything against me," stammered Monks. "I defy you to do it!"

"We shall see," returned the old gentleman with a searching glance. "I lost the boy, and could not recover him. Your mother being dead, I knew that you alone could solve the mystery if anybody could. When I had last heard of you, you were on your own estate in the West Indies, so I made the voyage. You had left it, months before, and were supposed to be in London, but no one could tell where. I returned. Your agents had no clue to your residence. You came and went, they said, as strangely as you had ever done, mingling with the same infamous herd who had been your associates when a fierce ungovernable boy. I paced the streets by night and day, but until two hours ago, all my efforts were fruitless, and I never saw you for an instant."

"And now you do see me," said Monks, rising boldly, "what then? Fraud and robbery are high-sounding words—justified, you think, by an imagined resemblance in some young imp to an idle fling of a dead man! You don't even know that a child was born of this maudlin pair."

"I *did not*," replied Mr. Brownlow, rising too. "But within the last two weeks I have learnt it all. You have a brother; you know it, and him. There was a will, which your mother destroyed, leaving the secret to you at her own death. It contained a reference to some child likely to be the result of this sad connection. This child was accidentally encountered by you, and you went to the place of his birth, where you destroyed the proofs of his birth and parentage. Now, in your own words to your accomplice Fagin, 'the only proofs of the boy's identity lie at the bottom of the river, and the old hag that received them from the mother is rotting in her coffin.'

"Unworthy son, coward, liar—you, who associate with thieves and murderers—you, whose plots have brought a violent death upon the head of one worth millions such as you—you, who from your cradle were bitterness to your own father's heart, and in whom all evil passions and vice festered, till they came out in a hideous disease that has made your face an index even to your mind—you, Edward Leeford, do you still defy me!"

"No, no, no!" returned the coward, overwhelmed by these accumulated charges.

"Every word!" cried the gentleman, "every word that has passed between you and this detested villain, is known to me. Shadows on the wall have caught your whispers, and brought them to my ear; the sight of the persecuted child has overcome vice itself, and given it the courage and almost the attributes of virtue. Murder has been done, to which you were morally a party."

"No, no," interposed Monks. "I—I knew nothing of that. I didn't know the cause. I thought it was a common quarrel."

"It was the partial disclosure of your secrets," replied Mr. Brownlow. "Will you disclose the whole?"

"Yes, I will."

"Sign a statement of facts, and repeat it before witnesses?"

"That I promise too."

"Remain quietly here, until such a document is drawn up, and proceed with me for the purpose of bearing witness?"

"If you insist upon that, I'll do that also," replied Monks.

"You must do more than that," said Mr. Brownlow. "Make restitution to an innocent and unoffending child. Carry the provisions of the will into execution so far as your brother is concerned, and then go where you please. In this world you need meet him no more."

While Monks was pacing up and down, meditating with a dark look on this proposal and the possibilities of evading it, the door was hurriedly unlocked, and Mr. Losberne entered the room in violent agitation.

"The murderer will be taken tonight," he cried. "His dog has been seen lurking about some old haunt, and there seems little doubt that his master either is, or will be, there, at dark. I have spoken to the men who are charged with his capture, and they tell me he cannot escape. A reward of a hundred pounds is proclaimed by the government tonight."

"I will give fifty more," said Mr. Brownlow. "What of Fagin?"

"When I last heard, he had not been taken, but

he will be, or is, by this time. They're sure of him."

"Have you made up your mind?" asked Mr. Brownlow, in a low voice, of Monks.

"Yes," he replied. "You—you—will be secret with me?"

"I will. Remain here till I return. It is your only hope of safety."

They left the room, and the door was again locked.

"Write and set the evening after tomorrow, at seven, for the meeting," said Mr. Brownlow to the doctor. "We shall be down there a few hours before, but shall require rest, especially the young lady. But now my blood boils to avenge this poor murdered creature. Which way have they taken?"

"Drive straight to the office and you will be in time," replied Mr. Losberne. "I will remain here."

The two gentlemen hastily separated, each in a fever of excitement wholly uncontrollable.

CHAPTER 49

Near to that part of the Thames where the buildings on the banks are dirtiest and the vessels on the river blackest with the dust and the smoke, stands Jacob's Island, surrounded by a muddy ditch, six or eight feet deep and fifteen or twenty wide when the tide is in, known as Folly Ditch. At such times, a stranger, looking from one of the wooden bridges thrown across it at Mill Lane, will see the inhabitants of the houses on either side lowering from their back doors and windows, buckets, pails, domestic utensils of all kinds, in which to haul the water up.

The houses themselves have crazy wooden balconies, with holes from which to look upon the slime beneath; windows, broken and patched; rooms small and filthy; dirt-besmeared walls and decaying foundations; every loathsome indication of filth, rot, and garbage; all these ornament the banks of Folly Ditch.

In an upper room of one of these houses, there were assembled three men, who sat for some time in gloomy silence. One of these was Toby Crackit, another Mr. Chitling, and the third a robber of fifty years, whose nose had been almost beaten in, in some old scuffle, and whose face bore a frightful scar. This man was an ex-convict, and his name was Kags.

"I wish," said Toby turning to Mr. Chitling, "that you had picked out some other crib when the two old ones got too warm, and had not come here, my fine feller."

"Why didn't you, blunderhead!" said Kags.

"Well, I thought you'd have been a little more glad to see me than this," replied Mr. Chitling, with a melancholy air.

There was a short silence, after which Toby Crackit turned to Chitling and said, "When was Fagin took then?"

"Two o'clock this afternoon. Charley and I made our lucky up the chimney, and Bolter got into the empty water butt, head downwards. But his legs were so long that they stuck out at the top, and so they took him too."

"And Bet?"

"Poor Bet! She went to see them," replied Chitling, his face falling more and more, "and went off mad, screaming and raving, and beating her head against the boards. So they put a straitjacket on her and took her to the hospital."

"Wot's come of young Bates?" demanded Kags.

"He'll be here soon," replied Chitling. "There's nowhere else to go to now, for the people at the Cripples are all in custody, and the place is filled with traps."

"This is a smash," observed Toby, biting his lips. "There's more than one will go with this."

"If they get the inquest over," said Kags, "and Bolter turns King's evidence, as of course he will, they can prove Fagin an accessory before the fact, and get the trial on Friday, and he'll swing in six days from this, by God!"

"You should have heard the people yell," said Chitling, "the officers fought like devils, or they'd have torn him away. You should have seen how he looked about him, all muddy and bleeding, and clung to them as if they were his dearest friends. I can see 'em now, the people jumping up, and snarling with their teeth. I can see the blood upon his hair and beard, and hear the cries from women in the crowd, who swore they'd tear his heart out!"

The horror-stricken witness of this scene pressed his hands upon his ears, and with his eyes closed got up and paced violently to and fro.

While he was thus engaged, and the two men sat by in silence with their eyes fixed upon the floor, a pattering noise was heard upon the stairs, and Sikes's dog bounded into the room. They ran to the window, downstairs, and into the street. The dog had jumped in at an open window. He made no attempt to follow them, nor was his master to be seen.

"What's the meaning of this?" said Toby when they had returned. "He can't be coming here. I—I— hope not."

"If he was coming here, he'd have come with the dog," said Kags, stooping down to examine the animal, who lay panting on the floor. "Here! Give us some water for him. He has run himself faint."

"He's drunk it all up, every drop," said Chitling after watching the dog some time in silence. "Covered with mud—lame—half-blind—he must have come a long way."

"Where can he have come from!" exclaimed Toby. "He's been to the other hideouts of course, and finding them filled with strangers come on here, where he's been many a time and often. But where can he have come from first, and how comes he here alone without the other!"

"He can't have done away with himself. What do you think?" said Chitling.

Toby shook his head.

"If he had," said Kags, "the dog 'ud want to lead us away to where he did it. No. I think he's got out of the country, and left the dog behind. He must have given him the slip somehow."

This explanation was accepted as the truth. The dog, creeping under a chair, coiled himself up to sleep.

It being now dark, the shutter was closed, and a candle lighted and placed upon the table. They drew their chairs closer together, starting at every sound. They spoke little, and were as awe-stricken as if the remains of the murdered woman lay in the next room.

They had sat thus, some time, when suddenly there came a hurried knocking at the door below.

Crackit went to the window, and shaking all over, drew in his head. There was no need to tell them who it was—his pale face was enough. The dog too was on the alert in an instant, and ran whining to the door.

"We must let him in," he said, taking up the candle.

"Isn't there any help for it?" asked the other man in a hoarse voice.

"None. He *must* come in."

Crackit went down to the door, and returned followed by a man with the lower part of his face buried in a handkerchief, and another tied over his head under his hat. He drew them slowly off. Blanched face, sunken eyes, hollow cheeks, beard of three days' growth, wasted flesh—it was the very ghost of Sikes.

He laid his hand upon a chair in the middle of the room, and seeming to glance over his shoulder, dragged it back close to the wall—as close as it would go—and sat down.

He looked from one to another in silence. If an eye were furtively raised and met his, it was instantly averted. When his hollow voice broke silence, they all three started.

"How came that dog here?" he asked.

"Alone. Three hours ago."

"Tonight's paper says that Fagin's took. Is it true, or a lie?"

"True."

They were silent again.

"Damn you all!" said Sikes, passing his hand across his forehead. "Have you nothing to say to me?"

There was an uneasy movement among them, but nobody spoke.

"You that keep this house," said Sikes, turning his face to Crackit, "do you mean to sell me, or to let me lie here till this hunt is over?"

"You may stop here, if you think it safe," returned Toby, after some hesitation.

Sikes said, "Is—it—the body—is it buried?"

They shook their heads.

"Why isn't it!" he retorted with a glance behind him. "Wot do they keep such ugly things above the ground for?—Who's that knocking?"

Crackit left the room, and directly he came back with Charley Bates behind him. Sikes sat opposite the door, so that the moment the boy entered the room he encountered his figure.

"Toby," said the boy falling back, as Sikes turned his eyes towards him, "why didn't you tell me this, downstairs?"

Sikes nodded, and made as though he would shake hands with him.

"Let me go into some other room," said the boy, retreating still farther.

"Charley!" said Sikes, stepping forward. "Don't you—don't you know me?"

"Don't come near me," answered the boy, still retreating, and looking, with horror in his eyes, upon the murderer's face. "You monster!"

The man stopped halfway, and they looked at each other; but Sikes's eyes sank gradually to the ground.

"Witness you three," cried the boy shaking his clenched fist, and becoming more excited as he spoke. "I'm not afraid of him—if they come here after him, I'll give him up, I will. He may kill me for it if he likes, but if I am here I'll give him up. I'd give him up if he was to be boiled alive. Murder! Help! If there's the pluck of a man among you three, you'll help me. Murder! Help! Down with him!"

Pouring out these cries, the boy actually threw himself upon the strong man, and in the intensity of his energy and the suddenness of his surprise, brought him heavily to the ground.

The three spectators seemed quite stupefied. They offered no interference, and the boy and man rolled on the ground together. The boy, heedless of the blows that showered upon him, never stopped calling for help with all his might.

The contest, however, was too unequal to last long. Sikes had him down, and his knee was on his throat, when Crackit pulled him back with a look of alarm, and pointed to the window. There were lights gleaming below, voices of conversation, and hurried footsteps crossing the nearest wooden bridge. One man on horseback seemed to be among the crowd.

The gleam of lights increased and the footsteps came more thickly and noisily on. Then there was a loud knocking at the door, and then a hoarse murmur from such a multitude of angry voices as would have made the boldest shake.

"Help!" shrieked the boy. "He's here! Break down the door!"

"In the King's name," cried the voices outside.

"Break down the door!" screamed the boy. "I tell you they'll never open it. Run straight to the room where the light is. Break down the door!"

Strokes, thick and heavy, rattled upon the door and lower-window shutters.

"Open the door of some place where I can lock this screeching hellion," cried Sikes fiercely, running to and fro, and dragging the boy, now, as easily as if he were an empty sack. "That door. Quick!" He flung him in, bolted it, and turned the key. "Is the downstairs door fast?"

"Double-locked and chained," replied Crackit, who, with the other two men, still remained quite helpless and bewildered.

"Damn you!" cried the desperate ruffian, throwing up the window and menacing the crowd. "Do your worst! I'll cheat you yet!"

Of all the terrific yells that ever fell on mortal ears, none could exceed the cry of the infuriated throng. Some shouted to those who were nearest to set the house on fire; others roared to the officers to shoot him dead. Among them all, none showed such fury as the man on horseback, who, throwing himself out of the saddle, and bursting through the crowd as if he were parting water, cried, beneath the window, in a voice that rose above all others,

"Twenty pounds to the man who brings a ladder!"

The nearest voices took up the cry, and hundreds echoed it. Some called for ladders, some for sledgehammers. Some ran with torches to and fro as if to seek them, and still came back and roared again. Some among the boldest attempted to climb up by the water spout and crevices in the wall.

"The tide," cried the murderer, as he staggered back into the room, "the tide was in as I came up. Give me a long rope. They're all in front. I may drop into the Folly Ditch, and clear off that way. Give me a rope, or I shall do three more murders and kill myself."

The panic-stricken men pointed to where such articles were kept. The murderer, hastily selecting the longest and strongest cord, hurried up to the housetop.

All the windows in the rear of the house had been long ago bricked up, except one small one in the room where the boy was locked, and that was too small even for the passage of his body. But he had never ceased to call to those outside, to guard the back. Thus, when the murderer emerged at last on the housetop by the door in the roof, a loud shout proclaimed the fact to those in front, who immediately began to pour round.

He planted a board, which he had carried up with him for the purpose, so firmly against the door that it must have been a matter of great difficulty to open it from the inside. Creeping over the tiles, he looked over the low parapet.

The water was out, and the ditch a bed of mud.

The crowd had been hushed during these few moments, but the instant they saw his intention and knew it was defeated, they raised a cry of triumph.

Those who were at too great a distance to know its meaning, took up the sound. It seemed as though the whole city had poured its population out to curse him.

The houses on the opposite side of the ditch had been entered by the mob. There were faces in every window and cluster upon cluster of people clinging to every housetop. Each of the three little bridges bent beneath the weight of the crowd upon it.

"They have him now," cried a man on the nearest bridge. "Hurrah!"

"I will give fifty pounds," cried an old gentleman from the same spot, "to the man who takes him alive."

There was another roar. At this moment the word was passed among the crowd that the door was forced at last, and that he who had first called for the ladder had mounted into the room. People at the windows ran into the street, each man crushing and striving with his neighbor, and all panting with impatience to get near the door, and look upon the criminal as the officers brought him out. The cries and shrieks of those who were pressed almost to suffocation, or trampled down in the confusion, were dreadful, and the attention was distracted from the murderer, although the universal eagerness for his capture was, if possible, increased.

The man had shrunk down, cowed by the ferocity of the crowd, and the impossibility of escape. But seeing this sudden change, he sprang upon his feet, determined to make one last effort for his life by dropping into the ditch, and attempt to creep away in the darkness and confusion.

Roused by the noise within the house that

announced that someone had entered, he set his foot against the stack of chimneys, fastened one end of the rope tightly and firmly round it, and with the other made a strong running noose by the aid of his hands and teeth almost in a second. He could let himself down by the cord to within a less distance of the ground than his own height, and had his knife ready in his hand to cut it then and drop.

At the instant when he brought the loop over his head previous to slipping it beneath his armpits, and when the old gentleman before-mentioned earnestly warned those about him that the man was about to lower himself down—at that instant the murderer, looking behind him on the roof, threw his arms above his head, and uttered a yell of terror.

"The eyes again!" he cried in an unearthly screech.

Staggering as if struck by lightning, he lost his balance and tumbled over the parapet. The noose was on his neck. It ran up with his weight, tight as a bow string, and swift as an arrow. He fell for thirty-five feet. There was a sudden jerk, a terrific convulsion of the limbs, and there he hung, with the open knife clenched in his stiffening hand.

The murderer swung lifeless against the wall, and Charley Bates, thrusting aside the dangling body that obscured his view, called to the people to come and take him out, for God's sake.

A dog ran backward and forward on the parapet with a dismal howl, and collecting himself for a spring, jumped for the dead man's shoulders. Missing his aim, he fell into the ditch, turning completely over as he went, and striking his head against a stone, dashed out his brains.

CHAPTER 50

Two days later, Oliver found himself, at three o'clock in the afternoon, in a traveling carriage rolling fast towards his native town. Mrs. Maylie, and Rose, and Mrs. Bedwin, and the good doctor were with him, and Mr. Brownlow followed in a post chaise, accompanied by one other person whose name had not been mentioned.

They had not talked much upon the way, for all were in a flutter of agitation and uncertainty. Oliver and the two ladies had been told by Mr. Brownlow of Monks' confession. The same kind friend had also prevented them from learning of the dreadful occurrences that so recently had taken place, until a better time presented itself.

But while Oliver had remained silent, his mind ran back to old times, and a crowd of emotions awoke when they turned into that road that he had traversed on foot—a poor, homeless, wandering boy, without a friend to help him.

"See there!" cried Oliver, eagerly clasping Rose's hand, and pointing out at the carriage window. "There are the hedges I crept behind, for fear anyone should overtake me and force me back! Yonder is the path across the fields, leading to the old house where I was a little child! Oh Dick, my dear old friend, if I could only see you now!"

"You will see him soon," replied Rose. "You shall tell him how happy you are, and how rich you have grown, and that you have come back to make him happy, too."

"Yes," said Oliver, "and we'll take him away from here, and have him clothed and taught, and send him to some quiet country place where he may grow strong and well—shall we?"

Rose nodded "yes," for the boy was smiling through such happy tears that she could not speak.

As they drove through the town, Oliver pointed out Sowerberry's, just as it used to be; there was the workhouse, the dreary prison of his youthful days, with scores of faces at the doors and windows that he knew quite well—there was nearly everything as if he had left it but yesterday, and all his recent life had been but a happy dream.

They drove straight to the door of the chief hotel. Mr. Grimwig was ready to receive them. There was dinner prepared, and there were bedrooms ready, and everything was arranged as if by magic.

When the hurry of the first half-hour was over, the same silence prevailed that had marked their journey down. Mr. Brownlow did not join them at dinner, but remained in a separate room. The two other gentlemen hurried in and out with anxious faces. Once, Mrs. Maylie was called away, and after being absent for nearly an hour, returned with eyes swollen with weeping. All these things made Rose and Oliver, who were not in on any of the secrets, nervous and uncomfortable.

When nine o'clock had come, Mr. Losberne and Mr. Grimwig entered the room, followed by Mr. Brownlow and a man whom Oliver almost shrieked with surprise to see, for they told him it was his brother, and it was the same man he had met at the market-town, and seen looking in with Fagin at the

window of his little room. Monks cast a look of hate
at the astonished boy, and sat down near the door.
Mr. Brownlow, who had papers in his hand, walked
to a table near which Rose and Oliver were seated.

"This is a painful task," said he, "but these dec-
larations, which have been signed in London before
many gentlemen, must be repeated here. We must
hear them from your own lips before we part, and
you know why."

"Go on," said Monks, turning away his face.
"Quick. Don't keep me here."

"This child," said Mr. Brownlow, drawing
Oliver to him, and laying his hand upon his head, "is
your half-brother—the illegitimate son of your
father, my dear friend Edward Leeford, by poor
young Agnes Fleming, who died in giving him
birth."

"Yes," said Monks, scowling at the trembling
boy. "You have the story there." He pointed impatiently to the papers as he spoke.

"I must have it here, too," said Mr. Brownlow,
looking round upon the listeners.

"Listen then!" returned Monks. "His father
being taken ill at Rome, was joined by his wife, my
mother, from whom he had been long separated,
who went from Paris and took me with her—to look
after his property. He knew nothing of us, for his
senses were gone, and he slumbered on till next day,
when he died. Among the papers in his desk were
two, dated on the night his illness first came on,
directed to yourself"—he addressed himself to Mr.
Brownlow. "One of these papers was a letter to this
girl Agnes, the other a will."

"What of the letter?" asked Mr. Brownlow.

"A sheet of paper with a confession, and prayers to God to help her. He had palmed a tale on the girl that some secret mystery—to be explained one day— prevented his marrying her just then. So she had trusted him, until she trusted too far, and lost what none could ever give her back. She was, at that time, within a few months of her confinement. He begged her, if he died, not to curse his memory, or think that their sin would be visited on their young child, for all the guilt was his. He reminded her of the little locket and the ring with her first name engraved upon it, and a blank left for the surname that he hoped one day to give her. He begged her to wear it next to her heart."

"The will," said Mr. Brownlow, as Oliver's tears fell fast.

Monks was silent.

"The will," said Mr. Brownlow, speaking for him, "talked of miseries that his wife had brought upon him; of the rebellious disposition, vice and malice of you his only son, who had been trained to hate him. He left you, and your mother, each an annuity of eight hundred pounds. The bulk of his property he divided into two equal portions—one for Agnes Fleming, and the other for their child, if it should be born alive, and ever come of age. If it were a girl, it was to inherit the money unconditionally. But if a boy, only on the stipulation that in his youth he should never have stained his name with any public act of dishonor, meanness, cowardice, or wrong. He did this, he said, to show his conviction that the child would share her gentle heart, and noble nature. If he were disappointed in this expectation, then the money was to come to you. For then, when both children were equal, he would recognize your prior claim upon his purse, who had none upon his heart, but had, from an infant, repulsed him with coldness."

"My mother," said Monks, in a louder tone, "burnt this will. The letter never reached its destination. The girl's father heard the truth from her. Goaded by shame and dishonor he fled with his children into a remote corner of Wales, changing his name so that his friends might never know of him, and no great while afterwards, he was found dead in his bed. The girl had left her home, in secret, some weeks before. He had searched for her in every town and village nearby. It was on the night when he returned home, assured that she had destroyed herself, that his old heart broke."

There was a short silence here, until Mr. Brownlow took up the thread of the story.

"Years after this," he said, "this man's—Edward Leeford's—mother came to me. He had left her, when only eighteen; robbed her of jewels and money; gambled, squandered, forged, and fled to London, where for two years he had associated with the lowest outcasts. She had a painful and incurable disease, and wished to recover him before she died. Inquiries were made, and were ultimately successful. He went back with her to France."

"There she died," said Monks, "after a lingering illness. On her deathbed, she bequeathed these secrets to me, together with her hatred of all whom they involved. She was convinced that a male child had been born, and was alive. I swore to her to hunt it down, to vent upon it the hatred that I deeply felt, and to drag it, if I could, to the very gallows. She was right. He came in my way at last. I began well, and, but for babbling whores, I would have finished as I began!"

As the villain muttered curses, Mr. Brownlow turned to the terrified group beside him, and explained that Fagin had a large reward for keeping Oliver ensnared, of which some part was to be given up in the event of his being rescued. A dispute about this matter had led to their visit to the country house for the purpose of identifying him.

"The locket and ring?" said Mr. Brownlow, turning to Monks.

"I bought them from the man and woman I told you of, who stole them from the nurse, who stole them from the corpse," answered Monks without raising his eyes. "You know what became of them."

Mr. Brownlow merely nodded to Mr. Grimwig, who disappeared and shortly returned, pushing in Mrs. Bumble, and dragging her unwilling husband after him.

"Do my hi's deceive me!" cried Mr. Bumble, with fake enthusiasm, "or is that little Oliver? Oh O-li-ver, if you know'd how I've been a-grieving for you—"

"Hold your tongue, fool," murmured Mrs. Bumble.

Mr. Brownlow stepped near the couple. He inquired, as he pointed to Monks, "Do you know that person?"

"No," replied Mrs. Bumble flatly.

"I never saw him in all my life," said Mr. Bumble.

"Nor sold him anything, perhaps?"

"No," replied Mrs. Bumble.

"You never had a certain gold locket and ring?" said Mr. Brownlow.

"Certainly not," replied the matron. "Why are

we brought here to answer to such nonsense as this?"

Again Mr. Brownlow nodded to Mr. Grimwig, and again that gentleman limped away with extraordinary readiness. This time, he led in two old women, who shook as they walked.

"You shut the door the night old Sally died," said the foremost one, raising her shriveled hand, "but you couldn't shut out the sound."

"No, no," said the other, wagging her toothless jaws. "No, no, no."

"We heard her try to tell you what she'd done, and saw you take a paper from her hand, and watched you too, next day, at the pawnbroker's shop," said the first.

"Yes," added the second, "and it was a "locket and gold ring." We found out that, and saw it given to you."

"And we know more than that," resumed the first, "for she told us often, long ago, that the young mother had confessed she was on her way, at the time that she was taken ill, to die near the grave of the father of the child."

"Would you like to see the pawnbroker himself?" asked Mr. Grimwig with a motion towards the door.

"No," replied Mrs. Bumble, "if he"—she pointed to Monks—"has been coward enough to confess, and you have talked to all these hags till you have found the right ones, I have nothing more to say. I *did* sell them, and they're where you'll never get them. What then?"

"Nothing," replied Mr. Brownlow, "except that it remains for us to take care that neither of you is employed in a situation of trust again. You may leave the room."

"I hope," said Mr. Bumble, "that this unfortunate little circumstance will not deprive me of my porochial office?"

"Indeed it will," replied Mr. Brownlow.

"It was all Mrs. Bumble. She *would* do it," urged Mr. Bumble, first looking round to ascertain that his partner had left the room.

"That is no excuse," replied Mr. Brownlow. "You were present at the destruction of these trinkets, and indeed are the more guilty of the two, for the law supposes that your wife acts under your direction."

Mr. Bumble scowled, fixed his hat on tight, and putting his hands in his pockets, followed his helpmate downstairs.

"Young lady," said Mr. Brownlow, turning to Rose, "give me your hand. Do not tremble. You need not fear to hear the few remaining words we have to say."

"If they have any reference to me," said Rose, "please let me hear them at some other time. I have not strength now."

"No," returned the old gentleman, drawing her arm through his, "you have more fortitude than this, I am sure. Do you know this young lady, sir?"

"Yes," replied Monks.

"I never saw you before," said Rose faintly.

"I have seen you often," returned Monks.

"The father of the unhappy Agnes had *two* daughters," said Mr. Brownlow. "What was the fate of the other child?"

"The child," replied Monks, "when her father died in a strange place, without a letter, book, or scrap of paper that yielded the faintest clue by which his friends or relatives could be traced—the child was taken by some poor cottagers, who reared her as their own."

"Go on," said Mr. Brownlow, signing to Mrs. Maylie to approach.

"My mother found the spot where these people lived," said Monks, "after a year of cunning search—ay, and found the child. The people were poor and had begun to tire—at least the man did—of their generosity. So she left the child with them, giving them a small present of money that would not last long, and promised more, which she never meant to send. She also told the history of the sister's shame, with such alterations as suited her. She bade them take good heed of the child, for she came of bad blood, and told them she was illegitimate, and sure to go wrong at one time or other. The people believed it, and made the child miserable enough even to satisfy us, until a widow lady, residing then at Chester, saw the girl by chance, pitied her, and took her home. In spite of all our efforts she remained there and was happy. I lost sight of her, two or three years ago, and saw her no more until a few months back."

"Do you see her now?"

"Yes. Leaning on your arm."

"But not the less my niece," cried Mrs. Maylie, folding the fainting girl in her arms, "not the less my dearest child. I would not lose her now, for all the treasures of the world. My sweet companion, my own dear girl!"

"The only friend I ever had," cried Rose, clinging to her. "The kindest, best of friends. My heart will burst. I cannot bear all this."

"You have borne more, and have been, through all, the best and gentlest creature," said Mrs. Maylie, embracing her tenderly. "Come, my love, remember who this is who waits to clasp you in his arms, poor child!"

"Not aunt," cried Oliver, throwing his arms about her neck. "Sister, my own dear sister, that my heart loved so dearly from the first! Rose, dear, darling Rose!"

Let the tears that fell, and the broken words that were exchanged in the long close embrace between the orphans, be sacred. They were a long time alone. At length a soft tap came at the door. Oliver opened it, and gave his place to Harry Maylie.

"I know it all," he said, taking a seat beside the lovely girl. "Dear Rose, I am not here by accident. Do you guess that I have come to remind you of a promise? You gave me leave, at any time within a year, to renew the subject of our last conversation."

"I did."

"Not to press you to alter your determination," pursued the young man, "but to hear you repeat it. I was to lay whatever station or fortune I might possess at your feet, and if you still adhered to your former decision, I pledged myself not to seek to change it. The disclosure of tonight—"

"The disclosure of tonight," replied Rose softly, "leaves me in the same position, with reference to you, as that in which I stood before."

"You harden your heart against me, Rose," urged her lover.

"Oh Harry," said the young lady, bursting into tears, "I wish I could, and spare myself this pain."

"Then why inflict it on yourself?" said Harry, taking her hand. "Think, dear Rose, what you have heard tonight."

"And what have I heard!" cried Rose. "That a sense of his deep disgrace so worked upon my own father that he shunned all—there, we have said enough, Harry."

"Not yet," said the young man. "My hopes, my wishes, every thought in life except my love for you have undergone a change. I offer you, now, no distinction among a bustling crowd, no mingling with a world of malice, but a home—a heart and home— yes, dearest Rose, and those alone, are all I have to offer."

"What do you mean!" she faltered.

"I mean but this—that I left you with a firm determination to level all imagined barriers between yourself and me; resolved that if my world could not be yours, I would make yours mine. This I have done. Those who have shrunk from me because of this, have shrunk from you, and proved you so far right. Such relatives of influence and rank that smiled upon me then, look coldly now. But there are smiling fields and waving trees in England's richest county; and by one village church—mine, Rose, my own!—there stands a rustic dwelling that you can make me prouder of, than all the hopes I have renounced. This is my rank and station now, and here I lay it down!"

*　*　*

"It's a trying thing waiting on lovers for supper," said Mr. Grimwig. "I had serious thoughts of eating my head tonight, for I began to think I should get nothing else. I'll take the liberty, if you'll allow me, of saluting the bride that is to be."

Mr. Grimwig lost no time in carrying this action out for the blushing girl. The example was followed both by the doctor and Mr. Brownlow.

"Oliver, my child," said Mrs. Maylie, "where have you been, and why do you look so sad? There are tears stealing down your face at this moment. What is the matter?"

It is a world of disappointment, often to the hopes we most cherish, and hopes that do our nature the greatest honor.

Poor Dick was dead!

CHAPTER 51

The court was paved, from floor to roof, with human faces. All eyes were fixed upon one man— Fagin. He stood there, listening to every word that fell from the presiding judge, who was delivering his charge to the jury.

Looking round, he saw that the jurymen had turned together, to consider their verdict. As his eyes wandered to the gallery, he could see not one face— not even among the women, of whom there were many there—with the faintest sympathy for him, or any feeling but that he should be condemned.

As he saw all this in one bewildered glance, the deathlike stillness came, and looking back he saw that the jurymen had turned towards the judge. Hush!

Fagin could glean nothing from their faces— they might as well have been of stone. Perfect stillness ensued—not a rustle—not a breath—Guilty.

The building rang with a tremendous shout, and another, and another. There was a peal of joy from the populace outside, greeting the news that he would die on Monday.

The noise subsided, and he was asked if he had anything to say why sentence of death should not be passed upon him. It was twice repeated before he seemed to hear it, and then he only muttered that he was an old man—an old man—and so, dropping into a whisper, was silent again.

The judge assumed the black cap, and the prisoner stood. The address was solemn and impressive, the sentence fearful to hear. But he stood, like a marble figure, without the motion of a nerve. The jailer put his hand upon his arm, and beckoned him away. He gazed stupidly about him for an instant, and obeyed.

They led him through a paved room under the court, where some prisoners were waiting till their turns came. As he passed, the prisoners assailed him with names, and screeched and hissed. He shook his fist, and would have spat upon them. But his conductors hurried him on into the interior of the prison.

Here, he was searched. Then they led him to one of the condemned cells, and left him there—alone.

He sat down on a stone bench opposite the door, which served for seat and bed, and tried to collect his thoughts. He began to remember a few disjointed fragments of what the judge had said, though it had seemed to him, at the time, that he could not hear a word. These gradually fell into their proper places. To be hanged by the neck, till he was dead— that was the end.

He began to think of all the men he had known who had died upon the scaffold, some of them through his means. They rose up in such quick succession, that he could hardly count them. He had seen some of them die—and had joked too, because they died with prayers upon their lips. With what a rattling noise the drop went down, and how suddenly they changed, from strong and vigorous men to dangling heaps of clothes!

Some of them might have inhabited that very cell—sat upon that very spot. The cell had been built years ago. Scores of men must have passed their last hours there. It was like sitting in a vault strewn with dead bodies—the cap, the noose, the pinioned arms, the faces that he knew, even beneath that hideous veil.

At length, two men appeared, one bearing a candle, which he thrust into an iron candlestick fixed against the wall. The other dragged in a mattress on which to pass the night, for the prisoner was to be left alone no more.

Then came the night—dark, dismal, silent night. To him it brought despair. The boom of every iron bell came laden with the one, deep, hollow sound—Death.

The day came and went, and night came on again. At one time he raved and cursed, and at another howled and tore his hair. Venerable men of his own persuasion had come to pray beside him, but he had driven them away with curses. They renewed their charitable efforts, and he beat them off.

Saturday night. He had only one night more to live. And as he thought of this, the day broke—Sunday.

It was not until the night of this last awful day, that a withering sense of his helpless, desperate state came in its full intensity upon his blighted soul. He had never been able to consider more than the dim probability of dying so soon. He had spoken little to either of the two men, who relieved each other in their attendance upon him. Now, he started up every minute, and with gasping mouth and burning skin, hurried to and fro, in such a spasm of fear and wrath that even they—used to such sights—recoiled from him with horror. He grew so terrible, at last, that one man could not bear to sit there alone. And so the two kept watch together.

He cowered down upon his stone bed, and

thought of the past. He had been wounded with some missiles from the crowd on the day of his capture, and his head was bandaged with a linen cloth. His red hair hung down upon his bloodless face; his beard was torn, and twisted into knots; his eyes shone with a terrible light; his unwashed flesh crackled with the fever that burnt him up. Eight—nine—ten. If those were the real hours treading on each other's heels, where would he be, when they came round again! Eleven! At eight, he would be the only mourner in his own funeral train; at eleven—

The space before the prison was cleared, and a few strong barriers, painted black, had been already thrown across the road to break the pressure of the expected crowd, when Mr. Brownlow and Oliver appeared, and presented an order of admission to the prisoner, signed by one of the sheriffs. They were immediately admitted into the lodge.

"Is the young gentleman to come too, sir?" said the man whose duty it was to conduct them. "It's not a sight for children, sir."

"It is not indeed, my friend," rejoined Mr. Brownlow, "but my business with this man is intimately connected with him. As this child has seen him in the full career of his success and villainy, I think it well—even at the cost of some pain and fear—that he should see him now."

These few words had been said apart, so as to be inaudible to Oliver. The man, glancing at Oliver with some curiosity, opened another gate, and led them on, through dark and winding ways, towards the cells.

They passed through several strong gates, and, having entered an open yard, ascended a flight of narrow steps, and came into a passage with a row of strong doors on the left hand. The guard knocked at one of these with his bunch of keys. The two attendants came out into the passage, and motioned the visitors to follow the jailer into the cell.

The condemned criminal was seated on his bed, rocking himself from side to side, with a look more like that of a snared beast than the face of a man. He continued to mutter.

"Good boy, Charley—well done—" he mumbled. "Oliver, too, ha! ha! ha! Oliver too—quite the gentleman now—quite the—take that boy away to bed!"

The jailer took Oliver's hand, and, whispering him not to be alarmed, looked on without speaking.

"Take him away to bed!" cried Fagin. "Do you hear me, some of you? He has been the—the—somehow the cause of all this. It's worth the money to bring him up to it—Bolter's throat, Bill; never mind the girl—Bolter's throat as deep as you can cut. Saw his head off!"

"Fagin," said the jailer.

"That's me!" cried the Jew. "An old man, my Lord, a very old, old man!"

The guard laid his hand upon his shoulder to keep him down. "Here's somebody wants to see you, to ask you some questions, I suppose."

Catching sight of Oliver and Mr. Brownlow, Fagin shrank to the furthest corner of the seat, and demanded to know what they wanted there.

"Steady," said the guard, still holding him down. "Quick, sir, if you please, for he grows worse as the time gets on."

"You have some papers," said Mr. Brownlow

advancing, "that were placed in your hands, for better security, by a man called Monks."

"It's all a lie," replied Fagin. "I haven't one—not one."

"For the love of God," said Mr. Brownlow solemnly, "do not say that now, upon the very verge of death, but tell me where they are. You know that Sikes is dead, that Monks has confessed, that there is no hope of any further gain. Where are those papers?"

"Oliver," cried Fagin, beckoning to him. "Here! Let me whisper to you."

"I am not afraid," said Oliver in a low voice, as he relinquished Mr. Brownlow's hand.

"The papers," said Fagin, drawing Oliver towards him, "are in a canvas bag, in a hole a little way up the chimney in the top front room. I want to talk to you, my dear."

"Yes, yes," returned Oliver. "Let me say one prayer. Say only one, upon your knees, with me, and we will talk till morning."

"Have you nothing else to ask him, sir?" inquired the guard.

"No other question," replied Mr. Brownlow. "If I hoped we could recall him to a sense of his position—"

"Nothing will do that, sir," replied the man, shaking his head. "You had better leave him."

The door of the cell opened, and the attendants returned.

The men laid hands upon Fagin, and disengaging Oliver from his grasp, held him back. He struggled with the power of desperation, for an instant. Then he sent up cry upon cry that penetrated even those massive walls, and rang in their ears until they reached the open yard.

Oliver nearly swooned after this frightful scene, and was so weak that for an hour or more, he had not the strength to walk.

Day was dawning when they again emerged. A great multitude had already assembled. The windows were filled with people, smoking and playing cards to pass the time. The crowd was pushing, quarrelling, joking. Everything told of life and animation, but one dark cluster of objects in the center of all—the black stage, the crossbeam, the rope, and all the hideous apparatus of death.

CHAPTER 52

Before three months had passed, Rose Fleming and Harry Maylie were married in the village church, which was the new site of the young clergyman's labors. On the same day, they took possession of their new and happy home.

Mrs. Maylie moved in with her son and daughter-in-law, to enjoy, during the tranquil remainder of her days, the contemplation of the happiness of those whom she loved with all her heart.

It appeared, on full and careful investigation, that if the property remaining in the custody of Monks (which had never prospered either in his hands or in those of his mother) were equally divided between himself and Oliver, it would yield, to each, little more than three thousand pounds. By the provisions of his father's will, Oliver would have been entitled to the whole. But Mr. Brownlow, unwilling to deprive the elder son of the opportunity of dropping his former vices and pursuing an honest career, proposed to divide it equally, to which Oliver joyfully agreed.

Monks retired with his portion to a distant part of the New World, where, having quickly squandered it, he once more fell into his old ways, and, after undergoing a long confinement for some act of fraud, at length succumbed an attack of his old disorder, and died in prison.

Mr. Brownlow adopted Oliver as his son. Moving with him and the old housekeeper to within a mile of the parsonage house, where his dear friends resided, he gratified Oliver's only remaining wish. Thus they formed a little group, achieving as close to perfect happiness as can ever be known in this changing world.

Soon after the wedding, the worthy doctor returned to Chertsey, but found that the place really no longer was what it had been. So he settled his business on his assistant, and took a bachelor's cottage outside the village of which his young friend was pastor. Here he took to gardening, planting, fishing, carpentering, and various other pursuits of a similar kind.

Before moving, he had managed to form a strong friendship with Mr. Grimwig. He was accordingly visited by Mr. Grimwig a great many times in the course of the year. On all such occasions, Mr. Grimwig planted, fished, and carpentered, with great ardor.

Noah Claypole received a pardon from the Crown for bearing witness against Fagin. After some consideration, he went into business as an informant, in which calling he made a great deal of money.

Mr. and Mrs. Bumble, deprived of their situations, were gradually reduced to great misery, and finally became paupers in that same workhouse in which they had once lorded it over others. Mr. Bumble had not even spirits to be thankful for being separated from his wife.

As for Mr. Giles and Brittles, they remained in their old posts. They slept at the parsonage, but divided their attentions so equally among its inmates and Oliver, Mr. Brownlow and Mr. Losberne, that to this day the villagers do not know to which establishment they properly belong.

Master Charles Bates, appalled by Sikes's crime,

wondered whether an honest life was not, after all, the best. Arriving at the conclusion that it certainly was, he resolved to amend the past. He struggled hard, and suffered much, for some time. But, having a contented disposition, and a good purpose, he succeeded in the end. From being a farmer's drudge, he became the merriest young cattle rancher in all Northamptonshire.

As for Rose Maylie, she continued to shine her soft and gentle light into the hearts of all who knew her. She took joy in performing charity abroad, and her domestic duties at home. She and Oliver passed whole hours together in picturing the friends whom they had so sadly lost, and took comfort in their love for each other.

Mr. Brownlow went on, from day to day, filling the mind of his adopted child with knowledge, and becoming attached to him, more and more, as his nature thrived. He saw in Oliver traits of his early friend that awakened old memories, melancholy and yet sweet and soothing. And the two orphans, tried by adversity, remembered its lessons in mercy to others, and mutual love, and fervent thanks to Him who had protected them.

Within the altar of the old village church there stands a white marble tablet, which bears one word: "AGNES." There is no coffin in that tomb, and may it be many, many years, before another name is placed above it! But, if the spirits of the Dead ever come back to earth, to visit spots hallowed by the love of those whom they knew in life, then the shade of Agnes sometimes hovers round that solemn nook.

AFTERWORD

About the Author

Born in Landport, Hampshire, England, in 1812, Charles John Huffam Dickens was the second of eight children. His father, John, worked as a clerk in a naval pay office, and his mother, Elizabeth, was a vivacious and charming person. His family moved to Kent when he was five, and five years later to Camden Town in London. During his early childhood, young Dickens spent a lot of time outdoors, reading adventurous novels from his father's collection of books.

Because Dickens's father managed money poorly, the family's circumstances changed often. Eventually, John Dickens had to go to Marshalsea prison for debt, and the entire family, except twelve-year-old Charles, lived there with him. Young Dickens stayed in London, working ten hours a day in a boot-blacking factory, affixing labels to jars of polish. He boarded nearby with other child laborers, and sent money to his family.

Though the Dickenses were released from the prison a few months later, they did not immediately remove their son from the factory, a decision that Dickens probably resented for a long time. After inheriting some money from relations, his parents sent him to private schools for a few years. He then apprenticed to a law office as a clerk, and learned shorthand. After working as a court reporter, Dickens began his journalistic career, covering parliamentary debate and election campaigns for a variety of newspapers.

In 1836, he married Catherine Hogarth, the eldest daughter of his friend George Hogarth. Hogarth had a large intellectual and musical family, which Dickens admired. He and Catherine set up house with Catherine's sister Mary, whom Dickens was extremely fond of. He enjoyed her earnest, intellectual qualities, which he might have found missing in his wife, of whom he complained of being too slow and languid.

After a brief illness, Mary died suddenly at the age of seventeen, in Dickens's arms, and he remained forever affected by her death. He wore one of her rings and kept a lock of her hair. He always considered her one of the most important influences in his life.

The same year of his wedding, Dickens published a collection of short pieces inspired by his journalism, *Sketches by Boz,* and it enjoyed success. He was then asked to complete a joint project of engravings with an illustrator, and this project became *The Pickwick Papers,* a novel about the adventures of a group of eccentrics.

This serialized novel, a little of which was published every week, made Dickens a household name while he was still in his twenties. From then on, he could write his own ticket with publishers. His readers enjoyed a steady supply of his work—over twenty-five books and many short stories. His better known novels include *Oliver Twist, David Copperfield, A Tale of Two Cities,* and, the work many critics consider his best, *Great Expectations.*

He was the first established writer of the Victorian Era—the time period during which Queen Victoria ruled England—and many people saw his as encapsulating the life of the times. He was especially known for the variety of memorable characters he created, and his witty observations about human society and behavior. Probably for this reason, his writing remains popular to this day, translated into films, plays, and musicals, and none of his work has ever gone out of print.

A prolific career probably came naturally to Dickens, who was renowned for his high level of energy and enthusiasm. He regularly went for long, vigorous walks of twenty to thirty miles, which seemed to energize him even more. In addition to writing, he loved acting, and participated in plays, musicals, and impromptu performances. His love of theater was evident in the effort he put into reading from his work for audiences, using distinct voices for all of the characters.

Although Dickens campaigned for social causes, and used his fiction to comment on social issues of the day, such as poverty and corruption, he was highly attuned to the commercial value of his work, and his own material interest in it. He had a keen sense of his audience, and he would change the course of a story according to his readers' reactions to previous installments. His talent for creating commercial success enabled him to support a family of ten children, plus provide occasional assistance for his parents and brothers. He enjoyed a comfortable lifestyle, and was considered a snappy dresser.

Dickens took a liberal stance about many social issues, but he was conservative about domestic arrangements. He expected a quiet, neat and order-ly house, and left all domestic duties to his wife. Letters and other documents indicate that Dickens was not especially sensitive to his wife and children, and he felt increasingly unhappy with his marriage. The couple separated in 1858, Dickens having become involved a year earlier with the actress Ellen Ternan, who would be his companion and mistress until his death.

In 1865, a train he and Ternan were traveling on wrecked near Staplehurst in Kent, and their car was the only first-class carriage that did not go plunging off a bridge. This event was to affect him deeply for the remainder of his life, and he did not produce much writing after it. He finished *Our Mutual Friend,* and began *The Mystery of Edwin Drood,* which he never completed. He died, after a stroke, on the five-year anniversary of the Staplehurst crash, at his home in 1870.

About the Book

Oliver Twist was Dickens's second novel, and like many of his works, it takes on the social issues of the day. Dickens cared a great deal about the plight of the poor and working class, who were seen as morally inferior by the upper classes and people who administered assistance to them. With *Oliver Twist*, Dickens gave his readers a highly accessible story about good versus evil, while also illustrating the injustice, corruption, and poverty that plagued Victorian society.

Dickens turns his keen eye first on the workhouse, a place meant to shelter and feed the poor, but which more often starved, sickened, and eventually killed them. People could be sent to the workhouse for a variety of reasons, including unemployment, bankruptcy, and petty crime. For Oliver, the workhouse is a place of slow torture, a combination of physical and emotional abuse, for which he is expected to be grateful.

When he leaves the workhouse, Oliver discovers the injustice and misery of the outside world. At the undertaker's, where he becomes an apprentice, death is merely a means of making money, and the suffering of the poor nothing to be concerned with, except as it interferes with business. Accordingly, at one of the funerals Oliver attends, the deceased pauper's family must wait outside in the rain for the pastor, while Mr. Sowerberry and Mr. Bumble stay warm inside by the fire.

Upon falling in with Fagin and his gang, Oliver learns about the world of petty crime, which, for many, was the only alternative to the workhouse.

Dickens shows how poverty turns children into corrupt little adults, like the Dodger and Charley Bates. Poor women, such as Nancy and Bet, must give up their most important attribute—virtue—and take up prostitution to survive. And Fagin seems to have lost his very humanity, for Dickens describes him both as a beast and a devil.

Some critics of the time felt that Dickens indulged in stereotypes. For example, he was harshly judged for making a Jewish character so villainous, and referring to Fagin simply as "the Jew." Many of the other characters also are extreme, including Oliver himself, who maintains an almost saintly attitude and speaks perfect English, despite his proximity to cruel and corrupt people, and his utter lack of education.

Because such extreme good and evil can seem unrealistic to a modern audience, it might be helpful to know that the Victorian reader saw paupers as inherently defective—that their natures dictated their circumstances, not the other way around. Dickens, who probably wanted to soften his reader's heart towards the poor, created a main character calculated to win people's sympathy. He also encouraged compassion for paupers by casting characters such as the beadle and the board members in an especially bad light, drawing attention to their cruelty and corruption.

Indeed, Dickens seems to relish exposing the flaws of people in power, doing so in great humor and detail. He shows the hypocrisy of Mr. Bumble, when he scolds Noah and Charlotte for kissing, even though just hours before he has kissed Mrs. Corney. Similarly, Mr. and Mrs. Sowerberry punish Oliver for being violent by thrashing him. Almost all of the public servants, who are responsible for the paupers' welfare, abuse the trust placed in them, and look out mainly for their own interests. Dickens is careful to show how these characters then become irate at the "ingratitude" of the paupers for the few crumbs that are left for them.

The one character who has both good and evil sides is Nancy. While Oliver and his friends battle villains, Nancy fights an interior battle, struggling to overcome years of vice and misfortune. In the end, she cannot save herself, but she redeems her life somewhat by saving Oliver. Ironically, it is her love and loyalty to Sikes, normally virtues, that speed her towards destruction. Her last act is a prayer to God, holding Rose Maylie's handkerchief, a symbol of goodness and innocence.

With the characters of Nancy, Oliver, and little Dick, Dickens shows the reader how good people can be victims of bad circumstances. Even Rose Maylie, seemingly a living incarnation of an angel, cannot escape the misfortune of her past, when she was vulnerable to other's misdeeds. Moreover, those who have fallen to vice can, according to Dickens, reform themselves, as Charley Bates does at the end of the story.

And yet, good circumstances do not always produce good people, as demonstrated by the villainous character of Monks. Though he comes from upper-class society, he is bad from his very cradle, and brings nothing but misery to those near him. Still, the compassionate Mr. Brownlow gives Monks a chance to reform. But, being an inherently bad person, he wastes it, instead falling back into vice and destruction.

In the end, good does triumph, in a variety of ways. Rose marries her true love, despite the stain on her past. Fagin, Monks, and Sikes perish, while the Dodger goes to prison. The Bumbles lose their positions, and end up in the workhouse, on equal footing with the people they have abused for so long. Even for Nancy, good wins out over evil, in the battle for her soul before her death. And finally, Oliver finds his true family, and a replacement father.

Oliver Twist not only shows the power of good over evil; its author also seems to tell us that we are not doomed *or* saved by our circumstances. His characters are able to change their lives despite their environments and the twist of fate that has put them there. Perhaps we can, too.